MAELSTROM

MAELSTROM

Chris Todhunter

Book Guild Publishing
Sussex, England

First published in Great Britain in 2011 by
The Book Guild Ltd
19 New Road
Brighton, BN1 1UF

Copyright © Chris Todhunter 2011

The right of Chris Todhunter to be identified as the author
of this work has been asserted by him in accordance with the
Copyright, Designs and Patents Act 1988.

All rights reserved. No part of this publication may be reproduced,
transmitted, or stored in a retrieval system, in any form or by any means,
without permission in writing from the publisher, nor be otherwise circulated in any
form of binding or cover other than that in which it is published and without
a similar condition being imposed on the subsequent purchaser.

All characters in this publication are fictitious and any resemblance
to real people, alive or dead, is purely coincidental.

Typeset in Baskerville by Ellipsis Books Limited, Glasgow

Printed in Great Britain by
CPI Antony Rowe

A catalogue record for this book is available from The British Library.

ISBN 978 1 84624 605 0

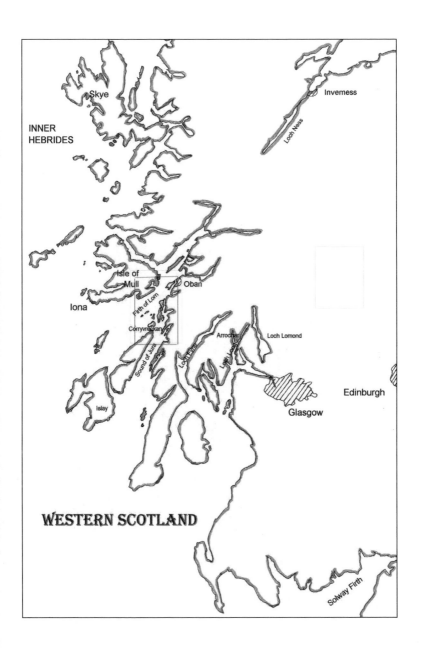

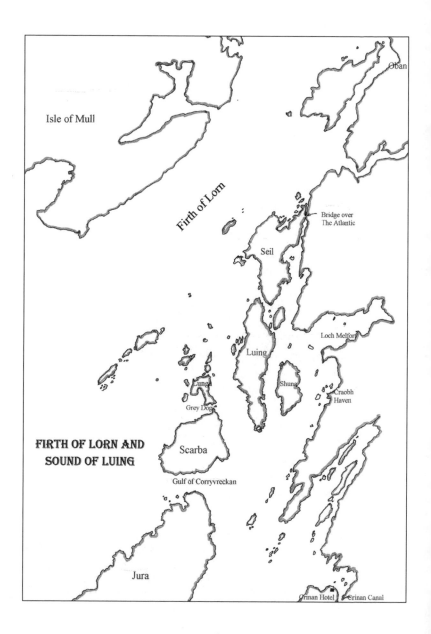

1

The barman came over, wiping his hands on a filthy dish towel.

'See here, pal, it's no healthy ye asking all these questions, an I dinnae want any trouble in here. Gaun hame while ye're still in one piece.'

Jack looked at his watch. Only a few hours left. He didn't know which ached more, his body or his soul. His knees were still knocking after his last encounter and it didn't seem he was making any progress here. He downed the last of his pint.

He felt everyone's gaze on him as he walked to the door, piercing eyes drilling into his back. An outsider. Unwanted. He didn't belong in the east end of Glasgow. But he needed to be a troublemaker. He was stirring the pond like crazy but nothing was coming to the surface.

The September night was cold and the air fresher on the other side of the door. It was a grim neighbourhood. The street lighting struggled to improve the gloom and succeeded only in benefiting the shadows and dark alleys.

He saw a figure about fifty yards away standing in the sickly sodium glow of a lone street light. Microskirt, purple tights, stiletto-heeled ankle boots, hair a peroxide mess. She'd be as good as anyone to ask. He set off towards her.

Two shadows unglued themselves from the darkness on either

side of the door he had just left. One confronted him, the other stood behind him, blocking any escape. They were close enough for him to smell fresh cigarette and none-too-clean body – overpowered by the pungent aroma of his own fear. A large car drew up alongside and, as if by magic, the boot lid swung up. The man in front of him didn't move but Jack sensed the guy behind approaching.

The moment he felt himself grabbed from behind he lashed out with his right foot, aiming to crash it down on his attacker's instep. The connection was good, the crunch satisfying, the howl rewarding and the punch to his kidneys painful.

His muscles spasmed and his resistance collapsed. They lifted him up as though he weighed no more than a sack of potatoes. He landed head first in the open car boot, his legs and feet followed. He twisted round, shifted his body weight and crashed his feet into the already closing boot lid, but he was too slow and the lid banged down, extinguishing all light. He smashed his heels into the side of the boot with all his strength.

As a gesture it was great. As a course of action it was futile. And his kidneys objected.

The vehicle moved off and he lost orientation; he could see nothing, didn't know which way he was facing, he could barely move his arms, and all he could smell was thick, sweet exhaust fumes. For a moment he feared he might throw up all over himself and the boot. He told himself to relax and go with the flow. Maybe he *was* making progress. He was clearly an irritant to someone. Perhaps he was being taken to the same place as Jenny. Even if he were locked up with her, at least they would be together and could give each other support. Even better, his absence tomorrow morning really would put the shit in the incense.

Eventually the vehicle slowed, bumped over rough ground, and came to a halt. The car rocked; doors opened and closed as occupants got out. When the boot lid swung up they hauled him out with the same lack of ceremony as when they'd flung him in.

He was in some kind of small park: rough ground that was dark, grassy and bordered by trees. He felt as much as heard the rumble of a train nearby. He stood awkwardly, moving his arms to ease the muscles and restore circulation. The talkative one spoke.

'Ye've been tell't, ye bastart piece o shite, an now ye'll get a kickin.'

In his heart he'd known this was coming; by now he was determined to give an honest account of himself. He had just enough time to transfer his weight to the balls of his feet before a fist the size of a melon slammed into his stomach. What little was in there exploded through his mouth in a technicolour display of tomato skins and diced carrots. He heard a surprised voice primly say something about a dirty wee bugger and a nice clean shirt.

He shook his head to try to clear the remains of his last meal from his mouth. The manoeuvre was still incomplete when a massive shock exploded on his face. His brain swam in an unaccustomed porridge of violence, the blood pounded in his ears, nose and eyes. The guy behind him grabbed his upper arms and held him while his colleague pummelled him with sledgehammer blows to the stomach, chest and solar plexus. Jack tried to double up to protect himself but couldn't move downwards more than a few inches, which was when an uppercut connected with his nose, bursting every blood vessel within range.

They let him sink to the muddy ground only so that they could engage their boots. He tried curling into a ball, but as the blows found his kidneys he jerked open. Most of the kicks to his front landed on his hands and arms, but still a couple connected with his face.

Then the rain of violence stopped as suddenly as it had started.

'Tha's the last warnin ye'll get. Now fuck off back tae whur ye came from and stop pokin yer nose whur it's no wanted.' One last kick in the stomach for emphasis. 'An clean yersel up. Ye stink.'

He heard them climb back into the vehicle and drive off. He could almost see the cloud of blue diesel smoke.

Tongues of fire crept up his back and licked at his hands and face. But he'd survived. Then the tremors started, the shaking and the pain. He was afraid to move in case he discovered anything serious.

He screwed up what little remained of his courage and uncurled slowly. Thunderbolts shot through his ribs and back. Blood flowed freely from a split lip and mingled with the discharge from his burst nose. He felt rather than heard the hesitant approach of curious onlookers.

'Ye aw right, pet?' *Extraordinarily enough*, he thought, *not altogether, no*.

They crouched over him and someone tentatively laid a hand on his back. At least it wasn't violent, he thought. And he was going to need some help to stand upright.

His rescuers, powerfully bathed in the acrid tang of cigarettes, cheap perfume and sweaty armpits, stroked his brow and made gentling noises. He was grateful for that. But he couldn't stay all night to enjoy it. Instead, he crawled onto his hands and knees, spat out another gobbet of blood, and muttered through thickening lips, 'p'ucking Hong Kong.'

2

Six months earlier

It was a desirable corner office on the third floor, overlooking Euston Square in the heart of London. A black-leather executive wheelie-chair was thrust back from the desk as though its owner had left in a hurry. The phone on the desk was ringing. Annabel Gray, Personal Assistant, sitting at a desk just outside the glass wall of the office, picked up from her extension.

'Jack Ross's office.' She listened. 'Oh hi, Bill . . . No, don't call him on his mobile, he's in a meeting at the moment. He should be finished around one.' She listened some more. 'Oh gosh, that doesn't sound too good. Tell you what, I'll go down and whisper in his ear and see if he wants to come out and talk to you. Bye.'

Her tall, elegant figure, clad in a bright-red dress that ended just above the knee, drew the usual lingering glances from the younger engineers whose desks she passed. More than one renewed his aspiration to be Operations Director one day.

Obligingly the lift was on its downward path as she arrived at the lobby; stairs were not an option with serious heels. Within moments she arrived outside the boardroom. She tapped lightly and went in. The Chairman acknowledged her entry with a slow blink of his lizard eyes, and returned them to the papers in front of him. Annabel went directly to Jack on the other side of the long table and whispered in his ear. Jack's eyes lost focus on the director speaking and he pulled his eyebrows together in concentration on what Annabel was saying.

'Forgive me, Rob,' he interrupted the speaker and turned to the Chairman. 'Nigel, would you excuse me for a moment while I take this call?'

The Chairman slow-blinked again in acquiescence. The eyes followed Annabel's rear-view on its way out before returning to the matter in hand.

The project management department was an open-plan space also on the first floor. Jack went straight to Bill Bruford's desk. Two extra chairs were already pulled up to it, one occupied by Bill's assistant, Wendy Spofforth, the other supporting the very ample behind of Terry Smith, commercial executive.

'OK, Bill, what's the problem?'

'It's the China–Vietnam pipeline, Jack. The ship laying it and ploughing it in has just reported that all the welds are splitting as the pipe goes off the back end. The client's hopping mad.'

It was on occasions such as this, standing with growing impatience on the platform listening to the announcement that trains were delayed due to a points failure, that Jack cursed the move of his office up to Euston Square. Commuting was fine when the office had been in Bracknell – after all it was why they had bought a house there, and convenience to the office meant that when he had to go home, pick up some clothes and hop on a plane at Heathrow, the whole exercise took little more than a couple of hours from problem phone-call to take-off from runway 1. But with the office in central London, Heathrow might as well be on the moon.

At least the underground was less packed than when he took it on his way to work. The mainline train to and from Waterloo was no better, but then you paid your money and took your choice, didn't you? You either lived in a broom cupboard in central London and walked to work, in which case you might keep reasonable hours, or you lived out of town, endured a mind-numbing journey and kept moronic hours to avoid the worst of the crowds, and sometimes even got a seat on the train.

Jack lived out of town. In a red-brick matchbox on a red-brick estate in a glass-and-steel town. He had seen prettier broom cupboards. As he walked into the kitchen and dumped his bulging briefcase on the table Sarah glanced up at the wall clock: it was a few minutes to four.

'Is this part of a new regime?' She looked surprised and delighted, her face bright and sunny. She was still in her tracksuit, freshly showered and still glowing, he presumed, from her keep-fit session at the gym. As he went over to give his customary peck on the cheek, she put her arms round his neck and gave him a warm kiss. Jack decided he must come home early more often. Inhaling the apple-blossom scent of her hair, he returned the hug and the kiss.

'I wish.' He disengaged with as much grace as he could muster. 'But I'm afraid not. Just coming back for a quick bite and then pack some gear before catching this evening's flight.'

The temperature dropped ten degrees.

'Flight? What flight?'

'We've got a major problem in China and the clients are insisting on a top-level meeting at their offices tomorrow.'

The chill was fast turning to frost and heading for ice. 'I see. And when do you think you'll get back?' Sarah's voice had taken on a dangerous edge. As usual, Jack failed to notice the warning signs.

'End of the week, I should think.'

'So what about Wednesday evening?'

'Wednesday evening?' His mental calendar showed a blank and his face reflected it.

'Yes. Tom's school play. Remember that? Remember Tom? Your son? The one who struggles at school and this is his crowning moment of the year? You promised you would be there.'

Too late, Jack realised the atmosphere was now ice. Not just a crisp covering of ice on a puddle, but the north-polar, load-bearing variety that would bring an ice-breaker to a juddering halt and freeze it in till the spring.

'Oh bloody hell! I'm sorry, Sarah, but there's nothing I can do about it, I do really have to go.' His distress was genuine but there was no way he could *not* go. Life just didn't work like that. Sarah knew that, didn't she? After all, it wasn't the first time he'd had to come home early, pack a case and fly off at short notice. It went with the job, she knew that, surely.

So what Sarah said next caught him thoroughly off-balance.

'I've about had it with your precious company. They get all your quality time and there's nothing left for me and the children. How's Tom going to feel when I have to explain to him that you don't care about his achievements? And another thing: it's always *me* that has to explain, never you, and I'm sick of it. Where are your priorities, Jack, and why don't we feature in them? So go to the other end of the world, spend your life at your beloved company's beck and call. You're always telling me that you have staff or managers to do things for you, but when push comes to shove you're always the one who has to go and never the others. It's not just once or twice, Jack, it's just about every time we try to organise something at home. It's always the same, and I've had about as much as I can take!'

Her voice ended in a screech. She spun on her heel, tried to find a door to leave through and had to end up dodging round Jack to get to it. She slammed it after her and Jack heard her sobbing through in the dining room.

Shit! He didn't think there was anything he could say at the moment to get her over this – other than that he wasn't going after all, but that wasn't going to happen. He judged it prudent to leave the scene, do some packing, and see how the land lay after that.

Twenty minutes later, bag packed, he went in search of Sarah. She had finished crying and had replaced it with the occasional sniff. 'I'm sorry, Jack, I didn't mean to fly off the handle, but I really am quite cross about this.'

'Yes I know, love, and I can't tell you how much I regret it . . .'

'Regret it? You didn't even realise what you were going to miss, did you? I suppose that's one of the worst things, you're just not aware of us here at all.' She reined herself in with a visible effort. 'I'm sorry, I didn't mean to get going again, but I feel like the hotel manager here and that was never part of my plans.' She was working at a paper handkerchief with her hands, as if wishing it was his neck. 'Jack, we've *got* to do something about this.'

He didn't have an immediate answer. He tried, 'Don't worry, darling, it'll turn out all right'.

She gave him an 'oh yeah' look. 'You'd better get going if you're to catch that flight.'

That wasn't true, he was running well ahead of schedule.

3

It had been an exhausting three days in Beijing. Jack had come to love the city on more relaxed visits, particularly the ancient parts: the Forbidden City, the classically reconstructed Summer Palace, and the Ming Tombs, which were a special favourite of his. But he had a basic problem with the food. It was not like the Sun-Luck Takeaway in the high street at home, and he really couldn't stomach boiled chicken's feet, sliced pig's ear and snake's bladders. He had managed to avoid fresh monkey brains and he meant for it to stay that way.

Climbing aboard the jumbo jet he felt the familiar sense of being on his way home. He had a meeting in Hong Kong tomorrow but all the time he knew he was on the downhill slope.

He was not at all surprised when the aircraft, which had stood motionless for an hour in the queue for takeoff, started its acceleration down the runway while he was still in the toilet. A shiver ran down his spine at the vivid memory of landing at Kai Tak airport fifteen or more years earlier, with an aircraft of the same airline hanging off the end of the runway, half in Victoria harbour, after a misjudged landing.

The flight itself was uneventful if somewhat unappetising. He declined the small box of animal body-parts and chopsticks, in anticipation of a decent meal when he got to Hong Kong.

The receptionist at the desk – Elizabeth Cheung if her name badge was to be believed – looked up as he completed his check-in and smiled. 'This is your key-card, Mr Ross: room 2210. I hope you have a pleasant stay with us.' As he picked up his bags he was already looking forward to a tall glass of San Miguel in the bar overlooking the harbour, followed by a nice juicy steak, when a familiar voice hailed him.

'Jack! Didn't know you were here?'

As he turned round his heart sank. Lydia Fox, one of the company's commercial managers, rumpled grey suit and all, was approaching him from the lobby.

'Lydia! I could say the same. What're you here for?'

'You know that oil rig we're bidding for in the South China Sea? This should be the final meeting with the consortium and hopefully should close the deal.'

'Good luck,' he said. She didn't smile. But then, Jack couldn't remember her smiling much in the office.

'As we're in Hong Kong,' she said, the round, horn-rimmed glasses making her look even more like an owl, 'I suppose we should eat something Chinese this evening.' She tucked a stray hair back into the tight bun on the top of her head.

'I guess you should. But for the last three days I've been fantasising about a nice juicy steak, some chips on the side and a glass of Chateau Something or Other to wash it down. I'll be eating here in the hotel restaurant.'

She tipped her head on one side as she considered it. Oh God, she was thinking of joining him! He could see a perfectly decent evening disappearing down the toilet.

'Sounds good. So when and where?'

He contained his irritation. 'I'm going up to shower and change, so how about an hour's time down in the lounge bar? First one there gets in a couple of San Migs.'

She put a hand on his arm. Actually, she had quite nice fingers, he noted.

'Deal,' she said, and smiled.

* * *

An hour later Jack was showered and on his way down to the lounge bar. Apart from the small matter of his meeting tomorrow, which he was not expecting to be too demanding, he was beginning to relax. The previous few days had taken it out of him: he'd had to face his irate customers, bright and alert, at 2 am his body time. Only now was he beginning to adjust – a sure sign it was time to go home. It was a bugger that Lydia had decided to share the evening with him, but he couldn't have told her to sod off.

He looked round the lobby bar and, not seeing her, found a table and ordered two San Miguels. The waitress, in a shimmering, deep-blue silk cheongsam with little flowers and birds on it, poured the beer into tall glasses, and Jack settled down to look out of the window at the teeming life on Victoria Harbour and across to Kowloon.

If he had enough beer perhaps he could survive dinner with Lydia after all. He knew her quite well within the company but not at all socially. Maybe once she'd changed out of her office clothes she'd tone down that starchy, know-it-all manner. At least she'd smiled at him.

As he addressed the serious business of getting himself outside his beer he watched the bustle of Hong Kong's business and social life across the lobby, on their way to check in, having checked out, or going to one of the many restaurants or bars within the hotel complex. He noticed one particular woman walking across the lobby wearing a short, lightweight cotton dress, belted at the waist, which conspired to conceal yet reveal a curvaceous, delightfully proportioned body. Her shoulder-length hair was a rich chestnut brown, glowing with health, and swung most attractively as she walked. Now *that*, thought Jack, I wouldn't mind dining with instead.

She was heading for the lounge, and paused briefly to look round for her friends. Catching sight of them at a table near Jack's, she smiled in recognition, and started off towards them.

Idly he glanced round to see who was meeting such an attractive woman, but couldn't see anyone nearby showing signs of reciprocation. She stopped at his table.

'Jack?'

Caught completely off-guard, he struggled out of his deep leather armchair and stood, rather more agape than was socially acceptable, before stammering, 'Lydia?'

'Someone else in mind?' Her smile teased him. How could this possibly be Lydia? Where was the bun? Where were those dreadful, horn-rimmed glasses? How had this creature, sinuous to the point of feline, been hiding under the dull grey trouser-suit and other disguises all these years?

'Lydia,' he repeated, knowing he sounded stupid. 'You look stunning.' And that perfume, he thought as it caught up with her, I'd never get any work done if she wore that in the office.

'Thank you,' she said with a *yes-I-know* smile, and settled into the deep armchair across the coffee table from him. She looked round her surroundings and, having clearly assessed them as being satisfactory, leaned forward, picked up her glass of beer and raised it to her lips.

'I've been looking forward to this,' she said. 'Cheers.' She grinned at him and took a mouthful. Some of the froth remained on the fine hairs of her upper lip; she curled the pink tip of her tongue up and licked the froth off.

Disoriented by the contrast between Lydia in glasses and starchy work mode, and Lydia sitting across from him now, Jack fought off a nagging concern that the balance of power was less clear than it should be, and settled down to redress the situation with what he hoped was intelligent and witty conversation. It was as though he barely knew this person; it might after all be a real pleasure to dine with such a charming companion all to himself. He smiled as he classified it as Work.

They selected one of the hotel restaurants where Lydia could choose something truly ethnic and Jack could have the steak he'd been dreaming about for the last week. They drained the last of their beer and headed off to the restaurant. Following Lydia up the short flight of stairs to the mezzanine floor disconcerted him even more. The vapour trail of her scent was having a narcotic effect on him as it was warmed by the heat of her body, and the movement of her limbs, emphasised by that dress which Jack was beginning to think was the work of the devil and all his angels, could only be dealt with decently and honestly if he averted his eyes. Thus far he was not having much success.

At length they arrived at the vestibule of the restaurant and were seated by the maitre d'. The view across Victoria Harbour towards Kowloon was as amazing as ever, with the lights of the myriad vessels crossing and re-crossing the harbour. He was sure the harbour was getting narrower by the month, as land reclamation and development between the Star Ferry terminals at Admiralty and Wan Chai on the Hong Kong Island side ate away hungrily at the available sea space. Won't be much longer, he thought wryly, before they build a bridge over the remaining two hundred yards of water separating the island from the mainland.

He was having a good time: that first glass of beer had uncurled his soul and his steak was fully living up to expectations. Relaxation was setting in after the stresses of Beijing – and, he had to admit, the atmosphere in which he had left home – and he was relieved to find himself enjoying Lydia's company. Thank God she'd decided to leave the glasses off. He wondered whether she could see anything at all without them.

'Well that was good,' he said, finishing the last mouthful of T-bone and putting his knife and fork into a tidy formation on his plate. 'You can get a bit tired of gristle and offal, you know.'

Lydia laughed, a rich, low note like a contented lioness. 'No, I don't know. Tell me.'

He told her of the meals he'd experienced in Beijing – although his hosts had described them, through the translator, as banquets – where meat as Europeans know it seemed curiously absent. 'And yesterday evening when we were taken to a restaurant called

MAELSTROM

The Peking Duck, I really thought I was in luck. I'm second to no-one in my appreciation of crispy Peking duck – well, down at the Sun Luck in Bracknell anyway – but this one took my breath away, I tell you.'

'What happened?' Lydia had paused in her eating, fork suspended over her bowl of *zha jiang mian*, great hazel eyes – unsullied by horn-rims – riveted on him.

'We were all sitting round this big round table with a space in the middle – which I supposed was for the beast when it came. After we've had a few cans of beer in comes a trolley followed by a chef all in his whites. On the trolley is a large dish with one of those silver dome jobbies on it. Everyone goes "Aaah" and the chef beams. When he's milked his entrance for all it's worth he whips off the silver dome as if he was performing on stage, and everyone goes "Aaah" again. But on the dish is one pathetic little chook for, what – six of us? How's that going to feed the starving multitude? I looked across at Bill who was obviously thinking the same. The look on his face said, looks like it's a Big Mac for supper tonight after the show.'

Lydia laughed again, a delicious gurgle. Jack was enjoying himself.

'Anyway, the chef picks up this enormous great carving knife and an evil-looking fork and does a few twirls, and I says to myself, *get on with it matey, I'm starving*. Eventually he starts carving. He cuts into the skin – which is crispy enough, I grant you – but underneath there's about two inches of gooey fat. Ugh! So he cuts all this skin and fat off and puts it on a plate so's he can get to the meat. But then what does he do? He only puts the plate with the skin and fat on our table and wheels the meat away. I couldn't believe my eyes! I would have laughed if I hadn't been so darned hungry.'

By this time Lydia was bubbling with laughter and Jack, with a couple of glasses of ridiculously expensive Australian wine inside him, was having the time of his life. His companion was making him feel witty, intelligent and appreciated, a heady cocktail from which he had not drunk much of late. But he knew to quit when he was ahead.

'So what about you, Lydia, how's your ethnic offering? Found any bull's whatnots or duck's feet yet?'

Her hand flew to her mouth as she gasped, 'God, I hope not!' Then she giggled. 'Actually, it's very good, I'm really enjoying it.' As she sucked another strawful of lime soda from her glass, she peered up at him and her eyes smiled. Even her mouth, wrapped round the straw, curved up at the edges.

Peace reigned briefly as they regained their composure.

'Is this your first time in Hong Kong?' he asked.

'Mm. First time in Southeast Asia, actually.'

'You're kidding.' His surprise was genuine. He leaned forward, forearms on the table. 'How long have you been with us?'

'Just over two years now.'

'And this is your first time in Southeast Asia? I'm amazed.'

'The company's sent me to the States a fair bit, to Japan, India and South America, but not here.'

'Well I never. What do you think of Hong Kong then?'

She looked out of the window and watched the teeming lights on Victoria Harbour and over on Kowloon-side. After a few moments, she turned back, leant forward and matched Jack with her forearms on the table. She looked at him, their eyes locked.

'I love it.' Her voice was quiet, husky. He could smell her perfume, or was it her breath? Both, maybe. Whichever it was, he breathed it in and savoured it.

Lydia broke the moment and sat back in her chair.

'What did you do before you joined the company?'

'Me?' His laugh was self-conscious. 'I was a sailor. Joined the Royal Navy with a shiny new engineering degree straight out of the cornflakes packet and spent ten years sailing the seven seas.'

'Girl in every port, then?'

'That's a wicked rumour,' he said, 'and just not true. Ask anyone in Lowestoft.'

Their laughter was shared, happy and warm. He was about

to put his hand out on the table for her to take – and then remembered that the circumstances weren't right. The happy warmth within him began to die as, unbidden, the memory of his furious wife, and the red-brick matchbox in cold, dark, wet Bracknell, engulfed him. He was in Hong Kong only because he'd had to endure a very uncomfortable couple of days with an irate client, developing work-around plans, revising contract prices and generally feasting on humble pie, and he was at the dinner table with a junior employee.

Ah well, it was nice while it lasted.

'Coffee?'

'Please.'

Lydia seemed to have picked up on the change in mood. Their conversation became more corporate and commercial. Coffee came and went, Jack signed the check. They rose from the table and, not without some regret, left the restaurant and headed for the lift.

'What floor are you on?'

'Twenty-second.'

'Me too.'

The lift came, but it was too full. The next lift was empty. The air conditioning in the lift was no more than modest, and her musk was warm, subtle yet pungent. Again he breathed it in and tasted it, seeking his fill before he lost it for ever. He looked down at her luxuriant, deep chestnut hair and discovered an overwhelming urge to caress, to bury his face in it.

With a massive effort he reminded himself that that kind of behaviour was off limits, and brought himself back down to earth and under control. All he could think was that it was such a damned shame.

They arrived at the twenty-second floor. Lydia stepped out of the lift, pausing almost imperceptibly for him to catch up as they turned to the right out of the lobby.

Outside room 2209 she stopped, took her key-card out of her shoulder bag and said, 'This is my room.' She turned and looked up at him. In a voice of golden honey that put Jack's blood pressure at risk, she said, 'Nightcap?'

He looked down into her deep hazel eyes. One of them had a fleck of gold in it. His knees threatened to buckle. Her musk had stirred things within him he'd forgotten existed. She'd captivated him at dinner with her charm, her wit, her eyes. And now here she was: warm, moist, inviting. He yearned now to taste her.

'Better not,' he struggled to say, 'we've both got busy days tomorrow.'

'Of course,' she replied with a brittle lightness. 'It's been a lovely evening.' She tilted her cheek up for a goodnight kiss. He leant down.

At the last moment they both turned their heads, and their lips touched.

The barrier crossed, they paused to savour the sensation, mouths open, inhaling each other's breath. A river of fire coursed through his veins and he felt her nipples taut against his chest. Their tongues touched, shyly exploring. She snaked her arms around his neck, his arms encircled her back, one hand caressing her neck under the glowing chestnut hair.

'Wait.' Lydia broke away breathlessly, unlocked the door and pulled Jack in after her. The lights were already on, obligingly low, and the king-size bed was turned down. She turned back towards him and they resumed their kiss hungrily. By now Jack was too far gone even to think of Sarah and the children and the implications of what was happening.

Bracknell belonged on another planet.

4

The cold woke him, his leg threatened cramp. There was a source of warmth on the other side of the bed; he snuggled up to it. With a jolt he realised where he was and who it was. The luminous dial of his watch told him it was a few minutes after five. He should get back to his own room. But he rather liked it where he was.

Glancing across at Lydia, who was lying three-quarters on her front towards him, he reached out and stroked the golden skin of her shoulder in a tentative attempt to waken her. She half-awoke and purred. He leaned across, put his arm fully over her shoulders and kissed her temple. Without opening her eyes she turned her face towards him and her mouth found his.

Oh Christ, Jack thought, I think we're both going to need some more.

It was not until after six that Jack finally summoned up the energy and will to slide out from under the covers, dress, and give Lydia a final kiss. Getting back to his room he abandoned thoughts of sleep even though he'd had precious little of it. He changed into his swimming trunks and headed off to the hotel's outdoor pool.

The hustle and bustle of the day was well underway, with the rumble of early morning traffic six floors below at street level. It was unusually mild for so early in the year but the water in the pool was bracing, and the swim gave his body the stretch he was looking for.

Back in his room he showered and shaved. His mind had not at that stage got as far as turmoil. He was still dazed from the experience of the night. The change in Lydia had confounded his equilibrium; she had blossomed from the starchy professional manager into something approaching a predatory lioness, rediscovering things in him he thought were long dead.

He dressed and went down to breakfast, picking up his copy of the *South China Morning Post* from the floor outside his room. The business pages redirected his mind to the realities of why he was in Hong Kong at all, and by the time he had finished breakfast he'd regained an even keel.

Managing to keep his mind more or less in focus, Jack coasted through his meeting on Harcourt Road and lunch with his hosts in a revolving restaurant at the top of a tower block on Queen's Road. Feeling groggy, he decided to catch up on the sleep he had missed out on the previous night. He awoke at five, showered and started to pack.

But his mind was elsewhere and gathering confusion. Clearly last night was only a one-night stand – the first in Jack's twenty-year marriage – and he was certain Lydia had known that he was firmly and happily married. For him, and doubtless for her, it had been a product of circumstance, purely a meeting of chemistry and opportunity. There would be no swooning with desire when next they met at the coffee machine back in the office – certainly not if she had tucked herself back into the grey suit, bun and horn-rimmed spectacles.

He didn't want to leave the matter hanging unresolved, but equally he had no idea how to resolve it. He rang her room on the offchance, but was not surprised when he got no reply. He tried to compose a brief note for her to pick up at Reception, but what he wrote seemed trite and pointless so he crumpled it up and threw it in the bin.

It would have to remain unresolved.

Jack adjusted the back of his seat in the Business Class cabin and settled to write up his notes on his laptop, a double gin and a small can of tonic water by his elbow. After an ineffective half-hour he closed his laptop and tried to read. But there was too much going on in his head. An evening meal was proffered but he had no appetite and waved it away. He made do with a second large gin.

He tried a film. With dozens to choose from surely there would be one to distract his swirling mind? He flicked the control. Crap, that one. Rubbish, the next. Seen it before, and it wouldn't be any better this time than the last. What about this? Give it go, he thought. Fortunately it was sufficiently brain-dead to cope with his mood for a while. But it didn't last long.

The turmoil in his mind was beginning.

It was slowly dawning on him what he had done. Not to put too fine an edge on it, he had cheated on Sarah. His wife. His best friend. The bedrock of his life, when he thought carefully about it. It didn't matter she'd been a bit cross when he left. Maybe she had a point? Maybe he didn't give his family the attention they deserved? And poor old Tom: yes, he remembered now how he'd promised to attend Tom's play this year.

He thought back to Tom's first day at his school, aged eight. His new uniform hung from his spare frame, his knobbly knees looking even knobblier. Tom had been both proud and apprehensive. Jack had glimpsed him on the edge of nervous tears, but Tom had bitten them back and replaced them with a watery grin. As they'd left him he'd forced out his usual, 'Tr-ro'. He'd never quite mastered 'cheerio'.

Tom had shone at nothing, but had been allowed a two-line part in the play each year – his moment of stardom when the audience hung, breathing suspended, on each of his half-dozen words. And Jack had missed it. Every year.

He couldn't remember the last time he'd attended any event at school for either of the children. No parent-teacher meetings; he realised Sarah must have gone to all those – alone. No prize-givings. Again, Sarah must have gone – alone. He didn't even know whether either of the kids had won any prizes. No concerts, no exhibitions, nothing.

Dammit, he wasn't much of a dad was he?

Should he make a clean breast of it, this fling with Lydia, when he got home, clear the air? He could imagine the scene. Light peck on the cheek. 'Have a good trip, darling?'

'Yes thanks, all sorted.'

'Meet anyone interesting?'

'Matter of fact, yes. Lydia was staying at the same hotel so, as we had nothing better to do, I shagged the arse off her.'

'That's nice, dear. Is she a good shag?'

'Since you ask, yes, very good actually.'

'Oh that's nice. I wonder if she'll be as good in twenty years when time, gravity and two kids have worked their magic.'

No, thought Jack, probably best not to go down that route.

Regret, shame and guilt, not emotions in which he regularly wallowed, were beginning their insidious corrosion of his emotional infrastructure and it was barely two hours into the flight. *Another eleven hours*, he thought miserably, *with only my own insufferable company*. Taking a few minutes to examine his immortal soul, he wasn't impressed.

By the time the plane was circling above the twinkling lights of London, Jack had worked out a number of things. Even though he'd allowed himself to slip out of touch with them, he knew that Sarah, Jenny and Tom were the most important things in his whole life. If he were to lose any one of them, never mind all three, he would need to check himself in for an indefinite stay in a psychiatric unit. Almost as bad, if he did not lose them as such, but lost their respect, he would not be able to live with himself – or, for that matter, with them.

But there was more to it than that. Twenty years ago Sarah

had had an effect on him similar to that which Lydia had had on him twenty-four hours ago. She had been beautiful, willowy, seductive, fun, alluring and all those other things that had made him hate to go away to sea, and made the homecoming earth shattering.

And the children. Yes, they had their hard-work aspects but, he supposed now he thought about it, they lit up his and Sarah's lives. The sound of their chatter in the house, albeit that it came at the price of piles of make-up brushes in the bathroom and a trail of filthy rugby kit from the front door to the kitchen on Saturdays, was a part of his life that he was not prepared to do without. It was true what Sarah had said: he was failing to spend any time with them, to treat them like human beings, to understand them, take pride and pleasure in them.

And what had he been doing about it? His toes curled as he acknowledged he'd been spending all his quality time in the office, and when he was not, he'd been exchanging body fluids with a woman who was not his wife.

By the time the landing gear squealed on the tarmac at London Heathrow at 05.08 on that Saturday morning, he had made the decision he was convinced would change all their lives immeasurably for the better. He would pack in his job in that dreary office on Euston Square. They would throw away their horrible matchbox of a house in Bracknell. And they would embark on the dream he'd harboured all these years but which had never seemed a realistic prospect – until now.

5

Jack was parking the car outside the house before it was 6.30 am. It was still dark, not quite freezing, the drizzle caught in the sodium glow of the street lights. How depressing, he thought; welcome bloody home.

He looked at home with fresh eyes. It was a truly miserable, undistinguished, red-brick house of outstanding blandness. Less of a house, more of an existence-pod, somewhere to survive on the basics of life before moving up the evolutionary scale. Glancing round at all the other houses on the development he saw a frightening sameness, a uniformity that sucked the soul out of a person. *Stick a few of them, what d'you call it, leylandii at the back end of the garden*, the estate agent had said, *and you won't even know you're on an estate*. Well I've got news for you, sunshine . . .

He let himself in quietly and showered and shaved in the downstairs shower room. Wrapped in a towelling bathrobe and armed with a tray of tea he went upstairs just as Sarah's clock-radio sprang into life. He drew a deep breath as he remembered how things had been when they'd parted at the beginning of the week. He'd called her twice from the hotel in Beijing: the first time she had been out, the second time conversation had been distant. Nothing to do with the mileage. Standing outside their bedroom, he was not surprised to find himself screwing up his courage. He hoped the little gift-wrapped jewel box would help.

As he opened the bedroom door it gave its habitual squeak at the half-open point – *I must get that fixed*, he thought. John Humphreys was shredding some unfortunate cabinet minister who didn't understand the concept of 'weekend' on the Today programme. Sarah was lying on her side facing away from the door.

'Hiya,' he said quietly, putting the tray down on his bedside table.

She rolled over, looked up at him sleepily – and smiled. Jack could barely conceal his relief.

'How was China?'

'Very Chinese. All bull's testicles and boiled duck's beak.'

She shuddered and said yuk. They laughed. And then hugged. And hugged some more. God, she smelled good, he thought, all warm and musky, traces of his favourite perfume that he could never remember the name of, only knew it came in a graceful and shockingly expensive bottle.

Much later, as they sat up in bed sipping their cold tea, Jack wondered whether this was the right time to mention his plans. Realising the sense of not spoiling a good moment, he decided to shelve it until they had breakfast inside them. Instead, he reached over to the tea-tray, picked up the jewel box and said, 'Happy Valentine's Day.'

'That was last month.'

'Oh. Sorry. I'll have it back then.'

'No you won't,' she said, and giggled.

Excited as a little girl she tore off the gift wrapping, but matured sufficiently to open the little jewel box slowly. As the lid rose, she caught her breath and her eyes sparkled. That was enough for Jack. With a little difficulty she slipped the eternity ring onto her finger, where the tiny sapphires and diamonds glinted just as he had hoped they would. It hadn't been cheap, even for Hong Kong.

As she threw her arms round his neck he whispered, 'Sorry, it won't happen again,' into her hair.

It being Saturday the children were not expected down much before lunchtime, so breakfast was a leisurely affair untainted by teenagers. Through the debris of cereals, toast and marmalade, Jack poured himself and Sarah another cup of tea.

'I was doing some thinking while I was away.'

'Oh yes?'

'You know how you've been saying for ages that I've got to get some balance into my life – our lives?'

Sarah gave a sharp intake of breath. 'Yes?' she said carefully.

'Well, I've been giving it some thought – and about how things were when I went away earlier this week.' He paused and took a deep breath. 'You're right: we can't go on as we are at the moment. But more than that, I reckon I've had enough of being an employee, working for someone else. I've got a few ideas, something I've always wanted to do.'

'Oh yes?' she said through the steam rising from her teacup. Her eyes looked bright but her tone gave nothing away.

Jesus, he thought, *this'll never work. It's a bloody silly idea. There's no way she'll wear it. There's a hundred and one reasons why she'll never wear it.*

But this is my chance. My only chance. If I don't bring it out now, it'll disappear for ever. Then I'll keep going with the company and as time goes on I'll get nearer and nearer my pension, so I'll stay just for that. And if I stay now and pack it in later, I'll be too old to get another job, too old to do what I really want to do.

'I want to run a boat on the west coast of Scotland.'

Sarah choked and spilt some tea on the table. She put her cup down and looked squarely at him.

'*What?*'

He repeated what he had said.

She gave him a puzzled look. 'But we don't live in Scotland.'

'I know. That's what this is all about. I want us to move up to the west coast of the Scottish Highlands, where I was raised as a small boy, and try our luck with the tourist industry up there. Ideally, we'll buy a decent-sized old house with a view over a sea-loch where we can moor a boat, and then we can run a family business based on taking holiday-makers round the islands.'

Some kind of barrier had gone up, there was that drop in temperature again.

'Forget it, Jack.'

He wasn't surprised. But this was his chance, and he'd fight for it. Besides, the eternity ring wasn't doing its job, was even mocking him as it caught the light from the fluorescent tube over their heads. It might have been different if the light it caught had been brilliant sunlight or something else worthwhile. But a fluorescent tube, for God's sake!

'I thought you'd be glad. No, let me re-phrase that: I thought you'd be over the moon.' Sod it, he thought savagely as he got up and took his breakfast things to the sink, there's no pleasing some people.

At the sink he turned round, frustration and irritation creasing his brow. This thing was slipping away from him. 'I'm confused: just what the hell do you want, if I may make so bold? Hm?'

'What I want, Jack, is for you to pay us some attention, to become part of *our* lives, instead of leading a separate life of your own and not even paying lip-service to us as people.'

'But,' he said – and it seemed perfectly reasonable to him, 'that's exactly what I'm proposing.'

'No you're not. You're proposing we all uproot ourselves from our lives here, move to some remote outpost at the far end of the planet and start all over again.'

Only to be expected – and only another hundred reasons to go.

'Hang on, Sarah, that's cobblers.' With an effort he reined himself in. 'In the first place, Scotland's not some remote outpost at the far end of the planet. They do have shops, you know.' He hadn't intended to be cutting, but he wasn't going to apologise for it. 'Look: I've now persuaded myself that I can do what you ask by pursuing my dream, my vision. I'm enthusiastic about it and now is the right time. For God's sake, Sarah, you can't play cat-and-mouse with my life like this.'

Her eyes flared. 'And just *who* is playing cat-and-mouse with people's lives? Just think for one moment what it means to the rest of us. The children have lived here all their lives. Their whole social circle is down here, everyone speaks the same language . . .'

'*Jeeesus wept!*' So much for a generation of political correctness and race relations. Ninety-nine reasons still to go.

'. . . and they're at a crucial stage in their education. It's not fair to lift them out, lock, stock and barrel and dump them a million miles from their friends.'

He couldn't believe what he was hearing. He'd stopped counting.

'I can't even begin to list the flaws in your argument,' he shot back. 'In the first place, you've been saying for years I'm in a rut. Well, if your analysis doesn't indicate a rut the size of the Grand Canyon I don't know what does. It damn-well sounds to me as though the kids *need* lifting out of their cosy mud-hole and being given the opportunity to test and stretch themselves. You complained the other day that we were getting boring – *I* was getting boring – and we needed some excitement in our lives. Well, here's a bit of excitement I'm offering you and the first thing you do is fling it back in my face. It's something for all of us to do together, where we'll all face the same challenges together and help each other deal with them. Sarah, don't you see, it's the answer to your prayers? And it's something I really want to do – before I get too old and decrepit.' He ended on a note somewhere between pleading and inspirational.

Sarah's face was impassive, unimpressed. 'And what about me?'

'Well, what about you?'

'I've got a life too, you know. I'm a southern girl, I need to be within reach of London. All my friends are here, my interests, the charities I work for. Jack, I'm just not prepared to give all that up when you can . . .' She came lamely to a stop, as if she didn't like where she might have been going with it.

'Go on,' he prompted, angry now. 'When I can what?'

'Well,' she hesitated, 'there are any number of jobs round here that you could do. Very well-paid ones that only involve ordinary office hours, so that you could see the children in the evenings and at weekends. Like Howard next door.'

He couldn't believe what she'd just said. 'You want me to be like Howard next door? Ha!' He was back up to full throttle. 'The man's got no testosterone. If he's your idea of excitement then he's certainly not mine. He doesn't lead a normal life, for God's sake! A normal life round here is what I lead: go to work when it's dark, come home when it's dark again, get grunted at by the kids as they come in from whatever den of iniquity they've been in, work all weekend, work over Christmas and New Year. *That's* normal, Sarah. Look about you: everyone's doing it, all our friends – except Howard, of course.'

'Don't try and confuse me with arguments, Jack. We're not going, and that,' she announced with the finality of a jackboot, 'is that!'

6

'What do you want for lunch, Jack? One of your disgusting fried egg sandwiches?' Sunday lunch was always a relaxed affair – the roast beef and Yorkshire waited till the evening.

He came through from his study with his half-moon glasses perched on the tip of his nose. He'd managed to get to forty before his reading eyesight had fully acknowledged middle age. The half-moon glasses did their job, but Jack had decided they also made him look judicial and therefore distinguished. He liked peering over them.

'They're not disgusting, they're packed with all the good things a body needs to stay alive, and an absolute godsend at the end of the night-time watches at sea. And since you ask, two eggs please.'

Sarah was artistically placing two perfectly cooked eggs on a slice of industrial white bread when an apparition more than six feet tall and built like a racing-snake suspended itself in the kitchen doorway. Its mop of dark hair cascaded – if a haystack could ever cascade – over its eyes. The fingers of its right hand were hooked over the door frame; the fingers of its left hand scratched its right armpit. It was dressed overall in black: t-shirt unrelieved by any slogan, black jeans.

'Morning,' it croaked. 'What's for breakfast?' It came in and inspected the contents of the fridge. The apparition's name was Tom.

As it was more-or-less the first time he had seen Tom since he had come back from China, Jack took the opportunity to ask him how the play had gone at school.

'OK, I guess.'

'Mum said it was really good – that you were terrific.' God, this was like drawing teeth.

'Whatever . . .'

Brick wall. 'Come on, Tom, tell me a bit about it. I *am* interested, you know.'

Tom rounded on him. 'Oh yeah? Well it doesn't seem like it, Dad. You never come to these things so it doesn't seem like you're interested at all.' He picked up a half-made sandwich and stalked off.

Sarah offered, 'That went well, didn't it?'

'Look,' said Jack, 'this is bloody ridiculous. *You* want to do something about it, *I* want to do something about it, I've got a plan and you haven't. Why don't we get the kids involved? They might help us to a solution. Let's face it,' he said with a rueful grin, 'with all this expensive education I want some payback in the form of intelligent ideas.'

Sarah looked at him levelly. 'We're not going,' she said with quiet determination.

I'm not ready to give up just yet, he thought. 'Come on, let's see what they say, eh?'

After a moment or two and with a visible effort, she let out a long breath and said, 'I'll go and get Jenny. You get Tom.'

The kitchen wasn't big at the best of times. With four people sitting around the circular table it was crowded. Jack ramped up his determination to escape. Sarah dumped a fresh cafetière and three mugs on the table. Jenny helped herself from a bottle of Vesuvio agua con gaz from the fridge.

It was more formal than Jack wanted, but at least he had their attention.

'Your mother and I have been thinking . . .'

'Not again,' groaned Tom. Jenny glared at Tom and hissed at him to shut up.

Jack tried again, this time giving it straight from the shoulder. 'I'm packing in work at the company and we're thinking of moving to Scotland.'

The shockwave was palpable and lasted for what seemed like minutes. Jenny was the first to speak.

'*What?*' she gasped. 'Did you say *we're* moving to Scotland?'

A big grin split Tom's face. 'Way to go,' he drawled.

Jenny was just getting into her stride. 'No way. Like, *no way.*' She turned to appeal to Sarah. 'Mum, tell me this is a joke. It's not true, is it? *Is it?*'

Jack realised this was going just as Sarah had predicted. The smile on her face could only be described as triumphant.

'Settle down everyone, and listen, just listen for a moment.' Sarah held up her hands, palms forwards, and closed her eyes until relative quiet had descended. She turned back to Jack with a wide *I told you so* smile.

Jack struggled to find inspiration, honest or not. 'The company is being taken over again and it's likely our operations will be merged with the new owner's operations.' He classified that as a white one, permissible for the greater good of humanity. 'That means my job is likely to go. If that happens, there isn't another similar job that I can see around that I would be interested in doing, even if I were to get it.'

He paused, warming to his theme. He certainly had their attention. He plunged the cafetière and poured himself a mug.

'Now, you all know I don't like hanging around at other people's beck and call . . .' Jenny muttered something about didn't they just know it. Jack ignored her. 'And I'm not prepared to do that here. So we're going to take charge of our own lives and futures, and,' his voice masterful, decisive, 'I've got plans to go into business on our own account.'

He looked round their faces. While Tom, at fifteen, hadn't

quite grasped the full significance of what Jack had been saying, he nevertheless entered into the excitement of it and clearly welcomed the idea of a change, any change. But Jenny was still looking incredulous and not a little mutinous. Jack continued.

'So what I want us to do is go up to the west coast of Scotland and run a motor-boating business.'

Tom leapt up in delight and punched the air. 'YESSSSSS!'

Jenny leapt to her feet, too. 'That sucks!' she yelled. 'That *so* sucks! What about what *I* want? What about my friends here? Where will I go to school? And there are no shops up there . . .'

Tom rounded on her. 'Aw, cool it, Jen, it's a great idea. Let's do it, hey?'

'You don't understand, Tom, it's just not an option. Is it, Mum?'

Jack caught the glance between mother and daughter. He'd known it would be uphill, that Sarah would have a hundred and one reasons. That was now two hundred and two.

He knew when he was beaten. He and Tom both.

7

Later that evening Jack was in no better a mood, but he could no longer avoid writing up the notes from his meetings in Beijing and Hong Kong. The ones he had failed to do on the flight. He picked up his mobile phone and briefcase and headed off.

With the door of his study closed, the noise of television and hi-fi were reduced to a manageable level. He docked his laptop, found the relevant directory, and cracked his knuckles. The mobile phone on his desk went *dink* as a text message came through.

He didn't get many of those, that wasn't the kind of life he led. More usually his messages came through as emails on his BlackBerry, and he kept his Nokia just for calls. He could never make up his mind whether the company was being parsimonious in not providing employees with mobile phones that took photographs, printed theatre tickets and mixed cocktails as well as doing basic telephony, or whether that was merely sensible. The IT department had handed him a new one less than a month ago, and he'd given his old one – eighteen months old, perfectly serviceable and with barely a mark on it – to Sarah, as it was better than her more elderly brick of a handset.

He reached for the phone and pressed the button. Apparently the message was from Jules. He didn't know a Jules. Julie? She didn't call herself Jules, and anyway she was in a different department at the office and so he didn't have her number in his mobile memory.

Chérie. As Jack's away –

Of course. It was his old handset, the one he was still familiar with. His own new one would still be in his briefcase, probably wedged between two particles of dust, the way technology was going these days. The text would be for Sarah. He pressed the *exit* button and put the handset back on the desk.

Hang on a minute. As Jack's away what? And *chérie*? Well, girls did call each other odd things when menfolk weren't about. Probably wanting to arrange coffee or Tupperware or something.

But he didn't recall mention of a Julie or Jules. There was *French Jules*, of course, Sarah's tennis pro in the summer and fitness trainer in the winter. Not someone he knew. Dangerous places, fitness clubs.

Jack looked at the handset, tempted to read the whole message and find out what was going to happen 'as Jack's away'. He resisted the temptation and turned his hand to writing up his notes on his meetings.

As he finished his notes and opened up his emails, he asked himself why little insidious doubts were always green. This wasn't a monster, this was more like rising damp or dry rot. It merely crept imperceptibly until it had eaten away the load-bearing structure, by which time it was too late for remedial action. But its aura was green, it gave off green phosphorescence, it smelt like green mould.

Jack reached for Sarah's phone and accessed the text.

Chérie. As Jack's away, maybe it's a good time for a little massage on that bad back? Donnes-moi une cloche. J

Bad back? He didn't know Sarah had a bad back. And why was it a good time when he was away? He went hot and cold. How much interpretation should he put on it? How could he find out? Should he have been reading Sarah's messages at all? His mouth went dry.

8

It felt as though the office got smaller every time she went in it. That was rubbish, of course, but the amount of clothes, books and bric à brac being brought in these days by charity-minded donors meant that the shop downstairs and the store-room at the back were full to bursting and there was only the office to expand into. It didn't help that head office invented more paperwork all the time, so the in-trays and out-trays added to the claustrophobia of it.

It would have been intolerable if Sarah's colleague had been grim to share an office with. In truth, Sarah had been afraid of that when Maggie first marched in some four years earlier. Where Sarah was warm and friendly, Maggie was a frizzy-haired, coiled spring of a terrier who feared no one. But she was fun – enormous fun, and they had become firm friends.

Sarah stared out of the window and said, deliberately off-hand, 'We're going up to Scotland.'

'That's nice,' said Maggie as she licked the flap of an envelope and applied a stamp. 'For a week or just the weekend?'

'Permanently, actually.'

Maggie's tongue paused in mid-air. She glanced across at Sarah, tugged her dayglo-green glasses down her long nose and peered over them at her. 'I feel another coffee coming on. I'll get it and then you can tell me all about it.'

She navigated her way through the assault course to the printer on top of which stood a kettle, a jar of fair-trade instant coffee and a carton of milk with a destroyed top, all artistically arranged on an opened-out newspaper. The lead of the kettle was ridiculously short and its cracked plug was rammed into an extension lead that crossed the office diagonally, stuck at intervals to the linoleum floor by green gaffer tape.

As the kettle boiled its head off, Maggie casually relocated granules of coffee in and around their none-too-clean mugs, splashed in the water and poured in a dash of milk. At least as much milk dribbled onto the newspaper as into the mugs. She absently rotated a teaspoon about three-quarters of a revolution in each mug, and tossed the spoon in the general direction of the newspaper, where it bounced, hit the wall and landed on the floor.

Successfully renegotiating the obstacle course without spilling a single drop, she dumped one mug on Sarah's desk with enough force to dislodge the top couple of millimetres of brown liquid onto the desk, then settled herself comfortably into her chair and said, 'Right, tell. And I want all the filth, the low-down and the dirt. What brought this on? Has Jack been having an affair? Is he having a mid-life crisis? Has he been fired? I'm all ears.' Maggie had an overdeveloped theatrical gland; she didn't do mundane.

'It's complicated,' Sarah started.

'Uh-oh. It's Jules, isn't it?' Maggie stirred a low-calorie sweetener gleefully into her coffee, using a well-chewed green biro with the name of a hotel chain on it.

'No. Yes. Partly.'

'Did Jack find out?'

Sarah avoided Maggie's eyes. 'Sort of. Jules sent a very stupid – and, I may say, unwanted – text through to my phone and Jack saw it.'

Maggie looked as though she'd swallowed an egg whole. 'Does he normally search through your texts and emails?'

'Well, not exactly. Until now I haven't had any that I wouldn't want him to see, but it's this stupid mix-up with our phones.'

'What's that then?'

'You know how Jack gave me his old mobile phone when he got a new one at work last month? Well, he's still prone to picking up his old one, forgetting he's got a new one. And I don't help, because I leave it lying round the house, wherever. But anyway, he picked it up thinking it was his, Jules sent his text through, and – well, I couldn't think quickly enough to explain it away.'

Sarah stopped to take a mouthful of coffee. Maggie stepped in with her unique mixture of sympathy and relish.

'How did he take it?'

'Hit the roof. You know Jack.'

'Yes. Silly question. Was he long on the roof?'

'Same as usual: quick up and almost as quick down. I just rode it out, let him rant on and he blew himself out.'

Sarah recalled how, when he came off the boil, he had taken it surprisingly well. He had taken her hand and looked at it, *really* looked at it, the way he used to twenty years earlier, when there was only an engagement ring on it. It had been a seminal moment for her.

Maggie broke into her thoughts. 'And then?'

'Well, I suppose the price I've had to pay is agreeing to our going up to Scotland.'

'Oh God, you poor child! How did all this come about?'

'Actually, we'd been talking round the subject for months. You know I'm fed up with the separate lives we lead . . .'

'You amaze me.' Her tone was as the desert.

'And I told you about how we had sort-of discussed it when we went away for our wedding anniversary in January, but I didn't get the feeling that anything would actually happen. Jack came back from the Far East last week, announced that he wanted a change and proposed we go up to Scotland.'

'Gosh!' Maggie's tone was unimpressed. 'And what are you going to do up in Scotland?'

'Jack wants to run a boat.'

'A boat.'

'Yes.'

'Tell me,' Maggie said as though speaking kindly to someone with a brain disorder, 'tell me about this boat. Are we talking a gin palace here? Perhaps a cast-off from the Aga Khan? No? An enormous speedboat, then, with loads of scantily-dressed models hanging off the rails?'

'Not quite,' laughed Sarah, 'it's much more modest than that. He's had this dream for years it seems, which is to take groups of tourists up and down the west coast of Scotland.'

'Sounds thoroughly dreary to me,' Maggie said. 'And you, what do you think of this hare-brained scheme?'

'At first I refused even to consider it. But then my bargaining power sort of – well, *shifted*, and I didn't feel I had any option but to agree.'

'But Scotland, for God's sake! Have you ever been there? No? Well I have and I'm here to tell you, my girl, that it's all mountains, porridge and hairy Scotsmen throwing telegraph poles. Ugh!' She gave a shiver of disgust.

'Now there's a thought,' Sarah giggled. 'But seriously, Maggie, I'm getting to quite – well, not *like* the idea, it's more a case of coming to accept it. Yes, it'll be a bit different from here, but Jack says they even have a branch of Tesco up there!'

Maggie gave her friend a withering look. 'That's all right, then.'

'On top of that,' Sarah continued, 'I've been on at Jack to give up or sort out his job for our benefit, and now he's decided to do so I can't very well turn round and tell him I don't like the alternative, can I?'

'You're a woman, Sarah. You can do whatever you like with

a man and his ideas. Let's face it, duckie, men don't understand us, thank God, and we ought to keep it that way. Keep them on their toes, keep them guessing, and keep them frustrated: it sharpens up their liver a treat.'

'Well, I was the one who got caught out.' Sarah spoke quietly, studying her still-full coffee mug.

Maggie became more serious. She didn't need to ask to understand that Sarah was putting a good face on a ghastly situation. Instead she asked how the children were taking it.

'Tom's delighted.' Glad of the change of emphasis, Sarah looked up more cheerfully. 'I wonder if this might not be the making of him. He's a handful at home, rebellious at school, poor academically and a downright pain generally. But he's brightened up tremendously since we told them about the idea and he's a different boy.'

'And Jenny? I'll bet she's thrilled.' Maggie poured a ton of lead into her sarcasm.

Sarah admitted that Jenny was a problem. 'She's very upset, thinks we're heading for the Arctic Circle to share a hovel with shaggy, long-haired cows.'

'You are, honey, you are. So how're you going to deal with it?'

'Jack's taking a few days off next weekend – says he no longer has a career to jeopardise. We'll fly up to Glasgow, hire a car, drive round and see what's what. We'll only make our final decision after that. Actually, I'm rather looking forward to it – in spite of myself.'

'Are you all going up?'

'Of course. Well, I suppose so. I hope so. But now you mention it, with Jenny indulging in a major sulk I suppose we must anticipate a bit of foot-stamping.'

'I'll bet you a manicure to a massage you won't get her to agree. She'll be a trouble, that one, a hell-cat. Rather than save your marriage, this'll put it under too much strain and you'll end up in the divorce courts, destitute and unhappy. Or worse still,'

Maggie said with relish, 'you'll end up with Jules. You're making a big mistake altogether, my girl, you mark my words.'

She downed the last of her coffee and looked up with a grin. 'Ooh look, it's time for lunch.'

9

Jenny Ross was one of those people for whom standard suburban life in the southeast of England was natural and comfortable. Worldly-wise to a level appropriate for a seventeen-year-old girl, pretty of feature, with golden hair and a sunny personality, she radiated wholesomeness. Academic success came easily to her and she displayed a mature diligence that led her teachers, rightly or wrongly, to nod their heads sagely and remark on a successful marriage of commitment and natural talent.

In her spare time she liked going into London or nearby Reading to dust out the corners of her debit card. Long since had she negotiated with her father to drop pocket money in favour of an allowance, even though to begin with the figure had been the same. How delicious it was casually to drop into the conversation with Amy and Laura that her allowance would cover whatever purchase she was focusing on. The other two noticed the reference and very soon they too were drawing an allowance. But Jenny had got there first – as she always did.

Life came easily to young Miss Ross.

'Mum, we're not serious about this Scotland thing, are we?'

The early evening news on the television was just finishing. Jack wouldn't be home for some while and Tom was in his room, where he had been most of the evening. Jenny, dressed in white t-shirt and much-patched blue jeans fraying at every available edge, was stretched out on the sofa concentrating on the application of cerise to toenail. Sarah's mug was empty; Jenny's was still half full of cold lapsang souchong.

'Yes, darling, of course. I thought we'd been over this?'

'Not really.' Jenny lost concentration on her artwork and looked up. She waved the tiny paintbrush around for emphasis. 'Dad calls me and Tom down for lunch. We're sat . . .'

'Sitting,' Sarah corrected primly, listening with one ear to the weather forecast.

'. . . *sitting* round the lunch table and Dad gets all formal. Out of the blue he announces we've all got to give up our lives here, move to . . . to . . . oh, I don't know, the other end of the known world. The next thing we know is that me and Tom are told that you and Dad have sorted it all out and we're going. I mean, come *on*. That's not exactly discussing it, is it?'

'Maybe not, but it doesn't alter the fact that it's what we're going to do. As a family. Dad and I have decided we are going to go up there and you and Tom will therefore have to come.'

'But I don't see why! What's got into Dad? Is he having a mid-life crisis, or is it the male menopause?'

'Behave yourself, young lady,' snapped Sarah.

'Sorry Mum.' Jenny recoiled slightly, more from surprise at her own forwardness than from the sharpness of the rebuke. 'But I don't want to move from here. I like it here, all my friends are here, everything I do is here. I'll be taking my A-levels next year and I want to do them with all my friends and in the school I know. I don't know anyone up there, they all speak a foreign language. And do they have any decent shops up there?' She leaned forward, replacing the congealing paintbrush in the bottle. 'Mum, don't you *see*? It's all wrong for me.'

Sarah kept her sigh to herself. She saw only too well that it was indeed wrong for Jenny – much as it was all wrong for herself. On the other hand, a part of her agreed with Jack that perhaps their life was too comfortable here, in their own rut, and that Jenny needed the challenge of a change. It was too bad about her friends and the shops, but she'd survive that.

'Look,' Sarah said as she got up, collected their mugs and put them on the tray, 'we'll all be going up for a look-round next weekend so that those of us who haven't been before can see what it's like, and get an idea about houses. We can explore the shops round there – I'm sure things aren't as bad as you imagine them – and we'll look round the local schools.'

'Mum, you're just not hearing me. I don't want to go up. I'm over sixteen so I'm legally entitled to make up my own mind. I'm going to stay down here.'

Sarah looked at her, eyebrows arched. She had not expected this previously compliant, sensible child to come out with such arrant nonsense.

'And where precisely will you be staying after your parents have gone away?'

'I'll stay with Amy and Laura. I've discussed it with them and they say I can stay with them.'

This was getting silly. 'And how much will their mother require for your board and lodging?'

Momentarily Jenny was thrown. But she rallied handsomely.

'We haven't discussed it yet, but I'll pay whatever is necessary – out of my savings, and I'll get a job packing shelves at the supermarket in the evenings.'

'Which will do wonders for your A-levels. Oh Jenny,' Sarah was at the same time exasperated and sympathetic, and also embarrassed because of the position she'd found herself in, 'don't you see how unreal all this is? We *are* going up to Scotland, you *are* coming with us, and there's an end to it.'

Jenny jumped up, four toes of the right foot painted, the remainder naked.

'This is *so* unfair! I thought you of all people would understand. Dad's got an excuse: he doesn't take any interest in us because he's never here and he doesn't know how selfish he's being. But you know what's important to us: I can't believe that you've agreed to give up everything we've got here.'

With a mutinous expression on her face she headed for the door, closed it behind her with more force than was quite polite and sprinted for her room.

Sarah felt shaken. Not for the first time, she was beginning to wonder whether she should have left everything just as it was. Jenny had a point – several points, actually. All the same points Sarah had made to Jack. But all those had been swept away when her indiscretion had come to light. Jules, for God's sake!

He was probably not quite forty, but he was trim, taut and terrific, skin burnished to a light bronze and fair hair kept on the pale side of gold by years in the sun – which was even more sickening than if it had been out of a bottle. On its own, that wouldn't have been enough to do it for her, but that was certainly good groundwork. No, what had toppled her was his French charm, the fact that he made her feel special. When she was having a lesson with him or having a cooling glass of fruit cocktail afterwards, she was the centre of his attention, she mattered to him. A feeling largely absent when she was at home. There she was the hotel manager, *chef de cuisine*, waiter, hall porter and chambermaid, all rolled into one. She appreciated she wasn't likely to be the only housewife who had ever felt like that, but that wasn't the point.

Equally, she didn't imagine that Jules didn't pay the same attention to any other attractive woman who had just sneaked over the magic thirty-nine line. But that thought was easy to lock away and ignore, especially when she was going weak at the knees as he fluttered his fingers down her naked back in the Treatment Room.

The first time it had happened she had suffered pangs of guilt afterwards, driving home in a state of terrified mortification. That was months ago. She had not allowed it to happen again – until last week. She had suffered a moment of vulnerability the day after Jack departed for China, not helped by a genuine twinge in her back which Jules was adept at massaging away. That had most definitely been the last time she was going to allow her defences to crumble, in any event, and she'd thought he had more sense than to push his luck – and in writing at that. When he'd asked how long Jack would be away, she'd said a week. He'd obviously taken it mathematically, whereas Sarah thought everyone knew a week's business trip meant back home on Friday evening or Saturday morning. Didn't they?

When Jack brought her phone to her and said she had a text from Jules, she'd assumed it was to say he was cancelling their next session. When she'd read the text she'd been puzzled at first, then her blood had frozen. Jack was still hovering with an unsuccessful air of inconsequence, and she was such an unpractised dissembler that she'd found herself babbling about how it all meant nothing and nothing had gone on – well, not much anyway. The more she babbled, the deeper the hole she dug.

After his inevitable eruption, Jack had managed to get it right – which wrong-footed Sarah utterly. Looking back on it now, maybe she should have shouted back at him and blamed it all on him. Instead, she'd let him come off the boil, apologise for his outburst and become magnanimous. He'd blamed himself, said he understood, and that was why he wanted them all to begin over again, so that they could function as a family.

Instantly she'd recognised defeat: the war had been lost in that one brief skirmish. Sarah truly didn't want to go up to Scotland: Birmingham would have been bad enough; even Oxford. It was true what she'd said, that her life was down here, and her children's lives. She didn't want to uproot herself and them. But Jack had won. He occupied the moral high ground; he'd forgiven her and blamed himself. They would all have a real chance to blossom.

It wasn't a case of blackmail. It had been more like a small nuclear device, rendering debate futile. The fall-out would be disastrous.

* * *

Jenny slammed her bedroom door and launched herself onto her bed in floods of tears. It wasn't a big room, but it was *her* room and she had it just as she wanted. She had grown up in it, known it for most of her life. The posters on the walls had changed as she had changed, but the teddy bears on the bed hadn't. She hugged a cushion to her stomach and her sobs began to subside. She saw Panda stare at her accusingly, as if he should have been providing the comfort, not an inanimate cushion. For God's sake, here she was, seventeen years old, an adult, and she was crying like a baby. It was all *his* fault. And now Mum appeared to be on *his* side.

She sniffed again and dragged the back of her hand across her eyes. She reached for her box of tissues and grabbed a handful. After a nose-blow and an eye-mopping-up job she felt a need to access the real world. She reached for her mobile phone.

'Hi, Amy!'

'Hi, Jen. You all right? Got a cold or something?'

Jenny sniffed again and rubbed her red eyes with a tissue.

'No. Just had a blazing row with Mum about Scotland. I thought she of all people would understand but she's supporting Dad.'

Jenny curled up on her bed, tucked her mobile phone between ear and shoulder, and occupied her hands with mangling the soggy tissue.

'Hang on,' said Amy, 'I'll put you on loudspeaker so Laura can hear.' Jenny heard a click. 'Can you still hear me?'

'Yeah. Hi, Laura.'

'Hiya.'

'Have you tried talking to your dad?' continued Amy

Jenny snorted derisively. 'Even if I ever got to see him, he'd never understand. He's like a little boy with this new idea of his and he can't see anything else outside that. I really don't know what's got into him. I think I preferred him the way he was, at least he let us get on with our real lives.'

'God, that's awful, Jen. Can't you do something?'

'Such as?'

'I don't know.'

Laura broke in. 'What about ringing Childline and telling them he's abusing you?'

'Don't be silly, Lo. It wouldn't take them a minute to find out that wasn't true, and it wouldn't achieve anything.'

'It would slow things down a treat while they investigated. And it would let your parents know how pissed off you are. You know, a bit like stamping on someone's foot just to get their attention.'

'Well, thanks for the thought, Lo, but maybe I'll take a raincheck on it.'

'Did you tell your mum you could stay with us while you finish your A-levels?'

'Yes, but she got all practical and said how much would your mum charge me for bed and breakfast. And I guess it's true your mum wouldn't agree unless my mum and dad had told her it's OK. But thanks for the offer, anyway.'

There was a glum silence.

'So what're you going to do?' Amy asked.

'Dunno. Mum said we're all going up to Scotland next week for a few days to look round but I don't think I can face it.'

'Well, come and stay over with us and let the others go.'

'Don't be silly, Ames,' Laura broke in. 'If we can't find a way to stop Jen having to go up eventually, it's best she goes up and finds out what it's really like, and then she can tell them in technicolour why the place is crap.'

Jenny thought for a moment. Laura was probably right, but just for the present she felt so anti-everything that she really couldn't bring herself to do that. The thought of a long journey with Mum and Dad – particularly Dad whom, right now, she felt almost as though she hated – made her just too angry.

'Oh, I don't know, Lo. I'd really like it if I could stay over with you guys for a few days. I feel like I've had enough of this place. Maybe I'd feel a bit better after a break from this madhouse.'

'Yeah, that's cool, Jen. Like Amy says, come and stay over. Maybe we can give you some ideas about how you can *really* screw the whole plan up.'

'You're mental, Laura,' Amy said, 'you know that?'

'Yeah, I know.' Jenny could almost hear Laura purring at the compliment.

10

Karen Olssen was no closer to deciding than when the letter had come unexpectedly in yesterday's post. Maybe a day out in the boat would help clarify things.

She crawled out from under the duvet, twitched the curtain a fraction and looked at the sky. There was sleet in the air, but the shipping forecast had suggested it would clear by mid-morning and they would have a good day. That meant she'd be able to see the snow-capped peaks of the mountains of Mull and Morven: she loved that.

She shivered, and switched on the two-bar electric fire before disappearing to the bathroom. The electric shower, although modern, was like most mod cons in the cottage: inadequate. It was always a toss-up whether she accepted tepid water in compensation for a decent flow of water; or whether warm water was more important than volume. It was warm water and a weak dribble this morning. She towelled herself off, ran back to the bedroom and leapt back into bed. She knew Ewan was on the verge of waking up anyway, but when she cuddled into his back for warmth he rolled over towards her, opened his arms and engulfed her. She giggled, as she always did when his bushy red beard tickled her face. This was always the best part of her day.

It was nearly a quarter to eight when they resurfaced, but they didn't have to be at the boat for another forty-five minutes. While Ewan showered Karen dressed and got the breakfast. The aroma of Colombian arabica medium roast did its usual trick and drew Ewan into the tiny kitchen still towelling his sandy hair. He never combed it, it always seemed to sort itself out, and anyway, it suited his weatherbeaten face with its crow's feet round the eyes.

He was wearing his red and blue Faeroes sweater – Karen didn't like the grey one his mother had given him last year after a trip to the Yorkshire Dales; it wasn't cheerful enough. In fairness, she conceded, his mum didn't like it much either.

'Any thoughts yet?' he asked.

She shrugged. 'Too soon. I need time. And coffee. And cereal.' Her rich Maine accent belied her Norwegian parentage. She played with her light-brown hair, which now lay in loose, thick braids over her left shoulder. Her sign of indecision, uncertainty.

'So do I,' said Ewan.

It took them no time at all to walk the hundred yards from their cottage in Ellenabeich on the Isle of Seil to the slate-built jetty. There they flashed-up the tiny outboard motor on the rubber dinghy and rode out to their eight-metre, rigid-hull inflatable, riding to a mooring buoy in the narrow sound between Ellenabeich and Easdale Island.

Ewan carried out the standard checks on the two 125-horsepower outboard engines, started them up and listened to them ticking over, checking the dials on his console. Karen meanwhile had secured the painter of the dinghy to the buoy and singled-up the bow-rope of the RIB. When he was satisfied, Ewan asked her to slip the bow-rope, and he gently motored alongside the slate jetty, ready for their first boatload of punters for the day.

By lunchtime they had run two two-hour trips with a full boat each time. The clouds had cleared and the sun glinted on the tiny wavelets. It was approaching spring tides and so the tidal streams throughout the day were running swiftly – drama for the customers. They'd spotted no whales but the dolphins were out to play, as were seals and puffins. It was good to be alive, Karen thought.

They wandered back to their cottage on Front Street for lunch, a small tub of Orkney pickled herrings and brown bread. The letter was still on the kitchen table – with a small splash of the sweet vinegar marinade to add character.

Dear Dr Olssen,

BENGUELA CURRENT PROJECT

You will be aware that I am assembling a team to research the decline in the krill and plankton stocks in the Benguela Current. Full details of the project are on our website: www.benguelaproject.ac.za. This is research of global significance, both scientifically and economically. I have been appointed Project Leader and I am seeking a Deputy.

Your name has come up too often to be ignored, and I have spoken to both Professor Balfour at the University of Delaware who supervised your doctorate, and Professor Baird at the Scottish Association for Marine Science at Dunstaffnage. Both of them spoke very highly of your scientific qualifications and experience, and your ability to lead a research project.

I would be grateful if you would consider becoming the Deputy Leader for this project. If you are interested, will you please contact me at your earliest convenience, and we can arrange for you to come down to Capetown as soon as possible for a quick chat, and then we can formalise things.

Yours sincerely
Dr Kees van der Stap
Marine Research Institute, University of Capetown

Karen casually ignored it. She had read the letter a hundred times and knew its contents by heart. Obviously she wanted the job; anyone would. But it was a long way from here – and from Ewan. Ewan would never in a million years move from the Hebrides: he'd been born on Raasay and had spent all his life on these waters.

Head said Benguela Project; heart said Ewan.

'Take it.'

'What?' Karen was jolted out of her reverie, knife and fork still poised over her herring.

Ewan nodded at the letter. 'Take it. Take the job. It's got you written all over it.'

'When I want your opinion, *Eòghann Mac a'Phearsain*, I'll give it to you. In the meantime, I'm thinking.' She looked at her untouched plate, then at his empty one. 'Want my fish?'

'Can't stand the damn things. I only eat them because you put them in front of me.' Ewan got up from the table, picked up her plate and tipped its contents into the bin. He brought her an apple which she munched while he washed up.

When they had put their boating gear back on, Ewan beckoned her over and folded her in his arms. They looked like two Michelin men in different dimensions: he towered a good twelve inches over her.

He kissed the top of her head and said, 'Take it.'

She said, 'No.'

He said, 'Stubborn woman,' and kissed her again. 'Let's find some customers to separate from their hard-earned wealth.'

They waddled, hand in hand, back to the boat.

There was a decent-sized crowd standing at the jetty. Many were already booked on the SeaFari boats, which ran from the same place and did pretty much the same thing as Ewan and Karen. Ewan never took bookings in advance, so took those people who would otherwise have been disappointed.

Without any difficulty he filled his boat, but not until after the pantomime he and Karen watched most days.

'Phwoar! Dad, can we do a boat trip please? Please?'

Dad, trying unsuccessfully to hide his excitement under a

veneer of *oh, all right then*, turns to Mum and says, 'Why not? You coming?'

Mum looks horrified as if to say *are you out of your tiny mind?* but says instead, 'Er, I think I'll sit this one out. I'll have a cup of tea and read my book in that tea-room over there.'

So Jack and Tom, with all the other passengers, climbed into the storm trousers and jackets Ewan provided, while Sarah looked on in amusement. After a demonstration of the lifejackets and a safety briefing, Ewan nudged the RIB away from the jetty and out towards the open sea. The south-westerly breeze freshened as they rounded the jetty, so the high-speed ride down the Sound of Luing was something of a thrill for fathers and sons. Karen pointed out the marine wildlife, which appeared with meticulous timing as the boat sped towards its main destination: the wild Gulf of Corryvreckan.

As the boat turned south-westwards round the island of Scarba, Karen told the customers about the Gulf.

'There are differing stories about the name and its origin. The one we like is that Corryvreckan was a sea-witch who lived in a cave just below the waves. If she was in a good mood, the waters were OK. But when she was cross she kicked up an awful row and the waters became rough.'

Karen always made sure she was looking towards the stern of the boat where Ewan was driving. Ewan, as always, rolled his eyes. She loved that bit.

'For those whose love of science is more highly developed than their sense of romance,' she went on, 'the other explanation is the presence of a huge rock pinnacle that sticks up a hundred metres – that's over three hundred feet – above the sea floor surrounding it.' She paused for the oohs and aahs to subside.

'As the water rushes along through the gulf it encounters this pinnacle which *forces*' (she accompanied the word with gestures for emphasis) 'the water to shoot upwards, and as there's only about another thirty metres to go before it hits the surface, you get this massive upwelling of water at the surface.'

'A bit like the Benguela Current,' Ewan interjected from the back.

'A bit like the Benguela Current,' Karen agreed. She turned to the rest of the boat. 'Don't worry about that; private joke.' She glared at Ewan.

'Now,' she continued, 'when there's not much lateral movement in the water – when there's not much tidal stream running – the upwelling never gets to the surface. But when there's a lot of tidal stream – midway between high-water springs and low-water springs, then it's moving at anything up to nine or ten knots, which in marine terms is going like the clappers. The water moving along the northern side of the Gulf – that's where the rock pinnacle is – throws millions of tons of water up to the surface and we get these gigantic eddies which really do become whirlpools, and there are quite big, sharp waves. Oh look,' she pointed to the east, 'look, you can see them just beginning to form.' She looked at her watch. 'Yes, I think we'll get quite a good performance today as the tides are about right for it.'

Ewan reduced speed as they approached the first eddies. Coming up fast from the south was a big, blue-hulled boat leaving a dramatic wake. The blue boat, *Porpoise II*, settled on a parallel course just a few metres away and matched Ewan's speed. A figure leaned out of the cuddy and called across to Karen.

'How's the old girl?'

'Brewing up nicely. Might get a good display today.'

'I'll go and play round the Grey Dogs then.'

'Take it easy, David, that could get nasty.'

David Ainsley patted his boat lovingly. 'That's why I've got nine hundred horsepower.' He gave a cheery wave and returned to the controls. The bow of *Porpoise II* rose as the stern dug down, and the boat leapt away leaving a thundering wake.

'Show-off,' muttered Karen as she and Ewan waved back.

For another ten or fifteen minutes they watched the turbulence growing in the water as the tidal stream increased in speed. Eddies expanded in size and intensity and occasional vortexes formed, giving the impression that they could swallow small boats whole. Ewan kept the boat as close as he dared to the big ones, occasionally allowing the stern to begin to be sucked towards the vortex. At that point he would push the throttles forward and, with two hundred and fifty horsepower from the two engines combined, the boat would leap away and out of trouble.

With a glance at his watch, Ewan eased the throttles open and headed westwards, out towards the open sea. He brought the boat close under the sheer cliffs of the exposed west coast of Scarba and everyone strained their necks skywards. As the boat followed the cliffs northwards they came to the tip of the island and a tiny gap a mere fifty yards wide before the next island, Lunga, started.

'And this, ladies and gentlemen, is *Bealach a' Choin Ghlais*. Those for whom Gaelic is not their mother tongue know it by its English translation, the Pass of the Grey Dogs.'

'Is Gaelic your mother tongue, love?' shouted some wag with a Lancashire accent at the back of the boat, to general merriment.

'In Penobscot Bay, Maine, we speak little else!' The volume of laughter left little doubt as to who'd won that round. When class had settled down, Karen resumed.

'Now, you know how the islands of Islay, Jura, Scarba and Lunga form a line from south to north? Well, when the tide rushes up the west coast of Scotland it's split by those islands; one mass of water rushes up the east side, between the islands and the mainland, and the rest passes up the west side, the open sea. The gap between that line of islands and the mainland narrows like a funnel – it's called the Sound of Jura. This squeezes the mass of water as it passes up that funnel, causing it to rise higher than the water to the west of those islands, which isn't squeezed like that. The result of this is that the water being squeezed in the Sound of Jura rushes through to the open sea whenever it finds a gap. The first gap is the Gulf of Corryvreckan, the one we saw earlier.' The boat gave an unexpected lurch; the passengers grabbed a handrail for balance. Karen rode the lurch.

'The second gap is the Grey Dogs, the one we're looking at now. In this one the water level on the east side can be six feet or more higher than the water level on the open sea side. In effect, it becomes a huge waterfall. And when the wind is blowing from the west the whole area to the west becomes turbulent and confused.'

The boat was standing about thirty yards to the west of the entrance to the Grey Dogs, which was protected by a group of islets and rocks.

'Can we go through it?'

'Ewan,' she called over. 'This gentleman here – what's your name?'

'Tom.'

'Tom wants to know whether we can go through it.'

'Aye, we can,' said Ewan in his slow lilt, 'when the tidal stream's not running too strongly. But it's still crazy at the moment and I wouldn't risk it for the next two, maybe three hours. You see that standing wave there?' He pointed to a trough in the sea beneath a wall of water, which stood almost two metres high. 'There, that's the dangerous bit – that would stop us dead in our tracks. I'll take you at slack water – Karen'll sell you another ticket!'

Tom didn't join in the general laughter. Instead he turned, awe-struck, to Jack and said simply, 'This is just *so* amazing.' He turned to Karen again. 'Which is the more dangerous – Corryvreckan or the Grey Dogs?'

She grinned. 'The Corryvreckan's a pussycat when the Grey Dogs are running.'

Back at Ellenabeich the boat spewed out its passengers, who stripped off their lifejackets and storm gear and gave them back to Karen. The big RIB returned to the mooring buoy, Karen squared away the storm gear and lifejackets in their trolley and Ewan brought up the fuel tanks.

'Decided?' Ewan was determined to push the issue.

Karen sighed. 'I think so.'

'Good.'

'How do you know it's good? You don't know *what* I've decided.'

'Maybe not. But I know which way it'll end up.'

'Pig!'

'Oink.'

Ewan indicated the trolley with all their boat gear in. 'Hop in and I'll push.'

'But there isn't room.'

'I know.' He grinned

She started hitting him playfully on the chest. He put his arms round her and she stopped, looked up at him.

'Go on,' he said quietly and seriously, 'tell me.'

'I'm not going.'

'That's the wrong answer. Why not?'

'Because I'm not leaving you, and you'll never leave here.'

'You've never bloody asked me, wumman! This place is getting too crowded: *Porpoise*, SeaFari and all the rest of them. It's getting like Argyll Square. I've never been outside the west of Scotland and I want to see the world before I die. I want to ride the Benguela Current.'

Karen bounced up, wrapped her arms round his neck and her legs round his waist.

'South Africa, here we come!' he shouted. A passing seagull squawked, jinked in its flight-path, and released a massive splat.

11

They had picked the car up from the long-term car park at Heathrow and were now immobile on the main road as they negotiated the crush through Staines and Egham. The delay to the flight had forced them down the jaws of rush hour. A light but determined rain was falling, the sodium street lights leaving a sulphurous orange on the greasy tarmac.

'Well, Tom, what do you reckon?' Jack glanced over his left shoulder.

'Yeah, really cool,' Tom replied. 'The boat trip was the best bit. Are we really going to get a boat?'

Jack was quite clear about this. Not only was it part of his dream, it was part of his financial plan. 'Yes we are. And we're going to do the same sort of thing – you know, boat trips, dolphins, whales, sea eagles and so on. And when you're not at school, or when you've left, you'll be my boat's crew – and you'll be paid a commercial wage, of course.'

'Oh wow!'

Nothing more to be said, thought Jack. Tom's on board. He spoke more quietly to Sarah. This was the important bit.

'And you, what did you think darling?'

He held his breath while she thought for a moment or two.

'I'll admit I was surprised. Actually, I thought it was lovely.

And I really liked those houses we looked at, particularly with all the daffodils just coming out. I could certainly see myself living in any of them.' Jack breathed a silent prayer of thanks that, with luck, they wouldn't be in their matchbox much longer.

'What did you think of Glasgow? Was there anything approximating a shop that caught your eye?'

Sarah cuffed him on the arm. 'You know what I thought of Glasgow. And the shops. They're every bit as good as Reading – actually, they're not much short of Oxford Street and Regent Street, but without the crowds. I suppose my preconception of Glasgow was based on pictures and stories of the Gorbals in the fifties and sixties, and I guess that's all been renewed now. I'll be able to tell Maggie she doesn't know what she's talking about. That'll be fun!'

A Harley-Davidson with cowhorn handlebars and rider with an upturned soup bowl on his head wove carefully between the lanes of stationary vehicles. Quietly, Jack asked Sarah what she thought Jenny's reaction would be.

'I really don't know, Jack. I'm worried she won't even give it a chance. It's a country area and Jenny's a town girl. Yes, Glasgow has bright lights and serious shopping but it's, what, a hundred miles away? And I can't say I particularly like the idea of her being in a permanent mood, not after she's been so easygoing.'

The traffic began to move and they eased past Imperial College. More Hell's Angels – not one of them aged noticeably less than sixty – meandered sedately between the lines of crawling cars.

'Can you speak to her?'

'I'll try. But when I called her from Argyll for a chat she wasn't very talkative and I don't know whether she'll be much more amenable now.'

Out of the corner of his eye, he watched Sarah absently drumming her fingers.

12

From: <u>L Fox, Commercial Executive</u>
To: <u>J Ross, Operations Director</u>
Sent: 29th April
Subject: Hi

Hi Jack

I'm so sorry I won't be able to go to your leaving party tomorrow evening – I did ask Rob if I could come back from the States one day early and he said if I wrapped the contract up by then for the target price, I could. So that means No. Shame.

Well, Jack, I'm so sorry you're going, and so quickly after – well, so soon. Was it anything I said?! Can we meet up after you've gone and maybe have a drink or something? I think you've got my home address and phone number.

Do keep in touch.

Love,
Lydia

From: <u>Jack Ross</u>
To: <u>L Fox, Commercial Executive</u>
Sent: 2nd May
Subject: Re: Hi

Hi Lydia

Thanks for your email. Yes, I'm sorry you weren't at the party; it went on longer than anyone had expected and migrated down to the pub. Luckily I'd booked a room at the Novotel, which turned out to be a wise move. Tell Rob he's a miserable old blighter with no sense of humour – although that's not quite how he looked at my party . . .

It was a bit sad leaving the company after so long, but there we are.

I'm not sure there'll be too many opportunities to meet up because we, as a family, are moving up to Scotland very soon to start a new life up there. The house is in chaos – packing crates etc, you can imagine.

I hope things go well for you all in the future.

All the best,
Jack

13

The idea had, of course, been Sarah's. Jack's preference had been to battle it out with Jenny but Sarah had seen the subtler way. It also made practical sense, a second car. And Jack had accepted the force of the fairness argument: Tom would undoubtedly be a major beneficiary in the acquisition of a boat, but Jenny wouldn't. Everything stacked up; there didn't seem to be any downsides.

The cost wouldn't be much of an issue, not once they had sold the Bracknell property. Although disappointing, the withdrawal of their purchaser from its sale hadn't been a major concern to begin with. It had been a finely balanced decision whether to call off the purchase of the house they'd set their hearts on in Argyll, but the Bracknell estate agent had been very confident that another buyer would be found quickly, so they carried on with the purchase. *Market's very, wossname, buoyant at the moment, won't be two ticks before you got a string of punters lining up at your door. Credit crunch? Nah. S'over. Money flooding the market again, piece of cake. Trust me. Good as sold.*

The village of Kilbeg was small, being little more than a cluster of a few dozen houses, a pub and two shops, some ten miles south of Oban on the coast road. It nestled on the edge of Loch Feochan, a sea-loch affording plenty of protection for boats at mooring buoys. The house they had bought was an imposing, stone-built Victorian villa that gloried in the name *Creag Mhor*, 'the great rock', after what appeared to be a prehistoric monolith in the back garden. Rather ungraciously, Jack suggested it was builder's rubble too big for the skip, which had grown moss and lichen instead. The house had been empty when they bought it, the previous occupant having shuffled off to a nursing home. It was in need of a pull-through with a pineapple and some modernisation, but that would have to wait until they had some money coming in.

Among her many worries Sarah had been concerned that they, and she particularly, would struggle to find friends, people with whom they could quickly forge a warm, comfortable relationship. Hugh MacDonald, the local GP, and his wife Annie had been warmly welcoming as soon as Jack and Sarah had arrived. Hugh and Annie were maybe twenty years older than Jack and Sarah, even though their daughter was the same age as Jenny. There was an element of relief in the MacDonalds that Lucy now had a like-minded friend of similar age in the village, a sentiment that Sarah reciprocated.

Lucy was probably the primary troublemaker, ScotRail the accomplice. Most Saturdays saw the girls taking the morning train to Glasgow for a day's shopping and bright lights, returning on the evening train. That Jenny was able to cover the short drive from Kilbeg to Oban meant total independence for the girls, satisfaction for Jenny, and relief for Jack and Sarah that she had settled so well.

There had never been doubt as far as Tom was concerned. As he was about to turn sixteen there was an understanding, implicit at first until it morphed seamlessly into reality, that he would leave school at the end of the summer term. It suited them both, as Jack would need crew for his boat and Tom wanted an outdoor job.

Hitherto not a major exponent of school team sports, Tom discovered an unsuspected pleasure in shinty as a member of the local club. A game that superficially resembled hockey, it was played, with robust enthusiasm and without the dead hand of most of the rules of hockey, throughout the Highlands. Team practice was on Tuesday and Thursday evenings, and matches on Saturday afternoon.

Jenny thus found herself explaining a social encounter to her Bracknell friends, the twins Amy and Laura.

'Name?' Amy demanded.

'Struan Campbell.'

'Sounds weird to me.' That was Laura. 'Where did you find him?'

'Shinty.'

'Where's Shinty?' they asked as one.

'It's not a place, you morons, it's a game.'

'Game? You mean, like Monopoly or something?'

'No. Like hockey or something. They play it with things like hockey sticks but aren't, and it's awfully rough.'

'So you play this shinty, then?' Jenny could hear the scepticism in Laura's voice.

'Don't be so silly, of course not.' *Like, yeah, as if I play a rough sport.* 'But Tom plays, and I take him down to the sports ground and pick him up again.'

'And how does this Struan fit in?'

'He's captain of Tom's team.'

Jenny could almost hear the *click* of the light going on at the other end. 'Ohhhh,' they said together. 'And so he saw you hanging around the bar and toilets . . .' Laura continued. Jenny mentally threw a cushion at her, and from the commotion at the other end Amy probably had.

'So yeah,' Jenny continued, 'we go out a bit. He's asked me to go to the Argyllshire Gathering Ball with him in August, which is all long skirts and kilts and sporrans and things.'

There was a cacophony of *oh wows* and *jammy old cows* from the other end.

It was a development that Sarah wished might have come

a bit later, but as Jack pointed out, Jenny was almost eighteen, a damned attractive young lady with a lighthouse of a personality, and Struan Campbell was a fine young man. He was nineteen, the son of the police constable in Kilbeg, and would be going up to Strathclyde University in the autumn to read law.

If Sarah was amused by the shock of peroxide yellow in his shaggy hair, Jenny hotly defended it as less a sartorial statement than a celebration of the end of winter. All the rugby club had done it: didn't she know? Well actually she hadn't known, but it was entirely in keeping with what Sarah had come to know of Struan. He brought a huge presence with him whenever he entered a room: although by no means a giant, he was over six feet in height, broad-shouldered and bursting with health and energy. He was fully a match for Jenny's kilowatt personality and they teased each other incessantly.

It was a matter of considerable relief to Sarah that there didn't appear to be much of the pink and fluffy in their relationship. Jenny and Struan both robustly defended their own space, their own activities. Struan had no interest in joining her and Lucy on their Saturday trips to Glasgow as they oiled the hinges of their debit cards, any more than Jenny intended to drape herself artistically over the stands on a cold and rainy day as Struan belted the inside out of a rugby or shinty ball.

Indeed, Sarah rather suspected that had she herself been twenty-five years younger and footloose, she might very well have been dazzled by him. Instead, she was delighted that the next generation was doing a pretty good job of it.

Although servicing a mortgage and a substantial bridging loan was challenging, Jack drew confidence from the estate agent that another buyer for Bracknell would be along soon and all would be well. In the meantime they were living off their cash savings, and income from what was becoming a steady flow of engineering consultancy work. He was confident that they would get the boat-charter business up and running quickly and cover their outgoings.

A growing pile of motor boating magazines on the floor by Jack's chair testified to the fact that finding the right boat was not proving easy. It was time to get off his butt, he'd concluded, leave the advertising magazines on the floor and do some footwork round the dealers.

He'd been doing that for almost a solid fortnight, going as far south as Lancashire, but the story was becoming monotonous: there didn't seem to be the right boat available at the right price. Orders for new boats, even if he could afford one, were being taken for delivery next year. Were his plans to be shattered so early on?

'Isn't the engineering consultancy work going well?' asked Sarah.

'Yes, fortunately.'

'Well why don't you forget the bit about the boat and just do the consultancy full time?'

Jack was horrified. 'No way, love. The boating's what we came up here for, remember? We can't give up just yet, it's far too early. The right boat's out there somewhere and I just have to find it, that's all. Barely scratched the surface yet.'

'That's all very well,' said Sarah, 'but it's now almost the end of May and the season's already started, you said. And haven't you got things to do to make it all legal before you start operating?'

'Yes – that's why we put the pressure on to come up here. It should be OK, all I have to do is try harder at finding the right boat.'

'Why don't you buy a cheaper boat this year, one that's available, see how it all goes and then upgrade when there is less time pressure?'

Jack shook his head. 'No, that'd be all wrong. In the first place that would get the business off on the wrong foot, wrong image. Second, it would tie up quite a few thousand quid and resale might be difficult and take a long time. Third, the loss on depreciation and brokerage fees would eat into our tight capital. No,' he confirmed, 'we've got to do it right, with the right boat, first time.'

Jack got back on the phone and started ringing all the brokers and boatyards he'd visited, just to make sure they were keeping an eye on the market for him. He also cast his net a lot wider, including all brokers and marinas right down to the south coast.

There were just no boats available. Those of the right kind and size were too old, too shabby or too expensive.

14

'Mr Ross?'

Jack's grip on the phone tightened as he recognised the slightly nasal twang from Clyde Yacht Brokerage.

'Something just came in which may interest you. She's barely three years old and there are only five hundred hours on the engines. Thirty-one feet in length, a combined saloon and three-berth cabin, and a very neat outside steering position. Ideal for the west of Scotland. Plenty of visibility all round, but good protection from the weather too.'

'What engine does she have? What sort of cruising speed does she make?'

'She's fitted with a very throaty engine – 260 horsepower Volvo Penta D4 diesel engine. Two propellers on a sterndrive. I couldn't say precisely what speed that would deliver, but I imagine you're looking at something over 30 knots.'

Jack's eyes lit up, but dulled again as he did a quick mental calculation. Even with a substantial discount on the new price it would still be a serious cost. It might well be what he had been looking for – fast, new, suited to the weather conditions. Would it have the kind of kerb appeal that would make passing car drivers lose concentration and steer off the road? He would have to see. But something like this wouldn't come cheap.

'Price-tag?'

The figure tripped lightly off the broker's tongue and Jack winced. Outside his bracket. Not do-able, not without bank finance. No more debt, he'd agreed with Sarah. He would turn the guy down. Now. Flat.

'Is there a photo of her on your website?' *Damn*, that wasn't what he'd meant to say.

'Not just yet. She's only just come in so we're still preparing her for market.' The broker seemed to pause as if considering something. 'Tell you what. I could take some pictures now on my own camera – very unprofessional, you understand – and I could email them to you. Shall I do that?'

No thanks. The boat's too expensive, it's beyond my means even if you offered me maximum discount. Do let me know if something more realistically priced comes along.

'Yes, please.' Jack cringed at his puppy-dog enthusiasm. 'Can't hurt just to look at her, I suppose,' he added more distantly, just to let everyone know it was all the same to him whether he bought the boat or not.

The hull was in need of a damn good scrub, marine growth thick on the waterline, barnacles encrusting the underwater working parts, sacrificial anodes not so much sacrificed as hacked to death. She'd obviously been in the water, unused, the entire winter; no maintenance, no preservation work, nothing.

But Jack couldn't deny she might, underneath the lack of care, just do. Mentally, he ran his hands lovingly over her lines. He imagined himself standing in the cockpit, preparing to ease away from the berth as crowds of onlookers watched enviously. 'Hey, mister, can I 'ave a ride?' No you can't, and get your grubby hands off my gleaming paintwork. But then a handsome couple dressed in immaculate boating rig come to the front and enquire whether they can charter this gorgeous boat for the day. The man eases out a soft leather notecase and starts counting fifty-pound notes into Jack's palm. They climb elegantly on board,

Tom slips the berthing ropes, and Jack eases the throttles forward. In no time at all the boat lifts her skirts onto the aquaplane and dances along at thirty knots. The girl laughs as she shakes her hair free, which the wind then whips into golden, gossamer strands flying about her Hollywood face.

'It's a bit grubby, isn't it?'

Sarah was leaning over his shoulder, looking at the first picture the broker had emailed.

'Mm, she could do with a bit of a scrub, but fundamentally she's a real possibility.'

'Are you buying it, then?'

Jack inhaled deeply. 'N-no. She's a bit pricey, unfortunately.'

Sarah turned away.

'Unless . . .' Jack spoke to her departing back. 'Unless, of course, I can negotiate him down.'

'Oh. Can you do that, then?'

'Who knows? You don't know until you try.'

'Are you going to? Try, I mean.'

Why not? Why the bloody hell not? Yeah, why don't I try? Maybe this rather nice boat can be ours.

'Yes,' he said. Then again, this time with more conviction. 'Yes, I am. I'll negotiate him down, and we'll bloody well buy the boat. She's . . .' he was going to say a beauty. She was certainly something that could accommodate his dream and he'd experienced real difficulty getting even this far. A beauty, though? Might be. He'd have to wait and see.

Seeing the boat for real the following day, Jack felt she could really be what he was looking for. The boatyard had been as good as their word. The weed and barnacles were gone, the paintwork washed and polished, the interior aired and freshened up. She was sleek, she gleamed; she looked substantial and *serious*. If she didn't draw the punters in, he thought, he hadn't seen the one that would.

'Gosh, isn't it lovely?' Jack was delighted that even Sarah

was impressed by this rather attractive piece of maritime real estate.

'I told you she was a beauty, didn't I? And incidentally, a boat, especially one like this, is a *she* not an *it*.'

'Ah. Have to get rid of that name, though.' Sarah was looking up at the bow while Jack checked out the propellers and shafts. He came round and joined her at the pointy end. *Salty Sal*.

'How bloody ridiculous! Yes, that'll get the push.'

At only five hundred hours on the engine log, the boat was not far off new: the engine looked almost new, the soft furnishings in the saloon didn't look shabby, the whole boat didn't even smell used – underneath the cleaning agent, of course. The only issue was the price.

Jack announced he was going to get down to the nitty gritty with the broker. He looked furtively round, checked the broker was out of earshot, and said he was going to 'jerk him about a bit'.

It took longer than Jack had expected and he was less successful than he'd hoped. The broker had come down a long way, and the original asking price was a massive discount on the price as new even two years ago. But there was still 'a funding gap', as he described it to Sarah.

'What does that mean?'

'Oh,' he said lightly, 'it just means we'd do some of it on hire purchase, just like if we were buying a new car.'

'Can we afford it?'

'I'm sure we can. Let's look at it this way. It's an expense we can set off against the income we earn on the boat. Less tax to pay.'

He knew Sarah wasn't stupid, and the look she gave him was eloquently sceptical. 'At the very least,' she said, 'let's go away and think about it, work out the sums.'

Jack grimaced. 'This is the boat, darling. There's no doubt in my mind. This is the beauty that will deliver my vision. I've searched high and low, I've negotiated my whatsits off, and for the boat that she is, it's a damn good price. I think we should go for it now.'

'Well *I* think we should just think about it for twenty-four hours.'

The broker was standing by, within earshot. He hadn't so far been a pushy type, and he had been good enough to keep Jack's name at the top of his list.

'By all means do that, Mrs Ross, but this kind of opportunity is unlikely to remain available for very long. I'm not trying to pressure you, but I don't expect this boat to remain on my books as long as another week. As you see,' they all looked round the cavernous boat shed, 'I have twenty or so boats available for immediate sale, but they're all petrol – I think I'm right in saying that many marinas on the west coast only have diesel – and these boats are, shall we say, beyond their first flush of youth.'

Jack turned to him. 'Can we have five minutes to talk about this, please?'

'Certainly, take as long as you need. In the meantime, would you like some coffee?'

He went away to get their coffee. Jack and Sarah looked at the boat and at each other.

'We'd be mad not to,' said Jack.

'Maybe, but would we be mad to, as well?'

'Look, love, this is an incredible bargain even if it's tad over budget, the boat is absolutely right, and if we miss this opportunity now we'd be kicking ourselves for the rest of our lives, saying oh if only . . .' He paused. 'I hate *if only*, don't you?'

'Yes, but what if? What if it costs us more to pay the finance charges than we earn on the boat? What then?'

Jack ran his hands through his hair. That was certainly one point of view, and she had identified the risk. But he couldn't go through his life being frightened of risk. Risks were there to be managed, not there to put you off.

'Then we admit that we've tried and failed, sell the boat, repay the loan and I stack shelves in a supermarket. But at least with the knowledge that we've *tried*.'

'I don't know, Jack, I'm not happy. It's a lot more than you had budgeted for and I'm worried about having to go to the bank for more money – on top of the bridging loan. I really think you should sleep on it. Twenty-four hours?'

'Yes, but what if someone else sees it tomorrow and buys it before we get back to him?'

'Jack, he's a salesman, it's a technique salesmen use. Don't be so naïve.'

Stung at being called naïve by his wife, Jack demonstrated his commercial maturity by telling the man they would think about it.

By the next morning Jack was still of the same mind. This was the right boat, it was a golden opportunity and he had reworked the financials. He called the broker.

'I'm sorry, Mr Ross, an offer was made and accepted late yesterday afternoon. But I'll keep my eye open for you in case any others come up.' Jack groaned inwardly. Proof if ever he needed it that he should grab every opportunity when it came along, none of this namby-pamby sleeping on it.

'Do you expect anything similar in the near future?' Jack could almost hear the broker pursing his lips at the other end of the line.

'Not really, sir. That was a rare opportunity I wouldn't expect to see repeated very often. By this time of the season it's only the lame ducks that tend to be left. Things start hotting up again at the end of the season. I'd expect to have a fair stock from November onwards. I'll give you a call then,' he finished brightly.

Jack thanked him and put the phone down. Sod it, he thought grimly, another year wasted. He'd be senile and broke before this dream became a reality.

15

'I hope you've paid the duty on that beer!'

With Jenny shopping in Glasgow and Tom playing shinty at Inverness, Jack and Sarah were having lunch at the *Tigh an Truish*, a pub by the Bridge over the Atlantic. After the defeat of the 1745 Jacobite uprising, the English government brought in laws designed to destroy the clan system by outlawing, among other things, the wearing of kilts. In the remoter areas – and the Isle of Seil qualified in those days – they retained their kilts at the risk of their heads. But when they took the ferry over to the mainland they changed into trousers, at the pub that came to be called the *Tigh an Truish* – the Inn of Trousers.

The sun glinted off the wavelets in the loch. The air smelt of the freshly cut grass on the banks of the water. The views up and down Clachan Sound, the tiny dribble of tidal water that allowed, somewhat fancifully, the bridge to claim it straddled the Atlantic, would have delighted the heart of anyone with a soul.

Jack was standing at the bar just about to take a pint of 80 Shilling and a glass of dry white wine back to their table. The voice was familiar but he couldn't place it. He looked over his shoulder. Standing behind him was a tall, athletic man in his mid-forties, with short, curly, fair hair, dressed in an Arran sweater and baggy, dark-blue corduroys an inch or so too short.

'Charles Burleigh-Wells, as I live and breathe.' They gripped hands, Jack's drinks forgotten. 'Charles you old pirate, how the devil are you?'

'Good to see you again Jack, very good to see you.' A wide grin split his features. 'Sarah with you?'

Jack indicated the table where Sarah sat. Charles strode over. She stood up to give him a hug and was enveloped by him. He finished by giving her a resounding smack of a kiss on her cheek then held her at arm's length to look at her.

'My God, you haven't changed a bit, Sarah. You're far too good for Ross, I've always said, and when you come to your senses and ditch him, you let me know.'

Sarah laughed in a flustered sort of way and gave him another hug.

'Good grief,' Jack cried as he returned with the two drinks, 'you're giving her ideas above her station! Sit down, for heaven's sake, while I get another glass.'

As Jack returned to the bar to order another pint, Charles perched on a tiny stool. 'Tell me, Sarah, what are you two doing up here? On holiday?'

'Let's wait for Jack to come back and then he can tell you. But from what you said a moment ago, do I understand that you're single again?'

'Afraid so.'

'Oh dear. What happened to – Philippa, was it?'

'Didn't work out. I spent too long at sea. She was far too pretty and vivacious a girl to put up with that and someone came along who could give her the kind of life I couldn't. He was an otherwise decent sort of chap – I'm friends with them to this day. Got delightful children – two girls and a boy, and I'm godfather to all of them.'

'But surely you have – *someone*?' asked Sarah.

'Oh yes,' he breezed, 'but nothing long-term, you know, it just doesn't seem to work like that.'

'Oh Charles,' she said, and put a hand on his arm. At that

moment Jack returned with another pint and resumed his seat.

'Well,' he said, raising his glass, 'here's to you, Charles, extremely good to see you again after all this time.'

'Amen to that,' said Charles and they all took a draught. 'So what're you doing up here? Holiday?'

'We live here.' Jack's expression turned from proud to pained. 'Oh all right then, I admit it. We've only just moved up. We chucked in life in the fast lane down south. And I'd always had this idea tucked away at the back of my mind that one day I'd come back up here and settle.'

'Delighted to hear it!' Charles screwed up his face, as though that would aid the recall of a deeply buried memory. 'Didn't you live up here as a boy? Or am I imagining that?'

'No, you're right. I was born on Skye and lived there until I was ten, then we emigrated to Southampton. My dad was an engineer on the old David MacBrayne ferries running between Uig and the Western Isles, and when they started to shed seafaring employees he got a job on the P&O container ships running out of Southampton. It broke my dad's heart, moving south. He took to the bottle, lost his job, drank himself insensible one day, and that was it.'

The three of them stared glumly at the surface of the table, as if trying to decipher the history of the initials that might have been carved into it but weren't. Jack realised it was up to him. He looked up cheerfully and pointed at his glass.

'So I'm carrying on the family tradition – although with less success.' Recognising it as the rescue attempt it was, the others laughed.

'What are you doing to keep body and soul together?'

'Just at the moment I'm doing some casual engineering consultancy. But the ultimate dream is to operate a fast motorboat in these wonderful waters and take paying groups of people round this superb coastline for the day.'

'I must say that sounds pretty damn good to me. Better than having to work for a living.' Charles roared with laughter at his own wit. When he had calmed down he asked, 'Will it actually make you a living?'

'Well that's the sixty-four-thousand dollar question, isn't it? It really depends on a number of things: finding the right boat – and at the right price; will there be enough holidaymakers willing to pay the appropriate amount of money, and what actually *is* the appropriate amount of money?'

'And the answers are?'

'I don't know, to be honest. But I guess this is really about our determination to make a go of it. It's less a matter of sitting back and seeing if it will happen, and more a case of bringing the sheer joy of it to the attention of the right people.'

Charles was watching him intently, fascinated. 'I must say I'm impressed. It sounds a bloody good idea to me, and you're obviously taking control of your life. I'm more than a tad jealous: I do a lot of sailing in these waters and I think they're the finest in the world, bar none.' He turned to Sarah. 'What about you, is this your idea of fun too?'

'Not the boating bit, but the rest is. I'm delighted Jack's going to do something he really wants to do. And I'm prepared to admit I really don't mind the change from Bracknell.'

'Ah, *Bracknell*,' said Charles in judicial tones. 'Got nothing against the place myself, in fact don't know it at all, but I think I follow your drift. My head office is in Croydon,' he said as though that explained everything. 'And what about the children? Children!' He laughed. 'They must be grown up by now. What do they think of it all?'

Between them, Jack and Sarah brought him up to date with the challenges that had faced Jenny and Tom. 'But I think we're all on an even keel now.'

'Relief all round, I should think.' Charles pinched a peanut from the bag in front of Jack. 'Where are you living now?'

'Kilbeg, just south of Oban,' said Jack. 'We've got a lovely old house on the edge of the loch, which is where we'll moor the boat. And it's not too far from the golf club at Glencruitten where I occasionally whack a few balls into the rough.'

'Good Lord, I'm a member there as well. I'm surprised I haven't encountered you as I look for my balls in the rough too. Maybe we ought to make a date to play a round each month. What do you say?'

'Good idea, I'd like that.'

'Now hang on, boys,' began Sarah, as if anticipating golf widowhood.

Jack jumped in quickly. 'We'll negotiate later.' Turning back to Charles he asked, 'And yourself? Are you still in the Navy?'

'No. I left – what, twelve years ago? Customs and Excise were recruiting and it seemed a whole lot more exciting than the service. So I did a bit of time on the big customs cutters and then got a bit of a mainstream career going. I am,' he announced with a modest smile, 'an Assistant Chief Preventative Officer'.

Jack and Sarah exchanged glances. Realising some reaction was expected of him, Jack said in hushed tones, 'An *Assistant Chief Preventative Officer*? No! Really?'

Charles laughed. 'Ouch,' he said.

'What's all that about, then? I mean, if you were in uniform, how many rings would that be on your cuff?'

'Three.'

'OK, that'll do, I suppose.' Jack chewed a handful of peanuts. 'So you're not the guy who stands at the ferry terminal watching hawk-like for people smuggling more than the duty-free limit of supermarket gin from the Outer Hebrides?'

'You've seen me then?' Other patrons turned round to see the source of a sudden burst of hilarity. 'No,' Charles said when he'd calmed down, 'I'm more involved with sea-borne detection and enforcement. Actually, it's all UK Border Agency these days, so technically I work for them. Although the way the politicians change the organisation every time the bell strikes, I expect we'll find ourselves coming under the Department of Health and Social Security next week. But anyway, what I do is mostly to do with intelligence and ships and things. Which brings me back to your plans. Tell me about this boat. What're you looking for?'

'Ideally, a new-ish sports cruiser, something about thirty or thirty-five feet long, with a diesel engine and looking drop-dead gorgeous. All for about five pounds. I found one a couple of weeks ago, just the job, but I slept on the idea for too long and when I went back to the broker, she'd gone. I felt sick as a parrot, I can tell you.'

'You're still looking then?'

'Certainly am. The season's well underway and if I don't get started sharpish we'll lose this season's business. And that'll do our bank balance a shedload of no good.'

Charles thought for a moment as he chewed on a handful of peanuts. 'Might be able to do you a small turn, my son.' He swivelled on his stool and called over one of the group he'd originally been with. He effected quick introductions.

'Gerry's trying to sell his boat. Aren't you, Gerry? Tell Jack about it.'

As Gerry obliged, Jack's eyes grew wide.

'Where's she lying?'

'Ardfern. Just down the road from here. Want to look at her? I've got her out of the water.'

'Too right we do.' Jack glanced at Sarah and reined himself in. 'Well,' he corrected himself, '*I'*d like to. How about you?'

Her look was indulgent and had *I suppose so, if we must* pasted all over it. Jack's demeanour took on that of a five-year-old who'd just heard reindeer hooves on the roof on Christmas Eve. He gulped the remaining contents of his glass and tossed a quick 'coming, Charles?' over his shoulder. Charles grinned at Sarah, downed the rest of his pint and jangled his car keys.

'Wouldn't miss it for the world. Lead on, Macduff.'

16

Almost a week later, Jack silently gave thanks that he had listened to Sarah. If he hadn't, he would now be the mildly proud owner of a boat that would have done the job. And quite well, too. He had longed to describe the boat in the boatyard on the Clyde as 'a beauty', but he'd known in his heart that it wasn't. Instead, he was now looking at the real thing, the full monty. Even the name worked: *Celtic Dawn*. And she was his.

Almost thirty-five feet of gleaming white glass-reinforced plastic sat proudly on the chocks. Jack's heart-rate increased just looking at it. Two enormous out-drives jutted out from the transom at the stern, each fitted with two large contra-rotating propellers. He tried to remain mature and nonchalant but failed as a wide grin split his face from ear to ear. It was all the more gratifying that a crowd was gathering to watch the spectacle. That's my boat, Jack wanted to tell everyone, but contented himself with his grin. They'd get the picture later when he went on board, turned the ignition, and shattered the afternoon air with the roar of his supercharged diesels. His vision was coming alive.

As the mobile boat-lift lazily straddled the boat he was already anticipating racing her at high speed along the magnificent coastline, spinning her on a sixpence in any one of the many tide-races among the islands, anchoring for lunch in a sheltered loch with the hot sun beating down, a dip over the side followed by a glass of Chablis in one hand and a slither of lobster or smoked salmon in the other.

Yes, he thought, this is it. Vindication of the conclusions he'd come to on the return flight from Hong Kong that cold March morning.

It had cost him pretty much the same as the first one would have, but there was no comparison between the two boats. The pain of arranging the bank loan and writing out the cheque for the full price dulled to insignificance as he watched the boat being put into the water. He could hardly believe that, in less than a week, he'd seen this boat for the first time, shaken hands on it with Gerry, arranged the bank loan, had the boat surveyed, and agreed the Bill of Sale. And now here she was, fully polished and 'tiddlyed-up' as Gerry had promised, gently gleaming in the morning sun. Even the weather was with him!

The whole family was there, mouths agape, eyes dancing. He banished the irreverent suspicion that for Sarah and Jenny this was just one giant bout of retail therapy and replaced it with an acknowledgement that they were, despite themselves, capable of enjoying the boat for what it was and the pleasure it would bring to all of them.

It took little more than an hour for the boat to be lifted off its chocks and into the water, the tanks to be filled and for Jack to familiarise himself with the controls, engines, bilge pumps, firefighting arrangements and VHF radio. While Sarah drove the car home, and with Tom and Jenny on board for the ride, he nosed the boat gently out of the marina at Ardfern and shaped his course down Loch Craignish, round the point through the *Dorus Mhor* and back north round the islands of Luing and Seil. He had leased a mooring buoy at the head of Loch Feochan, visible from both front rooms of their house. He spent most of that evening standing at the window of the living room, glass of lightly smoked 14-year-old malt from the Oban Distillery in his hand, just staring at the boat and salivating.

MAELSTROM

It was almost the summer solstice. This far north it wouldn't be dark until after midnight, and by three in the morning it would be light enough to get up and ogle the boat again. He'd get a thick ear from Sarah, of course, but that couldn't be helped.

Tom spent almost every moment of his time with his father on the boat. Together they crawled over every inch of it, getting to know how it worked, the controls, the plumbing, the valves, seacocks, electrics, everything about it. Time and again they practised coming alongside, with offshore winds and onshore winds, against the tide and with the tide. They cruised the coastline, the islands, the bays, sea-lochs and inlets. They became familiar with the tides, tidal streams, tide-rips and overfalls. Dolphins and seals, gannets and other diving seabirds accompanied them everywhere. Tom had difficulty identifying with precision one particular species that his father referred to frequently.

'Which are the shy-talks, Dad?'

Jack laughed and pointed at some passing seagulls. 'Those, Tom, and all their like.' When Tom was scrubbing down the weatherdeck paintwork later, he realised the spelling he'd imagined had been an error.

The whole family loved going for outings, particularly to Tobermory or Crinan for lunch. Family and friends came up from all over England to stay with them for a few days, lured by the appeal of the boat. It was an instant success; everyone loved it. Jack knew he had done the right thing in pursuing his dream, and this was the boat in which to do it. It had passed the Maritime and Coastguard Agency certification process and he was licensed by the local authority to take fare-paying passengers.

All he needed now was the clients.

17

Jack put three teabags in the pot. One extra kick of caffeine usually did it for him after a more-or-less sleepless night. He didn't think the extra teabag would make their financial situation noticeably worse. They could always re-use them tomorrow morning, he supposed.

The kettle reached its climax and the teabags did their thing. The refrigerator, however, did not. As he opened the door, his bleary eyes noticed a little red light burning on the indicator panel. Now what? He peered at it but the letters were too small. He looked again with his glasses on. It didn't tell him much: 'Fault'. How the hell did that happen? They could certainly do without a repair bill, just one more bloody expense. Not a good start to the day, and after a bad night as well.

And just to top it all, the milk had gone off. He wished they had a cat he could kick.

Sarah was less put out. 'We'll just have to get it mended, that's all.'

'Is it still under that ridiculous extended warranty they made us buy when we first bought the thing?'

'I doubt it: we've probably had it five years or even more.'

'Oh bloody hell. The cost of a repair will probably exceed its value.'

'That's all right,' she said cheerfully, 'we're probably due a new one anyway, and now's the time, I expect.'

'Oh bloody hell.'

'Do stop saying oh bloody hell, it's very monotonous and doesn't help at all.'

'Well how much does a new one cost?'

'The same as a piece of string.'

'Eh?'

Sarah rolled her eyes. 'It depends on the make and model you want.'

'A cheap one, then?'

'I don't know. Three hundred? Four hundred?'

'Oh bloody hell.'

'Jack, just what *is* the matter with you? Are you saying we can't afford three or four hundred pounds for a new fridge? Is that it?'

Jack drew his hands down his face. 'Not far off, I'm afraid.'

'Oh dear,' said Sarah. 'I didn't realise things were so tight.' She opened the door to the freezer compartment and retrieved a pint of milk in a plastic bottle which she had frozen for emergencies. It had defrosted almost entirely.

'Well let's have our tea, and you can tell me all about it over breakfast.'

They abandoned cereals and went straight to the toast.

'It's not going to plan,' Jack admitted. 'Unless we can find some way of getting punters to charter the boat we're going to run out of money. If your average tourist up here, in the depths of the summer, doesn't want what we're offering or at the prices that we need to make it viable, then our vision – OK, *my* vision – has to go down the toilet.'

'But I thought you were getting business?'

'We've had one booking.'

'Is that all? I thought you'd had some enquiries?'

'Enquiries yes. Bookings no. Other than that one.'

Sarah chewed her bottom lip for a moment. 'But we are getting some money from your consultancy work?' she asked, dolloping a small spoonful of thick-cut Seville on her unbuttered toast.

'Yes, but it's barely keeping us ticking over. We're haemorrhaging money on both the boat and the two mortgages. If we hadn't found tenants for the house in Bracknell we'd be bankrupt by now.'

He leant back in his chair and clasped his hands behind his head as he studied the ceiling. Two small spiders competed in a corner for prime cobweb space. At length he looked back down at Sarah. 'OK, it looks as though you were right and I was wrong. And I appreciate your not saying *I told you so*, even though we both know that.'

Her expression betrayed no triumph. She reached her hands out across the table to him. He accepted the invitation.

'Look,' she said, 'let's not dwell on the past, it's the present and the future we've got to deal with. There's still August to go which is the busiest month for tourists.' She glanced out of the window; the rain was belting down. 'Although goodness knows why.' She turned back. 'We'll go all-out on marketing for the business and see if we can't establish our reputation. And if things still don't work out you can sell the boat, do your consultancy full-time, and I'll get a job in Oban after the kids have gone back to school. Yes?'

He looked down at her hands, which held his. Her fingers were still long and slender. Their engagement ring – nine small diamonds set in a lozenge-shaped cluster – took him back twenty years. He thought about all the times she'd stood by him, most recently this adventure up here. And here she was, offering to rescue him again. And she'd not even mentioned the awful possibility of selling *Creag Mhor* and returning to the ghastly housing estate in Bracknell. A demon ran a swift videotape of a hotel room in Hong Kong in March. He punched the *stop* button savagely.

'Yes,' he said.

Without letting go of her hands, he got up from his chair. Sarah took the hint and entered his embrace.

'Love you.'
'Love you too. And thanks.'
After a few moments they disentangled. Sarah poured out more tea.
'So it's all down to getting charters in the next month?'
Jack nodded as he took a mouthful of lukewarm tea.
'What about my fridge?'

18

Jack and Tom sat outside the Crinan Hotel, overlooking the entrance to the canal locks and the magnificent bay into which the canal opened. Two antique Clyde puffers, *Auld Reekie* and *Vic 32*, winked contentedly at him. They had served their time, taking coal to the west coast and bringing whisky and barrels of herring back to the Clyde, and were now enjoying their retirement at permanent berths in the lock basin.

After more than two weeks of almost constant wind and rain it was a perfect mid-August day: sunny and warm, flat calm, with the sky a deep blue behind the slight heat haze. It was the kind of day when all should be right with the world. Jack was trying to remain cheerful, but increasingly finding it a struggle. He couldn't understand it, he'd been so sure that vast numbers of holidaymakers would jump at the chance of having his pulse-quickening boat at their disposal for a day.

At least today had been a wonderful passage down from Loch Feochan, with the opportunity for lunch while the boat was being serviced: fruit juice and big fat crab sandwiches. He wondered just how many more days like this they could expect to have before he had to put *Celtic Dawn* up for sale.

'We haven't had many customers, have we, Dad? I mean, we

can't really go on like this, can we?' Jack was surprised. He hadn't expected Tom to be aware of the commercial realities.

'Just the one, Tom.' He thought for a moment about putting a gloss, a positive spin on it. After all, he didn't see the need for Tom to be depressed about it too. But then, Tom wasn't stupid: he'd just demonstrated that. To deny his conclusions would amount to lying. He looked out over the bay and across to the islands and open sea. 'And no,' he continued, 'we can't go on like this.'

'I suppose we'll have to sell the boat, right?'

If he'd been trying to avoid it before, Tom's straight question brought reality into sharp focus, put some clothes on the scarecrow and gave it a name – failure; failure of his vision.

'I reckon so.'

'But we'll stay up here, won't we?'

When the fridge had broken down, Sarah had talked about getting a job locally. She'd said nothing about selling up and moving back to the south.

'Yes, we'll be staying.' The contrast between Tom now and Tom before was astonishing, and Jack could appreciate how it had come about. It would be a cruel and bitter blow for Tom to have that taken away as well.

'I reckon there's lots of things you can find to do if you're keen on an outdoor life. Maybe we'll find something else that you and I can do together, eh?'

Tom grinned and nodded his shaggy head. Jack felt buoyed by the grin and the nod.

'I'll go and pay the tab.'

They walked back along the road and down to the boatyard, paid the invoice for the boat's service and carried on down to the pontoon where the boat was berthed. Two men and a woman were on the pontoon admiring *Celtic Dawn*. With a feeling of pride, he gave them a cheery 'Afternoon' and swung himself on board.

'*Pardon m'sieu*, this is your boat?' The hand signals and expressive shrugs of the shoulders were even more Gallic than the accent. Jack couldn't explain why he felt thrown. The man, swarthy, fit, sixtyish, curly black hair salt-and-peppered with grey, had an air of Greek olives and retsina. Jack had difficulty matching this extreme Gallicness with the man.

'Certainly is. Beauty, isn't she?' Jack replied.

'*Bien sûr*. At what speed does it do?'

Jack shivered at the use of the word 'it'. Nevertheless, this was the kind of conversation he enjoyed. 'Cruises at just under forty knots; top speed given the right sort of conditions would be over forty-five knots. Can take six people comfortably from here to Iona in time for lunch, and be back here for tea.'

The man's skin was creased and leathery. He wore a heavy gold signet ring on his little finger. Grey chest hair curled out of his open-necked shirt. The eyes were obscured by wrap-around sunglasses, 'aviators' Tom would call them. Jack just caught a glimpse of disfigured skin on the left side of the man's face where it disappeared behind the sunglasses.

'What sort of trips do you make with it?' the man asked.

'Pretty much anything you would like her to do. Given reasonable conditions we could go right round the Isle of Mull, stopping at the islands on the far side – Coll and Tiree – or go up to the Isle of Skye and on up to the Outer Hebrides.'

'In jus' one day?'

'In reasonable conditions, no problem.'

The man thought about it. 'At where could I hire this *par jour*?'

Jack's heart leapt to the top of his throat and threatened to get stuck in his back teeth.

'Well,' he said, adopting a relaxed attitude, 'I suppose I could take a booking now – if I can fit you in, of course. As a matter of fact, I run this old girl . . .' he just thought he'd make the point, 'for precisely this kind of thing. Tell you what, if you're not busy, why not hop aboard and maybe we can go for a spin round the bay so you can see what she's like.'

The three, although clearly not boatmen by habit, clambered on board with tolerable agility.

'So,' he said when he'd given them an exhaustive tour of the boat – all of six minutes, 'shall we go to sea?' The man nodded. It was an order rather than a simple response to an invitation. 'Great. Tom,' he called over, 'can you get three lifejackets and bring them up here, please.'

'Lifejackets? *Pourquoi?*' asked the man lightly. 'We are expecting to sink?'

'Oh no.' Jack laughed. 'Apart from the fact that it's good practice, this little beauty accelerates and decelerates sharply, and anyone not holding on tight might get caught unawares. But don't worry, I'll look after you and in reality you won't need to inflate them.' He went on to show his passengers how to don them and, if they should fall into the water, how to inflate them. Then he and Tom put on their own lifejackets. Although they all looked the same, Jack and Tom's lifejackets would inflate automatically as soon as they fell into the water and dipped below the waves, whereas the lifejackets worn by his passengers needed to be inflated manually by pulling the toggle on the CO_2 bottle.

They cast off and, with only one engine in gear to keep the speed down, the boat pulled away from the pontoon. Jack turned her bows to point out towards the more open Sound of Jura. As they rounded the headland and moved out into the Sound, Jack put the second engine in gear and tickled the throttles a fraction. The great beast leapt forward as the superchargers kicked in and the bow rose dramatically. As he increased the engine revolutions delicately, *Celtic Dawn* slowly lifted her skirts and the stern rose as she started aquaplaning. Jack caught the man as he staggered. The other two, more sensibly, were hanging onto the rail already.

The giant diesel engines roared as he adjusted the throttles to get them to sing in tune. The speed log showed thirty-seven knots through the water already. He glanced astern to check that there were no other vessels in his stern arc and noted with his usual satisfaction the thundering wake, like an inverted waterfall. A wide grin creased his face as adrenalin was injected straight into his heart.

He called Tom over and indicated that he should take the wheel.

'There you are, Tom: course two-one-zero, thirty-one revs. Watch that yacht over there, but we shouldn't trouble her.'

Jack turned to his guests who were all standing in the stern cockpit where there was plenty of space. He particularly appreciated the steering position being in the stern cockpit at which he could stand. He had not seen another boat like it in any of the boating magazines; as far as he could tell, you were generally required to sit whether you were inside or out, and that would have irritated the hell out of him. He liked to stand.

'Well, *m'sieu*, do you like what you see?'

'*Mais oui*,' said the man, '*formidable*. Coluzzi?'

Coluzzi was pale, like an unhealthy Italian in need of a beach holiday, and carried a few extra pounds under his belt. Jack knew he was going to sound like one of those Al Capone caricatures in films.

'Just fine, Mr d'Astignac.'

Jack awarded himself a gold star. It would have been two if he'd said 'boss'. In any event, he was collecting names now.

'Marie-Claire?' D'Astignac raised a questioning eyebrow at the woman. Her '*bien sûr*' matched her olive skin, and Jack wondered whether he could expect the Secretary General of the United Nations tomorrow. D'Astignac and Marie-Claire conversed in rapid French, a thick dialect that put most words well beyond Jack's recognition. Coluzzi was ignored.

'So, what do you have in mind?' Jack asked. 'Normally a day's charter would involve my picking you up at a departure point of your choosing at ten o'clock, we would then go wherever you wished. This could be Tobermory for lunch and shopping, Iona for lunch and a tour round the monastery, or Port Ellen on the Isle of Islay to visit one of the distilleries – Laphroaig, Lagavullin or Ardbeg, for example. Anything that takes your fancy.'

'*Et le prix* – what price you charge for that day?'

Jack made a rapid decision. He quoted a figure almost twice what he had decided was a normal day's charter rate. 'Although for multiple days' charter,' he added, 'I'm quite happy to negotiate a discount.'

'That would be good,' d'Astignac replied. 'You see, we operate an adventure travel business – this is worldwide, you un'stand – and we are making a branch out into the Scottish islands where is much adventure and wildness. What we 'ave in the mind is that you with this boat will take p'raps two, three people to a remote island where they will start their adventure, and bring back, on your return journey, two, three people – with their baggage, you un'stand? – who are just finishing their adventure. Is this something you could do for us?'

'Absolutely ideal.'

'*Alors*, that is good.'

There was much nodding and smiling all round. Conversationally, Jack asked, 'Did you come over from Glasgow this morning?'

'*Mais non.* We stay last night *chez le* Crinan 'otel, where we again stay tonight, before we are returning tomorrow morning.'

'And then do you go back to France or are you over here for longer?'

'I return to *l'Amerique* tomorrow evening. However, I come to see our local associates of a regularity, so if I do not voyage with you this week, *sans doûte* my associates will, and I expec' I will join them on a future occasion.'

During the short conversation they had travelled a good few miles, and Jack judged it was time they were turning round.

'Tom,' he called over, 'come round to port and reverse course, please. When we're steady on course, increase revs to three thousand five.'

'OK.' Tom glanced over his left shoulder to check it was clear and brought the boat round in a gentle arc before settling down on a reciprocal course. He eased the throttles forward, the roar of the diesels increased to a whine and then, after they had been steady for a few seconds, he tickled the levers back a millimetre or two and the sounds of the engines balanced.

'I fancy we're now close to our maximum speed,' Jack told his guests. 'Let's glance at the speed log. Forty-four – yes, there we are – forty-five knots. That's over fifty miles an hour, and something like eighty-five kilometres per hour. Drinks a fair bit of fuel at this speed, so I don't keep her running at these revs for long.'

Jack reclaimed the wheel as they approached the entrance to Crinan Bay, and brought *Celtic Dawn* alongside the pontoon. Tom dropped the bow-line over a cleat and Jack did likewise at the stern before shutting down the engines. The silence was almost physical. Jack paused to savour it before he got down to business.

'Well, sir,' Jack began, 'I hope you like *Celtic Dawn*?'

'*Oui, tout à fait. Magnifique. Très impressif*,' d'Astignac gripped the rails and stared out over the ocean. If he had been able to see the eyes behind the aviators, Jack fancied they would have taken on a steely, faraway look. At last the hands relaxed and d'Astignac turned to him. 'May I have your details of contact? Is it that you have a card?'

Jack reached into a small locker in the saloon and fished out a leather wallet containing some papers. He picked out some business cards and handed them over. D'Astignac gave him one in exchange. Nothing from Coluzzi; nothing from the woman. 'Call me any time on my mobile phone, or on my office number any time after six pm,' he said. 'Before that time you can leave a message on the voicemail as I'll probably be out in the boat with clients.' *Yeah, right*, he thought.

'*D'accord, m'sieu. Merci bien* for the voyage, and I 'ope to see you again.'

Jack watched them as they walked up the gangway from the pontoon. As soon as they had disappeared he turned to Tom. 'You've heard the expression about not counting your chickens till they hatch?'

'Yeah?'

'Well stuff that. The chickens are coming home to roost, and with any luck they'll hatch and we'll barbecue them till the cows come home.'

Tom looked at him oddly. 'Do you mean you think we might get some business from these people?'

Jack laughed. 'Yes. Hope so.'

He glanced down at the business card in his hand: Marc-Antoine d'Astignac, Vice-President Operations, Coral Reef Enterprises, Inc.

Not Aristotle el Greco, then.

Jack set course for his mooring in Loch Feochan in a mood the like of which he didn't recall enjoying for weeks. The black thunderhead he'd been towing around for days had cleared away and he was already making plans and building castles in light, puffy, fair-weather clouds. In celebration he allowed Tom to play the boat in the bubbling whirlpools off Fladda in the Sound of Luing, and to wind the revolutions up to maximum speed through the Sound of Insch before heading into Loch Feochan at idling speed.

As they walked into the house Jack called out, 'We're back. God, I'm dying for a cup of tea. Get that kettle on, girl!'

Sarah came out of the kitchen and said, 'Perfect timing. I'd just put the kettle on for myself.' And then, noticing the lifting of the black cloud from Jack's brow, 'You look cheerful. One thing's to be said for your boat: it certainly improves your mood.' Jack had given up trying to get Sarah to see the boat as a lady.

'That and more,' replied Jack. 'We've had an enquiry, haven't we Tom? And it could be a biggie and maybe some repeat business. I wonder whether this could be the tide turning.'

'Oh yes? Are these holidaymakers here for a *very* long holiday?'

'No, I think it's business. French chap who runs an outfit that does adventure holidays and training for executives, or something like that. He needs to get his clients out to the remoter islands and back. I must look them up on the Internet. Anyway,' said

Jack with only the slightest of prudence, 'the chickens aren't in the bag just yet. Let's wait for the actual booking.'

Leaning against the Rayburn with a mug of tea he told Sarah all about the encounter with d'Astignac and his associates. Sarah's eyes lit up. She expressed cautious hope that this could be what they were looking for.

'Tell me about this Frenchman – what was he like?'

'I thought he was Greek, but he turned out to be very Gallic,' said Jack. 'French words spangled all over the place, he spoke as much with his hands as he did with his mouth, and shrugged every other sentence. Charming, self-assured. One of those chaps who could walk into a restaurant bollock-naked and make everyone else feel out of place.'

'Interesting thought. Tell me about the girl.'

'I don't know, really. Silent type, sort of dark and intense. She spoke a guttural sort of French with d'Astignac; I couldn't follow it at all. But then, even in Paris I could only cope with apples and oranges.' He crinkled his brow in thought. 'Don't know where the woman fitted in. Finance? Marketing?' He shrugged. 'Who knows?'

'Was she pretty?'

'Don't know, didn't notice.' He plastered an innocent look on his face. 'Tom,' he shouted through, 'was the woman pretty?'

A disembodied voice floated back. 'You must be joking. A hundred if she's a day.'

'There you are,' he said, 'ugly as sin, wrinkled old crone.'

Sarah laughed. 'How old was she then?'

'Oh God, I haven't a clue. You know I'm utterly incapable of guessing a woman's age. But if pushed, I would say mid thirties.'

'Ancient then?'

'Like I said, wrinkled old crone.' He kissed her on the nose. 'Not you, this French bird.'

19

Jack flew to the phone as he had done every time it had rung in the last two days. He hovered his hand above the handset, then lifted it slowly and importantly.

'Ross Cruises . . . Oh, hi Jenny . . . I haven't the faintest idea . . . no, I don't think so . . . OK, I'll tell him. Bye.'

Jack left the office, walked to the bottom of the stairs.

'Tom! Can you hear me?' A muffled response wafted from Tom's room. 'I'll take that as a yes, then. That was Jenny. She's been trying to call you on your mobile but she thinks you're sitting on it or something.' Another sound of indeterminate nature and meaning from upstairs. 'Don't mention it.'

As Jack returned to the office the phone rang again. He snatched it up.

'Patience, young lady, I've only just . . . Oh! I'm sorry Mr d'Astignac, I was expecting someone else. What can I do for you?' He listened for a few moments, reached for his uncluttered diary and thumbed through it irrelevantly. 'Now let me see . . . yes; I've just had a cancellation so that will fit in very nicely . . . yes, I can do that, that'll be fine. Right, we'll see you then . . . not at all, thank *you*, M'sieu d'Astignac.'

Jack replaced the handset with care and shifted a couple of paper clips from one part of the desk to another. He walked slowly and deliberately back to the foot of the stairs and called out loudly and distinctly, 'Tom! We've got a booking for the boat tomorrow. Breakfast at oh-eight-hundred, leaving harbour brief at oh-nine-hundred, and full speed ahead to Crinan for ten-hundred.'

An upstairs door crashed open and Tom shot onto the landing.

'Have we really, Dad?' Then, as if remembering he had street cred to maintain, he said more languidly, 'I'll have a word with the union and let you know what the going rate is.' Jack heard Tom walking slowly back to his room and closing the door with great maturity.

Sarah came into the hall and said, 'That's wonderful news. What will it earn us?'

'A month's bridging loan on this house, and all the fuel.'

'Is that all?' she said with a teasing grin.

'And a diamond and ruby necklace for both my girls. Only he doesn't know that yet.'

Jack and Tom were waiting, with *Celtic Dawn*, alongside the harbour wall at Crinan at the appointed time. Although it was more cloudy than a couple of days ago, and certainly less warm, it was still very fair, and there had been only a slight breeze to ripple the sea surface on their passage down. It should be a good day's boating, he thought.

After twenty minutes there was no sign of his clients and Jack began to wonder if he'd been had. A few minutes late is one thing, he thought, but twenty minutes, when one had to be conscious of and plan for the tides and tidal streams, was another thing entirely. He was just working up a head of steam when a large black Mercedes off-roader hove into view. Out got the girl who had been with the Greek-looking chap and Al Capone last Friday, and two men he hadn't seen before.

'*Allo, Jacques,*' she said. There was that guttural tone again. She introduced herself as Marie-Claire Casamajou and the two young men with her as Sean and Jamie, each with their big rucksacks in preparation for their adventure.

'Where to then, Marie-Claire?'

She was a striking woman, and not just because she was a good inch or two taller than Jack, athletic in build, with a strong, almost aquiline nose, and a determined line in eyebrows. Used to getting her way, he suspected, just the kind of character to be running the hard side of an adventure training business. The fit was obvious now he thought about it.

'Tobermory, Isle of Mull, if you please *Jacques*.' She tried a friendly smile with adequate results and Jack was prepared to give her benefit of the doubt.

They cast off. Jack eased the boat out into the Sound of Jura, handed over to Tom and gave him a course to steer. Sean and Jamie had gone forward into the saloon and sat reading their papers. Rather than mess around with boiling a kettle and making coffee at sea, Jack preferred to bring a couple of vacuum flasks on board. There was a convenient ledge for just this purpose by the steering position in the cockpit and Jack poured out three steaming mugs.

As he handed one to Marie-Claire she offered him a smile. He wasn't convinced it reached all the way to her eyes. There was something about this tall, angular woman that was a touch industrial, clinical. But at least she was making an effort. Her fingers wrapped round his on the mug. Jack was about to make a joke of it, something about being unable to let go until she let go, ha ha. But as he glanced up at her he caught a flash of something – was it in her eyes, or the set of her mouth?

She was watching his reaction, dammit. It was only momentary, or even less than that, but Jack was sure it had been there. A pendulum swung in Jack's mind, and stuck there, at the far end. The end that warned him there was something predatory going on, something with an agenda. But just what the hell was it? She wasn't *flirting* with him, was she? In front of his son? He almost laughed out loud. How bloody ridiculous!

Withdrawing his hand politely but firmly he decided to maintain a professional distance. And the best way to do that, he thought, was to take the upper hand, lead the conversation. Polite, social, professional.

'How did you get into this adventure business?'

'Uncle Marc gave me the opportunity.'

'Uncle Marc? d'Astignac? He's your uncle?'

'Yes.'

'Ah. Tell me about him.'

'There is not much to tell. When he came out of the army in 2003 he worked for a *compagnie* based in Miami that had enterprises all around the world. When I graduated from the Université Paul Cezanne . . .'

'Where's that?'

'It is one of the three *universités* of Aix-Marseille. *Alors*, when I graduated my degree was not in such high demand, you un's-tand, and I did not find it easy to get employment. And so, as I had been very enthusiastic at *université* for all the sports, and skiing and *parapente* and other things like that, my uncle suggested I join his company for this adventure holidays and corporate training.'

'What was your degree?'

'It was in economics and political science. And now you must tell me about yourself, no?'

Jack gave her a brief biography of the 'I was born at a very early age and now here I am' variety.

'So you live close by? At Crinan?'

'No. Just a few miles up the coast.' Normally, he would have talked a bit more enthusiastically about it, but the pendulum was still firmly stuck at the far end.

'And you have family?'

'Yes. My son Tom's on the wheel at the moment.' Tom turned and gave her a vague, diffident smile.

'And this is all your family?'

Bloody hell, woman, just leave it will you? He diverted the conversation. 'When you and your uncle came on board the other day, I couldn't quite place your accent. What part of France are you from?'

'*La Corse*. Corsica.'

'Ohhhh,' said Jack. 'That explains it. My French isn't very good, but even so I couldn't recognise many of the words.'

'I un'stand that. There is a kind of *patois*, a language that belongs to the island alone.'

'I've never been. What's it like?'

'It is ver' beautiful. Rugged. Mountainous. Napoléon Bonaparte, he was born *en Corse*.' Jack detected more than a hint of pride. A thought struck him.

'Corsica would be a very good place for adventure training. Why have you chosen Scotland?'

She thought for a moment, as if the idea had never struck her or the others.

'Oh, we have courses there as well. But Britain is more ... accessible, you un'stand? More convenient for clients.'

'Ah.' And the weather's more challenging, he thought.

The rest of the trip was functional. Jack pointed out the basking sharks and other marine wildlife as they went through the Sound of Mull, and Marie-Claire duly acknowledged them. Her enthusiasm was equally functional. Sunshine did break through on her face as the town of Tobermory came into view. All along the shoreline in the northern half of the bay the facades of the houses coquettishly displayed an array of yellows, blues, reds and greens of all shades, like a row of can-can dancers flashing multi-coloured petticoats. The sun was playing hide-and-seek with cottonwool clouds, bestowing its favours on selected houses capriciously. Briefly, real pleasure showed on

Marie-Claire's face, and Jack relented fractionally as he caught sight of the girl within the woman.

Celtic Dawn berthed at the pontoon. Sean and Jamie were exchanged for two new passengers whose names he didn't catch: like as not, Sean and Jamie as well. Rucksacks were offloaded, to be replaced by new rucksacks and holdalls. They were big and heavy. Jack decided he wouldn't have wanted to do a week's expedition carrying that weight of gear around. A boat was a much better idea: get up bright and early from your own bed, a day's boating at thirty or forty knots, and back home in time for a nice cup of tea and a sticky bun. Carrying that lot around, getting cold, wet and smelly, may do bucketloads for your character, he thought, but he was quite happy with the way his character was, if improvement entailed that lot.

The changeover complete, they wasted no time departing the berth and heading out of the bay and back down the Sound of Mull. The two passengers went down into the saloon, leaving Marie-Claire on deck to talk to Jack and Tom.

'I assume from your reaction that you hadn't been to Tobermory before?'

'No.'

'What did you think of it?'

'Ah, *Jacques*, it is very lovely, no?'

'Then you ought to come back one day and go ashore. Walk round the main street, go to the distillery, have lunch in any of the cafés, pubs and restaurants, go to the chocolate factory, then finish up with the finest haddock and chips, sitting on the jetty in the rain. Wonderful!'

Marie-Claire looked doubtful. It was only to be expected; she'd be much more accustomed to sitting outside a boulevard café, sipping strong black coffee in the boiling sun rather than the pouring rain. But today was sunny, and you could always fool yourself, he thought.

After a moment she spoke. '*Oui*.' She grinned at him.

He felt she'd given up running her hidden agenda and was leaving it at that. They'd never be friends, but that was OK by him.

She went forward to the saloon to join 'Sean' and 'Jamie'. Jack opened up their pack of sandwiches, poured out two more coffees, and took a spell on the wheel.

20

The same big Mercedes was on time on this occasion. He had not been particularly looking forward to this trip. The previous one had ended with civility on the surface but, as far as Jack was concerned, relief. He and Marie-Claire had not gelled.

The driver's door opened and Al Capone got out. Jack couldn't remember his name: he was the American who should have called d'Astignac 'boss' but didn't. The American waved enthusiastically and called over, 'Hiya, Jack.' Had there been anyone else around, Jack would have cringed with embarrassment and made like he had nothing to do with them. Fortunately there wasn't. Jack beckoned them over.

In an accent that Jack knew from gangster movies was from the Bronx, the American reintroduced himself as Tony Coluzzi and introduced two more adventurous young men, bulging with muscles and rude health. They appeared cheerful enough but not highly talkative, which was fine by Jack. Each carried his adventure gear in a large rucksack, which they hefted on board.

'Where to, Tony?'

'Didn't Mr d'Astignac tell you, Jack? Jeez, these guys. Lock Boys . . .' He struggled.

Jack helped him. 'Lochboisdale?'

'That's the one,' Coluzzi said gratefully. 'It's in the Western Islands somewheres. Ya know it?'

'Yes, Tony, I know Lochboisdale well. It's on an island called South Uist. Actually, it's less of an island than a series of puddles tied together by a few damp bits of ground and a long causeway.'

They cast off and, for the second time in less than a week, Jack headed *Celtic Dawn* out into Crinan Bay. As before, Jack shaped a course for the *Dorus Mhor*, the Great Door, a gap between Craignish Point and a series of offshore islets. Here the tide-rips were fierce and the boat, despite her power, was buffeted first one way and then the other. Jack and Tom revelled in it, Coluzzi looked distinctly uncomfortable, and the other two showed no reaction either way. After a short while, Sean and Jamie – again he hadn't caught their names, nor did he care – went forward into the saloon and read their papers.

Tom took the helm as their course took them through the eddies and whirlpools of the Sound of Luing, ever northwards to the entrance to the Sound of Mull, while Jack pointed out the features, seabirds and marine mammals to Coluzzi. The glazed look on Coluzzi's face told Jack that the man wasn't interested so he asked about the adventure expedition business.

'Well, it's just one stream of our business revenues, and I've been assigned to it.'

'What do you normally do then?'

'Coral Reef multi-operates: transportation, import/export, trucking, you name it. I do import/export. Anything you want, everything under the sun. You want a jumbo jet, I get it for you. You want a pack of pins, I bring it in for you. You want a boat-load of bricks sent to Miami, I arrange it for you.' He shrugged, encompassing everything. The shrug reminded Jack of d'Astignac.

'What about d'Astignac? What does he do?'

'He's my boss,' Coluzzi said. 'I work for him,' he added, as though there were the possibility of confusion about it.

'But he's French. How come a Frenchman and someone from the Bronx work for the same company?'

'I'm from Belmont,' explained Coluzzi with a hurt expression. 'The Bronx is over the other side.' As he had no idea where Belmont was, that meant nothing to Jack, nor what it was over the other side of. He asked about it, and Coluzzi began to light up. He told of how he came from an Italian family (*No, really?* breathed Jack) and how his real passion was cooking. Pasta, he explained, was the food of the gods when it was done properly, and it was really important to get the sauce just right and not drown the pasta with it. But it was the meat with the basil and tomato reduction . . .

Jack fixed a fascinated look on his face but mentally withdrew from the lecture. It was bizarre, he mused, that he was hurtling along at an economical cruising speed of 34 knots through the most magnificent coastal scenery in the world on a fabulously exciting boat while listening to an Italian from New York waxing lyrical about *bay-sil* and *tomayto*. When Coluzzi came to a natural break in his lecture, Jack grabbed the opportunity to ask about Marie-Claire.

Coluzzi shrugged. 'We don't interface too much. She comes, she goes. Sometimes she kicks the asses of our clients, hauls them up hills and back down again. But mostly she's all over the place. She's some hard-assed broad; I keep *my* ass out of her way.'

Jack nodded; that figured. Clearly not the customer relations manager. Instead, he asked how it was that Coluzzi came to be in import/export.

Coluzzi shrugged again, as though he had caught the habit from d'Astignac. 'It was my family. They said there was already too many cooks in the family and they wanted I should work in the other family businesses. d'Astignac, he came along later. The company wasn't doing too good and they brought him in to shake it up. He shook it up.' Coluzzi's heart didn't seem to be in it; Jack felt a bit sorry for him.

'Are you here on a permanent posting or just for a few days?'

'Oh, I'm here on permanent assignment. We're joint-venturing with an outfit here in Glasgow as part of our global highway. d'Astignac calls it business development.'

Jack could hardly contain his delight. This was truly good news: if he could encourage them to use him frequently, they would soon be financially secure.

Over the next five days there were two more day-charters. Jack was like a small boy on pocket-money day with the fat wad of cash he received at the end of each trip. He didn't remember ever having seen fifty-pound notes before, but before long they became as loose change to him. Not that he got much of a chance to use them – they went straight into the bank account without touching the sides. The overdraft was wiped out and a decent positive balance built up which would see them through the next couple of months. *This* is what it's all about, he thought gaily.

Lochboisdale was followed by Iona, a tiny island off the south-west coast of Mull. And finally Port Charlotte, a small harbour in the west of the Isle of Islay, sheltered from the westerly swell by being tucked inside a big sea-loch.

Marie-Claire did not appear again, and it was left to Coluzzi to go with Jack and Tom to Iona and Port Charlotte. He and Jack struck up something approaching a friendship. While pasta and sauce featured large in Coluzzi's library of subject matter, Jack was able to tune it out and let him chunter on. He assessed Coluzzi as being not altogether happy in his work, probably not suited to it and deeply unhappy in himself, and it seemed when he was out in the boat with Jack he was able to forget his woes for a while and relax.

For his part, Jack found himself chatting freely with Coluzzi. He sympathised with him for being in an unsatisfying job, and told him all about how they came to be up in Scotland. He explained about the initial reluctance of Jenny and how she had now settled happily and often went into Glasgow on Saturdays with Lucy MacDonald. And he admitted, perhaps injudiciously, that these charters were something of a godsend.

On the trips to Tobermory and South Uist, two adventurers and rucksacks were delivered to the destination island, and two adventurers plus gear were picked up. On the third, to Iona, the two adventurers were dropped off as normal, but of the three adventurers they picked up two were North American and one was, at Jack's best guess, Latin American. Coluzzi ushered them forward where they remained, uncommunicative, for the return journey. Their rucksacks were so new they had clearly been acquired just for their Highlands and Islands adventure.

21

The light rain had stopped by the time *Celtic Dawn* was passing the Sound of Islay. About forty miles to run, he reckoned, to Port Charlotte on the southwest corner of the Isle of Islay. A shade over an hour. The forecast reckoned the rain would clear mid-morning, to be replaced by light airs and broken cloud. That was fine by Jack; good boating weather.

He hadn't been to Port Charlotte before, but the chart didn't indicate any navigational problems. The pilot book said there was a small concrete jetty with a few metres' depth all the way round at low water, and a gently shelving sandy beach tucked inside. Piece of cake.

In fact, provided he tuned out the garrulous Tony Coluzzi, all in all this was turning out to be a very pleasant day's boating. By now Tom was doing the majority of the driving, and it seemed that Jack's primary activity was customer care.

It was a small price to pay, listening to Tony drone on, looking at his tattered photographs of his home and family in Belmont, his ancestral home and extended family in Naples, and demonstrating fascination in an analysis of the best wheat flour for pizza bread. If his attention ever wandered, Jack conjured up the vision of the roll of fifty-pound notes he would trouser at the end of the day.

With considerable relief, Jack watched Tom bring the boat round into Loch Indall, the inlet that ran deep into the Isle of Islay. He'd anchored in the loch many times in naval ships, seeking shelter from Atlantic winter storms.

Port Charlotte turned out to be a charming collection of whitewashed stone cottages, dominated by a whitewashed stone hotel. The small jetty was in good condition and the boat berthed quickly. Sean and Jamie leapt ashore with their rucksacks. After a brief word with their replacements, they headed off in the direction of the hotel.

The new Sean and Jamie stood on the pier, ready to stow their gear. Sean, or was it Jamie, was clearly not European. Latino? Jack wasn't sure, wasn't all that convinced he wanted to know. But it was the pile of rucksacks and holdalls on the pier that caught Jack's attention.

The bags were very big – he estimated sixty to eighty litres each, clearly heavy, and they were manhandled into the saloon and then the cabin with much grunting and wheezing. Job done, Sean and Jamie sat down, drew their red-tops or comics from the back pocket of their jeans and studied the pictures.

'I think we're good to go, Jack.' Coluzzi slapped Jack on the back. Jack was relieved Tony hadn't said *compadre*.

'Those're heavy bags you've got there, Tony. What's in them?'

'Don't worry about it, Jack. These guysa been on an adventure expedition, they got lotsa gear.'

'Yes, but . . .'

'Tell ya, Jack, don't worry about it. It's above my pay-grade, I don't ask questions, know what I mean?'

He glanced at Jack and shrugged. Jack tried to avoid putting two and two together, but his brain wouldn't let go. The only trouble was he wasn't sure what four looked like. He'd ignored a niggling thought on the previous trip, when they'd picked up three passengers who clearly weren't UK nationals, and didn't look as though they belonged with brand-new rucksacks. He didn't know whether this was all about those bags, or whether it was about the adventurers. But the niggle was becoming too insistent to ignore.

It wasn't as though he'd been offered ridiculous sums of money for the charters, sums so big they should have alerted him: no, he'd been asked what rate he charged, and it was he who had set the rates high. On top of that he'd looked up Coral Reef on the Internet and confirmed that one of their lines of activity was corporate training and adventure expeditions. Why, they even arranged flights. What could be more convincing than that?

He went through the options. Cigarettes? Spirits? Brandy? Had to be brandy: d'Astignac was French, Corsican, whatever; all Frenchmen smuggled brandy, had done for centuries. Maybe it was illegal immigrants? Those were the easy options, and for a while he suppressed the others.

On the other hand, he needed the money. It was good, extremely good. And it was keeping them solvent. It was funding the vision. It allowed the family to be a happy unit, it allowed him to play with this wonderful toy, it . . .

He laughed inwardly and bitterly. The only uncertainty was whether it was the pure stuff, or one of the modern derivatives. Not that that mattered much. One day, sooner rather than later, the Constabulary or the Revenue would be on the jetty watching him, as skipper, bring in a boatload of quality shit stuffed in rucksacks and holdalls. They'd enquire politely as to whether he was aware of the contents of the bags, and he would say, 'No idea, chief. See my mate Tony over there.' He could almost hear Dixon of Dock Green saying, 'A likely story. Let's have the keys to your boat, and mind your fingers as you get in that nice car with the flashing light on top.'

The day, four days later, had dawned with a slight mist over the loch and a heavy dew on the grass. The leaves were still green on the woodland trees but one or two of them were serving notice that, as it was early September, the season was over and they were about to shut up shop, undress, and turn in for the winter.

The red squirrels were now absent from the nut feeders that Sarah kept on the two big oak trees in the garden, just outside the kitchen windows. After all, why would squirrels waste their time with tired old peanuts when there were almost ripe hazels, acorns and the like to be had? Once they had stocked their winter larders they would be back for their breakfasts on the feeders, but for September they were busy at their harvest.

A similar compulsion drove Jack and Sarah into their garden: the warm, golden sun, the promise of autumn – and the untidiness of the crocosmia after their brilliant, flame-red flowering throughout August. Armed with secateurs and shears, Sarah had spent most of the day slashing and burning. For Jack, by contrast, a light tidy of the garden involved the big black ride-on mower, the fourteen-inch chainsaw and the petrol strimmer.

At about four o'clock it was by common consent time for a break and a mug of tea. As soon as Jack immersed his hands in warm soapy water the phone rang. Tom had gone into Oban earlier in the day, declaring his intent to get the two o'clock bus back rather than wait for a lift from Jenny. As it was her birthday, she and Lucy had said they would do some after-school shopping. He'd obviously missed the intended bus and this would be him ringing to beg a lift. Rinsing off the soap, Jack grabbed the towel and rubbed a layer of garden dirt into it. He strode to the phone calling out, 'Patience Tom, Daddy's coming.'

'Hiya, Jack, Tony here – Tony Coluzzi.' Jack's heart sank. It'd been such a nice day, it didn't deserve ruining like this. 'Can ya fix another trip for us Tuesday? Can ya do that for us?'

He'd have given anything for the call to be from Tom, and he would gladly have gone into town to give him a lift. But there was nothing else for it, he would have to deal with this right now. At least he'd had time to rehearse his exit strategy.

'No can do, I'm afraid, Tony. The boat is due her end of season service tomorrow and then she comes out of the water for the winter.'

'But Jack,' wailed Tony, 'we need ya! And besides, it ain't the winter yet, it's still only September, ain't even the fall. What ya doin' taking the boat out of the water so soon?'

Jack improvised hurriedly. 'Unfortunately there's nothing I can do about it, Tony. It's an insurance requirement. After tomorrow I have no insurance for paying passengers and the general public, so it wouldn't be in your own interests if I took you out anyway.'

'Jack, Jack,' purred Tony, 'we're OK with that. We don't need your insurance – we can provide that for ya anyways, believe me. Look, I'll tell ya what I'll do. I'll pay two grand a day. How's that for ya? Uncle Sam's greenbacks, in hand, no tax, no questions asked. What d'ya say, Jack?'

Jack didn't have to reconsider more than a couple of seconds. Two grand would have been nice – very nice. 'Sorry, Tony, it's beyond my control I'm afraid. I just can't do it. I'd like to help, but really I can't.'

'Jeez, Jack, that's a real shame. I know Mr d'Astignac is on his way over and he was looking forward to it so much. He's going to be real disappointed ya can't do this for us. Real disappointed.' And he rang off.

Jack didn't think for one moment that would be the end of the matter. In fact, he reckoned, it would get a whole lot worse before it got better.

22

Tea was the highest priority. He was gasping for it and Sarah admitted she was dying of thirst. Waiting for the kettle to boil allowed his inner man to reflect on the depth and nature of the trouble he was in. He hadn't come up here just to land himself in more dilemmas than he had left. Nor for that matter, as he warmed the pot, had he come up here to service an industry that was abhorrent to all right-thinking people. Mechanically he tipped the water out, dropped in a couple of teabags and filled up with boiling water.

As he let it brew, he considered the options. One was to go straight down to Iain Campbell in the village and tell him the whole story. A dash of milk in each mug. Undoubtedly Iain would know who he should talk to. A quick stir of the pot and pour out the tea. Would it be the guys in Albany Street in Oban? Do they have a CID? Or a Drug Squad? Two spoons of sugar in his, wind it in. Or would it be straight down to Glasgow to see the cavalry? No. It would be – a quick slurp of tea: *Jesus!* that's sweet! Oh shit, he forgot he'd given up sugar a few weeks ago. *Concentrate, man.* No, he had a vague memory that Argyll came under the headquarters at Dumbarton. Big building on the left-hand side in the middle of that parkland. Just after the 40-mph speed restriction started on the dual carriageway and he always expected a dozen patrol cars to come screaming out of the gates and haul him over for doing 45.

Damn, he was letting detail get in the way. The question was, as he carried a tray of biscuits and the mugs out to the garden, should he be telling the police? Maybe he should leave it for a bit. Maybe . . .

Sarah tugged her gardening gloves off and gratefully accepted the mug and a biscuit. They both sat down on a flat bit of *creag mhor*, the big rock that gave the house its name. Maybe he should open it up with Sarah, see if she had any ideas? Unfortunately he'd have to go back a bit and explain his concerns in the first place. Was today the right day to do that – Jenny's birthday?

It didn't take him long to decide it wouldn't do any harm to leave it till tomorrow. He could see the benefit of the West Highland approach to time: they didn't have a word conveying quite as much urgency as *mañana*. He'd leave it for now. Instead, they talked about what plans they had for the garden later in the year: rhododendrons here, azaleas there. A gravel path here, some wild flowers yonder. Bloody d'Astignac could wait.

After another hour in the garden they were ready to call it a day. Jenny's car pulled into the drive as they were tidying up the implements and putting them away. Sarah waved and called over, 'Had a nice day, darling?' Jenny didn't appear to notice and headed straight into the house. Jack and Sarah exchanged *oh dear what have we done now* glances.

She was nowhere to be seen when they went inside, and there was no reply when Sarah called upstairs and repeated her question. Sarah said she'd have a quick wash and change and then see what was what. Jack went to the study to check emails, faxes and the like.

There were none of any significance – Jack didn't think he needed any pills for penile enlargement, or not that his wife had mentioned recently. He opened a drawer and saw two fifty-pound notes that they hadn't banked but retained for cash expenditure. Was it a quandary? Not really. Making money was one thing.

Making it from drug smuggling was another thing entirely. No contest. Withdrawing was absolutely the right thing to do. Yes, it would cause d'Astignac problems, but they weren't insurmountable, he'd find another way. There was no real reason for d'Astignac to give *him* a hard time about it. Was there?

He didn't know. He was out of his depth. He would put it out of his mind.

He went upstairs to shower and change. Sarah wasn't in the bedroom or bathroom, and the smell of her soap and perfume suggested she'd finished whatever it was she had to do. He heard low voices in Jenny's bedroom.

The shower washed away the grime from his body and the problems from his mind. The PM programme on Radio Four put it all back – the problem, at any rate. It seemed that a Royal Navy frigate operating in the Caribbean, acting on intelligence received, had stopped and searched a Panamanian-flagged freighter and found almost a tonne of cocaine on board. He wondered what a tonne of cocaine looked like. Was it bagged up, like bulk wheat or soya meal, or fertiliser that you got from the garden centre? Was it wrapped neatly in bricks and stacked on a pallet? Or was it stuffed into rucksacks and holdalls, ready to be offloaded into a Toyota Landcruiser with blackened windows?

His already acute imagination could hear the report on the PM programme now.

> *Earlier today, police and Customs officials intercepted a consignment of cocaine in the Inner Hebrides. After a furious chase and the exchange of shots, the fast motorboat* Celtic Dawn *was holed at the waterline. Half a tonne of cocaine was seized, together with a number of firearms. The motorboat was sunk by gunfire and the skipper, Jack Ross, was reduced to tears. A police spokesman said, 'That's his fucking problem. We don't approve of drug smugglers, and I hope he gets banged up for the rest of his natural.'*

Sarah had planned a special dinner for Jenny at home in the evening, leaving her free to go into Glasgow with Lucy MacDonald the following day, Saturday. The two of them would spend her birthday money in ways that only girls in their late teens know.

Jack tried to slam the lid on his concerns and his overactive imagination. 'You're looking cheerful for your birthday.'

Jenny gave him a weak smile as she sat down at the table. Although it wasn't dark outside, the candles on the table danced in competing drafts, making the dining room cosy.

He broke off from the d'Astignac problem long enough to congratulate himself on just how far he'd come in his relationship with his seventeen-year-old daughter – no, make that eighteen as of today – that he'd noticed she was looking peaky. Only a few months ago he wouldn't even have been *here*.

'Something troubling you, darling?'

Nowhere near what's bloody troubling *me*, he thought sourly. He didn't see the look Sarah flung across the table at him.

'Bad day at school? Miss McGillivray playing up again?'

'Can we just leave it, Dad?'

Fucking d'Astignac, thought Jack. He could have done without this today. Jenny was obviously upset – was it the present they'd got her that wasn't right? Or, worse, the present they'd failed to get her? What was it she'd wanted? And what had they got her? Bloody Coluzzi, wanting him to do another trip.

'Did we get your present wrong, Jenny?' He looked across at Sarah and mouthed something about what had they got her.

Sarah replied, 'Just leave it, Jack. Jenny's not feeling too good at the moment. It'll pass.'

What really pissed him off was they must have thought he was stupid. All those big rucksacks and bags. And then just shrugging his shoulders and saying it's above his pay-grade. There was no way on God's earth he was going to continue smuggling that shit. And now that he was super-Dad he wasn't going to risk it, not just to amuse d'Astignac and line his pockets, how bloody *dare* he!

'It's that bloody McGillivray woman again, isn't it? I've a good mind to go round there and picturise the old witch . . .'

'No Dad, it's not Miss McGillivray.' Jenny thrust back her chair and stood up, resting her knuckles on the table. 'I'm bloody pregnant, OK?' Her voice wobbled.

'Eh?'

'I'm pregnant.' She was trembling.

Jack looked at her as she stood there, leaning forward with her hands on the table. She was challenging him. Bloody d'Astignac and now this.

He shot out of his chair as he roared, 'What the *hell* did you have to go and do that for? Who's the father, eh?'

'*Sit down*!' said Sarah sharply, but Jack didn't hear.

'What the hell were you playing at, you stupid girl,' he yelled. 'Your mother and I have brought you up to be decent and this is how you behave.'

Faced with this onslaught, Jenny began to cower away from him.

'Who was it, eh?' roared Jack. 'Who's the father?'

Jenny mumbled, 'Struan.'

'Ha!' he barked. 'Ha!' he said again, not knowing what to do with the information. He changed tack. 'What're you going to do about your A-levels? You've about buggered them up, and with them your life. God, what *possessed* you, girl?' He was beginning to come off the boil, experiencing the familiar suspicion of an over-reaction somewhere. He shook his head in dismay and stomped out of the dining room. Jenny overtook him in the hall as she ran to her room in floods of tears.

Sarah came out of the dining room behind him with a stony look on her face. 'Nicely done, Jack,' she said acidly. 'That was about the worst thing you could have done. She needs support and love, and what do you do? You behave like the most pigheaded man I have ever come across in my entire life. You'll be damn lucky if she ever speaks to you again.'

He suspected she was right but he was nowhere near ready to

admit it. He threw his hands up in the air, breathed 'Women!' in exasperation and went to the living room to solve both this and the d'Astignac problem with whisky. Sarah followed Jenny up to her bedroom.

He reached for the Oban 14. There was only a dribble in the bottle and a search failed to reveal a spare. Damn and blast the sodding stuff! A rummage in the back of the cupboard threw up a bottle of Islay Caol Ila cask-strength left over from Christmas. He splashed a hefty two fingers in a tumbler, ignored the water and tossed back a large gulp. It caught the back of his throat and brought on a violent coughing fit. He went to the kitchen for a glass of water. Tom had quietly made himself scarce.

As he dried his eyes and caught his breath, Jack had the opportunity to calm down. He admitted to himself that it was less a case of Jenny having behaved badly. It was himself who had just made a complete idiot of himself. The only justification he could come up with for his reaction was that, to him, she was still his beautiful little girl, and no man should be laying his hands on her. At least, not without his permission, which he was not yet ready to give. On top of that, he might have – would have – reacted differently if d'Astignac hadn't been rattling around inside his head.

But he knew that was no excuse. He'd made a bad situation worse. *Christ*, he thought bitterly, *what have I done?* He had some serious fence-mending to do. He went up to Jenny's bedroom where there was a low murmur of voices but no audible crying. Knocking quietly, he slowly opened the door and poked his head round. Jenny was sitting on her bed, her usually china-blue eyes now poker-red, twisting a hopelessly inadequate and sodden handkerchief in her hands. Sarah was sitting on the bed next to her, holding her close. They looked up as he opened the door.

'Um,' he started, 'I just . . .'

He felt the hostility in both pairs of eyes.

'I don't think now's the time.' Sarah spoke with equal measures of frost and caution.

'Yeah,' Jack mumbled. 'Sorry.'

When they went to bed that night Jack almost froze in the atmosphere. Jenny had not wanted to speak to him, remaining in her room. Conversation with Sarah was little better than monosyllabic.

'That phone call, just before supper,' he began, waiting for a reaction. None came. 'It was Coluzzi.'

'Who's Coluzzi?'

'One of the guys chartering the boat. With d'Astignac.' Again he waited for a reaction which failed to materialise. 'I told him I didn't want to carry on with the charters.' Stony silence. 'I don't think he was all that happy, but he's got no choice. Has he?'

'I wouldn't know, Jack. Just don't create any more problems, that's all.'

Ah, he thought, the Sunshine School of Problem Management: *That's your problem, Sunshine.* Clearly not the time to share his own worries.

After a foul night's sleep Jack woke with a raging headache. Sarah's side of the bed was empty and cold. He glanced at his bedside clock: 06:44. The smell of coffee brewing wafted up. Fortified by a handful of paracetamol and a violent shower he searched out the source of the smell.

At least the coffee was still in the mug as she handed it to him, not in separate batches flying in loose formation. Maybe she had slept off the worst of her anger.

'About last night,' he began. 'I think I over-reacted.'

Sarah turned and looked at him, one eyebrow arched in eloquent sarcasm.

'Yeah all right,' he muttered, 'I acted like a moron, I know. I need to apologise to her.'

'We'll just have to hope that she's prepared to give you the benefit of the doubt, won't we?' she said, none too kindly but with the hint of a thaw. 'She's meeting up with Lucy and they're going into Glasgow on the ten-past-eight train. I'll take her a cup of tea and see if she'll grant you an audience.'

Jack held his breath as he waited to see whether he would be forgiven. By way of answer, Jenny came down and did her best to avoid him. He cornered her and tried to tell her how sorry he was for last night. She gave him a fragile smile and told him that she was OK now. With both of them treading on eggshells Jack could only hope that, once she'd got out of the house and into the company of Lucy, she would cheer up. After a good day's shopping in Glasgow she might even have forgiven him. A bit.

23

The text came through on Sarah's phone at six thirty-five that evening. As she was not much of a mobile phone user and even less accustomed to receiving texts, when her phone went *dink* she didn't react. Jack looked up from his newspaper.

'Text.'

'Hm?'

'Text. You've got a message on your mobile.'

'Oh, have I?' She rummaged in her handbag on the sideboard, dug out her mobile phone and pressed buttons gingerly. 'It says it's from Jenny. She'll be on the train by now, won't she?'

Jack looked at his watch. 'Should be: it was due to leave about fifteen minutes ago. Probably telling us it's been delayed.'

Sarah brought up the message and read it.

'Oh, how careless of them!'

'What is?'

'The girls have missed the train. She says they're "staying over", whatever that means.'

'Give her a ring and tell them I'll come and get them. Bloody expensive exercise, staying the night in Glasgow, and I'm not sure it's entirely wise. I could be there in a couple of hours, which will give them time for a nice evening meal and a glass of wine.'

Jack folded his paper and got up. 'Tell you the truth, it'll give me an opportunity to make amends a bit. Maybe they can get a local train out to Balloch or somewhere like that: that'll make the car journey a lot shorter and get them home quicker.'

He left Sarah to call the girls as he went out to get the car. He waited, the engine running, until she came out. 'I can't get her, it goes straight through to voicemail every time I try. I've left her two messages to call me. I hope she's all right.'

He wasn't concerned. 'Maybe they're in an area of poor coverage. Look, call Annie MacDonald. I expect she's received the same from Lucy. Tell Annie I'm on my way and when one of you eventually makes contact, give me a call and let me know where to pick the girls up, OK?'

An hour and a half later Jack turned off the A85 and pulled into Balloch village at the southern end of Loch Lomond. Parking by the railway station, he punched the quick-dial for home into his mobile.

'Established contact yet?'

'No, neither has Annie. Both of us get diverted through to voicemail. We've both left messages saying that you're on your way to pick them up and to call back as soon as they get their messages. But we've heard nothing.' Sarah paused for a moment. 'Jack, I'm worried: do you think anything's happened to them?'

Jack wasn't exactly worried, but neither was he totally relaxed.

'I shouldn't think so, love. After all, if anything had actually happened to them they wouldn't have been able to text us saying they'd missed the train, would they?'

'No,' Sarah agreed doubtfully, 'I suppose not.'

Expensive mobile airtime went unused for a few seconds.

'I imagine they're in some noisy basement club or bar, taking advantage of the full evening in town, and then they'll get a garret room in the station hotel where they'll pick up your voicemail messages before catching tomorrow morning's train home.'

'Yes I expect so,' Sarah said in a voice that didn't quite match the words.

'So I'll turn round and come home,' Jack continued. 'If you hear from them before I get home let me know, and I'll turn round again and pick them up.'

Weary and disappointed, he headed for home.

24

Jamie Barr yawned and eased his back in his seat as the vehicle thundered along the carriageway. He'd made good time from Ayr, less than an hour, and once on the other side of Glasgow he'd stop for a mug of tea you could stand the spoon up in, and a decent plate of Lorne sausage, two fried eggs, a couple of slices of Stornoway black pudding, and a good spoonful of baked beans. That service station on the M80 just south of Stirling. He let out a foetid belch and scratched his vast gut. He was losing weight rapidly, he reckoned, and needed to get that plateful inside himself.

Passing junction 1 he wished he was on the Haggs Castle golf course, just disappearing over his right shoulder. Despite his extreme bulk he was a keen golfer, playing off a handicap of twelve. He laughed every time he thought about how he pissed off the slim, athletic members at Ayr, with their twenty-plus handicaps, every time he thrashed them.

He was in speed camera country so glanced at his speedo. It hovered just below the limit. It was no problem anyhow, as there was still not much traffic about at that hour on a Sunday morning. His ample paunch rumbled, and not for the first time. It deserved respect; it deserved listening to. He had a Yorkie bar somewhere in his emergency ration stowage, and he fumbled for it now. A small bag attached to the inside of the driver's door, just level with the base of his seat, just at the right height for rummaging in. He experienced a surge of anticipation as he searched. Ah, there it was: Yorkie. Milk chocolate Yorkie, with nuts. That'd put a few pounds where they rightly belong. He transferred the chocolate bar to his left hand on the wheel, and began expertly unwrapping it with his right.

His mobile phone erupted. He paused in disrobing the Yorkie and punched the green button.

'Aye?'

'Jamie, ye wee bastart, where's yersel the noo?'

It was his brother Ronnie. Also driving a container lorry but down from Dundee. They'd said they would try to meet up for breakfast.

'Ronnie, ye wee shite, I'm on the M77 near tae Glasgow. Just joining the M8 and – *shit*, I've dropped ma Yorkie. Just hud oan while I – oh shit, Christ Almighty, whit the fuck . . .'

It was multiple lanes joining multiple lanes, and then lanes merging. Unobserved by Jamie, a black Audi A8 4.2 TDi saloon was alongside his forty-foot container trailer as he eased onto the M8. The lanes and traffic could accommodate them both until Jamie leant down to retrieve his Yorkie, inadvertently pulling the wheel towards him. Jamie's lorry lurched to the right, squeezing the Audi between itself and a thirty-ton bulk cement truck.

Jamie's alarm was at the shuddering along the length of his rig and the horrible grinding noise. The horn of the Audi, which the driver was frantically punching, didn't even feature. Jamie corrected his swerve, clicked his indicator left and headed for the hard shoulder. The driver of the cement truck had the same general idea and was also heading for the hard shoulder. The Audi, meanwhile, was being squeezed like a lemon, the bodywork ripped to shreds on both sides by the wheelnuts of both lorries. With thirty tons on one side and thirty-eight tons on the other, the Audi didn't stand a chance.

By the time the two HGV drivers understood fully what was going on and had come to a halt on the hard shoulder, the black

Audi was a wreck. Jamie levered himself down from his vehicle and tried to peer into the shattered windows of the car, all the while stabbing a sausage-like finger repeatedly at the 9 button on his mobile. The inside of the Audi was fully obscured by airbags that looked like someone had stuffed in a hot-air balloon and then ramped up the gas. Jesus, it was a mess.

'Which service do you require, caller: police, fire or ambulance?'

'Er, all three, I think.'

The phone rang urgently – that would be Jenny. Sarah got to it first.

'Oh darling, we've been so worried – oh, sorry Annie, I thought it was Jenny.'

Jack listened to the one-sided conversation. Sarah seemed to be relaxing. She covered the mouthpiece and turned to Jack. 'Lucy's home,' she whispered. But then her face took on a frown, she caught her breath and her free hand flew to her mouth.

'Drugged? What do you mean, drugged?' As she listened, Sarah stared unseeingly at Jack, her hand still at her mouth. After a few moments, she said, 'You'd better speak to Jack,' and handed the phone to him.

'Hello, Annie, what's happening?'

'Well I'm not sure. Lucy's just come back from Glasgow in a dreadful state. She's incoherent; Hugh thinks she's been drugged. Is Jenny home yet?'

'No: didn't she drop Lucy off at home?'

'No she didn't. We didn't see who it was – it seems she was sort of dumped, just dumped outside the front door. That was about five minutes ago.'

'Is she hurt?'

'No, thank goodness. She's just like a rag doll: can't speak, can't focus, doesn't know whether it's Easter or Christmas. We've asked her whether Jenny came back with her but she's got no idea what we're talking about.'

'Has she said when she last saw Jenny?'

'We just get blank looks from her.'

The conversation ceased while Jack chewed over the implications of all this. Sarah was watching him for signs of hope. He kept his face neutral.

'Look, Annie, can we come over and talk?'

'Of course.'

Jack put the phone down pensively.

'What did she say, Jack? Did Jenny come home with her? Is she on her way?'

He rubbed his eyes and the bridge of his nose, giving himself time to think. 'Lucy doesn't seem to have any idea where Jenny is. They didn't come back together and Lucy's in a very confused state. I really don't know what's going on. Let's go round to the MacDonalds, pool our thinking, and see if we can get some sense out of Lucy. C'mon.'

It was raining a fine west-coast mist of rain as they stepped outside, but it was warm, and only a few minutes' walk to the other end of the village where the MacDonalds lived. Annie opened the door to them as they walked up to the porch of the fine Victorian stone house, almost identical in style and layout to their own. They climbed out of their anoraks, shook the water from them and hung them up.

As Annie brought them into the large, slate-flagged kitchen and put the kettle on the Rayburn for a fresh pot of coffee, Hugh came through from the living room shaking his head.

'I'm fairly sure she's been sedated – tranquillisers or depressants.'

'Who would do that? How?' Jack was having difficulty making sense of it. Sarah looked as though she'd given up trying.

'I don't know, Jack. It's a whole problem area. There are reports of things like flunitrazepam or GHB . . .' Jack wrinkled his brow in incomprehension. Hugh explained, 'Flunitrazepam. Rohypnol is the brand name you might be familiar with. It's a strong form of valium. A sedative. Or gamma-hydroxybutyrate – that's a depressant. Either of them could be slipped into someone's drink or food, and they can lead to drowsiness, impaired motor function, loss of memory.'

Jack's eyes narrowed. 'Is that what they call the date rape drug?'

Hugh looked away and hid his eyes. His big hands, gnarled by arthritis, gripped the back of a wooden chair. Jack began to comprehend what Annie and Hugh were going through. They had said Lucy was like a rag doll, and now with all this talk of date rape drugs, the implications didn't bear thinking about.

'Yes,' he croaked. He cleared his throat and spoke more firmly. 'Yes.' He turned back to Jack and Sarah, back in control. 'Someone could have slipped it into her breakfast fruit juice this morning or whatever – I don't know. In fact,' he threw his hands up in exasperation, 'I don't really know very much at all.' He rubbed his red eyes. He and Annie were well into their sixties, Lucy was their one and only, the apple of their eye. Jack suspected they'd had an even worse night than he and Sarah.

'At least she's home safely – or relatively safely.' Jack thought they could do with some encouragement to look on the bright side. Hopefully Jenny would be along directly; and there was no reason to think she'd be in the same condition as Lucy.

'Yes,' said Hugh, breathing out noisily as if relieved he was over the danger of crumbling. 'Any news of Jenny?'

Jack and Sarah accepted cups of coffee and sat down at the kitchen table. Sarah's hands weren't steady. 'No. I was wondering whether we could talk to Lucy and see if she can tell us anything?'

'You can certainly try, although we haven't got much out of her so far. I've asked Flora Cameron from the practice to come round and check her over. She should be here in a few minutes, so when she's finished you're welcome to talk to Lucy.'

Jack leant forward on his elbows and addressed a very fine knot on the well-scrubbed pine kitchen table. 'We've been trying to phone Jenny since about half past seven this morning but all we've been getting is her voicemail. I assumed she was sleeping off a heavy night in the clubs last night. Not that she's much of a drinker, but then two glasses of white wine spritzer is over the top for her.'

One of seven or eight bells high up on the kitchen wall jangled – the original Victorian bell, operated by ropes and pulleys between the front door and the kitchen.

'That'll be Flora,' said Hugh and went to let her in. Annie picked up the conversation. Her hands were no more still than Sarah's; her fingers worried at a hangnail which was beginning to bleed.

'That's pretty much the same for Lucy. She can party all night on a glass of water so we thought she'd had too much to drink and needed to sleep it off.' Annie wrinkled her forehead in thought. 'But the girls must have left Glasgow at about half past seven this morning to get here at nine-thirty and there isn't a train at that time. I've no idea how much a taxi would have cost – must have been astronomical. And why hasn't the taxi dropped Jenny off yet?'

Jack's mind was beginning to whirl. If Lucy was home by now, why wasn't Jenny? Where could she have gone without Lucy? And why? Puzzlement was being elbowed out of the way by unease. Were there any other clues?

'Have you checked Lucy's handbag? I mean, was it stolen? Was anything stolen from it – money, credit cards, phone? Did she have enough money to pay for the taxi?'

Annie said that Lucy still had her handbag but no, she hadn't checked inside it. 'That's a good idea – I'll do that when Flora's finished.'

Jack felt rather than heard his mobile phone ring. He retrieved it from his pocket and saw a number he didn't recognise.

'Ross.' He got up and wandered from the kitchen to the MacDonalds' dining room. The view from the bay window looked across the valley to the mountains, rather than towards the loch and islands like *Creag Mhor*.

'*Jacques, ici* Marc-Antoine d'Astignac.'

Jack's heart skipped a couple of beats. Not the best time.

'I am desolated, *Jacques*, that you will not be available to carry out our charter on Tuesday. Is it possible there is anything I can say or do which may assist you to change your mind?'

This was a bloody nuisance. The man was becoming a pain, and right now he had serious things to deal with, so as far he was concerned, d'Astignac could just fuck off.

'I'm sorry, Mr d'Astignac, forgive me if I can't focus on your particular problem at the moment. I'm having a bit of a crisis of my own here which is rather occupying my mind.'

'*Quelle dommage*,' said d'Astignac, all solicitation and concern, '*Je suis desolé de l'écouter*. What is the nature of this crisis?'

Before he could stop himself, Jack replied, 'My daughter has failed to return from a trip to Glasgow and the circumstances are such . . .' he faded away, ending up, 'It's very worrying.'

'*Vraiment? Quelle dommage*,' d'Astignac repeated, his tone dry as a camel's backside. *Dommage* be buggered, Jack thought savagely. He didn't want any sympathy from d'Astignac.

d'Astignac continued. 'I imagine that you will wish to attend yourself to this crisis, and so I shall terminate this call and call you . . . per'aps later this morning, to ask whether you have been able to reconsider yourself to my request. *Au 'voir, Jacques.*'

As the connection was cut, Jack stood pensively for a while, tapping his mobile against his teeth. Problems on two fronts; he could do without that right now. He considered switching off his mobile to block the inevitable second call – but then realised that Jenny might call at any moment and ask to be picked up from wherever.

'Who was that, Jack?' Sarah came through from the MacDonalds' kitchen and met him in the hallway. 'News of Jenny?'

'Hm? Oh, no. That was d'Astignac. Said he was sorry to hear I wouldn't be doing his charter on Tuesday. Asked me to reconsider.'

'Oh,' said Sarah, deflated. 'I thought it might have been something to do with Jenny,' she added hopelessly. She took Jack's hand and they went back into the kitchen. Hugh was back, and a short, homely woman in her late fifties with gold-rimmed half-moon glasses perched on her nose was leaning her ample backside against the Rayburn rail, thanking Annie for a mug of coffee. Annie introduced her as Flora Cameron, Hugh's partner in the local medical practice.

Sarah asked her, 'Is Lucy all right?'

'Fundamentally, yes, I think so,' said Dr Cameron, 'but I can't add to what Hugh's already worked out. I guess it's a depressant or sedative that's got her in this state. I've taken a blood sample which I'll send to the lab tomorrow. If it's a sedative it'll show up for quite some while, but if it's one of the depressants I doubt it'll tell us much unless she's been given an enormous dose.'

'Why won't it tell us much?' asked Sarah.

Hugh replied. 'GHB is always present in the human body, it's a natural substance associated with neurological function. But we don't know how much, and it varies from person to person, according to what part of the body and what time of day.'

Dr Cameron continued, 'If she'd been given a large dose of anything then I'd expect her to have suffered convulsions, vomiting, respiratory depression, that sort of thing. No sign on first examination of any of that.' She mused for a moment or two. 'These things are normally used either to pep-up a party – tiny doses for that – or in slightly larger doses to incapacitate someone while . . .' Dr Cameron glanced uncomfortably at Hugh and then at Annie. Annie nodded her permission. 'While *advantage* is taken of them. I was just telling Annie and Hugh that mercifully there is no initial indication,' she was choosing her words carefully, 'that any advantage was taken of Lucy.' The doctor studied her feet for a moment.

Jack saw a ray of hope, a straw he clutched with mounting desperation. 'I expect they went to a party last night, and somehow things got out of hand, they had a bit of this whizzo stuff, got separated and . . .' He ended vaguely with a shrug and a questioning look at Flora Cameron.

She thought carefully for a moment. 'Just thinking about the timing of it, I'd guess that Lucy was administered the drug just a few hours ago rather than last night. As I was examining her she was already showing signs of increased awareness, so who knows? – she may be able to answer a few questions fairly soon.' She glanced at her watch. 'Heavens! I must dash, I'll be late for church. Thanks for the coffee, Annie. I'm sure Lucy'll be right as rain very soon. Get her to drink lots of water, and administer oodles of TLC – she'll need it.'

As Dr Cameron left in a whirl, Sarah sank slowly onto a chair, her face crumpled as tears started to flow. Jack's ray of hope had been dashed as the implications of what Dr Cameron said unfolded. He got down on one knee beside Sarah and hugged her to him, making *shushing* noises. He knew exactly what had hit her: Dr Cameron had prescribed lots of tender loving care for Lucy. Jenny was, at best, in the same state as Lucy, but there was no one there to give *her* any TLC.

Jack's mouth went dry. It was clear Jenny would not be walking in through the door in the next few minutes, sober or sedated.

The thinking part of him said he had to report Jenny as a missing person. But on what evidence? OK, she hadn't come home last night, but they knew that was because the girls had missed the train. All right, she hadn't appeared this morning – but there was still the ten o'clock train from Glasgow and that wasn't due in for a while. Was she truly 'missing' or had she just not turned up yet? How the hell do you even *report* a missing person? And to whom? Do you ring 999 even though it's not an emergency? Do you ring your local nick even though she probably disappeared a hundred miles away, on someone else's patch – or was it a manor?

Only one way to find out. Sarah was beginning to regain control of herself and Jack's knee was hurting anyway. He stood up stiffly, excused himself and went out into the hall to make the call. He speed-dialled Iain Campbell, the local police constable – Struan Campbell's father.

'Iain. Sorry to bother you at home and on a Sunday morning at that, but I need some advice.' Jack recounted the events of last night and this morning.

'Aye,' PC Campbell drawled in his west-coast lilt, 'no doubt about it, treat it as a Missing Person. Ring the Police Contact Centre – it's all one big call centre nowadays for the whole Strathclyde Region. I have the number here somewhere.' After a moment's rummage he read it out. Jack thanked him and cut the connection. He dialled the number, his mind in a churn, his imagination overactive.

'Strathclyde Police Contact Centre, Trisha speaking. How can I help you?' A bright young woman, sounded on the ball. Thank goodness not a call centre operated from the other side of the world with impenetrable accents. Was Trisha a uniformed constable, he wondered, or maybe a detective sergeant?

'I'd like to report a missing person, please.' He felt terrible. The contents of his stomach were turning to battery acid. 'At least, I'm not sure if she is missing or not and I was wondering . . .' He tailed off.

'Don't you worry about that, sir' said Trisha, 'we'll sort that out. Now, can I take some details please.' Jack felt reassured – the first small glimmer. Trisha was right on the ball, the faint *clack* of a keyboard spoke of a computerised form being filled in. The days of an elderly desk sergeant filling in a paper form, licking a blunt 2B pencil, were obviously well past. Jack supposed it was progress. He responded woodenly to her questions.

'So what makes you think she might be missing? I mean, instead of just not home yet?'

He summarised the events. His adrenalin high, he had difficulty being succinct.

'Can you think of any reason why she might have *chosen* not to come home?'

Jack squirmed.

'Possibly,' he admitted quietly. 'You see, we did have a bit of a row on Friday evening and things were still a bit fragile when she went off with Lucy yesterday morning. But she's a pretty resilient girl and a day shopping in Glasgow would normally cheer her up and I was hoping she would have forgiven me by the time she came home. Oh God,' there was a hint of wail in his voice, 'I hope it's only that. But I still can't get her on her mobile.'

'Right you are then, sir, I've got all that on the report which I'll pass to the duty inspector now. We'll start by contacting all the other divisions for incident reports that may match, and we'll contact all the hospitals. And when the inspector has done a risk assessment we'll get back to you and report on progress. Now, if I could just take some more details . . .'

While it was still in his hand, Jack's mobile phone warbled. 'Ross.' He walked out of the hallway back to the dining room. It was d'Astignac.

'*Jacques*, I am asking myself if you have had the opportunity to reconsider our request?'

'No, Mr d'Astignac, I haven't.' The man was becoming a nuisance. 'As I told Tony, I can't do it – insurance and all that; and as I told you, I've got other things on my mind at the moment. I'm quite happy to look at things afresh next year when the boating season starts again, but in the meantime, Mr d'Astignac,' Jack's tone was rising towards belligerent, 'I'd be grateful if we could bring this to a close and I could get on with – other things. Yes?'

'*Hélas, Jacques*,' d'Astignac's voice dripped with oily reasonableness, 'life is not that simple. I have contracts to honour, obligations to meet, and I need you.' There was a pause at the other end. Jack assumed he was expected to fill it. But he waited, forcing d'Astignac to continue. 'When we spoke earlier, you told to me your daughter had failed to return from Glasgow last night. As you know, *Jacques*, I have associates here in Glasgow, and I am ringing from their office, as a matter of fact. The staff, they are mostly local people, of course. I have taken the liberty of making the enquiries amongst those who have the ear to the ground. They are hearing *les chuchotements* that *une jeune fille* is being held by an unknown group. It is possible, is it not, that this *jeune fille* is your daughter?'

What the devil was going on here? How *dare* he start making enquiries about Jenny's whereabouts? This was an intimate family matter that was no concern of d'Astignac's –

Cold sweat broke out all over Jack's body. Was he being particularly dumb?

'Mr d'Astignac,' he had difficulty getting the words out, never mind sounding civil, 'are you telling me you know something about my daughter's disappearance?'

'I am telling you nothing. What I am suggesting is that I may be able to help you in your difficulty. And that may assist you towards being more reasonable when I ask for your help.'

Well, that was as plain as a garden fork up the transom.

'*Cependent*,' d'Astignac continued, cool as the ice cubes in a gin and tonic, 'per'aps you would like me to try to make contact with this group – as a go-between only, *vous comprenez?*'

'*You bastard!*' Jack shouted down the phone. 'If you harm a single hair of her head, I swear to God I will tear your throat out with my bare hands, do you hear me?'

The silence at the other end was deafening. Eventually d'Astignac spoke.

'*C'est chiant, Jacques* – this is most tedious. I must emphasise that I have nothing to do with this sordid matter, I am only trying to help you.' There was another pause. He continued in a very quiet tone. 'As you must try to help me.' If it was cold sweat before, Jack's spine was solid ice now. 'Do we have the understanding of each other, *Jacques?*'

Jack had to un-grit his teeth. 'Yes, I understand, d'Astignac. I understand only too well.'

'And per'aps I should add that going to the police would be . . .' he paused as if trying to identify the choicest word, 'unhelpful. I am advised that, if the perpetrators detect that the police have been informed, they are likely to terminate . . .' he made it sound like the snip of scissors, 'all communications with my associates – and who knows what else may occur?' Jack imagined the Gallic shrug. 'It seems, *Jacques*, that I am your only hope. Do we understand each other?'

'Yes, you bastard, I hear you loud and clear.' Jack cut the connection and, denied the satisfaction of slamming the phone down, slammed his open hand down on the dining room table instead. And now he had a sore hand.

25

His jaw still clenched and the muscles aching, Jack returned to the MacDonalds' kitchen. Sarah asked who'd called. It took him half an hour to tell how and why he had got mixed up with d'Astignac, what he suspected was the purpose of the boat trips, d'Astignac's barely veiled involvement in current events, and to answer all their questions. Hugh MacDonald said he must, of course, go to the police at once and tell them everything.

'But tell them what?' asked Jack wearily. 'd'Astignac will deny he knows anything about Jenny, that he ever said she'd been kidnapped. I mean, it was me who brought it up – like he manoeuvred me into it. We've got no demands for ransom or anything like that. And he made it clear that if I do go to the police then all bets are off for Jenny. No, d'Astignac has got us well and truly forked.'

As the others sat round in glum silence, Jack's mind was beginning to unfreeze.

'Hang on a minute,' he said. 'It's no use d'Astignac telling me not to go to the police; I've already done it. I'm certainly not going to ring them up and say she's just walked in the door when she hasn't. Nor am I going to say, just forget about it, I've changed my mind. No,' he said defiantly, 'the police can crack on with it.'

'But shouldn't they have the full picture? I mean, about d'Astignac and his crew?'

'Good point, Hugh. I'll go down and see Iain Campbell and talk him through it. If nothing else, he'll be able to tell me who I should contact. Can't help feeling it'll be a Glasgow job rather than one for the Kilbeg community police constable.'

Jack felt much better with something decisive to do and the prospect of progress to be made. He looked across at Sarah. She'd been almost silent throughout and he could understand why. She was looking close to shell-shocked, her clasped hands reflecting the tension in her neck.

'Come on, darling,' he said gently as he got up, 'let's go home and get cracking on this search, eh?'

Sarah barely reacted; a slight, disconnected glance at Jack. Annie noticed what was going on.

'Jack, why don't you go home and get going on things, and Sarah can stay here and have lunch with us?' Jack waited for Sarah to answer, but she didn't appear to have the capacity. 'After all,' Annie continued, 'you'll be busy with things, and at least Sarah will have some company here. What do you think?'

'Thanks, Annie, I think that'll be for the best. You're a star.' Jack turned to Sarah who was by now watching him hungrily, as if relying on him to give the lead. 'Are you OK with that, darling? I'll come and pick you up later this afternoon when I've got things going with the police.'

Hugh and Annie came with Jack to the front door. 'Jack,' said Annie, 'I can't tell you how much I feel for you both. We'll look after Sarah. But you'll have to be strong for the two of you.'

'I know. As long as I've got something I can do that at least makes me think I'm contributing, I can keep going. But I'm worried that really it's all in the hands of other people now, and all I'll be able to do is run round like a headless chicken making squawking noises.'

'Nonsense!' said Hugh. 'You get out there and do everything you possibly can. Every little bit counts. You may find the one little piece of the jigsaw puzzle that completes the whole picture and allows the police or whoever to do the job they do.'

Hugh gripped Jack's hand in his own gnarled one. Jack found it surprisingly strong, and drew strength from it. Annie reached up to put her arms round his neck; he hugged her close.

'We'll look after her for you. You just do whatever you have to do.'

As he walked back home his mind was both numb and overworking. He didn't know whether he was in a better place than last night because he now knew the worst, or a worse place because it was now pretty much beyond doubt that d'Astignac's crew had their hands on Jenny. At least the not knowing was over – for a while – and he could start doing something about it. But what?

His mobile trilled in his pocket. Caller ID said it was Charles. *Bugger!* He'd forgotten all about it. He was supposed to be meeting him at the club for a round of golf. He looked at his watch: he was nearly half an hour late. Golf? In this situation? The thought would have been laughable if it hadn't been so serious.

'Charles, I'm dreadfully sorry, I'd forgotten all about it.'

'Not to worry, old man!' Jack held his mobile an inch or two away from his ear.

'Look, I'm sorry, but I can't make it today. Something's – something's cropped up and it's rather cocked up my arrangements.'

'Not a problem, dear boy. I'm sure I can find someone else in the bar to play a few holes with. I do hope it's nothing serious. Is everything all right?'

That was such an all-encompassing question that Jack found he couldn't answer it directly.

'Jack?'

'Well, it's a bit of a bummer. But nothing to worry yourself about.'

Jack and Charles had gone through Dartmouth together, ending up in HMS *Coventry* during the Falklands war as sub-lieutenant watch-keeping officers at the age of twenty-two. They had shared their successes and cock-ups, sea-sickness, runs ashore in Portsmouth, Gibraltar and many other ports, thick heads the next morning. They had consoled each other as girlfriends came and went. They had been as brothers.

When the bombs came inboard, ripping the heart out of *Coventry* and starting fires everywhere, Jack had been on the bridge and Charles in the operations room. It was not until some hours later, recovering in HMS *Broadsword* from flash-burns and oil ingestion, that each knew for certain the other had survived. They shared equal fury when they discovered the Ministry of Defence had informed Charles' parents he'd been killed.

Three years later they had found themselves serving in the same ship again. By that time Charles was already married and heading for divorce. But Jack met Sarah when the ship was in the Pool of London on a goodwill visit. Charles had teased Jack mercilessly, who had to Charles' intense satisfaction blushed furiously, and less than twelve months later he had been best man at their wedding.

You didn't have secrets.

'Tell you what. Why not come and have a coffee, it's less than ten minutes beyond the club, and I'll tell you all about it.'

'I'll do that.'

Jack watched with more than a little envy as Charles' silver-blue 1963 Aston Martin DB4 with its burgundy upholstery drew up next to his grey Mondeo. Charles had always been flamboyant and could carry it off: Jack wasn't and couldn't.

He took Charles through to the kitchen and got such pleasantries as there could be out of the way while the kettle boiled. They sat down at the kitchen table with a cafetière and a plate of plain digestives between them while Jack brought Charles up to date. Without any interruptions, it took him thirty-five minutes while Charles listened intently. When Jack had finished, Charles' eyes remained fixed on him, which he found disconcerting.

'Why are you looking at me like that?'

'Sorry, didn't mean to.' Charles removed the intensity from his eyes. 'I know these people, that's all. Well,' he corrected, 'I know *of* them.'

Jack's eyes narrowed. 'Then why the devil didn't you tell me?'

'I didn't know you were mixed up with them. Until now.'

'Well for Chrissake who are they and what do they do in office hours? This is your Customs hat talking, isn't it?'

'I don't play golf with them, if that's what you mean.'

'Very funny. Who *are* they, and how do you know them?'

Charles got up to stretch his legs. He walked over to the window and gazed, hands in pockets, out over the glen. The bracken was beginning to turn brown on the hillsides, and the earliest trees were starting to tinge their leaves with gold.

'That's one hell of a view, isn't it?'

After a few more moments drinking in the autumnal scene, he turned round. To Jack he was just a tall silhouette against the brightness of the window.

'The United States Drug Enforcement Administration has been watching d'Astignac's outfit for the last few weeks, aware that they've been developing a new route for their controlled drugs. The US DEA tell us this outfit is an unofficial sideline for a legitimate if slightly shady commercial operation called Coral Reef Enterprises, Inc. They're based in Miami and operate, among other things, a fleet of ships carrying dry cargoes in small container ships and unboxed general cargo vessels – tramp steamers they used to be called. Being in Miami they're ideally placed to bring narcotics from South and Central America, or from transhipment hubs in the Caribbean to ports on the eastern seaboard of North America. Until recently Coral Reef arranged onward carriage to Europe via other shipping interests or traders who would bring the contraband into the usual gateways in western Europe – Spain mostly. With all these links of the chain in so many different hands, intelligence was relatively easy to gain and our European colleagues were doing a fair job intercepting these cargoes and some minor operatives.'

This was a new side to Charles that Jack had never guessed at.

'It may be that these measures were hurting Coral Reef – or maybe they were getting greedy, wanting to reduce their third party costs, we don't know. In any event, they stopped using the usual gateways a few weeks ago.

'And then, all of a sudden, we heard from Lloyds Intelligence that some of their tramp steamers were crossing the Atlantic, calling in at the Azores for bunkers, and we asked ourselves why their trading pattern should have changed. We concluded that they were looking for other access routes to the European markets.

'The trail went cold for a bit and then you can imagine our surprise when one of those tramps turns up on one of the inner Hebridean islands to discharge some very dull, unexciting cargo. They even cleared Customs!

'So of course we crawled all over the ship and the cargo and found nothing. But what had escaped our attention was that a couple of the crew were due for a crew change. So they came ashore with their discharge papers, and got the next Caledonian MacBrayne ferry to the mainland, train to Glasgow and a flight back to wherever.'

As he talked, Charles abandoned his silhouette position in the window, sat down again and took a slurp of lukewarm coffee.

'When we eventually noticed this, we screened their luggage carefully and discreetly before they got off the Caledonian MacBrayne ferry, sniffer dogs and what-have-you, but there was nothing. And of course we didn't know where they were going to be landed from their ship until too many hours after they had actually landed. This meant that there was always a dead period of a few hours that we couldn't cover.'

Charles was looking intently at Jack again, as if willing him to join in or draw a conclusion. Jack wilted under the piercing blue eyes.

'What?' he said.

'But what you've been telling me just now is pure gold – or dynamite, call it what you like.'

'What? What's pure gold . . . dynamite . . . whatever?'

'You've given me the final link – your boat. Don't you see?' Charles' eyes narrowed in excitement and he leaned forward earnestly. 'We've never been able to get to them in time. We didn't know quite how they were bringing the contraband in the last few miles; we lost sight of it before we could get to the steamer, and once that had happened . . .' Charles threw his hands up. 'It was anyone's guess where it had gone and thus how it ended up on the streets.'

'Yes, but why me? Why did they bring in someone from outside the criminal fraternity?'

'I don't know for sure, but my guess is along these lines. First of all, a local boatman knows the waters, the harbours, the area generally. If they brought someone in from out of the area, they would take a long time to acquire all that local knowledge. And they might stick out like a sore thumb, too.'

'The weakness in that argument is that I'm not a criminal and I might not want to do it. As I don't. And they can't make me.'

'Are you sure about that?' Charles' look drilled into him. 'I mean, it's not as though you're under any kind of pressure from them at the moment. Is it?'

Jack let out a long breath and put his head in his hands. 'They've got me over a barrel, haven't they?'

For a while Charles said nothing, just watched his friend. At length, he spoke up cheerfully. 'Buck up, chum. If we approach this whole thing strategically, there's a good chance you'll get out of it without raising a sweat.' He reached for the cafetière and refilled both their mugs. They didn't bother with milk. 'From my perspective, if you didn't do Tuesday's run d'Astignac would probably set up an entirely different route in, and then we'd be set back for absolutely bloody months.'

Jack felt rather than saw Charles looking keenly at him again. 'But that doesn't get me any further forward, does it?' he said.

'I mean, I'm not free of these bastards just because the Revenue men are sniffing round, nor is Jenny any safer, is she?'

'That's true – if we don't arrest them. On the other hand, if we do arrest them . . .' He let the implication hang. 'That's what I meant about approaching this strategically.'

They sat in silence, contemplating the contents of their coffee mugs. Heavy rock opened up with both barrels from an upstairs room.

A wry, minimal smile creased Jack's face. 'It must be later than I thought. Tom's alarm clock.' Charles smiled briefly in reply. 'I was going to call Iain Campbell and see who he thought I ought to tell about d'Astignac. I'd better call him, I suppose.' Jack got up and headed for the door.

Charles spoke before he got there. 'Who's Iain Campbell?'

'The village bobby.'

'Hm. I don't suppose he'll have much idea who you should talk to.'

'Possibly not, but he's all I can think of. I mean, think about it. If I were to call that Contact Centre again and say, "Hi, I've been running drugs for a smuggler called d'Astignac and now he's kidnapped my daughter, I just thought I'd mention it," they'd think I was a joke caller, wouldn't they?'

'You could be right. So I've got an idea.'

'Not like that idea you had when we were midshipmen and we nicked a policeman's helmet in Gibraltar? That was *not* a good idea. Five days Required on Board in Gib was a less than good result.'

'No,' Charles said with a restrained chuckle, 'not like that. There's a Detective Chief Inspector in Strathclyde Police I know well – used to be attached to the Scottish Drug Enforcement Agency, which is how I got to know him. I'm not sure what he does now, I think CID in Glasgow. I'll give him a bell and he can tell us who we should speak to.'

Charles wandered off and spoke into a mobile phone the size of an after-dinner mint, while Jack considered the strange turn of events. He hadn't known much about HM Customs and Excise – UK Border Agency as Charles had told him they all were now – beyond the people at a presumably functional level who stood by the Nothing to Declare exits at airports and ferry ports. He was now beginning to appreciate where the serious work of intelligence, planning and enforcement was done, and at what level. None of this had occurred to him as they had downed a sociable pint at the *Tigh an Truish* at Clachan Seil months ago. Evidently Charles had felt no compulsion to expand on his function as an Assistant Chief Preventative Officer, not after Jack had teased him about the dreadful mouthful of a rank. If Charles had told them a bit more about it, then Jack might have sought his advice some time earlier – possibly avoiding Jenny's abduction altogether. If only . . .

He cursed the vagaries of life just as Charles came back to the table, folding his micro-light mobile phone down to the size of a postage stamp.

'Any luck?'

'As it happens, Duncan Grant is still in CID – said something about being with a specialist unit or somesuch at headquarters. So he's very pleased I called and he'll take it on from here. I also,' he continued without a pause, 'called Jim Francis. He's skipper of HM Customs Cutter *Vanguard*, which operates in this area and on the lookout for just this sort of activity. She's alongside in Oban at the moment, and he agrees it would be a good idea if the three of us had a meeting on board. Get your car keys.'

Charles turned to go. Noticing that Jack remained sitting at the table, he stopped mid-stride.

'Ah,' he said. 'I'm making assumptions I'm not entitled to, aren't I? What's your position here: are you going to do the op with us? I'm not putting pressure on you; I just want to know whether Tuesday's a goer or not.'

Jack knew it was the only realistic option. This way, if everything went OK, d'Astignac would get what he wanted and return

Jenny, and Charles and his people would pick up d'Astignac and his crew, lock them up and throw away the key. On top of that, it was something Jack could do to be involved and help in Jenny's rescue.

'Count me in. I'll do anything I can to help. But – it's on the understanding I'm doing it for Jenny. So everything else comes second. Are we agreed?'

Charles barely paused. 'I'd say the same if I were in your shoes.'

26

Detective Chief Inspector Grant pressed buttons at Strathclyde Police Headquarters, 173 Pitt Street, Glasgow. Within three rings a nicotine-stained Clydeside voice answered.

'Cox.'

'Brenda, sorry to bother you at home.'

'No problem, Duncan, I was about to settle down with a glass of something volatile when I could swear I heard you thinking about dialling my number.'

'There's a young girl disappeared and the strong indications are that she may have been abducted. Could be connected to drugs and organised crime. We're right on the edge of the first twenty-four hours.'

'Why isn't one of the Divisional CIDs handling it?'

'Because there's no known location other than a general presumption of Glasgow. And we'll need to work with Serious Crime and SCDEA.'

'Sounds very jolly. Where are you?'

'Pitt Street. Can you get the team together, a couple of spare uniforms, HOLMES suite, incident room, that sort of thing. Meanwhile, I'll speak to Control and one or two other people, and let's meet here in – what, two hours? Thanks.'

Grant broke the connection and rang the Control Room.

Sergeant Ronald Gillespie answered in his slow drawl. Grant could envisage his walrus moustache and pebble glasses.

'Ronnie, Grant here. Have we received any MISPER reports yesterday or today about one Jennifer Ross?'

'Aye, we have. Her father called in about 10.30 this morning. We've been ringing round the divisions for incident reports and round the hospitals but so far nothing.'

'Right, I'll come down and take it over.'

He cut the connection and made two further calls.

They drove up to Oban in convoy. Jack would have loved to have gone up in Charles' Aston Martin, but he'd need his own car to get back as Charles would be going straight back to Glasgow.

As he followed Charles onto the Northern Light House Board pier at Oban, he looked with interest at *Vanguard*. Painted battleship grey she looked as though she belonged in the Royal Navy; but the large 'HM Customs' painted on the side was a bit of a giveaway. She was of a betwixt-and-between size, neither one thing nor the other. At forty-two metres she was smaller than a mine hunter or a River Class patrol boat, and bigger than a P2000 fast patrol boat. Mind you, he thought, with her narrow beam and lovely sleek lines, she could probably deliver a fair turn of speed. Tidy, businesslike vessel, he reckoned.

They climbed the gangway and were met at the top by an officer in a white, short-sleeved shirt, dark trousers and a white-topped peaked cap sporting the Revenue and Customs portcullis device under a crown and surrounded by gold laurel leaves. His epaulettes showed two and a half gold rings.

'Charles, welcome aboard.'

'Thank you, Jim. Can I introduce Jack Ross, skipper of the sleek streak of white lightning called *Celtic Dawn*. Jack, this is Jim Francis.'

'Glad to meet you, Jack. Let's go up to the bridge and see what's what.'

They made their way onto the bridge where Francis phoned

down for some coffee to be sent up. Jack was almost caffeined out but he went along with it.

Francis took them to the back of the bridge where there was a chart table, higher than normal desk height and with six shallow drawers below, each the full width of the table and designed to stow charts flat. Above it was a shelf with pilot books, nautical almanacs, tide tables, Admiralty List of Radio Signals and the like. On the bulkhead to the side was taped a quick-reference chart showing the west coast of Scotland with its offshore and inshore islands, sea-lochs, canals, bays and harbours.

'I like that,' said Charles, tapping the chart, 'very imaginative.' Someone with a highly developed sense of humour had fixed a small wooden cocktail umbrella over the yellow shading symbolising a beach somewhere on the Ardnamurchan peninsula.

They remained gathered round the wall-chart. Charles announced that Jack was up for the operation on Tuesday and asked Jack to run through the facts of his encounters with d'Astignac. Charles picked up again when he'd finished.

'Jim, you'll be in charge of marine operations on Tuesday, but essentially I want to be at the dockside with a reception committee when Jack returns with d'Astignac and the contraband on board. That very simple fact will give us a clean sweep here, it will provide the continuity of evidence for the USDEA in Miami to clean up there, and it'll give security for Jack and his family. What I need from you, Jim, is two things: monitor the incoming Coral Reef ship; and ensure a safe and comfortable passage for Jack from his pick-up point back to wherever d'Astignac directs him.'

'That shouldn't be too much of a problem.' Jim looked at the chart. 'Jack, do you know where your pick-up point will be?'

At that moment, a steward arrived with a tray of coffee and biscuits. He opened the top drawer of the chart table and solemnly retrieved a folded chart. Its condition horrified Jack. There were blotches and stains, rings and splodges all over it. With relief, Jack read the legend scribbled in thick black felt-tip pen: **KNOCKER WHITE'S COFFEE/TEA MAT – TOP SECRET**

– HANDS OFF. The steward placed mugs on the filthy chart, poured out coffee, left a milk jug, sugar bowl and the biscuits, and disappeared.

'Pick up point? No. So far I've always picked them up at Crinan at ten o'clock and delivered them back there. Destinations have been Tobermory on Mull, Port Charlotte on Islay, Lochboisdale on South Uist, and Iona.' As he spoke he indicated on the chart the variety of directions from Crinan.

Jim Francis stroked his beard. 'Hmm. There's no pattern, nothing that gives any indication where they might go next. If *Vanguard*'s hanging around down by Islay,' he tapped the chart, 'and the Coral Reef vessel goes in to Stornoway up here on Lewis,' again he tapped the chart, 'that's a difference of . . .' he opened out a pair of dividers to twenty miles on the latitude scale, and stepped them up from Islay to the Western Isles, 'over 300 miles. My maximum speed is 26 knots in a calm sea, so that would take me the thick end of twelve hours. By then of course the vessel will have discharged her cargo and be 50 miles offshore. Even if we manage to find her, which is unlikely if she wants to evade detection, she'll be outside territorial waters so I couldn't arrest her.'

'I thought territorial waters was two hundred miles?' Jack asked.

'That's the Exclusive Economic Zone – over which we have jurisdiction only for management of natural resources. The UK claims only twelve miles for territorial waters. As you can see, I need to be as close as possible when she arrives at her destination, and I need grounds to suspect that she is carrying or has discharged contraband.'

Jack felt two pairs of eyes boring into him – a sensation that was making him feel like a pin-cushion. He looked from Charles to Jim and back again.

'What, me?'

'I'm afraid so. That's why you're the crucial link in this entire operation.' Charles was looking steely-eyed again and Jack felt sweat break out in his armpits.

'What I need from you as soon as you possibly can,' said Jim, 'is an indication of where d'Astignac wants you to go to. And then, when any baggage is brought on board and you begin your return journey, I'm afraid you need to form an opinion as to whether you honestly and reasonably think, given everything that you know about the circumstances, that it might be or contain contraband.'

'Bloody hell! You don't ask much, do you? It all sounds very lawyerish.'

'I'm sorry about that, Jack, I wish it could be any other way. As Customs officers, like the police, we have to have a certain understanding of relevant bits of law. And if we don't get it right, you wouldn't believe the amount of multi-coloured shit that will blow back our way.'

Jack looked anew at Jim Francis. He didn't seem to be much older than late thirties – forty at the most. Sandy-coloured hair, thick but neatly trimmed beard, eyebrows that would inevitably become shaggy one day, steady blue eyes. He had to have a staggeringly wide range of skills and qualities to do this job, which Jack had never been put in a position of even thinking about. An ability to make quick decisions while avoiding rocks and shoals, making judgements about courses to intercept while the deck beneath his feet was heaving in a lively sea. And on top of all that, he had to have knowledge of law and be able to apply it, otherwise smugglers went free and his career could revert to the exits at Heathrow. Jack looked at him with new respect.

'Can you do that for me? I'd be counting on it.'

If Jim Francis had to do everything that seemed to be necessary then he, Jack, could do his own small bit.

'Yes, I'll do it.' Jack squared his shoulders, generating within himself some pride that others would be relying on him – after everything that had seemed to go so badly wrong in the last few days. And it was action that his soul craved, action that would be a key part of ending this whole stinking mess. 'I'll need to be in communication with you from my boat. VHF?'

'Use channel 72 to call me on *Vanguard*. You'd better use some spurious call-sign for me, and also we'll need to dream up a bland subject for the call. Call me "Highland Radio": it doesn't exist as a VHF station so it won't confuse anyone. I might get a rap over the knuckles from the coastguard, but I'll buy them a pint or two later. Request a weather forecast or something from me. That should give you the opportunity to slip in your destination. And then do the same once you're heading for home.'

Charles broke in. 'When you're heading back to your return port, let Jim know where it is. I'll be monitoring Channel 72 – I've got a mobile VHF in my Land Rover – and I'll pick it up. It's vital that I know where you're returning to so I can get my team and the police in place for when your guests step ashore. If we're not waiting for them when you come alongside, we've had it for this trip.'

'I understand.' Jack turned back to Jim. 'Just one thing I'm nervous about. It's this thing about making a judgement about whether they've got contraband on board or not.'

'The purpose of that is that I can't arrest the ship unless it's within territorial waters *and* I have reasonable grounds to suspect that it has been involved in the commission of an offence – in this case, landing contraband. Once the vessel sails, it'll be out of territorial waters with an hour – assuming they head straight out and don't bimble along the coast for a jolly – and my chance has gone.'

'That's all very well, but how do I make this judgement? I mean, they're hardly likely to load ten tea-chests all neatly labelled as Finest Grade Heroin or whatever.'

'Just use the same analysis as you did last time, when you began to suspect you weren't just ferrying a couple of climbers and their sleeping bags. You said yourself that your suspicions were aroused when they were loading far more than any adventure trainees would need for a few days out on the hills.'

'Yes, but how do I know it's *contraband* and not just – oh, I don't know – party poppers?'

'Don't worry about that side,' said Charles. 'It's enough that we have shared the available intelligence with you, and therefore you're entitled to put two and two together and suspect illegal drugs. After all, it's only that your *suspicion* has to be reasonable, it's not actual *proof* admissible in court that Jim requires for an arrest.'

'Holy shit, this is way outside my comfort zone.'

'Well, I can certainly understand that. But don't let it get out of proportion and scare you off from making a judgement at all. After all, I reckon it's highly unlikely that the issue of the arrest will come to court, or that you'll be the prime witness if it did.'

With an unsteady hand, Jack returned his coffee mug to Knocker White's top-secret coffee mat. His mind was swimming with all the twists and turns of events of the last twenty-four hours, until his thoughts were interrupted by Jim.

'Can I have the SBS?' Jim was looking fixedly at the chart.

Jack wasn't sure he'd heard right. If he had, he didn't like the sound of it.

'Thinking?' Charles asked.

'I'm thinking that I'll be outside the Hebrides dealing with the Coral Reef vessel, while Jack will be inside the islands, heading back to the mainland. He'll have d'Astignac, or at least some of his outfit, plus the contraband. And where there's controlled drugs there are probably firearms. I think Jack should have some heavy-duty back-up. After all, we exercise enough with M Squadron for just this purpose. Now is one of those times, don't you think?'

'Now hang on just a tiny wee minute.' Jack's comfort zone had already receded to a speck on the horizon. 'What's going on here? Are we experiencing mission creep here? Christ almighty: covert signals on the VHF, making judgements on contraband that determine whether or not this . . . this *drugs bust* is going to be a success, going to court as a witness, and now we've got Special Forces haring around armed to the teeth! Aren't you forgetting what this is all about?'

Jim and Charles looked at him as if he'd just turned up as a Christmas tree fairy with kinky boots. Charles recovered first.

'I'm sorry, Jack, you've got a point. You're in this because it's the best way to help Jenny and rid yourself and your family of these vermin. And although my paid responsibilities are to catch these people and lock them up, I'm with you on your personal mission.'

'Well thanks, Charles.' Jack was still waiting to be convinced.

'But Jim's right. You could do with some back-up from the SBS. If we just tuck them away and out of sight behind some rocks, they can keep a fatherly eye on you – just to make sure nothing goes wrong.'

What can go wrong, thought Jack morosely. What can *possibly* go wrong?

27

'Are we all here?' asked Grant. Detective Sergeant Cox nodded. 'Right, let's get on with it.' He turned to address his team. In addition to Cox there were three detective constables, dressed casually to blend in with any crowd, and three constables who, if they hadn't been called in off duty, would have been uniformed. A particularly scruffy, ill-kempt individual sat at the back, in a corner on his own.

'Sorry to spoil your Sunday afternoon, ladies and gentlemen, and thank you for coming in. This operation is a race against time to save a young woman from the tender mercies of a gangland group, here in Glasgow.'

He gave them a summary of the relevant facts relating to the abduction. He kept the operation on the coast confidential for the moment.

'As you are all aware, the first twenty-four hours after an abduction are critical, and the chances of finding the victim alive or even at all diminish rapidly after that. We are at that point.' His eye glinted under the fluorescent strip light.

'To begin with, we're talking old-fashioned police-work. We need to interview Jenny's friend Lucy, the one who did come home, we need photographs of the kidnapped girl, and we need to pull together and analyse our available intelligence on our resident gangs and their operations. There's CCTV footage, and there'll also be a lot of footslogging round the seedier bars and nightclubs. Call in some favours from all the professional girls you know and any and all of your informants: that will produce the best leads.

'Brenda, organise a press conference for tomorrow morning. Stuart, I want everything we've got on recent abductions, registered sex offenders and all the rest of it. Meantime, I've arranged a meeting with the Serious Crime Squad and the SCDEA. Brenda, I want you in on that. Shona, call the parents of Jenny's friend Lucy, see what initial information you can get from them and Lucy if possible, and make arrangements to take a formal statement from her first thing tomorrow morning. We could ask one of the Oban bobbies to do it, but I'd rather you got a feel for the case direct from Lucy. Brief me when I've finished with Serious Crime and the Agency.'

Their planning session onboard *Vanguard* was drawing to a close. When they had worked through everything they could think of on the operation, Jack brought the conversation back to the kidnap.

'That's your operation sorted. Now what about Jenny? I've got to go home now and tell Sarah that everything's just fine and dandy and Jenny will be home directly.'

Jack looked from Charles to Jim and back again.

'I can't answer for the police, of course,' Charles said, 'but I do know that Duncan Grant will do everything in his power to get Jenny back as quickly as he can. Look, from what I know of him I suspect he's up to his eyeballs on this case right now. Why don't you give him a ring first thing tomorrow morning and find out what progress he's making? He'd probably want to talk to you and fill in any gaps in his background knowledge.'

Jack had appreciated early on that, realistically, Jenny wouldn't be coming home on her own. But that left him with a lot of dead time to fill in before he could get going on this operation on Tuesday. On the one hand he knew he had to go home and tell Sarah what was going on, and just be with her. On the other hand, he'd feel totally useless, sitting around doing nothing and relying on everyone else to get his daughter back. What happens if they can't do it? He'd spend the rest of his life knowing that he'd sat at home, thumb in bum and brain in neutral, not making any kind of effort to save her.

Although it got him into trouble periodically, activity was how he defined himself; inactivity was his enemy, the thing he avoided at all costs.

But right now he'd have to go home and be with his wife.

'God, this stuff gets more disgusting by the day.' The scruffy individual who had sat in the far corner during Grant's briefing looked morosely at the thin plastic cup of liquid of indeterminate brownish-greyness, powdered milk floating undissolved on the top. He added three sachets of sugar in an attempt to mask the flavour, and rearranged it with a streak of plastic that was called, in his view fraudulently, a stirrer.

Detective Inspector Moira Cathcart kept a deadpan expression as she placed her glass of water carefully on the table. DS Andy Anderson, Serious Crime Squad, looked at it disdainfully. She opened her briefcase, brought out a small plastic bottle of Cairngorm Spring Water and pointedly turned the bottle so that Anderson could read the label. Anderson observed that, as the bottle hadn't been opened, it was unlikely the glass had anything other than tap water in it. Cathcart said she hated detectives who used their professional skills outside office hours.

The door opened and Grant came in. He was fifty-two years old, and only his eyes were remarkable. They used to be of a pale blue that could variously be described as ice, steel-grey, flinty or merely pale blue, depending on the circumstances. But following a police raid many years ago which got out of hand, one of them had been replaced by a glass replica that failed to change according to circumstance. It being Sunday, he was not in his usual rumpled grey suit. Instead, he had relaxed to a threadbare tweed jacket, grey flannels, and a knitted tie with his Tattersall check shirt.

He dumped his very thin sheaf of papers on the table and sat down. 'Brenda Cox will be joining us in a minute or two. Thank you both for coming in this afternoon.' There were general murmurs to the effect that it was not a problem. 'We shouldn't be long here. I just want to make sure we're all in harmony and functioning like the well-oiled machine the Chief Constable believes us to be.'

He summarised everything he knew about the case, including the drugs and gangs. Brenda Cox joined them just as he was finishing, and nodded to the others in recognition. There was a shuffling and rearranging of chairs before the conference resumed.

Grant turned to DI Cathcart and said, 'Why don't you kick us off, Moira? What can you tell us about this lot?'

The role of the Scottish Crime and Drug Enforcement Agency was to tackle, at a national level, all serious organised crime. As such, it was in constant touch with all the international law enforcement agencies: the US DEA, the FBI, Europol, Interpol and many more besides. It had a directly employed workforce but this was supplemented by secondees from the police and Customs. Detective Inspector Moira Cathcart was on secondment from Strathclyde Police CID.

She nodded at a pile of files in front of her. 'This is what I have so far from what you told me on the phone, Duncan, but I haven't read through all of it yet.' She indicated multi-coloured tabs sticking out of the files. 'I expect I'll be reading bits out as we go along. In another twenty-four hours I'll have a much more coordinated view. In the meantime, let me tell you what I have got.' She reached for the top file.

'Let's start with this chap d'Astignac. The Serious Organised Crime Agency have a detailed dossier on him which they emailed over to me. There's an issue with his identity,' she announced as she settled into her briefing, 'his name's not d'Astignac. That's the name of a man he killed before he joined the Foreign Legion.'

'Oh, very pleasant. Does he have a real name?'

'Efstathios Chrysostomou Antoniou.' Cathcart hadn't practised saying the name out loud and stumbled over it. 'Greek. Comes from Komotini, a market town in the north-east of the country. Komotini is about ten kilometres from the Bulgarian border and not much more from the Turkish border.

'The family, it says here, had a long history of trading across the border – I take that to include smuggling, and I suppose it'd been going on for so many centuries that it was regarded as legitimate and respectable trade.'

'Makes sense. That means it's probably in his blood, and I can guess where all this is leading. Go on.'

'You're right. When he was very young, early twenties, he was sent by the family into the Mediterranean to find more business, open up opportunities. Instead he seems to have found love.'

'How sweet. Where?'

'Corsica. Put one Marguerite Casamajou up the duff which seems to have upset her fiancé, chap by the name of Marc-Antoine . . .'

Grant and Anderson joined in the chorus. 'd'Astignac.'

Cathcart said something obscene about being privileged to share a room with Glasgow's finest brains.

'So with, no doubt, a price on his head and an assumed name that the rightful owner wouldn't be needing for a while, he legged it to the mainland and joined the Legion in 1978.'

'Hang on,' said Grant. 'If he's French – or apparently French, why's he joining the *Foreign* Legion?'

DS Anderson interjected. 'Being French isn't a bar. Anyone can join, French or not.'

Both Grant and Cathcart looked at him.

'How do you know that?' A grin cracked slowly over Moira Cathcart's face. 'You did, didn't you? You went and joined the Foreign Legion.' Anderson turned red and looked at the table. Cathcart turned to Grant. 'Did you hear that, Duncan? He joined the Foreign Legion.'

'No I didn't,' said Anderson, by now bright red. 'I only looked into it. Decided against it as I didn't think I could cope with the language bit. Can we get on with this briefing, please?'

Grant smiled. Cathcart returned to her files. 'He was commissioned two years later.'

'That's unusual,' said Anderson. 'The officers are normally from the regular French Army, or NCOs commissioned after very long service. Any indications why?'

'Yes. It seems he was quite bright, resourceful, had an eye for the ground and a knack of avoiding the enemy. The others seemed to follow him around like sheep. I guess with his background that makes sense.'

Brenda Cox brought it back to the here and now. 'Well that tells us a great deal about what we're up against. And Mr Ross, poor sod.'

'I suppose so. Anyway, he got plenty of experience. Chad–Libyan campaign 1983 to '87, Rwanda 1990 to '94, and on the Ivory Coast from 2001.' She read on for a moment. 'According to Legion headquarters in Aubagne, he was discharged without a good character reference in 2003.' She peered at them over her glasses. 'I wonder why?' She pushed her glasses back up her nose and carried on reading. 'Ah yes, here it is.' She laughed. 'You wouldn't bloody credit it, would you? Twenty-five years in the Legion and some stupid little recruit did for him. Says here he was running a little import/export business on the side, including controlled drugs. Then one day some rookie went and asked the sergeant-major where he could get some more weed as Captain d'Astignac was away on leave. What a fucking moron!'

There was incredulous laughter round the table, sympathy and serves-him-bloody-right in equal measure.

'Anyway,' DI Cathcart continued, 'without a good character reference, it was inevitable he would gravitate towards a criminal career. Got a job with a Colombian cartel improving the security of their shipments from Colombia to Florida. Then moved further along the supply chain to Coral Reef Inc in Miami, who were experiencing their own difficulties of distribution. Either their shipments to Spain were being compromised or they were being elbowed out by the competition.'

'So what are they doing up here?'

'Well, it seems d'Astignac is chummy with a wholesaler here in Glasgow.'

'Who?'

'Hang on a moment.' She put down one file and flipped through another. 'Yes, here we are. About ten years ago two brothers came over from Bulgaria on student visas. Their names were Kayvan and Haluk Celenk.' She pronounced it Selenk.

'It's pronounced *Ch*elenk,' said Anderson.

'You know them, then?' asked Grant.

'Oh yes, I know the brothers Kayvan and Haluk. They never returned to Bulgaria but instead secured work visas which turned into rights of residence here.' He took another mouthful of coffee. 'Don't you just love it?'

Grant and Cathcart both snorted.

'Anyway,' Cathcart continued, referring back to her file. 'They set up in business, importing and exporting just about anything that moves – from refrigerated transport of ritually slaughtered meat for the ethnic minorities in Glasgow, to the export of luxury goods for the filthy rich in the Balkans. About three years ago we began to suspect that their business was expanding to include less-savoury trades, like controlled drugs of course, but also people-trafficking via the Balkan countries. Now there was no way they could muscle in on turf in Glasgow or anywhere else, so they've carved out a niche as intermediaries, wholesalers if you like. They aren't the only ones, of course, but they've certainly got a big slice of the market here.'

'How does d'Astignac come to be talking to people like that?' Cox was shaking her head in puzzlement. 'I mean, didn't you say he was French Foreign Legion or something?'

'Remember what I said about where this Frenchman came from? Komotini in the north-east of Greece. Now, the Celenks are a Turkish family established on all sides of the Bulgarian–Greek borders, so I guess they're old trading partners of d'Astignac – Efstathios thingummy or whatever his name is. It wouldn't take much for d'Astignac to lift the phone and say, "Kayvan me old mucker, I've got a proposal." And so here he is. Here we all are.'

'So if we've got all this intelligence,' asked Grant, 'why aren't the Celenk brothers behind bars? Or do I know the answer to that?'

'You know the answer to that,' Anderson said. 'We've had one or other of them in court any number of times, but they've got the same brief as the other gangland bosses who get off every time. That plus a good dose of witness and jury intimidation.' He grimaced as he drained the last of his coffee. 'Bloody awful, that.'

'Tell me about it,' Grant said mournfully.

'I meant the coffee.'

'Oh.' Grant looked at his notes again. 'What about this Coluzzi character then?'

DI Cathcart changed files. 'New York Mafia. Third generation of an Italian immigrant family. That's mainland, not Sicily. Twenty-eight years old. Nothing remarkable about him, not attended law school or anything, not high up, not low down. There's nothing here indicates why he's with d'Astignac – or even that he *is* with d'Astignac. Mr Faceless.'

'Hmm. What about this third person,' he glanced down at his notepad, 'Marie-Claire Casamajou?'

Cathcart changed files again.

The passport in his hand was dark green, the legend *Republique Tunisienne* embossed in gold below Arabic writing.

'Inès Rafrafi,' he said, looking at the photograph and comparing it with the tall woman standing in front of him. Pride, even a certain imperiousness, burned from her eyes. Below the almost aquiline nose a slight smile played about her mouth, and he could imagine humour there. He would like to know this woman better. He motioned to her and they both sat.

'It seems you have many passports.'

She shrugged. 'I need many passports.' He was surprised at the fluency of her answer. He had spoken in mainstream Russian even though his people were Altaic citizens of Chechnya, his mother tongue Nogay Turkic.

'Nine?' He smacked one down on the table. 'Antoinette Didier. French.' Another passport landed on the table. 'Marie-Claire Casamajou. French.' Another added to the pile. 'Ileana Prasnaglava, Romanian.' More passports followed quickly. 'Greek. Bulgarian. Turkish.' He dumped the last two on the pile which had already spilled sideways.

'Go to Greece a lot?'

She shrugged again. 'It's a nice place.'

He picked up one of the passports. 'So is Pakistan if all these visas are anything to go by. And Russia. Where do you go in Russia? I mean, it's a big place.'

'I need a cigarette.'

He reached into a pocket of his soft leather jacket, pulled out a packet of Sobranie Black Russian and spun it across the table at her. She looked at it with disdain before digging into her shoulder bag for a Diyarbakir. He didn't know whether to be insulted or impressed. He wasn't used to having a Sobranie treated like a Marlboro Light; they were the one luxury he permitted himself. He wasn't sure about the Diyarbakir, but he recollected his grandfather, a Turk, having them hand-made for him.

She extracted a cigarette with long, claw-like fingers, and returned the packet to her shoulder bag. She arched an enquiring eyebrow at her interrogator.

He dug into another pocket and extracted a wafer-thin Dunhill carbon-fibre lighter. A flame sprang to life as he reached over, and she leant forward and sucked the flame into the tobacco. The flame clicked off and they both relaxed into the backs of their hard wooden chairs. She directed a stream of smoke up towards the bare lightbulb, where it failed to dissipate.

'You were telling me where you went in Russia.'

'Here and there.' It was his turn to cock an eyebrow. He picked up a passport at random and flicked through the visa pages. 'Pyatigorsk.' He flicked another page. 'Grozny. Tbilisi. This is not exactly *Russia*, is it?' He tossed the passport back on the table and regarded her for a long moment.

'OK,' he said. 'Tell me why you want to join us.'

'I don't.'

He frowned. 'I thought that's why you're here.' Then he laughed outright. It was a vibrant, healthy laugh – that of a young man with ambitions to fulfil. 'Tell me why you *are* here.' His dark eyes twinkled.

She drew on her cigarette again, held the smoke in her lungs then exhaled. She regarded him through the smoke. There was a Balkan Sasieni pipe tobacco tin on the table with the marks of countless stubbings-out. She tapped the aromatic ash from her Diyarbakir into it. She looked up at him and held his eyes, steady.

'I have a proposition for you.'

'For *me?*'

'I have access,' she said with studied nonchalance, 'to dirty nuclear waste.'

'Go on,' he said without giving anything away other than that dirty nuclear waste would be of intense interest to him. This was no matter of amusement. He would have to treat her seriously.

'It is in tiny quantities, and I can supply it to you as spent pellets from the reactor, or as treated waste in glass form. In either case they will be well packaged to prevent radiation leakage. Should the packaging be ruptured at any stage by, say ... PVV 5-A or Semtex in a public place – like the Moscow metro – who knows what political concessions may follow?'

Her eyes remained locked on his. A small smile played around the corners of her mouth. He reached for his packet of Sobranie, extracted one without breaking her look, and only looked down when he lit it. He restored both packet and lighter to his pockets.

She drew one last time on her Diyarbakir, blew a luxurious plume of grey-blue smoke into the atmosphere, and stubbed the half-smoked cigarette out in the Balkan Sasieni tin. He was sure it was a deliberate display of careless excess, like a Hermès crocodile handbag or some other ridiculously expensive accessory.

He waited for her to finish, then asked, 'How much?'

'That depends whether you want it treated or untreated. One pellet untreated would be ten thousand US. One pellet equivalent, treated, will be fifty thousand US.'

He processed the information in his mind, drew on his Sobranie, then spoke.

'Why?'

She gave him a quizzical look. 'I assume you're not asking why those are the prices?'

He laughed. 'No. I'm asking myself why you do this. What sort of person I am dealing with here. What makes you tick.'

She shrugged. 'It's simple. A girl has to make a living, no?'

He tipped his chair and his head back and laughed long and hard. 'Oh dear,' he said, wiping his eyes, 'I like your sense of humour, Inès.' When he had calmed down, he continued. 'A girl who needs to make a living becomes a hairdresser, or works in a shop. Or works on the streets. She doesn't sell heroin or cocaine, armaments or explosives. She certainly doesn't peddle stuff that glows in the dark to people like me.' He got up from his chair, went over to the window and looked out. The sky was uniform iron-grey, the mountains in the distance clear. He avoided looking at the damaged buildings closer, those reminders of what they were doing – had done – to his country.

'People like me,' he continued, still looking out of the window, 'are straightforward. We blow things up, kill people, frighten the shit out of the government, until we get what we want politically.' He turned round, deliberately a silhouette against the brightness of the window. 'But you – I can't make you out. That worries me. You see, I thought you wanted to join our cause. You were brought here so that we could talk – about you and about your aspirations in our cause. And then I could decide whether to welcome you, or . . . not. Instead, you come up with this . . .' he fluttered with his hands, 'this proposal. So we cannot have this talk before I have to decide whether to work with you – or have you disposed of.'

The woman was relaxed. 'I am happy to talk.'

'I'm glad about that.' He left the window and returned to his chair at the table. He offered her a Sobranie again. She shook her head, but accepted a light for her Diyarbakir.

She blew a plume of smoke towards the ceiling and regarded him through the haze of their mutual cigarette smoke. 'Where do you want me to begin?'

'The beginning.'

'I was born thirty-five years ago in Tunisia. I never knew my father. He died in the feuds before I was born. We lived in the mountains and I walked five miles every day to be taught the Kor'an in Ghat. I learnt well and was then sent to the school in Sabha. From there I won a scholarship to the university in Sfax.'

'What did you study?'

'Modern languages: English, Turkish, Russian.'

'I didn't think education would be free in Tunisia?'

'The village school was. Thereafter, my education was paid for by my uncle.'

'Ah.'

'He had experience in security services, and he found employment in Colombia. Then he began a business in Florida where he could develop his interests both . . . tax-paid and duty-free. By that time I had worked in countries all the way round the Black Sea, and I found that I was useful to people. I had an ability to facilitate transactions, to find sources of goods that were in demand. It was not long before I became a merchant in my own right.'

'And your uncle?'

'He also had this ability. He suggested we form a joint venture, I think he would call it, in order to expand both our markets –

his in cocaine, mine in heroin. I was able to source armaments, he had a ready market for them. Our businesses work together well. We work together well.'

'I'm sure you do. And I find myself, for the moment, satisfied. I shall have to make some enquiries, of course.'

'Of course. But you would agree that a girl has to make a living?'

Again he allowed himself a laugh, long, carefree, uninhibited. Her eyes flashed in amusement, the angle of her shoulders changed to draw attention to her breasts, so that the atmosphere changed. He knew he was attractive to women, but above all he wielded power over others, a natural ability to dominate a room. He had never experienced refusal.

He rose from his chair and said, 'Come. We shall eat.' He waited for her to stub out her Diyarbakir in the Balkan Sasieni tin, and he drew back her chair as she rose to follow. Instead, they paused briefly in each other's space, testing each other's pheromones, their animal instincts. Like two young warriors who were used to seizing the moment, they hurled themselves into a mutual embrace of fiery intemperance, and clawed each other's bodies where they stood.

'Marie-Claire Casamajou.' Moira Cathcart drained the last of her glass of water and unwrapped a Kit-Kat Chunky. 'One of a number of aliases: Antoinette Didier, Inès Rafrafi, Aysel Yilmaz. And more. She's of interest to a whole raft of law enforcement agencies around the Mediterranean and Middle East. Let's see.' She ran her finger on again for a few moments. 'Yes, here we are. She's got her fingers in a broad range of nasty little activities: heroin, armaments – oh, you'll love this, Duncan: spent nuclear fuel. And she's peddling it round terrorist organisations, presumably to sellotape to small bombs.'

'What the hell's someone like that doing up here?' asked Anderson. 'Is this guy Ross mixed up in terrorism, nuclear waste bombs and the rest of it? Jesus Christ, what a shit-heap.'

'Those,' said DI Cathcart, 'are exactly the sort of questions the Director General and others are asking. The upshot is that this is now a multi-faceted and inter-service bag of nails. There's a note here,' she said, speaking round a mouthful of cholesterol-enriched calories, 'says any involvement with her is to be reported to MI6, MI5, the Met's CO15 *and* SOCA for Interpol. Wow! Can you imagine the baggage that goes with that lot?'

'Thank you, Detective Inspector, you make my day. Blessings be upon you and may you have a thousand sons.'

Cathcart mumbled something about two being bloody plenty.

28

'Shit,' Grant mumbled as they headed down the stairs, 'that's the last thing we want. This poor kid Jenny sounds like she's mixed up with a serious bunch of bastards of international proportions.' They reached his office. 'Thanks Brenda, I'll call Burns. No, wait – I'll come with you and see what Shona has found out.'

They turned back along the corridor, almost colliding with a cleaner, a floor mop and a bucket.

'What the . . .' Grant exclaimed as he recovered his balance. 'Cleaners on a Sunday evening – whatever next?'

'They're civilian contractors, Duncan. They're contracted to clean when the offices are empty-ish. It seems to work quite well.'

'Oh. I hope someone keeps an eye on them when they're in here. I mean, there would be rich pickings in the Anti-Terrorist Branch offices, wouldn't there?'

'That's why we have a clear desk policy, remember?'

'Oh,' Grant said again, 'I suppose it is.'

Cox pushed open the door to their incident room. DC Stuart Sutherland's back was towards them as he was going through CCTV tapes. Even though compact disks and hard drives had replaced video tapes years before, there was still a tendency to refer to them as tapes. DC Shona Macleod was standing behind

Sutherland looking over his shoulder, pointing something out on his screen.

'Shona, the boss wants briefed.'

Shona Macleod turned round, picked up her notebook, and came over to join them. She had passed her sergeant's exams only a few months ago and was hoping to be promoted at the next vacancy. The only question was whether the wedding would come before her stripes, or the other way round.

'I had a long conversation with Dr MacDonald, and then with Lucy. Piecing the events together from what they said, she and Jenny had gone into Glasgow on the morning train and done some shopping. Things began to go wrong when they went to Marco Polo's, an upstairs wine bar on Gordon Street, for some lunch. Neither of the girls drink very much, so as usual they ordered a lime soda and a panini.'

'What's a panini?' asked Grant.

'A posh crusty roll, sir. It's Italian.'

'Oh.'

'Anyway, about ten minutes after they'd started drinking their lime sodas they began to lose focus and control of their arms and legs, and some person or persons helped them down the stairs and into what Lucy thought was a taxi. She says she can't remember much with any kind of clarity until she got home. She has vague impressions and memories but they're only things like being in a car, or in a room. Dr MacDonald said he thought she might have been given something like Rohypnol, and had it expertly topped up until she was brought home. Anyway, Lucy's still very shaken up and frightened, and a good night's sleep will help, so I've made an appointment for a face-to-face interview at their home at oh-nine-hundred hours tomorrow.'

'Good. Has any medical analysis been done?'

'Dr MacDonald said his partner at the medical centre took a blood sample, but whether that will tell anyone much is an open question. He'll send a copy of the results down here.'

'What about the Rosses?'

'I rang their home but only their son was in. It seems that Mrs Ross was a bit shaken up and was with the MacDonalds.'

'And Mr Ross?'

'He was out.'

'So you'll see the Rosses tomorrow morning after you've taken a statement from the MacDonalds?'

'Yes, sir.'

'Good. Thanks Shona.' Grant turned to DS Cox. 'Go and see what's turning up on CCTV while I talk to Burns. I'll come back down here after I've spoken to him and we'll get people out on the streets asking questions.'

Grant punched some buttons on his desk phone, calling his boss, Detective Superintendent Arthur Burns, deputy head of Strathclyde Police CID.

'Duncan Grant here, sir. Sorry to call you on a Sunday evening, but I thought I should keep you informed about a possible abduction that seems to have taken a nasty turn.'

'Tell me.'

Grant summarised what he knew. 'I've just been meeting with the SCDEA. There's flags against the name of one of the suspected drugs gang, posted by SIS, MI5, CO15 and Interpol.'

There was silence at the other end for a couple of moments. 'Damn.' Grant observed that Burns was one of the senior officers who swore politely. 'Have you sent your team out onto the streets?'

'Not yet: I'll get them out . . .' he looked at his watch, 'within the hour.'

'Well hold fire on that just at the moment: if there's a flag against the case I'll call Rufus Buchanan now and get back to you asap.'

As he drove back to Kilbeg from Oban, Jack was fired up with energy and a certain sense of hope. But he was not happy with the idea of doing nothing for the next thirty-six hours and leaving it to others whom he didn't know to bring this to a successful outcome. That wasn't the way he was hard-wired. He resolved that he would set off early the next morning, see this DCI Grant chap and offer his services to the rescue. Grant would of course gladly grasp the offer – after all, weren't the police in every force seriously undermanned? So he would go home now, tell Sarah that everything was well in hand, she would cheer up, Jenny would be rescued on Monday once Jack was down there to stiffen their resolve, he would do the final drugs run on Tuesday, the whole gang would be picked up by the police and he would be free of them for ever. Pretty straightforward in his opinion.

From the moment he picked Sarah up from the MacDonalds', shortly before 5 pm, the plan didn't seem to go quite right. Sarah was more distraught than Jack had realised she would be. As he began telling her about the powers of rescue that were being unleashed even he realised she was not on the same wavelength. She could only cope with the here-and-now.

'I suppose I'd better get some supper, then,' she said without enthusiasm.

'Oh, don't worry about it, love, I'm not hungry.'

'It'll give me something to do.'

'Fair enough,' he said. He felt at a loose end, that if he tried to help in the kitchen he'd only get in the way. 'I'll just go and check the emails.'

As Sarah disappeared into the kitchen, Jack headed for the study. He'd tried to call it the office in an attempt to create a commercial environment for the boat business, but neither the idea nor the word had stuck. Apart from the usual junk there was only one mail of any interest: from Maggie. Jack detested the woman, a spiky, prickly, army-surplus-wearing harridan, and he could never understand how or why Sarah had become friendly with her. Sarah's one attempt, as far as Jack was aware, to entertain her in their house in Bracknell had been a disaster, and they had always met on more neutral ground. Providing he never had to encounter her, Jack had grown to accept that Sarah liked her and he'd decided he wouldn't stand in the way.

An email from Maggie would probably cheer her up. He went through to the kitchen where he found her mechanically preparing omelettes and toast.

'Email from Maggie, darling. You go and read it while I do the omelettes.'

'Oh. Thanks, I'll do that.' Sarah visibly brightened. 'And by the way, it's scrambled eggs I thought I was doing, not omelettes.'

'Ah.'

Jack wasn't all that sure his culinary offering would be one as distinct from the other, but he didn't think he was going to lose any Michelin stars on it.

Sarah was longer at the emails than Jack had anticipated, which suited him fine as his cookery had taken longer than he had expected. When she came back he was just tipping lumps of scrambled omelette onto cold slices of toast.

'How's Maggie? Lost the edge from her acerbic wit?'

Sarah stopped in the doorway and looked at him, her face drained of colour.

'Who's Lydia?'

29

Detective Superintendent Burns took longer calling back than Grant had expected.

'Duncan, did you know that Rufus Buchanan's in hospital?'

'Good grief! No, I didn't. What's wrong with him?'

'Road traffic accident this morning. Both his legs are broken. His wife said he was on his way to play golf at Gleneagles and his car was squashed between two lorries on the M8.'

'Bloody dangerous game, golf. Anyway, where does that get us with the flag?'

'I've just spoken to the Chief Constable. He's just about to go away for his twice-delayed holiday, and this throws his authority plans into disarray. Grimwade's the only ACC who's got spare capacity at the moment so the Chief Constable has put him in charge of Buchanan's shop. He said something about showing Grimwade a bit of deference – it's political I think, and the Chief Constable's effectively asking us not to rock the boat.'

Grant detected a certain disdain in Burns' voice. Rufus Buchanan was Assistant Chief Constable (Crime) whose remit included CID and serious crime. Gilbert Grimwade was Assistant Chief Constable (Admin) whose remit included the collection, analysis and submission of data for government policing targets. That, and pencils and forms in triplicate. The job suited the man.

With Buchanan unoperational, Grimwade must have jumped at the chance to play real cops and look steely-eyed.

Burns continued wearily.

'I spoke to Grimwade. He insists the investigation must at this stage remain absolutely covert. You are to do nothing whatsoever that might spook the Celenks or anyone they're working with, because of other parallel operations that you have told me you're aware of. That means you can't make any enquiries out on the streets or among any of your other contacts or informants, until I'm given the word. And absolutely no press conferences.'

Grant exploded. 'But that's *monstrous*, sir! We've got a young girl's life on the line here and you're telling me – Grimwade's telling us – to tie one hand behind our backs!'

'Those are the words I used.' Burns' tone was bleak. 'I couldn't shift him. That's why it took me so long to get back to you. I think he's mesmerised by the peripheral stuff – the Customs operation on the coast, the MI5 and MI6 flags – scared shitless he'll get the blame if this operation is successful and the other services feel we screwed theirs up. He latched on to the fact that this chap – what's his name, d'Astignac? – threatened Ross if he went to the police. I'll be having another go at him at tomorrow morning's Ops Meeting.'

Grant kept his face stony as he pondered this own-goal.

'Fuck's sake, sir. That's all I'm saying: fuck's sake.'

'Listen up, everyone. Slight change of plan.'

The team turned round from their desks and paid attention. Grant nodded at Cox, who summarised the effect of the intelligence they had learned at their meeting with the Serious Crime Squad and the SCDEA. She also updated them on what Shona Macleod had learned from the MacDonalds.

'We're in gangland here,' Grant said as he helped himself to some coffee, 'serious organised crime. Our villains are wholesalers, intermediaries. They supply everyone. They aren't tied by turf. Wherein lies our problem. One of our problems.'

He added two spoons of sugar and stirred vigorously. His audience was on the edge of their seats; he wanted them like that.

'Jenny Ross could be anywhere in Scotland's biggest city.'

He took a slurp of coffee and rocked backwards and forwards on his heels. One of his shoes squeaked.

'And here's the nausea. This abduction is only a small bit in a very much larger operation, so it's gone right to the top of the Command Team. And the Command Team have decreed that we can't go out onto the streets, we can't make our usual enquiries. We can't even do a press conference. We can do nothing overt, nothing to alert other villains to our awareness of the abduction.'

A buzz of muttered *jeeez* and *fuck's sakes* ran round the room.

'In short, ladies and gents,' he finished up, 'we've got our right arms tied behind our backs until this restriction is lifted.'

The look of disgust on his face said it all.

'But that's no excuse to give up,' he said with determination, and more confidence than he felt. He sat on the edge of a desk and swung a leg. 'We know that Jenny and her friend were lunching at a wine bar on Gordon Street. Stuart, you're going through all the CCTV tapes covering the area at the time. Have you got anything yet?'

Stuart Sutherland shook his head.

'Keep going. Shona, go to the wine bar itself this evening, have a couple of glasses of tap water on the taxpayer, and just get a feel for the place. While I'd dearly love you to talk to the staff, that kind of thing is off limits for the moment.'

As the team began to make moves, Shona Macleod came over to Grant.

'What do you think the risks are to Jenny if we can't find her within the timeframe?'

Grant sucked his teeth noisily. Although he'd deliberately not briefed the whole team about the Customs operation on the coast, he decided now that Shona should know the background. Quickly, he explained about Jack's involvement with d'Astignac and the connection into the Celenks in Glasgow. 'Whether or not it's been discussed with Celenk – which I doubt – he won't want any loose ends, and a young girl who's been a reluctant guest of his organisation is a loose end. I suggest there are two likely scenarios. The first is probably preferable: a quick and merciful bullet or knife and a concrete coffin on some construction site. Alternatively, there's a commercially more attractive option for him. Export, in a drugged state, for sale on the back streets of Belgrade or to a harem somewhere in the Middle East. A blonde teenage virgin would collect a high price, I imagine.'

'Do we know she's a virgin, sir?'

'That's not the point.'

The timing couldn't have been worse, not even if he'd planned it with the precision of a Swiss clock-maker. At Sarah's report of an email from Lydia and the coldness of her eyes, he had thought he'd better go and see what it said. Sarah hadn't, at that stage, followed.

The email was open on the screen. He sat staring at it, reading the email over and over. What was the word? Nemesis: the chap who followed you around when you'd done something iffy, crept up behind you and walloped you over the head when you were least expecting it. It must have arrived just as Sarah was reading Maggie's email.

From:	Lydia Fox
To:	Jack Ross
Sent:	6th September
Subject:	Hi

Hi Jack
How are you keeping? I was talking to Sally in HR the other day and she said you're up somewhere in the west of Scotland not too far from Glasgow.
  I'm coming up for a conference in Glasgow in a couple of weeks and I'll be

staying at the Ramada. I wonder if you'd like to come over for a drink and, you know, talk about old times in Hong Kong? I wonder if I'll get Room 2209 again!

Love
Lydia

On the face of it, now he read it again, there was nothing to indicate conclusively to anyone else that this was not an entirely innocent, if inappropriate, invitation for a gin and tonic. Guilt, however, had turned it into a smoking gun in Jack's mind, and the blankness in Sarah's eye spoke of suspicion. As a consequence he'd found himself intellectually unequipped to find a smart way to avoid a full confession. He'd squirmed while he told it, and squirmed even more when she observed, coldly, that he'd failed to admit his lapse while she was owning up to hers. She'd supposed that he'd done it deliberately – retaining the moral high ground to use as a bargaining lever for his plan. Blackmail, she'd called it.

He'd seen on her face the hurt, followed by anger, disappointment, and finally sheer sadness. As she'd got up from her chair he'd gone over to her and tried to put his arms round her. She'd shrugged him off, frozen him out. He'd have preferred it if she'd had a good old go at him, he could have grovelled and maybe they could have moved on. That might have been the case if Jenny's predicament hadn't been so much in the foreground.

Left alone, he concluded that his presence in the house was unlikely to be highly productive in the immediate future. He went upstairs, threw a few things in his old grip bag and went back into the study to print off a dozen small photos of Jenny Tom had taken only a couple of weeks ago. She was laughing, her hair glinting golden in the sunlight, and looking so beautiful he almost cracked. He gritted his teeth and shook his head to clear it of this destructive emotion. Finally, he went in search of Tom.

'Look, Tom,' he said, 'I've got to go to Glasgow now. There's things I can do there to kick-start the search for Jenny. I've got to do it, I can't just leave it to others.'

'But Dad, you won't get there till late, what can you do?'

'I'll get a hotel room and see the police first thing tomorrow morning. I want to make sure they know everything about it, and they're doing everything they can.'

'Oh, yes, I forgot to tell you. Someone from the police rang a bit earlier while you were out and Mum was at the MacDonalds.'

'There you are then, they do want to see me, and it's best I see them face to face first thing tomorrow.'

'Can I come with you?'

Jack looked at his son. Not long turned sixteen, tall but not yet comfortable in his gangly body, worried for his sister and wanting to help do something about it. Jack would love to have his company.

'No, Tom, not this time. This is something I have to do on my own. Besides, Mum's a bit cross with me at the moment, she's also very upset about Jenny's disappearance, so she needs lots of love and support, and you're the best one to give it to her at the moment. Will you do that for me?'

'Yeah, OK, sure.'

He looked disappointed, but Jack knew he realised it was the right thing.

'When're you coming back?'

'We've got a boat trip to do on Tuesday, you and me, so I'll be back well before then. With any luck I should be back tomorrow evening, but if I need to stay longer I will. At the latest, I'll be here by . . .' Jack calculated for a moment, 'eight on Tuesday morning. We'll need to leave here with the boat by eight-thirty to get to Crinan for our clients. Make sure you leave your mobile switched on so I can call you whenever, OK?'

'Sure.' Tom was perking up with all this talk of action. 'Dad?'

'Mm?'

'Look out for yourself, OK?'

Jack had no intention of getting himself into anything iffy. This was an intelligence-gathering job. 'Count on it.' But his grin was an effort.

30

As he headed off into the night, a light west-coast rain fell without conviction. It was the worst kind of rain: too much for the intermittent windscreen wipers, not enough for them full-time. It was an irritant, but not the issue at the forefront of his mind.

He had no real idea what he was going to do. He supposed he'd find himself a hotel room, maybe step outside and see where the nightlife was, ask a few questions, then get himself a decent night's sleep. In the morning he'd go round the police station, talk to this Grant chap, offer his services, and they'd have Jenny safe and sound by tea-time. He couldn't shift from his consciousness a memory of the last time he'd left home having shot the relationship to pieces.

He had just about two hours to work his turmoil through his system before hitting the Glasgow traffic and needing to be mentally alert. At least the setting of the windscreen wipers was no longer an issue: it had stopped raining, but the road was still slick. Finding a 24-hour car park under the M8 flyover in Anderston, he grabbed his holdall and walked up into Argyle Street. Given that it was 10.30 on a Sunday evening he was shocked, but not really surprised, he supposed, to be propositioned at least half-a-dozen times by ladies of the night, and offered quality shit, horse, crack, skag, smack or whatever by other seedy characters. He felt out of place, a country boy, and began to appreciate the enormity of what he was getting himself into.

Not far along Argyle Street he found a hotel that was still open, and paid up-front for a room for two nights. He took the tiny lift, slow and wobbly, to the sixth floor. As he opened the door to his room a combination of stale cigarette stench and lack of oxygen hit him. He went to open the window but, as it looked out onto the street down below, it was either stuck fast or designed, with quaint regard for his health and safety, not to be opened. All in all, the room was not cheery. Oh well, it least it was a base, somewhere to lay his head if he got the chance.

He began to think about what he would do now that he was here. He'd been shaken by seeing street whores and drug dealers close-up. He realised this was not a game, and life here, at this time of night, was raw. Squaring his shoulders, he took his wallet out of his pocket, extracted a few small notes which he trousered, deposited his wallet in his bag which he stuffed in the wardrobe, and went out into the night.

Turning eastwards out of the hotel he walked along Argyle Street a few hundred yards and entered the vast tunnel under Central station. The darkness, even under the street lights, felt claustrophobic. It heightened the city smells: diesel fumes overlaid with the promise of urine and vomit. Jack hoped it was just his imagination.

The first bar he came across was packed. At least it hid his embarrassment and indecision. He had no idea how to start, not a clue. He extracted one of the small photos of Jenny – God, how lovely she looked, and here he was trying to locate her in bars in downtown Glasgow – and wondered if he should just go round every table and every punter standing at the bar and ask whether they had seen his daughter. It was sheer madness! Even if it was the right thing to do, it would take him forever.

Nevertheless, he was here now and he would have to get on with it. Surely once he'd made a prat of himself once it would get easier and easier, right?

He navigated his way to the bar through the throng. The bar staff consisted of a young man with a ponytail and a spiky-haired girl he reckoned barely old enough to be in the place. They were rushed off their feet and there was a crush at the bar waving empty glasses. Ignoring the curses and elbows, he eased his way as close as he could get and tried to catch the barman's eye. The barman, however, was far too experienced for that: he could tell when someone was queue-barging. Jack had to wait his turn, plus a bit more. Eventually his turn came.

'Whit d'ye want, pal?'

'Er, actually I'm not here for a drink, I just . . .'

'The fuck y'here for, then?'

Jack held up the small photo. He felt bloody ridiculous.

'I'm trying to find my daughter – she's missing. Have you seen her?' As soon as he'd spoken the words, he realised just how pathetic, how hopeless the whole enterprise was.

The barman took the picture and studied it for a moment.

'Naw, I nivver,' he said as he shook his head slowly. 'Och, she's a wee stoater, so she is. Oi, Polly,' he called over to the barmaid, 'seen thon wee lassie? She's gone missin.'

The girl left a pint of lager running and stretched out her hand for the photo.

'Naw,' she said slowly, still studying it. 'When'd she go missin?'

'Yesterday,' said Jack.

The girl handed the photo back, still shaking her head. 'Poor wee thing.' Her pint of lager had just come to the top of the glass.

'Well thanks, anyway.' Jack took the photo back and was grateful that he had been treated gently. With a *frisson* of guilt, he realised that his relief at not having been treated like a complete wally outweighed his disappointment that he was no further forward in finding Jenny. At least he found the courage to move on to the next pub, and the next, and the next, reversing his course and exploring the side streets.

When he came back to Hope Street he turned right into it and worked his way up. Not bothering with the punters at all, he walked straight to the bar, waited his turn, and produced the photo. In each case, he was treated with tolerance bordering on sympathy, followed by the inevitable shake of the head.

Eventually he came to a nightclub where he was stopped by the door manager. Jack was surprised. He hadn't realised he looked disreputable or dangerous. When queried, the door manager looked him up and down and said pityingly, 'Ye're no seriously goin clubbin dressed like tha, are ye, pal?' Jack looked down at his stone-washed chinos and green Marks & Spencer crew-neck jumper, and realised he stood out like a lighthouse on boost. He just hadn't given it any thought; he was utterly naïve, a child in Sin City. He took the point and was about to walk on when it occurred to him that a bouncer was as good a prospect as anyone else.

He explained his purpose and brought out a photo. The bouncer studied the picture carefully, all the time sucking his teeth and shaking his head. He handed the photo back.

'Listen, pal, it's no a pure dead brilliant idea tae go round askin questions like this. It's probably best tae leave it tae the polis: they know the rules o the game, see?'

The advice was kindly meant but Jack had difficulty not bristling at it. However, the bouncer's size and obvious physical capabilities persuaded him not to make an issue of it. He thanked the bouncer for his advice and moved on. He was going to be helping the police tomorrow, but that didn't mean he couldn't get a head start now, did it?

It was by now midnight and nightlife appeared to be in full flow. Having worked his way up to Waterloo Street he turned left into it. He was immediately accosted by a series of working girls, one after the other, who wanted to know whether he was looking for business. He declined each offer politely, instead showing them his photo of Jenny.

He wasn't encouraged by their reaction. Careful study of the picture, a hardening of the eyes as if to say, what do you think you're playing at, showing me a picture of some child who's led a sheltered, comfortable life? And you're worried about what's happened to her? Just look at *me*, look at all of us, do you think we care about this privileged wee brat? If you're not buying what we're offering, just fuck off and leave us alone to earn enough money to keep the pimps off our backs, a few shots of heroin and, with any luck, something for food.

They had a point, however it was expressed or implied. He wasn't sure they were much older, underneath the haggard lines, pebble-dashed make-up and last month's peroxide rinse, than Jenny. The bile rose in his throat.

He carried on from bar to nightclub to bar, getting into some but not others, showing his picture of Jenny to anyone he thought might remotely pay any attention to it, but getting a nil reaction every time. No one repeated the advice of the bouncer earlier in the night, no one gave him a hard time.

It was getting towards 3 am and the remnants of the drinkers and clubbers were leaving or being thrown out. There was surprisingly little in the way of vomiting and brawling, but given that this was Sunday night and not the roughest end of town, he guessed it made sense. His feet sore and his body weary, he made one more attempt before admitting defeat for the night: an elderly prostitute, more raddled than those he had seen so far, losing out to the younger, less junked-up girls he'd spoken to earlier. He showed her Jenny's picture and explained that she was missing and did she have any idea how he might track her down?

'How missin?' She had a voice like a chainsaw, destroyed by alcohol, cigarettes, heroin and any number of social diseases from the past.

'Well, I don't really know,' he said wearily. 'I seem to have got caught up in an argument with some people and . . .'

'An *argument*?' she said, her expression shot through with

disbelief. 'An argument, ye say? Listen pal, ye dinnae get caught up in *arguments* with Weegies who take your wee girl. I tell ye, leave it tae the polis, ye dinnae want to get caught up with the likes o them.'

'But I can't just leave it,' said Jack, his voice almost a wail. 'I'm her father and I have to do everything I can to find her. Don't you see?'

She looked at him for a good few seconds. He was awaiting the barbed wire fuck-off-and-leave-me-alone brush-off.

'Och, I wish . . .' leaving it unfinished. She studied him a bit longer as if considering whether to vouchsafe further information, her breathing rattling in her chest. 'Listen, pet,' she said at length, 'it's no here ye need lookin. Ye'll no find any information from *this* lot,' she said contemptuously. 'Ye need lookin further *tha* way,' she nodded in an easterly direction, 'out tae the Calton, or Bridgeton. But if ye'll take my advice ye'll gaun hame an leave it tae the polis.'

He thanked her and turned for his hotel.

'Are ye sure ye're nae lookin for business?' she called after him. He shook his head slowly as he looked at the photograph in his hand.

His poor Jenny. As Dr Cameron hinted, in need of TLC and no-one there to give it.

31

An insistent beeping dragged him slowly out of his deep and troubled sleep. He didn't know what it was, where he was or what day of the week it was. He rolled over, extricated his arm from the blankets and tried to focus on his watch.

Where was that damned beeping coming from? He staggered out of bed and over to the excuse for a dressing table, found his mobile which he had set less than five hours ago, and stabbed the right buttons to make the damned thing shut itself up. He remained standing, awareness slowly returning to him of where he was, what he was doing and why. God, he felt crap.

He stumbled to the bathroom. After a few unsuccessful attempts to find the light-switch, he looked outside the door and flooded the tiny compartment with sterile light. It was about the only thing anywhere near sterile. The shower was surprisingly powerful but as he couldn't get a decent balance between scalding and freezing he opted for freezing.

The buffet of cereals, toasts, buns, ham, cheese and full cooked in the cafeteria would normally have been inviting. Jack grabbed a glass of industrial orange juice and a cup of strong black coffee and found himself a table. Going back to the buffet for something solid he tried to select something he could force down. He failed. His throat just wasn't in the mood. He went back to his table, downed the orange in one, the coffee almost as quickly, signed the check and went to Reception to ask where the main police station was.

Discovering it was only a ten- or fifteen-minute walk away he set off back the way he had come the previous night, through what had been the red light district. How different it all looked now the red lights had been turned off. It was a respectable, business-looking district, imposing sandstone buildings so intensely Classical, Gothic or Georgian as to be at once recognisable as Victorian. He wondered if the workers heading for their offices had the slightest idea what went on the moment they turned their backs.

Emerging on the other side he found the corner of Pitt Street and West George Street. A brick block-house. Strathclyde Police Headquarters. Shit. He didn't feel quite so confident that this Detective Chief Inspector would take him on to help his team, not now that he was faced with the solid reality of a massive organisation of professionals. He felt a minnow in a vast pond.

On the other hand, these were the boys that were going to find and get back his Jenny. So he screwed up his courage and his hope and marched up the steps into Reception. It didn't look entirely as he had expected. Far from the floor being covered in cigarette butts and the place looking and smelling like the waiting room on a 1960s railway station, this was plush, smart and immaculate, more like the headquarters of a small yet moderately successful merchant bank than a police station. There was no desk sergeant hiding behind a sheet of bulletproof glass. Indeed, there were two smartly dressed female receptionists who enquired politely of him how they could be of assistance.

Jack had no idea even how to start.

'Um, my daughter's missing, and I reported it yesterday, and I was hoping to see . . .' was as far as he got before the fragrant and charming receptionist smilingly headed him off at the pass.

'Oh dear, I think you've come to the wrong place. This is the headquarters of Strathclyde Police. I think you want the Divisional

Office for Glasgow Central, which is on Stewart Street.' She spent the next minute or two explaining how easy it was to get there. 'It's only five minutes and you can't miss it.'

It was not until almost half an hour later, as Jack was still trying to cross the major roads which seemed to act as fortifications for the police station, that he realised she had assumed he was driving. Stupid cow! And stupid bloody police for hiding their office away from pedestrians. He was not in a good mood when he arrived.

Even though it was still early there was a queue. Jack felt deflated, an anti-climax to his courage-screwing-up exercise. But the queue slowly cleared and he got to the desk. The civilian bar officer was harassed rather than bored – obviously the first flurry to start off the working week.

'Now then, sir, how can I help you?'

'I'm looking for Detective Chief Inspector Grant.'

'Is he expecting you?'

'No.'

'I see. Can you tell me what it's about?'

'Umm, it's about a missing person – my daughter, she's missing.'

'I see, sir.' A uniformed sergeant was rummaging behind the desk on another mission. The bar officer said to Jack, 'If you'd bear with us just one moment, Sergeant Murray will deal with you . . . Next!'

Jack distinctly heard Sergeant Murray mutter, 'Thanks, Jim.'

The sergeant found what he'd come for and put it on one side. He started rummaging for something else, asked Jim where he kept his missing persons forms, then looked up at Jack.

'Now then, sir, your name is?'

He gave his name. And Jenny's.

'Now, when did you last see her?' Jack realised he was filling in a standard form for missing persons. All he was missing was the blunt 2B pencil.

'Look sergeant, I reported all this to the police yesterday morning. Do we have to go through it all again?'

The sergeant's look said, far more eloquently than any words, *well why the fork-end didn't you say so earlier.*

'Have you got the report number with you, sir?'

Embarrassed, he mumbled that he hadn't.

'Not to worry,' said the sergeant, happy to have captured the procedural high ground, 'I'm sure we can find it.' The queue to the side of Jack was hugely enjoying the exchange and his discomfort. Jack wasn't.

'Look sergeant,' he said again, this time urgently and more quietly, 'can I please see DCI Grant? I understand he's looking after the case and ... and ...' Jack struggled to come up with a convincing reason why the Senior Investigating Officer would want to see him, rather than being dealt with by some lowly detective constable, 'and I wish to make a statement,' he ended up triumphantly. The sergeant's expression betrayed his scepticism, but he'd obviously had enough of Jack. He punched some numbers on the desk phone. After a few moments he spoke, all the while watching Jack as though he was suspect number one.

'Brenda, I've got a Mr Ross here, says his daughter's missing, he's already made a MISPER, and that Mr Grant's SIO.'

He listened for a few moments before saying 'Right' and putting the phone down.

'If you'd like to go over to Force Headquarters in Pitt Street – that's out of the door here, turn right ...'

Jack interrupted him wearily. 'Thank you, Sergeant, I've just come from there: they sent me here.'

The sergeant gave him another old-fashioned look – as if considering whether to nick him for wasting police time, or maybe have him sectioned under the Mental Health Act.

'When you get there, sir,' he continued, keeping a wary eye on Jack, 'go to the *back* door,' the sergeant paused to emphasise that Jack was to use the equivalent of the tradesmen's entrance, and that charming and fragrant receptionists weren't for the likes of him – 'the *back* door, and ask for Detective Sergeant Cox.'

Thoroughly hacked-off by this inauspicious start, Jack thanked the sergeant and the bar officer as civilly as he could, the latter already talking to the next customer. Without missing a beat, the bar officer flicked a glance in Jack's direction and slipped a 'don't mention it sir' into the sentence he was speaking to the next customer, neatly splitting an infinitive in the process. Jack exited the front door, turned right as directed by the sergeant, and retraced his steps to Pitt Street.

Twenty minutes later he was walking down West Regent Street to the corner with Holland Street, and saw an entrance at the back corner of the Headquarters building he hadn't previously spotted. He didn't think he'd ever seen so many dark-red bricks holding up a building. Obviously intended to put off your average hardened criminal. There was a constant flow of dark-shirted police officers, and the occasional one dressed in civilian clothes, entering and leaving the building. He realised with a cringe of embarrassment that he must first have gone to the Chief Constable's ceremonial entrance – the one he used probably only on the Queen's Official Birthday or the State Opening of Parliament. He felt more comfortable with the tradesmen's entrance. He found a reception desk just inside the door and asked for Detective Sergeant Cox.

'Is she expecting you, sir?'

'Yes: I've just come from Stewart Street and the desk sergeant there . . .'

For the second time in under an hour he was headed off at the pass. 'If you'd take a seat over there, sir, she'll be down in a moment.' The bar officer pressed a couple of numbers on her phone and spoke quietly into it.

Jack went over and sat on a hard, moulded plastic chair that turned out to be surprisingly comfortable. A few minutes later the inner door opened and a short, middle-aged woman with bobbed hair that had once been blonde emerged, looking round the waiting area. Dumpy, that was the word Jack would have used if pressed; dumpy.

As he was the only person waiting, the woman made eye contact and came over to him.

'Mr Ross? I'm DS Cox.' Jack stood and shook the proffered hand. 'Let's go and find somewhere quieter to talk.' She returned to the reception desk, signed him in and gave him a plastic security pass to clip to his non-existent lapel, went over to the inner door, punched in an access code on the adjacent wall, and led the way in.

As they settled in Meeting Room 3, Brenda Cox offered him coffee. He was by now foot-sore, thirsty and not a little cross, so gladly accepted. When it came Jack recognised the small plastic cup of plastic-tasting light-brown stuff made with plastic milk, clearly produced by a sister machine to the one in Jack's late office in London. But it was hot and wet, he supposed.

DS Cox began to draw the story out of him but after a while asked him to pause while she got the big man down. Jack's first impression of the Chief Inspector was that he wasn't at all big height-wise, but stocky – an ideal match for the dumpy detective sergeant. He introduced himself but Jack had difficulty dealing with the glass eye, which never quite looked at him. Jack resumed the story and recounted everything: the boat, the smugglers, the row with Jenny, his encounter with Charles and the meeting on board the Customs cutter. For some reason he never quite clarified to himself, he didn't mention his search round the bars and clubs last night.

'Started off early this morning, did you? After all, it's only . . .' Grant consulted his watch, 'nine-forty now.'

Jack felt wrong-footed. 'No. I came up last night, took a room on Argyle Street.' He scratched his ear. 'To tell the truth, I wasn't all that popular at home yesterday evening and so it was an excuse to get out as much as anything else.' Grant and Cox kept their gaze steadily on him. Jack experienced an urge to jabber under that steely scrutiny. He continued with his original plan even though he was fairly sure by now he knew the answer.

'Er, I was also wondering whether there was anything I could do to help. After all,' he rushed on, 'I'm not busy until tomorrow morning and . . .' he tailed away.

'I understand your desire to help, Mr Ross, but it's probably best left to us, don't you think? We're not dealing with very nice people here, there's drugs, very probably firearms, and likely other kinds of thuggery. Dealing with people like that is what we're trained to do; it's our job.' Grant spoke kindly, and Jack knew he was right. He acknowledged his own naïvety.

Grant drew the interview to a close. 'You've been most helpful, Mr Ross, and the photos you gave us of Jenny will be very useful. Right now I've got an officer in Kilbeg interviewing Lucy, we're going through all the CCTV tapes, we're scouring our intelligence network files, and we're nosing around on the ground. We'll find her, Mr Ross, don't you fret, and we'll find her quickly. Now, I suggest you go home and give your family lots of moral support. That's the best way you can help Jenny.'

Jack was dismayed but not surprised. He thanked them. DS Cox signed him out, gave him her card and said to ring her if he had any more news.

32

Shona Macleod thanked Dr MacDonald for their help and went back to her car. Before going to the Rosses she just wanted to read through the statement she'd taken from Lucy, and she wouldn't do that sitting in their front drive.

There were parking spaces along the road forming the centre of Kilbeg village – the usual collection of handsome stone villas and white-painted cottages strung along a main street, a pub, post office-cum-village shop, and butcher. She couldn't remember the last time she'd seen a butcher's shop; for her, meat purchasing was an activity carried out between the pre-packed dairy produce aisle and the tinned veg aisle. It brought back memories of meat that had flavour.

Shona parked and popped a couple of polo mints into her mouth. She rubbed her temples before re-reading Lucy's statement. It was in Shona's own handwriting and the rather stilted style beloved of coppers in every force in the land: 'I was proceeding in a northerly direction when . . .' But the account of the facts was Lucy's.

. . . Jenny and I went into Glasgow most Saturdays, and Saturday 5th September we did the same as usual. We took the 0810 hrs train from Oban, which arrived at Queen Street at about 1130 hrs. We

looked round some shops in Buchanan Street and Princes Square Shopping Centre, and then went to Marco Polo, an upstairs wine bar in Gordon Street at about 1330 hrs. There, we went to a table by the window and we did not have long to wait before a waiter came and took our order. We both ordered a lime soda and a panini . . .

Mmm, thought Shona, plenty of flavours there to cover up something slipped in them.

. . . The lime sodas came quite soon and we drank them quickly because it was a warm day and we were thirsty. They didn't taste any stronger than they normally would. When the food came we asked for more lime sodas, which came after we had started eating our food. I am not able to say whether they tasted different because, once you have started eating, drinks taste different anyway . . .

I'll bet that idea had crossed someone else's mind too, thought Shona.

. . . We had almost finished our food when I began to feel tired and sleepy but without actually wanting to go to sleep, a bit floppy. The feeling came over me quickly once it had started, and I was worried that I would disgrace myself and the waiters would throw me out because they thought I was drunk. Instead, the waiters were very kind and helped me to stand up, walk out of the restaurant, down the stairs and into a car which was waiting for me just outside the door. I do not know whether Jenny was feeling the same way, or if she needed to be helped as well. But as far as I can recall, she got into the car with me . . .

We should be able to get the vehicle index number from CCTV footage.

. . . Once in the car, someone gave me some water to drink from a cup or beaker. I was very thirsty and drank as much as I could. I went

to sleep after that. I don't remember very much after that, except I can dimly remember being half-awake, being very thirsty, drinking more water and going back to sleep. Sometimes I was in a vehicle, sometimes I was in a room. I cannot be more specific. The sleep was very deep. The next thing I remember with any clarity is waking up in a car, drinking more water, and being in a half-awake state, a bit like when I was taken ill in the restaurant, and then being helped out of the car in front of our house in Kilbeg. I don't remember Jenny being with me in the car.

Bastards, she thought. She'd seemed a nice kid, Lucy. Short by comparison with today's eighteen-year-olds, but slim, with long, dark, crinkly hair. Shona could see that, in other circumstances, Lucy would have an easy smile and a nice way with her. Although she'd only known Jenny for a few months, they'd clearly hit it off quickly, and Shona wondered whether in seeing Lucy she was also seeing Jenny. Lucy had said that, although it was Jenny's birthday or near enough, Jenny had at first seemed preoccupied, not as bubbly as usual. However, all that had evaporated once they'd started serious shopping in Glasgow and her sunny personality has reasserted itself.

There wasn't much that either of Lucy's parents could add, so it was on to see old man Ross.

She drove down towards the bottom end of the village, and stopped by the loch. She had to admit the view was heart-achingly beautiful, and she was reminded of how it had been in the cottage at Ballachulish after her mother had died and her sister Màiri had taken over looking after the wains. Back in those days she only had her Gaelic name, *Seònaidh MacLeòid*, a part of her personality that didn't quite belong in Glasgow. Happy-sad times; typical West Highland times; where the history of massacres, burnt villages and whole communities cleared off their ancestral lands was part of the psychological make-up of the clan families even now.

With an effort she cleared her head of the memories. She was now Shona Macleod, international jet-setter – well, she took the occasional holiday in Majorca – and law enforcement agent. Looking behind her she could see three handsome, stone-built villas, each in about half an acre of garden. One of those would be the Ross residence, she reckoned.

Within a couple of minutes she was ringing the bell at the front door of *Creag Mhor*, a very fine house whose bay windows had a commanding view over the loch. She was wondering whether the sleek boat riding to a mooring buoy was Mr Ross's when she heard the door open behind her. She turned and looked up at the tall, lank teenager who had opened it.

'I'm Shona Macleod, Strathclyde Police.' She produced her warrant card. 'I phoned yesterday evening. Was it you I spoke to?' He looked like the owner of the voice on the phone.

'Yes.'

'I was in the area trying to get a few details about the disappearance of Jenny – is that your sister?'

'Yes.'

'I'm sorry.' Shona felt sorry for this gangly youth, so thin his Adam's apple was his most prominent feature. He looked a nice enough young man, even handsome in a spare way, but he had an aura of sadness about him. Not helped, she admitted, by his black t-shirt and black jeans. Nor by the fact his sister was missing. 'I wondered whether your father or your mother was in, and I could have a few words?'

'I'm sorry, they're out at the moment.' He had a rich, deep, English voice, which Shona found both pleasing and melancholy. 'Um, would you like to come in anyway?'

'Thank you.'

'Where have you come from? Oban?'

'Glasgow.'

'Oh, I see. I wonder – no, don't worry, probably not. Would you like a cup of tea or coffee or something?'

'Yes please.' Brilliant! That would give her an opportunity to find out lots more informally. She followed him into the kitchen. It was a big room with a slate floor – much bigger than the cottage kitchen in Ballachulish, and you could fit the tiny wee kitchen in her Pollokshaws flat into this ten times over. Still, it was a homely place, with a dark green Rayburn under an extractor hood at one end, an island of units and worktop delineating the cooking area, leaving a large informal dining area dominated by a pine kitchen table and four wooden chairs.

She leant her backside against a conveniently placed worktop and asked conversationally, 'What's your name?'

'Tom. What's yours? Oh, you said: Shona something. I'm sorry, I didn't catch the last bit.' Tom filled the kettle and switched it on.

'Macleod. Shona'll do fine.'

'Are you a detective?'

'Yes. Detective Constable.'

'Oh, I see.'

He didn't sound all that thrilled or impressed. But then, his sister was missing so he wouldn't be all that bubbly, would he?

'What do you do, Tom? I mean, are you at school, college, or uni?'

'No. I'm not very good at that kind of thing so I gave up school at the end of the summer term. I was working for Dad on the boat, until . . .' His voice trailed off, and he concentrated on the kettle as if willing it to hurry up and boil. He did not have long to wait.

'Um, tea or coffee?'

'Coffee, I think, as it's coffee-time. Is that OK?'

'Yeah.' He spooned instant coffee into two mugs, poured the boiling water in, fetched a bottle of milk from the fridge, tipped some into one mug, and glanced questioningly at Shona.

'Please,' she said.

He poured in some milk, stirred both mugs and handed one to her. They both sat down at the table.

'Where're your parents?'

'Well, Mum's a bit knocked sideways by all this, and actually she's asleep upstairs – well, I suppose she's asleep. Dr MacDonald gave her some tablets – Valium, I think – and they make her sleepy.'

'And your Dad?'

'He's gone to Glasgow.'

'Glasgow! How?'

'Well, he came home yesterday evening from a meeting he'd had at Oban. We had supper and I cleared off up to my room because it was all so depressing. I heard Mum and Dad having a row, I don't know what about but I can guess.'

'What do you think it was?'

'I think Mum blames him for . . . I don't know; somehow for Jenny's disappearance.'

'And you think it was just about that?'

'Well, there was the bit when Jenny announced she was pregnant and Dad hit the roof.'

'I'm sorry, what was all that?' My God, thought Shona, some families come awfully complicated.

'Friday was Jenny's birthday and so Mum put a special supper on for us in the evening. Jenny came back from Oban all quiet and depressed and I guess she told Mum all about it. I expect Mum was hoping to tell Dad about it later when he could hit the roof and it wouldn't matter.'

'Does he often hit the roof?'

'Sometimes. He gets the wrong end of the stick sometimes and over-reacts.'

Shona wasn't at all sure she liked the direction this was going. 'Does he get violent?'

'Dad? Oh no, he's not violent. It's silly really. He hears something, assumes the worst and then hits the roof. He simmers down within five minutes, realises what a wally he's been and apologises to everyone. It never lasts long with him.'

'And so that's what he did on Friday night when he found out Jenny was pregnant?'

'Yes. Only poor old Jenny took it really badly, you know? Well,

I suppose I can understand that. I mean, she wasn't feeling too good about it herself, and then when Dad . . . you know . . .'

'I can imagine.'

'So things weren't all that great on Friday evening. I kept to my room, I can tell you, kept right out of the way.'

'And how were things on Saturday? Was everyone feeling a lot better?'

'Well Jenny went into Oban with Lucy to get the early train to Glasgow – that's just after eight o'clock. Or I guess they did, I don't usually make it up that early, not unless I'm helping Dad with the boat. But when I came down there was still this atmosphere, if you know what I mean?' Tom cocked a questioning eyebrow. Shona nodded.

'It was like everyone was – I don't know, walking on eggshells. I kept out of the way again. I really hate it when things are like that.'

'Does it often happen?'

'Oh no, not really. I guess it makes it worse when it does happen.'

'So do you think,' and here Shona was careful not to lead her witness too much, but she had to get the point cleared up, 'do you think Jenny was still angry with your Dad about what he'd said the previous evening, and might she have stayed overnight in Glasgow just to teach him a lesson?'

'No. No way. Jenny's not like that. No chance.'

'Tell me what she is like, then.'

Tom thought for a moment. 'She's – usually – happy and cheerful. She's one of those people who walks into a room and the whole place lights up, you know? She gets the pick of the boys, and she's always the centre of attention. She's not like me at all.'

Tom said it matter-of-factly, but Shona felt there was an undercurrent of pain there. Not envy of Jenny exactly, more a case of disappointment that he didn't feel he compared well with his sister, that life came easily to her but not to him.

'Do you get on well with each other?'

'Oh yeah. Occasionally we have a spat, but mostly we're good mates.'

'Do you get on well with your Mum and Dad?'

'Yeah. Mum's – well, she's Mum. And Dad, I've got to know him more since we came up here.'

It was Shona's turn to cock a questioning eyebrow.

'When we lived down in Bracknell, we hardly ever saw him, he was busy all the time. But when we came up here and got the boat, well, it's been great. It's like he treats me more as an equal – and he pays me to crew the boat.' Tom grinned, and she acknowledged by returning the grin.

'Tell me about the boat trips.'

'They're great.' Tom's face lit up. 'We've only just started doing them. For months we weren't getting anything, and then just this last couple of weeks we've been doing lots of trips and . . .' He stopped suddenly.

Shona nodded in encouragement. 'I know about d'Astignac and what he's mixed up in.'

Tom's demeanour changed. It was as if his batteries had run down. 'I never liked them. But Dad said you aren't paid to like your customers. I think he was getting pretty desperate for some business. If we didn't get any by the end of the season we were going to sell the boat. Dad and I talked about that. And Mum and Dad used to – well, not fight, really, more discuss intently, you know?'

'I can guess.'

'I think things were tight with money and I got the impression they were talking about selling up here and going back to Bracknell. But I asked Dad about that and he said not.'

'Would you like that – to go back to Bracknell, I mean?'

'No! No way.' Tom looked out of the window and thought for a moment. 'I love it up here, I feel I belong. And although we're in trouble at the moment it's like being up here has been the best thing, you know?'

'I know, Tom. Believe me, I do know.'

She let the silence hang.

'Well,' she said finally, 'I'd best be getting back.' She got up, took her mug to the sink and rinsed it out. 'Thanks for the coffee.'

She said she hoped his mum would be up and around soon, and headed for the door. Tom came with her. At the door, she turned to thank him again, and felt she now understood a bit about why this rather fine young man had an undercurrent of melancholy. Very West Highland, she thought.

'We'll be in touch.'

'Shona . . .'

'Yes?'

'You'll get my sister back, won't you? Please?'

Shona hated this bit. She could never give the assurance they wanted. She took his hand and gave it a squeeze.

'We'll shift heaven and earth, I promise you that, Tom.'

33

DS Cox let Jack out at Reception and returned to Grant's office.

'Poor bastard, doesn't know whether it's arsehole or Easter. Didn't even finish his coffee, ungrateful wee bugger.'

'Yes,' agreed Grant, ignoring the last comment, 'and I didn't like giving him the confidence *spiel* when we've got our hands tied behind our back. Still, we've got some things we can be getting on with. Shona's taking a statement from Lucy MacDonald?'

'She's out there now. With any luck she'll be back early afternoon, but if she gets anything particularly useful she'll give me a call before she sets off.'

'CCTV?'

'Stuart's going through the tapes and I'd be surprised if we don't get some clues shortly. But what I'd really like to be doing is disturbing the underworld and seeing what rises to the top. *That's* where we'll get our critical lead.'

'I know,' agreed Grant. 'Go and find out how we're getting on with the CCTV stuff.'

Blinking into the sunlight as he went down the steps into West Regent Street, Jack felt knackered. He was deflated: his fine plan to join Grant's cavalry on his white horse and rescue Jenny single-handedly had turned to chutney. It was inevitable, if only he'd sat down and thought about it. He wasn't firing on all cylinders as a result of lack of sleep and energy. He walked up to Sauchiehall Street in search of a café and sat down with a strong coffee and a bacon sandwich. He topped it up with two Mars bars and felt the rush of sugar hit his brain and muscles. The second Mars bar defeated him so he re-wrapped the remains and stuffed it in his pocket.

Energised, he determined that he could still do this thing. The last working girl he'd spoken to last night had told him to head east, to the Calton and Bridgeton. He didn't know those areas so he needed to explore them and see what there was to see. For that he needed a map of the city and his car.

But first he was in desperate need of less-conspicuous clothing. At the first likely retail outlet he bought well-washed jeans, a t-shirt and a windcheater made from a particularly tasteless nylony stuff that even in these circumstances made his flesh creep. He gritted his teeth at the price he paid for dark trainers. Passing a newsagent on his way back to the car park, he picked up a street plan and studied it when he got back to the car.

Cox found DC Sutherland hunched in front of a monitor, three plastic cups of machine-fed coffee on the table to his right – all of them three-quarters full but cold – and one large Styrofoam cup of piping-hot black Americano, four sugars please.

'What have you got for me, Stuart?'

'Not much, Sarge.'

'Don't call me Sarge.'

'No Sarge. Sodding CCTV on Buchanan Street was on the blink over the weekend. The council isn't paying for weekend repairs due to pressure on the budget, they tell me. I'm just running the disc from the Hope Street camera. This is opposite Gordon Street where the wine bar was, so I'm hoping we'll get lucky that it's looking along Gordon Street at the crucial time. I'll give you a shout if there's anything there.'

At that moment Sutherland sat up in his chair. 'Hang on just a wee, cotton-picking second, something's occurring.' His right hand reached out for a pencil to note down the time on the screen and instead it encountered a plastic cup of cold coffee. He jerked his hand away and overbalanced another cup, and in an effort to save that he knocked over the Styrofoam cup of still-hot coffee. With four sugars. The liquids intermingled and spread all over the desk, spilling onto Sutherland's trousers. He leapt up with a cry of 'shit!' then looked down at his wet jeans and wailed, 'Fuck's sake, sodding stuff, and it's hot! Jeesus!'

DS Cox ignored the pantomime and was studying events on the monitor.

'Stuart, go and get yourself cleaned up, there's a good detective.' As Sutherland walked gingerly off to the toilets in a manner suggesting he'd found a novel place to stow his golf clubs, she called after him, 'and get someone in here with a mop and bucket.'

What was intriguing DS Cox was a group of figures – four, she counted, two males, two females – emerging from the wine bar. The two females were being assisted by the males into a BMW X5, a large 4x4 beast, dark in colour, but which colour couldn't be detected on the black-and-white screen. She rewound the disc to see when the BMW had arrived at the kerb. Two minutes and about twenty seconds before the group of four had emerged from the wine bar. She rewound again, this time to see when the girls had arrived, and if she could identify two males who might have followed them in.

After rewinding and fast-forwarding for about five minutes she had identified that the girls had gone into the wine bar thirty-two minutes before they had come out. Assuming they had ordered drinks within five minutes, and five minutes later the tranquillisers had been introduced into their drinks, and again assuming within, say, another ten minutes they had finished their drinks, that left a very adequate twelve minutes for the drug to take sufficient effect for them to be 'escorted' from the premises. If all that was correct, then a male or the two males must have made a move – a social, chat-up type move, Brenda guessed – fairly quickly, the girls must have been drinking non-alcoholic drinks judging by the fast onset of the sedative effect, and, judging by the fact that Lucy had not so far mentioned vomiting or breathing problems, the amounts of tranquilliser administered had been very carefully measured and timed. We're dealing with very sophisticated criminals here, she thought.

Freezing a frame and magnifying it, Cox was able to note down the index number of the BMW. *Gotcha*, she thought. At that moment Stuart Sutherland returned, still more preoccupied with his wet jeans than with catching criminals.

'Stuart, while you've been drying the parts no one wants to think about, I've been doing some police work. Here,' she handed him a piece of paper with the index number of the BMW, 'go and get the registered keeper details on that.'

Jack spent the rest of the morning driving around the eastern end of the inner city, trying to get an idea of the kind of pubs and bars where he might get more focused information. He didn't expect the area to come alive for this kind of thing until late evening onwards. Although packed together tightly, mostly the housing stock looked to be in good condition. Brand-new terraced housing and recently renovated tenements jostled for space. In days gone by, he could imagine, this would be where the crowded slums, closes and backs would have been.

The area was essentially a series of village centres stretched out along the main arterial roads – London Road, Gallowgate and Edinburgh Road – with the residential housing surrounding each village centre in-filling between the main roads and merging with the next village. The shops seemed to be the same wherever he looked: a Spar grocer, a post office, a solicitor's office, and at least two betting shops. On the edge would be a Social Work Services office, and usually somewhere within the residential area a medical or health centre.

He had no sense of menace or foreboding. Local residents walked the streets, mothers with their prams and toddlers, pensioners with their shopping trolleys. Folk stood outside the front door of a shop, an office or a pub, puffing away in the open air out of reluctant respect for the no-smoking laws. These areas were clearly places where respectable, law-abiding citizens lived their lives. Not for the first time he experienced simultaneous and conflicting emotions: this was not the place to get leads about criminal activity; relief that he would not be facing up to hard men this evening.

'You're not going to like this, Sergeant.'

'Try me.' Cox knew it was serious: Sutherland hadn't called her 'Sarge'.

'Registered keeper of that index number is one John Thomas McDingle Ross.'

'McDingle?' Cox's eyebrows shot up.

'That's what it says here. Of Creag Mhor, Kilbeg, Argyll.'

For a moment, Cox didn't say a word. She could see two options. The first was that Jack Ross owned the BMW and was intimately involved in the kidnap of his own daughter. That didn't figure. From her brief meeting with him she didn't think he was the type. And what motive could he possibly have? The other option was that Jenny's abductors had a warped sense of humour and had fixed false number plates to the BMW deliberately showing the numbers of Ross' own vehicle. A two-fingered salute to the polis. To her personally. Both options merited a four-letter expletive.

'Make and model registered for that index number?'

'Grey Ford Mondeo.'

'Sick bastards.'

Night time changed the east end dramatically. Jack had waited until it was dark and then got going, taking his grip bag with him in the car. He'd already paid the hotel. If he wanted to come back to sleep, he could do it. But he didn't anticipate it would be necessary.

By now it was just shy of 8.45 pm and fully dark. The lamps on the main streets – Gallowgate, London Road, Edinburgh Road – delivered joined-up illumination. Off the main roads there were shadows, many broken or failing lamps. Working girls were amassing. Was it only twenty-four hours he'd been here, since Sunday evening? It felt like a lifetime. But time was pressing: in twelve hours he had to be back at the boat.

The traffic system denied him access to Argyle Street and an easy passage to Glasgow Cross. Instead he went round in two-and-a-half circles, unintentionally joined the M8, disappeared south over the river, escaped and succeeded in crossing King George V Bridge only to be denied a right turn along Argyle Street. Turning left instead, he slipped down James Watt Street and turned left into Broomielaw. At least he was now travelling in the right direction, and it should have been a simple matter of making along Clyde Street, High Street and turning sharp right into London Road. Instead, he inadvertently crossed High Street, negotiated St Andrew's Square and only then turned into London Road. Following the one-way arrows he drove west, away from his target area, but finally turned sharp right twice into Gallowgate. Finding a vacant roadside parking space unexpectedly, he screeched to a halt in it.

Setting off on foot he started his quest. The previous night's experience had been good: he no longer felt embarrassed at the questions he had to ask, and he reckoned his clothing would mark him out less as a country boy and interloper. His accent alone would do that, but there was nothing he could do about it.

Within a few hundred yards he encountered the first pair of working girls; it was a mutual encounter but entirely at cross-purposes. Jack was as pleased to see them as they were him but, no, he wasn't looking for business, either aloneski or two's-up. Instead he showed them the picture of Jenny. This bit was Jack's weak point, when he looked at the picture of his lovely girl, laughing innocently, safe in the bosom of her loving family.

They shook their heads and lost interest.

Across from the station was a pub. He crossed the road and went in. It was busy but not yet fully crowded. As he had learnt the previous night, he waited his turn at the bar. The barman took the picture, looked carefully at it and slowly shook his head.

Gritting his teeth and squaring his shoulders, Jack moved on.

34

Jack looked at his watch: 9.25. Time's beginning, just beginning, he thought, to run out. He didn't know whether he was being naïve but he was disappointed to have got nothing. Not a flicker, not a wink. A feeling of dread was developing in the pit of his stomach. Tomorrow morning he had to be at the boat at eight-thirty, and by then he had to know where Jenny was – or at least have clues.

Another working girl walked slowly along in leather boots which continued right up over her knees, practically to where the hot-pants stopped. He was beaten to her by a car. Passenger window down, brief conversation, and she was in and gone with a screech of tyres. He was sure he saw a baby seat strapped in the back. Bastard, he thought furiously. Why the hell do they have to do it, these guys? And then he thought of his own shame, what, six months ago?

He shook his head roughly to unburden himself of these thoughts. Get your head back into gear, he told himself, and focus on hookers and hit-men. *Come on, get a grip!*

A pub: an ugly, foetid place. He walked in. Things were busier. A longer wait at the bar. When his turn came he had to shout to make himself heard, but it was the proffered photo that made what he said understood. The barman shook his head, made an appreciative remark – or a remark that Jack chose to take as appreciative – then took it over to another man standing at the far end of the bar. They conversed briefly, the barman nodding in Jack's direction.

The other man detached himself from the bar and made his way over to Jack. He was of no more than average height, slight build, even a bit weedy. His head was close-cropped but not shaven, his features undistinguished, even forgettable. His look lacked humour.

'The fuck ye lookin for?'

Jack was nonplussed, off balance. The fuck he was looking for his daughter. The fuck he was looking for help. The fuck he was not looking for trouble.

'I'm looking for my daughter. She, er, went missing on Saturday somewhere in Glasgow and I'm just making enquiries . . .'

'She drinks here?' He indicated with a nod of his head.

'No, I don't think so.'

'So whit the fuck ye askin here for?'

He hadn't expected this line of questioning. It made sense, of course, and it was hard to answer. His mouth went dry.

'Just asking.'

'Aye, well,' the man said, 'doan't. Just fuck off, see?' The man turned, walked casually over to the far end of the bar and resumed his place, draped round his pint of heavy. He remained staring at Jack, stony-faced.

Jack found his knees shaking. His first encounter with something approaching a rough customer – and, let's face it, rough customers is where it's going to be at – and he had turned to a jellified wreck. Jesus!

He suddenly felt his bladder muscles about to give way. 'Where's the toilet?' The barman nodded at a door beyond the end of the bar. Oh God, he'd have to go past that ugly bastard again. Well, at least he could use the crowded bar as an excuse to make a wide detour.

Keeping his eyes lowered, he made it to the Gents. No one

was in there. The urinal was a long aluminium trough which, try as he might to avoid it, resulted in splashing onto his trousers. Just as he had started, he was joined by two others who silently stood on either side of him. Although the trough was not small, he felt hemmed in and wished they had stood just a few inches further away from him. It was a personal space thing.

For a change of scenery, Jack looked upwards and studied the cistern which released a constant dribble of water to cleanse the trough. The aluminium reverberated as his two silent neighbours began their business. A couple of seconds later he became aware that his right foot was in receipt of a flow, then his left foot joined in. He looked down and saw that his neighbours were directing their stream against his feet, and beginning to work their way slowly up his legs.

'Oi!' he exclaimed angrily, 'what the hell are you playing at?'

'Nuthin,' the one on his right replied. 'Gonnae shut yer face now an fuck off hame, pal?'

They waggled their dangly bits, stowed them away, and unhurriedly left the Gents.

Earlier in the day Jack had been looking for an air of menace that would start giving him clues. Now he had found menace and he didn't like it. For the second time in almost as few minutes he found himself trembling, aware that he didn't belong here, he was well out of his depth, and his reserve of courage was not equipped for this sort of thing. Twice the previous evening he had been advised to leave it to the police – probably for this very reason.

Jack escaped outside, evaded the smokers at the front door, walked some yards along the street, round a corner and paused to draw in lungfuls of fresh air, knees trembling. He began to calm down and review his situation.

Time was getting on: he had only a few more hours to get any information, otherwise he would be forced to leave it to the police and head back home. So far he had got nowhere. He had wet, smelly trousers. He was honest enough to admit that he was scared, and had scant self-confidence left. Maybe he should call it a day.

And yet . . . had he done everything in his power to find Jenny? He got out his picture of her. Gently he massaged it with his thumb, as though he could feel her, could give her strength wherever she might be, and he drew strength from her to do whatever might be required of him.

No, he decided, he had not done everything he possibly could. If he packed it in now he would know he was quitting just because of a couple of lousy deadbeats with a poor aim in the Gents. And maybe he hadn't got nowhere. Why was he being warned off? Because he was getting close. Obviously! *Buck up, Ross, where's your grit? Pull yourself together man and stick with it.*

He squared his shoulders in his revolting nylony jacket and looked across the road. Yes, there was another pub across the road. One more go at stirring this stinking cesspit to see what floats to the top.

The door opened directly into a single bar or lounge, a big room. Bench seats edged around the walls, covered in a plastic fabric which, although smoking in public bars had now been banned, was damaged from years of cigarette burns. Tears had been repaired by patches and glue, knife-slashes by stitching. The ceiling was low, the atmosphere oppressive.

With an effort Jack maintained his renewed self-confidence – and he reckoned a pint of beer would do wonders for his courage.

The bar was busy so he was able to take some time to survey danger-spots. He looked at the men standing at the bar. Either they were all hard men, or none of them were. He realised he just couldn't tell. Looking further round, mostly the clientele was male, a lot of youngsters. There were some women present, grandmas sitting quietly next to grandpas, contemplating their port and lemon. He could see no obvious threats.

There was still time for him to survey the beer pumps and select a quality local beer. There was none. One industrial beer masqueraded as a bitter, the rest were all lagers and strong ciders.

What hope could there be for these people with no decent beer available?

When he brought out his change he showed the barman his picture of Jenny. He misunderstood Jack's motives.

'She work round here, then?'

'No. She's my daughter. Went missing a couple of days ago. I'm just looking.'

The barman took one more brief look at the picture before handing it back.

'No seen her round here.'

Jack took his beer over to a free table by the wall and sat on the bench seat, back to the wall. He took a couple of mouthfuls of the metallic swill in his glass, wiping the minimal froth from his lip with the back of his hand. He looked at the picture of Jenny again, turned to the older couple sitting at the next table and asked if they had seen her. They looked only briefly before shaking their heads and resuming the silent contemplation of their alcohol.

He looked up and round to see if there were any other punters that he could profitably approach. As he did so, he caught sight of the barman looking at him with a mobile phone clamped to his ear. The man was looking at him as he spoke, not just gazing in his general direction for lack of anywhere better to look. Inwardly, Jack groaned.

After a few more words, the barman nodded and disconnected. Wiping his hands on a dish towel he excused himself from the group of punters he was yarning with and came over to Jack's table, a look of exasperation on his face and concern in his voice.

'See here, pal, it's no healthy ye asking all these questions, an I dinnae want any trouble in here. Gaun hame while ye're still in one piece.'

35

Jack checked himself out. His ribs and back hurt like hell; his nose and mouth felt like they'd had a botox job. But nothing else seemed to be damaged. His brain was still functional, as were his legs and arms.

Slowly and gingerly he rose to his feet. The women did their best to help him, fussing and clucking more than anything else. But he was grateful to them for their kindness. He stood there, legs trembling and feeling very wobbly.

'Aw, pet, whit the fuck have ye done tae *them*?'

'Well, I don't really know,' he said. Even to his own ears, his English accent sounded plummy. It had an instant effect on the women who presumably had expected to be rescuing one of their own.

'Whit's sumbdy like yersel doin here, mixing wi dug's keech like *them*? Shouldn't ye be back in Buchanan Street or somewheres fancy like tha?'

He was expecting the same kind of *fuck off and stop bothering us if you're not going to buy* that he'd received from all the other working girls. Instead, they fussed even more. 'Aw pet, whit have they done tae yur face? Are ye aw right?'

While they clucked, he peered at them through a rapidly swelling eye. In the dim light they were thin to the point of skeletal, their skin sallow, hair suffering from a combination of lacquer and unwash. It seemed they were abandoning business for the night, as they insisted he come back home with them and be cleaned up. What a contrast to the way the street girls in the posh end of town had treated him the previous evening. He guessed it was the old primeval thing: if you save a life, you're bound to it for ever.

It was only a few minutes' careful walk to a newly refurbished and smartly presented tenement block just past the old brewery on Duke Street. There they climbed to the first floor and one of the women let them into a flat. First things first, she announced throwing off her nylon leopardskin, and immediately put the kettle on. The other led Jack to a sofa and cleared some space on it, where he collapsed in a grateful heap. He was by now very shaky, shocked, and unsure that his legs would last much longer. His face and ribs were painful and breathing was only possible through his mouth.

While one was making tea in the kitchen, the other woman disappeared and he took the opportunity to glance round the room. Clothes, used plates and mugs cluttered every surface. The carpet was greasy and approaching threadbare. The sofa he was sitting on – he hoped it was cheap leather rather than vinyl but suspected the latter – was dirty, with cigarette burns and various stains curdling on it. But he was beyond caring.

The other woman returned with some white pills and a glass of water. He eyed the proffered pills dubiously.

'C'mon pet: they're paracetamol. Ye doan think I'm gonnae give ye anythin more excitin, dae ye?'

There were three in her grubby hand. He would be glad of them all. He took the pills with an unsteady hand and gulped them carefully down. His lips swollen, their seal round the rim of the glass was inadequate and water dribbled down his t-shirt as he drank.

The other woman returned with tea, and a rag wrapped round something. Shoving more rubbish further up the sofa, she sat down next to Jack and with surprising gentleness put the rag and its contents over his bruised nose and mouth. He winced.

'C'mon, pet, this'll get the swelling down.' Jack replaced her hand on the ice pack with his own, and she got up, handed the tea round, and sat down on another chair.

'Well, pet, I wouldnae usually be askin any questions, but ye're nae from round here, are ye?' she said, opening a new packet of cigarettes, offering one to her friend, and lighting them. In the garish glare of the single, unshaded 100-watt lightbulb, the older one's skin had a yellow tinge – no trick of the lighting – a darker shade than the previous evening's street girls had. The other one's skin was merely pale and unhealthy. Their clothing, which he'd previously thought of as merely garish, he now realised was sad, down-at-heel and ill-kempt. He suspected they were addicted to some form of drugs, but his own background did not equip him even to guess. Perversely, he hoped it was not cocaine or some derivative of it, knowing that he had been a part, albeit unwittingly, of the supply chain of a small amount being marketed on the streets.

Although speech was difficult, Jack began with introductions. It seemed he had been rescued by Betty, the yellow-skinned one who was now clearly even older than she'd looked, and Maureen, the brunette who might just have been her daughter. It turned out she was her wee sister.

'Your sister?' Jack didn't even try to hide his amazement.

'Aye,' said Betty matter-of-factly. 'I couldnae have left her at home, now could I?' Betty picked a non-existent strand of tobacco from her tongue, as though her Silk Cut was a Senior Service.

'Why not?'

'It's all a long time ago now.' Betty was distant; Maureen slackly studied the floor. There was a silence that Jack felt contained a Pandora's box of memories, grief and regrets. He didn't push. Instead, he continued with his story.

In a version that referred only briefly to his argument with d'Astignac's outfit and what he understood they did for a living, but which majored on his struggle to track down any leads over the last couple of days, he haltingly recounted his attempts to find his daughter and the events leading up to the present.

'Och, I wish we'd had a da' like ye,' said Betty, glancing across at her sister, 'don't we's, Maureen?' Her sister nodded silently, eyes still vaguely on the threadbare carpet.

'Why, what happened?' enquired Jack. Betty's eyes suddenly gained focus, flashing fire, the line of her mouth bitter. This time, Jack pushed. 'Did he die? Did he leave your mother?'

'Better he had,' said Betty. 'The drunken, wife-beating, child-molesting piece o scum.' She spat the last word. 'From as early as I can mind he would come home from the shipyard blind drunk most nights, yelling at me ma, clouting her tae kingdom come. When he'd beaten her tae a pulp, he'd climb intae ma bed an dae terrible things, *terrible* things tae ma wee body.' As she relived it, every muscle in her body seemed to go rigid, her face a rictus of remembered pain and humiliation, eyes fixed unseeingly on a point just above Jack's head. 'By the time I was fourteen, I was past caring, but one night the bastart climbed off of me and went tae Maureen's wee bed an started on her.' Betty's eyes suddenly focused angrily on Jack. 'She was *four years old*. The sick, perverted *bastart*!' She continued glaring at Jack as if he'd been the one. After what seemed a lifetime, she lost some of her tension and exhaled. Jack glanced briefly across at Maureen; silent tears were streaming down her cheeks. Betty continued.

'It was as if he was gonnae give her the kind o hell he'd given me for six years. Well, I couldnae let him dae *tha*. So the next day I just walked out the door with Maureen an hopped on a bus tae the centre o Glasgow. We didnae have any money so we got thrown off about six buses afore we got tae Argyle Street. An then we just walked on tae Glasgow Cross.'

Betty paused. Jack was riveted.

'So what did you do next?' he prompted. 'How did you survive? What did you do for money?'

Betty's bloodshot eyes bored into him. He knew what was coming; at fourteen she was just about the right age to become a shoplifter and pickpocket. He'd never thought *Oliver Twist* existed these days. It wouldn't have been long before she was caught and the two of them put into care. He felt unutterably sad, his own minor problems looking like a flea-bite through a telescope used the wrong way round.

'The only way I knew. I went on the game.'

Jack's blood froze. At *fourteen*, for chrissake? Poor, poor kid.

Betty continued, matter-of-fact. 'We was picked up by a man who gave us food an shelter for a few days. Then we was put in a stinking hovel on wer owns, an I was telt tae get out on the street and start earning so's I could pay the rent. An if I didnae pay the full amount any week when the man came round, he'd fair belt me an take his payment the other way.' She took a deep drag of her cigarette. 'But at least he left Maureen alone.'

Betty squared her shoulders, and Jack sensed that she was proud of what she'd done for them both. To him she was a hero. He felt humbled in their presence: he had, by contrast, enjoyed a comfortable, privileged upbringing and adult life; he'd shamed and jeopardised his family by his stupid involvement with d'Astignac, and he'd failed to treat his lovely daughter with the humanity she deserved when she – just like him – had made a mistake.

As if Betty could see into the turmoil in his soul, she consoled him.

'Aye, an that's why it'd have been better if he'd died or gone off. If he'd been a proper da like yersel, none o this would've happened.' Jack suspected there were equal amounts in what she said of envy of him as a father coming to look for his daughter, and encouragement to him not to beat himself up too badly. He was grateful, but didn't know what to say. She came to his rescue by asking what he planned to do next.

He explained that he had to be back home by about eight tomorrow morning to carry out his part of the plan.

'I've got absolutely nothing to show for the last couple of days, other than a busted nose and sore ribs. I'm no closer to finding anything about where Jenny might be. The police don't appear to have made any progress . . .'

'Aye, useless cunts. It's no their fault, mind; it's just that they're on the outside and cannae always find out what's happening on the inside, intit?'

He looked at his watch. It was not quite eleven. There was still time, although precious little of it. And what he'd learned from Betty and Maureen had stiffened his resolve to do d'Astignac's run the next day, to play a part in putting him and his scum away behind bars for a very long time.

'I don't have to be on my way till about half-past five so if I get going again there are still a few more places I can ask round in case anyone knows where she might be.' He pulled himself together and forced himself to his feet.

The two women exchanged a glance.

'Just hud oan a wee minty, pal, ye're gaun nowheres,' said Betty. 'Ye've a face like a skelpit arse; they've given ye a warnin tae take note of; and ye're fair peely wally an needin big zeds the night. Ye'll stay here the night till ye're needin tae go home, an me an Maureen'll find out who's huddin yur wee girl, won't we's, Maureen?'

'Aye, so we will. Jack's nae hope of ever findin anythin out hereabouts, but.'

'So ye curl up on yon sofy an we'll find out where yur wee bairn is.'

It made sense. If he went out with a face like a car accident everyone would avoid him. He wasn't getting anywhere, and these two were already halfway there: they probably knew who it was that had given him the kicking, or who had ordered it, and they might even be able to find out where Jenny was. And he was damn glad of the opportunity to sleep.

Betty got up, declared she had an appointment with Mr H, and disappeared off to the bathroom. By the time she emerged, refreshed and restimulated, Jack had curled up and was asleep.

36

DS Cox had been in since before 7.00 and was ploughing through print-offs from the Serious Crime Intelligence network and incident reports from the divisions. Acres and acres of data but nothing that gave them the slightest indicator. She was still smarting from having discovered that the vehicle in Gordon Street was stolen and the number plates switched.

The only other results from CCTV were no better. Stuart Sutherland with the wet trousers had worked it backwards so that the first sighting of the big BMW had been joining the Great Western Road at Drumchapel, and the final sighting after picking the girls up was in upmarket Pollokshaws, heading towards Strathbungo. Cox strongly suspected that the point of origin of the BMW was nowhere near Drumchapel, and its destination was nowhere near Pollokshaws.

This investigation is going nowhere, she thought, at least not until the ACC lets us play detectives again. She and her team needed to be out on the street, talking to the working girls, talking to their informants. She needed to be ripping apart the bar staff and waiters in Marco Polo: the statement Shona had got from Lucy MacDonald strongly suggested that one of the staff was in the pay of the Celenks and had spiked the girls' drinks. The leads were there to be had, they just weren't allowed to follow them. That was the trouble with ACCs: Buchanan shouldn't have had his bloody RTA, and Grimwade was about as much use as an udder on a bull. Jesus Christ Almighty, it made you so fucking cross!

Her mobile phone did somersaults on the desk.

'DS Cox.'

She listened for a moment, then frowned.

'Where are you? How do you know this?' Again the pause. 'That was extremely unwise of you, Mr Ross. I thought we'd made it very plain to you that you should go home and not try to play amateur sleuths. Apart from the fact that it can be very dangerous, it could also compromise anything that we're trying to do covertly at the same time.' Pause. 'Well, yes, as it happens, very good progress. But,' she said with an irritated sigh, 'I suppose it can't do any harm if you tell me what you've got.' She reached for a pencil and a pad. 'OK, shoot.' She scribbled as Jack spoke at the other end. Finally, she said, 'Well thanks for that Mr Ross, I'm sure it will be most helpful. But I really must impress on you that you mustn't do that again and you really should leave that kind of thing to us. Will you promise me that?' Satisfied as to the point she rang off.

But she was pissed off big time. She hated it when her hands were tied behind her back by the Ivory Tower. She hated it when rank amateurs tried to play detectives. And she *really* hated it when they came up with the goods and the professionals, forced to obey higher powers, couldn't.

Knocking on DCI Grant's door, she poked her head round. He looked up as he was extracting a file from the middle of a pile on his desk. The files and papers above slid lazily to the floor where they dispersed far and wide. 'Shit,' he said succinctly. 'Is it going to be one of those days, Brenda?'

'Might be, might not be.'

'What's that supposed to mean?'

'Just had a call from Mr Ross. Says he's got a name.'

Grant looked up in surprise from his tidying-up exercise. His glass eye glinted in the fluorescent light.

'How the hell did he manage that?'

'Said he'd been asking around in the Calton and Bridgeton areas, and the word on the streets is Davy McBride.'

Grant groaned, a combination of irritation that he hadn't been able to find that out, and frustration that a thoroughly out of place member of the public had.

'Wee Davy McBride? About ten feet tall and built like the proverbial sewage facility. I knew him some years ago when I was at the London Road office. Nasty, violent psychopath, but he was just a small-time thug and housebreaker at that time. How interesting that he's now an employee in bigger organised crime.' Grant mused for a while. 'Even if we brought him in, we'd get absolutely nothing from him. Might put a tail on him, though, and that might lead us to the locus. Any indication of what area we're supposed to be looking in? If they've got any sense they'll have gone to somewhere like Drumchapel or Maryhill.'

'Shettleston, he said.'

'Bingo! That's what we need. Get in touch with the duty DI at Shettleston Road and see if there have been any reports from the beat officers of anything out of the usual.'

Grant got up from his desk, yawned a mighty yawn and stretched his back.

'And ask him if he's got any ideas about possible holding places. I expect he'll laugh in our faces, what with the number of run-down industrial premises, lock-ups and so forth in the area. But at least we might be able to narrow the search for the needle down to a handful of haystacks.' Cox turned to go. 'And get a tail on McBride'.

John Humphreys and Sarah Montague were just announcing the eight o'clock headlines on the *Today* programme as Jack parked the grey Mondeo in front of *Creag Mhor*. Getting out of the car was more a matter of crawling, then unfolding slowly. He let himself into the house and went through into the kitchen. Tom was already there, as he promised he would be when Jack had called him on his mobile thirty-five minutes earlier.

'Dad! What's happened to your face?' Tom looked aghast.

'Oh, that?' Although he still ached he was well drugged-up and his spirits were high. 'Does it look bad?' He went to the downstairs toilet and looked at himself in the mirror. All things considered, it could have been worse. Yes, his nose was a bit fatter than usual and there was discolouration from the bruising. His top lip was more noticeable: it was definitely a thick lip, well swollen, but no obvious splitting because all the damage had been done inside where the skin had been punctured by his teeth. But the swelling, he thought, was nowhere near as bad as it might have been but for the ice pack. Although he was still trembly and shaken up, he realised he'd been let off very lightly. He knew why. A serious kick in a vital place could, at best, have hospitalised him, and at worst, killed him. And d'Astignac needed him.

He walked gingerly back into the kitchen and helped himself to another handful of paracetamol. While he was at it, he wondered if ibuprofen would help, so he added some to the cocktail.

'Dad, you're hurt!' Tom looked concerned and a little frightened. His father was not in the habit of disappearing for two days into the rough end of a city and returning looking (and smelling) very much worse for wear.

'I've got a lead to where Jenny is,' he declared.

'Why haven't you brought her home, then?'

'We'll have to leave that to the police, Tom. I spoke to them a few minutes ago and they have it in hand.'

Tom clearly had a dozen questions on his lips, but Jack was weary from the drive, his face and body were stiff, and he was in serious need of a mug of strong coffee, a shower and a change of clothes. But first, he had a question for Tom.

'How's your mother?' Jack asked quietly.

'She was in a pretty bad state on Sunday evening after you went down to Glasgow. Dr MacDonald came over first thing on Monday morning to see her and gave her some pills. She's to take them every four to six hours.' He turned and opened one of the kitchen cupboards, reached inside and gave a packet to Jack to read.

Valium, 5mg, two to be taken four times a day. Poor Sarah. As he held the packet, his eyes glazed over. His lovely wife who was accustomed to laughing and smiling, who had stood by him during this mad adventure, was now distraught and on Valium. Just what the hell had he done to his family?

He pulled himself together as much as he could and handed the box back.

'Thanks, Tom.' His voice was quiet. 'And thanks for looking after Mum.'

37

DS Cox had been doing her own ringing around. Specifically the duty Detective Inspector at Shettleston Road Police Office. She had informed him of the operation in his area, and asked him whether there had been any reports from beat officers of any activity that might suggest kidnappings, unlawful imprisonment and the like. He looked through the log, read out a couple of entries, but they weren't of any help.

'Any ideas where they could be holding her?'

'It'd be quicker to suggest places where they *aren't* holding her, Sergeant. But if you were to press me, I'd probably choose an empty lock-up deep in the heart between London Road and Shettleston Road. Must be a dozen of them to the square inch.' The duty DI paused to see if Cox would react. She didn't. 'If we searched them all it would take about a week.' He paused again. 'How long have we got?'

'Not long. Intelligence says if we don't get in there by close of business today then we may be too late. And as we're treating this as an abduction and it's been forty-eight hours already, it's probably too late anyway,' she added drily.

'Are you taking the piss, Sergeant?'

'I wish I were, sir.'

'Jesus Christ!' The DI paused for a few moments. 'Look, I need some pointers, something that tells me where to start looking. Have you got anything else, anything at all?'

Cox was reluctant to admit that their biggest stumbling-block was an ACC (Crayons and Plasticine) with his thumb so far up his arse he could brush his teeth without opening his mouth.

'Well, other than a watch on McBride, nothing. I'll get back to you if anything turns up.'

'You do that, Sergeant, I'll be waiting for your call.'

Cox put the phone back on its cradle carefully and ceremonially snapped a pencil in two. It gave no relief. She got up from her desk and kicked a wastepaper basket as hard as she could. She decided that her Chief Inspector needed to share her frustration.

She went to his office. He was out.

Detective Superintendent Burns' door was ajar. Grant knocked and poked his head round.

'Morning sir, got a moment?'

Burns was standing behind his desk, sorting through the pile of papers in his in-tray. He looked up. 'Come in, Duncan. How're you getting on?' Burns continued looking through his mail.

'I think we're on the move, sir. We've got a name, someone I used to know when I was at London Road, and a general location. If he's involved in this kidnap then we're making progress. But if he's not, then we aren't, and I need to know one way or the other very soon.' Grant paused to be sure he had Burns' full attention. 'I want to bring him in. I appreciate what the ACC said yesterday, sir, but I really would like at least to try to get approval to bring him in for questioning. I think we can do it quietly and any extra time we buy ourselves can only increase our chances of a successful rescue.'

Burns clicked a switch on his desktop intercom.

'Laura, find out if Mr Grimwade can see me now for five minutes. Thanks.' Turning to Grant, he said, 'Depends what his diary's like, I suppose. On such small matters great things depend, eh, Duncan?'

The intercom buzzed urgently. 'The ACC can see you now, sir.'

Burns led the way as they went round to the front of the building and up to the top floor of the Ivory Tower. The temperature was rumoured to be about three degrees lower than further down the building and the atmosphere so rarified that, if you didn't come down to the lower floors regularly, you lost all sense of reality.

Access to the great man's room was through his PA's office.

'Morning, Rachel,' said Burns cheerily. Rachel smiled at him. Grant felt very grubby in his none-too-clean, somewhat rumpled, grey flannel suit. Rachel almost wrinkled her nose in disgust. She motioned that they should walk straight in.

'Morning, sir. You remember DCI Grant?'

'Ah, yes,' said the ACC who clearly did not. Assistant Chief Constable (Administration) Gilbert Grimwade was a short, balding man with the trace of an accent from somewhere near Birmingham, gold wire-rimmed glasses and the air of a self-important bank manager. 'Everything going well, Grant?'

Grant opened his mouth in preparation for telling it like it was but Burns suavely hijacked the question, just as a good staff officer should in case a foot-soldier placed his foot somewhere near his mouth.

'Yes and no, sir.'

Ha, thought Grant, that's why I'll never be a senior officer.

'It's in relation to the Border Agency operation on the coast,' Burns continued, 'the one we discussed at yesterday morning's ops meeting. You recall I raised a connected kidnap that Grant is handling at the moment? Grant's team have been working night and day . . .' Burns nodded at Grant's less than crisp condition, 'and have found a lead. But it is the only one, sir, and there are other circumstances which are causing major concern.'

Burns outlined to the ACC the fact that there had been no

leads resulting from intelligence and covert activities, the involvement of the Celenks, and the nature of the risks to Jenny Ross. On top of all that, Customs had said they appreciated that Jenny Ross' life came first, and it was a police call.

'Yes, I understand all that,' snapped the ACC, 'but I don't see why another few hours will make any difference to the victim's situation, when to strike too early on this would jeopardise a very significant drugs operation. This operation has an extremely high political profile, not merely for the force and the region, but nationally as well. In addition, inter-service cooperation is a measurable target and this operation on the coast is a prime opportunity to cooperate; I am not prepared to jeopardise the opportunity to meet or even exceed our targets.'

Government-imposed performance targets were a red-hot issue throughout the service generally, no less than with Grant himself. He was about to dismiss targets with a few pithy and well-chosen words when Grimwade cut across him.

'And I don't have to remind you of the importance that the Intelligence Services *and* Interpol have placed on specific persons who are the target of this operation . . .'

Aye, Grant thought bitterly, *which lowly detective sergeants dug out and which I passed on up the chain of command, so don't give me any bullshit about MI5 or MI6.*

'So this will remain a covert investigation while I'm in charge of the department.'

Grant was horrified at the arrogance of the pompous little shit. He glanced across at Burns, whose jaw was clamped tight, his hands clenching and unclenching. In an effort to clarify precisely what the issues were, Grant thought the time for pussyfooting around was over and only blunt would do. He impaled the ACC with his good eye and spoke sufficiently loudly to brook no interruption.

'We're talking about the life of a young girl here, sir, and the impact on her family if we get it wrong. It's my professional opinion that the risks to this girl's life are already too high but if we act now in the manner I propose, we have as good a chance of rescuing her unharmed as we'll ever have. I also consider that there's a reasonable chance we can avoid jeopardising the drugs operation. If we don't act as I propose now, at this instant, we're playing games with the victim's life. If necessary, sir, I will put that in writing in an email.'

The ultimate threat. Not just protecting one's backside but the chance of a leak to the newspapers.

'If that was your idea of a threat or blackmail, Grant, forget it. The fact is that there are issues here so far above your head you couldn't imagine it. This is why I wear these badges of rank,' he tapped one shoulder, 'and you don't. For the last time – no overt move on the Celenk gang until you have my express permission. That's an order. Is that clear?'

Grant could barely get his throat to function. Didn't the man even have the grace to realise how much proverbial would hit the rotating if he carried through the threat?

'Yes, sir.'

'And if you can't achieve a satisfactory result within the overall constraints,' continued the Assistant Chief Constable (Stationery and Forms in Triplicate), 'I'll find someone who can.'

Jack and Tom had made a comfortable passage in *Celtic Dawn* down to Crinan where they had arrived just after 9.30. Steel-grey clouds joined seamlessly with the gunmetal sea, chasing away the last of Jack's optimism from his Glasgow trip. The paracetamol/ibuprofen mix was holding off the worst of the aches, but he had to be very careful: any sudden moves woke the sleeping dragon wrapped round his ribs and he wasn't keen to do that. The shower had braced him up a bit, made him feel smarter, more professional, more on the ball. So too did the uniform he and Tom wore: dark-blue polo shirt, white chinos and trainers, dark-blue fleece against the cold, and fluorescent red foul-weather gear for the wind and rain. Although there was not much more than a north-westerly breeze at the moment the forecast was for showers, and for the wind to strengthen throughout the day and back into the west.

He would be interested to know where d'Astignac wanted to go today. Somewhere new, or one of the small ports they had previously been to? He hoped it wasn't a long journey; he wasn't sure he could put up with their company very long or that his body would put up with the movement of the boat. Just do the job, he told himself, keep your nose clean, and the Revenue men would clear up here, and the police in Glasgow.

His earlier confidence about the inevitability of Jenny's rescue was not so much evaporating as being submerged beneath the weight of things that still had to be done and the risks still involved. Apprehension gnawed at his guts.

Ten o'clock came and went. OK, so he couldn't expect them to keep to naval time, but he had understood they were staying at the hotel by the lock basin so they clearly weren't being held up by traffic. Besides, there was an enormous Toyota Amazon Landcruiser with darkened windows in the car park, which couldn't realistically belong to anyone other than out-of-townies intent on carrying a large quantity of material they didn't want anyone else to see. When 10.30 came and went he was getting worried. Had they changed their minds? Had something gone wrong? Had the police in Glasgow somehow spooked them and all options were off? Just where the bloody hell were they? There wasn't much deck on his boat to pace, so he paced the quayside instead.

At 10.40 he observed, with some considerable relief, d'Astignac, Coluzzi and two gophers sauntering down from the hotel towards where he was berthed. With his altered state of awareness of the true facts, he had to agree with Tom that d'Astignac did carry an air of Mediterranean menace: the French connection. It gave him the willies.

Coluzzi was the same as ever: padded, Italian, American.

'Hiya, Jack, and how are *you* today?' he called while still some distance off. Jack refrained from giving him the full medical details that the question always tempted him to give. Instead he just waved. But as they got closer Coluzzi's face screwed up in concern.

'Hey, Jack, what happened to your face?' Jack remembered Betty's description of it. Had a nice turn of phrase, the Weegies. But he knew that the swelling was down a lot, only slight discolouration, and he didn't speak with too much of a lisp with his split lip. Provided he didn't do anything too imaginative and energetic, the heavy doses of paracetamol were keeping the worst of his ribs in order.

'Not altogether pretty, is it?' he apologised. 'Had a minor car accident over the weekend and my face hit the steering wheel before the airbag sprang into action. Maybe I should get a new car one day.'

'Yeah, maybe you should, Jack.' Coluzzi seemed satisfied; his surprise and concern had seemed genuine. But then, thought Jack, what do I know? I've misjudged every character and every situation in the last week.

d'Astignac, on the other hand, was inscrutable, an impression reinforced by the aviators sunglasses he wore despite the leaden sky. He didn't mention Jack's face, didn't show surprise or concern, feigned or not. The consummate professional. Jack could have done without d'Astignac's company today.

'So,' Jack said with an effort at cheerful bonhomie, 'where to today?'

'I think the Island of Iona, today, *Jacques*, if you please.' Jack used to find the French accent very attractive; but not now, never again.

He went down to the saloon and checked the tide tables. With high water – a very high water, so a strong spring tide – shortly after 6 pm tidal conditions in the area would be interesting. He'd have enjoyed them in any other circumstances.

Back up on deck he started the big Volvo engines and watched the dials for smooth running. Despite his aching body and the desperate situation, he grinned and his heartbeat picked up with the throaty throb of those engines. Life wasn't all bad, not with a boat like this.

As Tom slipped the head rope Jack slipped the stern rope and they headed slowly out into the bay. When he had stowed the ropes and fenders, Tom came back to the cockpit and took over the wheel. Jack went to the VHF, switched it to channel 72 and picked up the handset.

'Highland Radio, this is *Celtic Dawn*, channel 72, over.'

The speaker crackled into life, Jim Francis's voice acknowledged and Jack transmitted again.

'This is *Celtic Dawn*, outward bound from Crinan to Iona, four passengers, request local weather forecast, over.'

Jim replied with the inshore waters forecast he had copied down from the radio earlier that morning. Jack thanked him and checked out.

d'Astignac was watching Jack throughout this exchange, eyes obscured and inscrutable. Surely just asking a local shore station for a forecast wasn't suspicious? Was it?

38

Neither of them spoke until they were back in Burns's office.

'That's how it's going to be, Duncan. There's politics here way above my level. I'm sorry. It makes the job hard – but not impossible.'

'Yes, I know, sir.' Grant paced up and down, pent up energy burning inside him. 'I just don't think it's worth the risk. It's so *bloody* frustrating. One lead, that's all we have.' He looked at his watch. 'And time's running out.' Grant spun on his heel and faced Burns, his right hand clenched tightly. 'For two pins, sir, I'd . . .'

Burns stopped him just in time.

'I share your sentiments, Duncan, but I don't want them voiced.' He waited for Grant to recover his composure. 'Given the constraints on the operation, what will you do now?'

'Just keep watching McBride's place. It's all we can do. As the duty DI at Shettleston said to DS Cox, without another whisper of information we've got pretty much no chance. If we can question McBride there's a chance he'll let something slip that will give us that whisper. If we don't get it, this case will turn into a slow-time search for a dead body. Or worse. Basically, Shettleston's too big an area to go prising all the boards off the windows and doors of every lock-up and disused industrial shed without giving about a week's warning to the abductors that we're looking for the girl. Grimwade's certainly right on that score – it wouldn't help Jenny Ross at all.'

He ran a hand through his thinning hair and sat down.

'Best use of time is to plan the rescue operation, even though we don't know where and how she's being held. So I'll get on down to the incident room, if you don't mind, sir. But what I will need – when we get the go-ahead – is the Tactical Firearms Unit to go in first. Can I ask you to organise that for me, sir? Thanks.'

On his way down to the incident room, Grant rearranged himself psychologically. It had been a severe blow, Grimwade stopping him bringing in McBride. He had two options. The first was to obey his orders. That would mean it could be many hours before he was allowed to pull McBride in for questioning. And what if McBride genuinely didn't know where Jenny was? They would be back to square one. And by that time, Grant feared that Jenny would be an embarrassment to Celenk and either dead or in the process of export.

The second was to ignore the order and pull him in anyway. There was a chance he could do it in such a way that word did not get back to Celenk, at least for a period of time.

If he did that and managed to narrow down the place where Jenny was being held, Grant knew that he couldn't go in without the Tactical Firearms Unit, and he knew he wouldn't get them unless and until Grimwade had approved the operation. Two months previously there had been a monumental cock-up with an operation in which firearms had been authorised, and two innocent members of the public had been seriously injured. When in doubt, overreact, and so all firearms-led operations now required written approval from ACC level or above, until the inquiry into operational procedures and lessons learned had been completed.

He was in a dilemma, blocked either way.

But Nelson, as he was in the habit of saying to himself, wasn't the only one with a duff eye.

Cox looked up as Grant walked in and pointed to a brown paper bag on her desk. 'I've got you an egg and bacon sandwich, Duncan.'

'Thanks. Life's not all bad, then.'

He tucked in and discovered how ravenous he was. Having devoured the first mouthful, he asked whether there had been any sign of McBride so far.

'Not much. Lights on in the house, that sort of thing, but so far he's not put in a personal appearance. Shall I bring him in? If he's there, of course.'

Grant used his second mouthful of breakfast to give it thought.

'Ideally I want him to lead us to where Jenny is. It makes sense to give him the morning to do that. But if he doesn't do it by, say,' he looked at his watch and calculated, '1300 hours then we need to go the riskier route. That means getting McBride in for some light gardening, and digging it out of him.'

'Will that give us enough time?'

'I don't know. But even if we brought him in now, God alone knows whether he'd crack. He's the stubborn type, who'll just sit there with his arms folded and demand his solicitor. He's an overconfident, supercilious bastard, who survives on the phrase *prove it*.'

Grant looked morose. Cox on the other hand was looking pensive.

'Anyone associated with him who might know anything? I mean, does he have any mates who he usually goes on jobs with?'

Grant screwed up his face as he dug deep into his memory, and suddenly his brow lost some of its gloom. 'He had a brother-in-law; thick as an MP's expense-claim file. Followed McBride round like he was on a lead. What was his name?' He chewed a mouthful of tea as he dredged his memory again. 'Got it. Kelvin Morrison. Also resident in the Calton area, from memory. Get his address from London Road Office if we haven't got it, and get a DC and one out in a car at his address. Follow him everywhere he goes. If either he or McBride haven't led us to the premises by the end of the morning, he's the one to pull in: he'll break. That of course assumes he's involved and knows anything.'

That's what he'd been looking for: the third option. Perfectly clear if you look down Nelson's telescope the wrong way.

DC Shona MacLeod went down to the CID car pool and signed out a rusting Vauxhall of non-descript colouring: battleship grey was her best guess. Used pizza boxes and KFC cartons jostled for room on the back seat and in the foot-well.

PC Chalky White sauntered by in plain clothes, fingers deep in the pockets of his designer jeans with the precision tears and artfully arranged frayed edges.

'Hey, Chalky, you're late for work.'
'Time's a relative concept. Einstein said.'
'Who's Einstein?'
'Fuck's sake! You detectives worry me.'
'I thought you wanted to be a detective?'
'So?'
'Hop in, then, and make it snappy.'

Chalky grinned a big beam. Shona tossed him a bunch of keys.

'Here, you drive, I want to be hands-free.'
'Where are we to, then?'
'I've got an address in the Calton and a photo of a man alleged to live there. We've to sit outside and watch for him. If he comes out, we're to follow him and keep Control informed.'
'Is all? Jings! And here I was, thinking we'd be wading in with bulletproof vests kicking the shit out of a gang of drug-pushers.'
'You read too many of them crime novels, Chalky. Detectives detect: shit-kicking is done by shit-kickers.'

With a surprising skill in one so young that secretly impressed Shona, Chalky wove the car through the remnants of the rush-hour traffic and ten minutes later pulled up behind two other parked cars about a hundred yards short of the address Shona had given him in the Calton district. The area was densely packed residential housing, mostly small terraced houses and low tenements. All of it was newly built or refurbished, and most of the occupants had made an effort to keep their areas smart, clean and tidy. Shona noted with disgust the plethora of cars parked in the neighbourhood: new 4x4s, black BMWs and sporty Audis. Inconspicuous rusting Vauxhalls were conspicuous by reason of their absence.

The address was for a three-storey tenement block; the flat number suggested the second floor. They settled down to wait. Always the worst thing. The mind begins to wander, the eyes glaze over and, quick as a flash, the key event occurs unnoticed.

'Is it true you're getting married?'

'Aye.'

'When's that, then?'

'Two weeks on Saturday.'

'Who's the lucky man, then?' Chalky ventured, pushing his luck.

'He's in Special Branch. Seven feet tall, plays football for Celtic in his free time, and eats four Shredded Wheat for breakfast.'

That was rubbish, of course: no one eats four Shredded Wheat for breakfast. Shona wasn't going to tell Chalky that. But it shut him up as they settled down to wait.

With the boat steady on a course of 288 degrees along the south coast of Mull, d'Astignac and Coluzzi joined their two gophers in the forward cabin, the door shut. Tom had the wheel, and he and Jack exchanged looks of relief as the clouds of oppression lifted. Jack noticed a fender rolling around on the foredeck and tried to go forward to secure it. But as he stepped up his ribs stabbed him and he couldn't control a sharp grunt. Tom glanced round. When he'd got his breath back, Jack asked Tom to hop forward and secure the fender while he took the wheel.

A few minutes later Tom dropped lightly back onto the after deck and retook the wheel.

'OK, what really happened?'

'How do you mean?'

'Oh, come on, Dad, I'm not stupid. You disappear off to Glasgow on Sunday evening to look for Jenny, you're away all day Monday and you reappear this morning looking like you've been in a train smash. It's obvious you're hurt, and quite badly. What's going on? What happened to you in Glasgow?'

As much as his ribs would let him, Jack sighed. He supposed it was only to be expected; he was only kidding himself that he was in a fit state even to be a passenger on a boat at all, never mind in charge of the boat and leaping around on it. He was heavily dependent on Tom – and he was bloody glad to have him along for that and for the company.

'I . . . ran into some trouble.'

'How come?'

'Well, when I got to Glasgow, all my good ideas about how I was going to find Jenny sort of evaporated. When I landed on the streets with her photograph, I realised I didn't know anything at all about where to start asking, who to ask, or how to go about it. It seemed a hopeless task when I actually started trying to do it.'

He recounted the deflation he felt when his ridiculous offer to help the police was turned down. His need for clothes with a bit more street cred provided a moment of levity in an unhappy tale. But as his narrative approached the events in the men's toilet in the pub in Bridgeton Cross Jack began to tremble, and his words faltered as he relived what he now realised was outright physical fear. He was glad of the strength of Tom next to him, and when he felt Tom's arm slip round his shoulders he was not embarrassed when his trembling slowly became great, silent sobs. Tom's arm just tightened.

After a while he was able to recover himself sufficiently to resume the story of his beating and subsequent rescue. His composure crumbled a second time when he thought of Betty and Maureen and the hell that had been their lives, and that it was they – not him – who had found the information he had passed to the police.

With a massive effort he brought himself under control a second time. His handkerchief by now a sodden mess, he found himself in serious need of a second. Tom reached into a locker and fished out the rag they used to wipe the dipstick for the daily engine oil check. The resulting oil streaks on Jack's face were lost in the general artwork.

As a semblance of equanimity was restored with much clearing of throats and copious quantities of water drunk from bottles stored in the starboard rope locker, Tom kept his eyes on the distant horizon and said as quietly as the engine noise would permit, 'Well, *I'm* proud of you, Dad.'

Jack was too choked to reply.

39

A male of medium height and substantial girth, with dark close-cropped hair and eyebrows that met in the middle, stepped out of the front door of the likely flat on the second floor landing, and walked towards the stairwell.

'Heads-up, Chalky. Let's have a look at that photo again.'

The photo was a bit grainy but the figure was obviously the same. Fat round the waist, dark eyebrows low over the eyes and meeting in the middle. In the photo the head was shaven, but allowing for a couple of days' stubble and an hour or two at the Anthony Mascolo beauty salon and coiffure shop it was unmistakably him. Kelvin Morrison.

A few seconds later he appeared at the front of the close, walked in the opposite direction and got into a black BMW M3 of that year's registration. Only a few months old! Out-bloody-rageous, thought Shona, whose own pride and joy was a two-year-old Peugeot 207 on which she still had a year's hire purchase charges to pay.

She picked up the radio mike and called in to Control, reporting the sighting, index number, and that they were following. She hoped the M3 wouldn't disappear at a rate of knots that they couldn't hope to match.

Instead, he motored at a sedate and law-abiding pace down to Bridgeton Cross and slipped into a roadside parking space. The Vauxhall carried further on down the road, turned into a side street, did a three-point turn and parked close to the junction with London Road, so that they could just see round the corner and follow whatever direction the M3 went off in.

Morrison got out of the car and crossed to the small grocer's shop on the corner. They could hear the bell jangle from where they were as Morrison swung the door open. Chalky looked at Shona.

'Should I . . . ?'

'No. Just ciggies.'

A minute later Morrison emerged, unwrapping the cellophane from a packet of cigarettes and dropping it casually on the ground as he sauntered back to his car.

'How did you know?'

'I'm a detective, remember?'

PC White marvelled for a couple of moments then tried his own brand of policing.

'That's two offences we can get him banged-up for.'

'Oh yes?'

'Dropping litter and failing to pay for his parking.'

'Aye, right. That'll see him in Barlinnie secure wing for most of his natural.'

Morrison returned to his car, did a tyre-screeching three-pointer and drove straight home. Shona radioed in to Control and then opened her mobile and called DS Cox.

'Nothing, Brenda, other than the fact he's at home. And that his day is so full he can't walk down the shops for ten minutes for his fags. His only crimes today, my back-up constable tells me, are littering and failing to pay for his parking. Just thought you'd like to know.'

'OK. If he's not showing signs of taking us where we want him to take us, the boss says bring him in. Use any pretext other than the right one, we don't want his missus telling all and sundry that the polis is onto him. Try littering and parking.'

'You're joking! Aren't you? He'll never fall for that!'

'Aye well, it's up to you, whatever you want to think of. But anyway, the boss wants him brought in and it must be quietly. Take him to Shettleston nick for interview. I'm going up there now, so I'll tell them to expect you.' Shona heard the disconnection. She muttered foul oaths and poked PC White in the ribs.

'Come on, Chalky, come and try a bit more detecting.'

'Why? Where're we going? What's going on?'

'We're going to ask Mr Morrison to accompany us to the station and assist us with our enquiries.'

'What enquiries?'

Shona explained. Chalky White's face broke into a big grin.

'Hey, are we going to arrest him for dropping litter and failing to pay for his parking space?'

'Have you got a better idea?' asked Shona sardonically. God, she hated it when these youngsters thought they were God's gift. 'C'mon, get your arse into gear. And this heap of rusting garbage.'

PC Chalky White continued with his unofficial detectives' training and experience by assisting Kelvin Morrison – a good few inches taller than himself – to a hard wooden chair on one side of a hard wooden table. They were accompanied by a uniformed constable of B Division, and Chalky was hard pressed not to strut in front of the uniform. He was sufficiently well acquainted with hubris, however – the chap who would ensure that DS Cox came in and said in a loud voice, 'Thanks PC White, you can go and change into your uniform now.'

But when Cox came in she winked at him and said, 'Thanks, Chalky.' He left, and Cox seated herself across the table from Morrison.

'Now, Mr Morrison. Kelvin. I'm Detective Sergeant Cox, and

I need a few words with you about the social ills of dropping litter and not paying for your parking.'

'What the fuck . . . ?' Cox could see both Morrison's brain cells in conflict. He might be a violent psychopath, she thought, but he would come second in a game of noughts and crosses with a five-year-old. 'Have ye's brought me in here just to talk about *tha*?'

'In a manner of speaking, yes. But I'm quite happy to widen the conversation a wee bit. Just so's it doesn't get *boring*.'

'I'm out o here, so I am.' Morrison started getting up. The uniform behind him, no mean physique himself, placed a gentle hand on Morrison's shoulder. 'I know my rights. I want a brief.'

'I'm sure you do, Kelvin,' Cox soothed. 'After all, you've been through all this many times before, haven't you?'

'This is whit this is all about, intit? Polis harassment, so it is. I want a brief.'

'Sit down, Kelvin. As you well know, you get a lawyer when I say, and not before. Besides,' Cox tossed a packet of cigarettes on the table, 'I don't think you need one.'

Morrison eyed the cigarettes suspiciously; but resistance was futile. He licked his lips and reached for them. He extracted one, placed it surprisingly carefully between his lips, then slipped the packet into his shirt pocket. He stared at Cox with an attempt at arrogance.

She beamed back at him, as if to say, *that's my boy*. Cox leaned forward and flicked her cigarette lighter almost – but not quite – under the cigarette. Morrison leaned forward slightly, cupped his hand round the lighter, and sucked the heat into the tobacco. With the first drag of nicotine-laden smoke into his lungs he sat back in his chair, enjoyed the sensation, and then exhaled like a dragon.

The relationship was established to Cox's entire satisfaction. Best of friends. Bosom buddies.

'Now then, Kelvin. I just want a wee chat.'

*   *   *

Duncan Grant was fretting. He looked at his watch again; still no word from Cox on Kelvin Morrison. If Morrison refused to talk, or he had no connection with the abduction, Grant would be in serious trouble for disobeying the direct order of two senior officers. The depth of the trouble would be even greater if Morrison *was* involved and his absence spooked the Celenks and the landing operation on the west coast. He didn't care: he knew he had done the right thing morally. And he would have been prepared to bet many pints of beer that if Rufus Buchanan hadn't been in hospital he would have given Grant the go-ahead immediately.

He knew he should have more patience, but SIOs weren't paid to be patient. He extracted his mobile and was about to ring DS Cox when he realised she could be interviewing Morrison right now – she might be at the crucial moment, and the ring of her phone might break the beautiful moment. Or she could have it switched off.

He strolled along to the incident room and found a uniform loafing. She was about his grand-daughter's age. He gave her his mobile and said, 'Can you do a text thing for me please? I haven't got my glasses with me.'

She smiled at him, knowing full well it was rocket science to him. 'What do you want me to say, sir?'

'Oh, just: Any news?'

When she had done that, she asked who he wanted to send it to, clicked all the right buttons, and handed the infernal contraption back to Grant with a smile. 'There you are, sir, all done.' He smiled his thanks with his good eye.

He didn't have long to wait. Within a few minutes Cox rang back.

'Anything from Morrison?'

'Not yet.'

'Is he involved, do you think?'

'No doubt at all, right up to his great, fat, stinking eyeballs, which I am about to extract, mount on a toasting fork and return to him with a salt and vinegar dressing.'

'I take great strength from your confidence, Sergeant,' he said drily, and disconnected.

40

An hour after stepping ashore from *Celtic Dawn*, d'Astignac rang Jack on his mobile phone to say that they were ready to be picked up. Before weighing anchor and with only the clueless Coluzzi on board, Jack called 'Highland Radio' on Channel 72 and was able guardedly to let Jim know that he was about to load a large pile of cargo he could see on the jetty with his binoculars, and would shortly be departing.

As he manoeuvred alongside the tiny slipway Jack was alarmed at the number and size of grip bags and backpacks awaiting loading. He counted twelve of them, and from the difficulty d'Astignac's gophers had with lifting them, passing them down to the boat and stowing them in the saloon, cabin and heads, he reckoned they must have weighed something like thirty or forty kilos apiece. With a shock he calculated that there was close to half a tonne of whatever – raw cocaine? – on his boat. There was no way that was innocent on any analysis; he could see what Jim meant.

Bastards!

As Jack eased the boat from the slipway, the gophers – Sean and Jamie had been joined by one other, Eric he reckoned – went down to the saloon, presumably to ensure that no-one stole their evil cargo, while d'Astignac and Coluzzi remained standing in the stern cockpit with Jack and Tom. Jack kept his face impassive, black eyebrows pulled low over his eyes and his square jaw set.

The boat was sluggish at low revs with the thick end of half a tonne of cargo on board, but Jack knew there was plenty of spare power in the engines to get the hull up onto the aquaplane where the most efficient performance was to be had. Once they were into the open waters of the Sound of Iona he increased revolutions; she struggled a bit getting up onto the plane, but once there she was as sweet as anything, even moving more comfortably over the sea with the extra ballast.

As they left the Sound of Iona and turned onto a course of 108 degrees to take them across the open stretch of sea to the gap between the islands of Jura and Scarba, Jack broached with d'Astignac the subject that had been gnawing at his guts.

'Have your people been able to establish any news about Jenny's whereabouts?'

'*Oui. Un chouïa* – a small amount. I shall call the office,' d'Astignac announced tersely. He conversed on his mobile phone for a few moments, giving absolutely nothing away. Jack half suspected there was no one on the other end. When d'Astignac rang off he turned to Jack with a grimace. Jack doubted it was an attempt at a smile.

'*Mes associés* still work on it. There is much that they have to do, but they have optimism they will be successful.'

Small mercies, thought Jack, and d'Astignac is milking this situation for all it's worth. He told himself to keep calm, they were on the home straight, and all he had to do was deliver these crooks back to Crinan and it would all be over.

'Back to Crinan?'

'If you please, *Jacques*.'

He reached for the VHF mike.

'Highland Radio this is *Celtic Dawn*, fully laden from Iona to Crinan; request weather forecast, please.'

* * *

The air was so thick even Cox was having difficulty breathing. The duty sergeant had already popped his head round once and asked for a quiet word, pointing out that police stations couldn't be seen to be quite so obviously in breach of the Smoking, Health and Social Care (Scotland) Act 2005. Cox slipped him her spare packet of Marlboro and the duty sergeant left her to it.

'No, I don't think it's a good idea for you to be going home right now, Kelvin.' Morrison was sweating and Cox was confident it had nothing to do with the heat. 'All I want to know is where you've been delivering groceries to.'

'Fuck off,' he pleaded, 'I'll be in pure deid trouble if I breathe a word.'

'Will you?' She feigned horror. 'Surely not? After all, I don't want to know what groceries you've been carrying, or to who, or who asked you to do it. No, no, that's not it at all. I just want to know *where*; just so's I can check you haven't been dropping sweetie papers, or not paying your parking dues.'

'Och, Sergeant,' he groaned, way out of his depth, 'I just cannae dae it, I'm sorry.'

It was almost the end of the line. She looked at her watch. So be it.

'I'm very disappointed in you, Kelvin.' She sighed. 'I'll get a car to take you home.'

Morrison's relief was palpable. He put his head in his hands.

'We'll find her, you know.' She spoke quietly. Morrison's head shot up, eyes wide. 'And when we do we'll let Celenk know it was you. We won't even look for you in the concrete foundations of the new multi-storey at Easterhouse. Come on, the car's waiting.'

He groaned.

If Grant had been fretting before, by this time his blood pressure was stratospheric. Still no news from Brenda Cox, who presumably was even now removing Morrison's intestines with a blunt garden implement at Shettleston nick in an effort to extract the key piece of information that would unlock this whole mess.

He had been shuffling pointlessly between his office and the incident room, barking at anyone in his way. He almost had a heart attack as his mobile warbled.

'Boss, we've got what we need. Jenny's being held in a tenement on the Craignure Estate, just down from Shettleston nick. It's currently all boarded up, awaiting a council decision whether to demolish or repaint. Anyway, it means we can now watch it for any signs of movement.'

'About time too,' he barked. Then, realising that she had been doing all the hard work and he had contributed nothing, he softened his tone and told her she had done well.

'Can Shettleston provide surveillance for us, Brenda?'

'I'm already on the case. DI Robertson is organising all his available CID people in unmarked cars and deploying them round the tenement. I'm just about to brief them what to watch out for and what to do if anything happens. Shona Macleod and Chalky White are already here, so if you can get Stuart Sutherland and anyone else in plain clothes to join us we'll be on a roll.'

'I'll do that. You get that building wrapped up tighter'n a midge's arse so no one takes Jenny out, while I get the Firearms Unit organised. Speak to you shortly.'

Grant's shoulders squared back, the twinkle returned to his eye: the man was on a mission. Rather than run straight up to see DS Burns, he thought for a few minutes about how he would play it. This was all going to be about managing his senior officers, not about police work. When he was ready he picked up a random file from his desk, went up to the second floor and knocked.

'We've had a breakthrough . . . at last, sir. A tip-off that an apparently disused tenement on the Craignure Estate is where Jenny is being held. I've got the place under surveillance now so that no one goes in or out without our knowing about it. On top of that, Customs expect they'll be mopping up their operation over on the coast within the next hour or so.'

'That's very good news,' Burns said warmly, 'well done. I knew you could do it within the ACC's constraints.' What sanctimonious bollocks, thought Grant, until he saw the twinkle in Burns' eye.

'That being so,' Grant phrased the next bit very carefully, 'I thought it would be prudent policing to start making plans for a rescue based on the assumption that this tip-off is correct. And set things up ready for the executive order.' He looked at Burns expectantly.

'I assume you have plans already?'

'Yes sir. I can't see any subtle way of doing it. After all, no one goes casually knocking on the door of a boarded-up tenement, enquiring if the occupants would care to buy the Encyclopaedia Britannica. I see no alternative to a forced entry. This would need to be armed and very swift.'

'Because?'

'The background to this operation is drugs. I'm not sending in unarmed officers.'

'I'm happy with that. Go on.'

'There's not much more in outline, sir. Tactical Firearms clear the place of weapons. If Jenny's in there we arrest her captors. I'd have a medical team standing by.'

'Isn't that a bit over the top, Duncan?'

'I hope so, sir. But prudent, if you get my drift.'

Burns leaned back in his chair, steepled his fingers under his chin and thought for a moment or two. He looked at his watch; Grant saw the movement and glanced up at the wall clock: 2.35 pm. He'd spoken to Charles earlier and his assessment had been that the west coast operation would be complete in – what? – not much more than an hour. Not much more than an hour to go before Jenny ceases to be an asset and becomes an embarrassment – assuming she's still in the country.

Grimwade had better give the word, Grant thought sourly, *or I'll string him up by the most painful extremities I can lay my hands on.*

DS Cox was sitting in her own car watching the rear of the tenement block. Her mobile phone trilled: Shona Macleod.

'Brenda, a blue Transit van pulled up in the front close a few minutes ago and two guys got a wheelchair from the back. They're up on the top floor now, walking along the balcony. Yes, they're standing outside the far door at the eastern end waiting to be let in.' She paused for a couple of seconds. 'They've gone in.'

'OK Shona. I think it's time we went active. I'll tell the boss.'

Cox broke the connection and speed dialled Grant. 'I think they're preparing to take Jenny out as a medical case. Wheelchair just gone in. She's probably drugged to high heaven. I think your export scenario could be the one.'

Still in Burns' office, Grant pressed the disconnect button.

'Things are becoming more pressing, sir. It looks like Jenny Ross is about to become export goods for the Eastern European filth market.'

Burns' eyes opened wide, and he appeared to make up his mind. He reached for the telephone on his desk and pressed a button.

'Rachel, is Mr Grimwade free?' He paused for the answer. 'What do you mean, no? In the *air*? Whatever for?' He paused again for the explanation. 'Thanks.' Looking up at Grant, he punched another button on his desk phone. 'It seems he's on his way to London for a conference and the Chief Constable's on his way to Tenerife or wherever. Do it – just do it. I would've said that a long time ago if the Chief Constable hadn't asked me to humour Grimwade – but then, I doubt the Chief Constable imagined this scenario would crop up or Grimwade would be such a . . .' Burns left it there. 'Just do it, Duncan, and I'll square up with the Duty ACC shortly.'

Grant ran down the stairs to the incident room. All he had to do now was ring the duty Inspector at the Firearms Unit at Springburn and tell him he had authorisation for a Tactical Firearms team. He'd fax the written authorisation over to him. With any luck they'd be on the scene within thirty minutes.

He was also glad that he'd planned in a medical team. Brenda was probably right that Jenny had been drugged. And heaven only knew the state of her physical condition apart from that. Back in his office he rang Cox.

'Brenda, we've got the approvals. A Tactical Firearms team will be with you in about thirty minutes, as will a medical team on standby. I'm leaving Pitt Street now. Don't do anything to spook them, for God's sake. If they leave with the wheelchair and occupant, follow them at a distance and keep me informed.'

'Got that, Boss.'

He cut the connection and rang the Support Unit at Springburn. Impatiently he waited for a reply. After an interminable period a constable answered. He asked to be put through to the duty inspector. After another interminable wait the duty inspector told him that the shift team – team leader Sergeant Wallace – was out on another operation.

'Sorry about that, sir, but we do have to respond to incidents as they arise.' Grant knew that very well, he just wasn't in the mood to accept it calmly. 'If you give me the location where you want them, sir, I'll get them to go direct to you as soon as they finish their current op, and give you a call when they're on their way.'

Grant slammed the phone down. Damn! There was no way he was going to let unarmed officers go in first. They were preparing to take Jenny out in a wheelchair; he *had* to gain entry to the flat before they did that otherwise he would lose the initiative.

If Wallace turns up late and this op turns to chutney, he thought, *I'll give that fucking Grimwade to Brenda Cox so she can eviscerate him with a blunt spoon.*

41

D'Astignac and Coluzzi came out of the saloon onto the deck.

'We have a new destination, *Jacques*, if you please.'

'Oh?' *Shit*. Charles had been emphatic that he needed to know d'Astignac's ultimate destination. Jack kept his voice neutral, unconcerned. 'Where to then?'

'Oban.'

Jack calculated swiftly. Crinan was something like an hour's drive from Oban. If he alerted Charles now, he and his team just about had time to get to Oban. But even then, Jack would have to keep the revs down. If Charles got held up by lorries on the bendy coast road, and Jack had a good run to Oban, d'Astignac would be off and away before Charles arrived there. And they'd have no idea of the vehicle or vehicles d'Astignac was using, switches made, and all the rest of it. D'Astignac had anticipated well, planned well, and timed it well.

If Charles got the information now, there was a chance – a slender one – that he could relocate in time. Jack reached inside the saloon for the VHF mike.

'Highland Radio, this is *Celtic Dawn*, over.'

That was odd: he didn't remember turning the volume down. He heard no squelch or click of the transmission switch. Reaching inside the saloon again he looked at the volume level. The knob was in its usual place. He turned it up to maximum and clicked the transmission switch twice.

Concrete hardened in his stomach: the radio was dead. He looked round the back of the radio and saw the power lead had become disconnected. He supposed the movement of the boat and the vibration of the engines had been to blame, and he had to admit that it was not one of his daily checks. He picked up the lead and was in the process of reconnecting it when there was a sharp *phut* behind him and the radio erupted in front of him. The heavy Perspex window of the saloon beyond the radio developed a spider's web of cracks, centring round a neat hole.

Jack spun round and saw Coluzzi holding a small handgun. The barrel was thicker than he would have expected – until he realised it was a silencer. Smoke curled lazily out of the muzzle.

'What the fuck . . . ?'

It took a moment or two for Jack to connect up all the images and sounds in his mind.

'Did you just do that?' he asked Coluzzi. 'With that . . . that gun?' Coluzzi didn't answer. The look on his face was unconcerned, as if to say, *don't see me, mate, see the Boss.*

Jack exploded. 'What the *hell* do you think you're playing at? How dare you bring that thing on my boat – and without asking me first? This is – this is piracy. And you shot out my radio. That is about the stupidest thing anyone can ever do at sea. Jeesus! Give me that thing, and just fuck off out of my sight. Over the side or into the saloon, I don't care.'

Coluzzi didn't move. Neither did his unconcerned expression.

'*Move*, damn you! Don't just stand there like a . . . like a . . .' He couldn't think what. Instead he looked at d'Astignac. 'He's your boy, just get rid of him.' Jack turned back to face forward, and muttered, 'Jesus H Christ. Fucking gangsters.'

d'Astignac's voice was cool, unconcerned. 'This is not a game, *Jacques*. Our new destination is Oban. And I want myself to be certain that there are no more . . . unnecessary . . . weather forecasts.'

'Yes, but the radio: the *radio*, for Chrissake! You should know better, d'Astignac!'

d'Astignac cocked an enquiring eyebrow. A flicker in the back of Jack's mind hinted that he'd given something away, but he was so furious he didn't care.

'And get rid of that fucking gun! I don't allow guns on my boat, d'you hear?'

He just had time to register the glance passing between the two of them. Coluzzi stepped up close behind Tom and held the gun in the small of Tom's back. In a voice like a blow to Jack's solar plexus, d'Astignac said, 'Do I have to remind you that I control the fate of both your son *and your daughter*?'

Wordlessly, Jack looked from d'Astignac to Coluzzi to Tom. Coluzzi shrugged. d'Astignac he could understand as an evil bastard, especially as he knew his military background. But Coluzzi; Tony? Why, they were almost mates. Pasta and sauce from Tony, all about his family from Jack . . . Suddenly he twigged. He had played into their hands. He had given Coluzzi all the information they needed: they had all the power, all the leverage. Marie-Claire had been the first to try to extract the information, and when that hadn't worked Coluzzi had been wheeled out with his reluctant gangster spiel. They'd played him for a fool.

While he seethed inwardly, he gritted his teeth and maintained a veneer of composure. There was nothing for it but to alter course for Oban. He took over the wheel from Tom.

'OK,' he growled, 'I'll take you to Oban. You can put that gun away, it won't be necessary.'

'Coluzzi will keep the gun exac'ly where it is.'

'I said, PUT THAT FUCKING GUN AWAY. I will *not* have it pointing at people on my boat.'

Both Coluzzi and d'Astignac ignored him.

Jack could feel his whole rescue plan slipping away from his control – as much as it ever had been within his control in the first place. But he wasn't ready to give up yet, not by a million miles. Not after everything he'd been through.

'Tango Alpha One this is Scarba Lookout, over.' The Marine positioned on the top of the island of Scarba with a pair of powerful binoculars and a radio had noticed the boat's alteration of course.

'Tango Alpha One.'

'Target altering thirty degrees to the north, lining up for passage to north of Scarba. Over.'

'Roger, out.'

The radio operator in the lead RIB, Tango Alpha One, turned to Corporal Cyril Gogerty, Royal Marines, in command of two Pacific 22 rigid inflatable boats of Four Troop, M (Maritime Counter-terrorism) Squadron, Special Boat Service. The two RIBs had stationed themselves in the Sound of Shuna, just out of sight but handy if needed inside the islands.

'Goggs? Scarba lookout reports target altering thirty degrees north to a course which will take him to the north of Scarba.'

'Roger.' Gogerty turned to Lance Corporal Peter Short, cox of the boat. 'Let's have a look at that chart, Lofty.' Together they pored over it. 'What the fuck? He can't be serious: if that report is correct, the boat's heading for Bealach a – I give up, can't pronounce it: the Grey Dogs. He'll be in real trouble if he does that.' He looked up and called over, 'Sparks, call Scarba lookout and get him to confirm target's course.'

After a hasty radio conversation it was confirmed that *Celtic Dawn* was indeed heading for the Grey Dogs.

'Shitty death!' exclaimed Gogerty. 'We need to be over there, standing by.' He looked at the chart again and selected a point about a mile to the east of the Grey Dogs, from where he could watch the progress of *Celtic Dawn* towards them through binoculars, yet merge into the background behind him of the island of Luing.

As soon as they were under way, Gogerty called up Jim Francis on board *Vanguard*.

'*Vanguard* this is Tango Alpha One. Target is three or four miles west of Scarba, was making towards Corryvreckan. Then sharply altered course twenty degrees north towards the Grey Dogs. Target's intentions unknown and not understood. Am positioning myself to render assistance if necessary. Over.'

'Roger, Tango Alpha. Do you think he's still heading for Crinan?'

'Unlikely. Repeat, *Celtic Dawn's* intentions unclear.'

Jim Francis acknowledged and relayed that to Charles Burleigh-Wells in his blue unmarked Land Rover.

'Has Jack called you with a change of destination?' Charles asked.

'No. But maybe they've changed destination to somewhere like Easdale or Oban, and disabled the radio.'

'You could be right. If that's the case, d'Astignac's taken the gloves off or Jack's done something to piss them off. Either way, I don't feel comfortable with this – and Jack's probably even less thrilled. Tell the Marines to be ready to stick to them like glue.'

Jim Francis acknowledged, and Charles signed off with the fervent hope that his tightly planned operation wasn't heading for a ball of chalk.

DCI Grant's dark-blue Vauxhall Vectra pulled up behind DS Cox's silver two-litre Audi S3 Sportback. Cox got out of her car and climbed into the passenger seat next to Grant. He asked drily whether she couldn't have rolled up in something just a little more conspicuous. Equal to her boss's humour, she observed that elderly, mid-range family saloons were more conspicuous in this deprived area than shiny new Audi sport cars. Grant snorted. Cox went smoothly into briefing mode. She said they were just out of eyesight of the target flat, and described the disposition of the other detectives.

'How many people in the flat?' Grant asked.

'We only know of the two who came with the Transit van and the wheelchair, and one person who let them in.'

'Let's assume at least one other. Leaving aside Jenny, that's at least four. Not bad for an empty and boarded-up flat.'

Grant's mobile vibrated quietly from somewhere inside his jacket. He answered, listened to his caller, thanked him and disconnected.

'That was Burleigh-Wells. He thinks something's gone pear-shaped on his operation. Not necessarily that it's going wrong, but he gets the impression that the temperature and pace have changed. He still thinks that, whatever it is that's happening, they are well within his grasp and it's perhaps only a matter of a few minutes before the gloves are off.'

'Well,' said Cox cheerfully, 'that's all we need to get our operation underway. Any sign of the cavalry?'

'Not just yet. They were out on an op when I called earlier. I was hoping that was Sergeant Wallace calling to say he was on his way.'

There was silence in the car for a few moments.

'I'm not wearing my jackboots, Duncan. Do you have yours?'

'There's no way we're going in there without the entire Armoured Division.'

'What are the risks as we wait?'

Grant sucked his teeth noisily.

'Once they've got her out of the flat, we lose the initiative. As we follow, the risk increases that they would see us and then the situation develops into a stand-off and a possible shoot-out. And if we wait until she's arrived at their destination, which I suspect is a ship, once they get her on board she can be secreted away very quickly in a place where it would take days or weeks to find.' He was silent for a while. 'I doubt we have that kind of time.'

'So we're glued here until Wallace arrives?'

'That's pretty much it.'

42

As Jack turned the boat to a course of 075 degrees towards the Grey Dogs, the motion eased. A strong swell was running, but as it had a long wavelength and the wind waves were going with them, it was not uncomfortable in the boat. The only uncomfortable thing was Jack's blood pressure and the sound of fury pounding in his ears. He would *not* tolerate a gun in Tom's back.

Jack kept the revs high and noted they were making thirty-two knots through the water. For what he had in mind, he'd need to get the revs up as high as possible. Any less and there was a risk it wouldn't work.

He estimated they were no more than five miles away from the Grey Dogs. At thirty knots, three miles in six minutes; five miles in about ten minutes. He teased the throttles up a hundred revs. Thirty-four knots. That brings it down to about eight minutes. But during that time they had travelled another mile, so four miles to run, ease the throttles up another hundred revs, let her settle. Glance at the log, thirty-seven knots. That's about six minutes to run.

Jack had a momentary doubt about his plan. His ribs were hurting like crazy and his vision was none too clever. Sean, Jamie and Eric were still down in the saloon: should he call them up on deck? Of course he should, he knew that. But then he thought about what this bunch of filth stood for, and what they were doing to his children, not to mention Sarah and himself. Let them rot down below, he thought.

His resolve hardened and his hate intensified. He was going to need all his courage for this. He hoped to God it wouldn't fail him at the last minute; that Tom would realise what was going on; that both of them would be lucky. Luck would be important.

Luck? He wasn't too sure about his recent luck. What if the police aren't able to rescue Jenny? What if the speed of the boat's too much? What if the speed isn't enough? Were the tides right? Had Ewan MacPherson known what he was talking about?

The first outlying island of Lunga came abeam to port. Less than a mile to go, he thought. He glanced across at Tom who was looking quizzically at his father as if to say, Hey, Dad, what're you doing?

Gritting his teeth against the stabs of pain in his ribs, Jack surreptitiously but clearly tightened the belt of his lifejacket and looked pointedly at Tom's lifejacket. Tom took the hint; he tightened his belt, glanced back at Jack and grinned.

Jack tickled the throttles up to their maximum revs, more than three thousand nine hundred. The engines screamed in response. By now they were slicing through the water at forty-six knots. One thousand five hundred yards a minute. Twenty-five yards a second. As they got closer to the gap the passing scenery began to flash by.

d'Astignac looked sharply across at Jack, about to demand that they slowed down. But then he saw what was in the fifty-yard gap ahead: a huge standing wave of ten feet or more from trough to crest as the water from the east side of the island cascaded over into the waters on the west side. Exactly what Jack was looking for, and just what they had seen when they'd been here six months previously in Ewan MacPherson's boat.

By the time d'Astignac had realised the implications of what he was seeing, the boat was upon the gigantic wall of water. At the last second Jack heaved the wheel full over to starboard, the boat heeled seventy degrees onto its starboard beam and the exposed bottom of the hull smashed into the wall of boiling water, the stern just catching the jagged rocks on the north side of the gap. The stern splintered into shards of fibreglass and wood, the fore part of the boat sheared off in one piece with its three occupants still inside, and filled rapidly with water.

Jack, d'Astignac, Coluzzi and Tom were all flung haphazardly into the angry maelstrom. Only Jack and Tom's lifejackets inflated automatically. With a combined shout of glee and yell of pain as his cracked ribs objected to the abuse, Jack surfaced instantly. His first thought was for Tom but he was unprepared for the sight he now encountered. Even though he'd anticipated it, planned it even, he watched in horror as his pride and joy, the beautiful *Celtic Dawn*, was smashed on the rocks of the Grey Dogs, pounded by the towering wall of water.

He tore his fascinated gaze away from that scene of carnage and searched desperately for Tom. He caught sight of him perilously close to being mixed up with the wreckage of three and a half tonnes of crushed boat as it circulated and was pounded again and again on the rocks of Eilean a' Bhealach.

Jack tried desperately to swim over to Tom but was held up like a cork by his lifejacket, on his back, and so couldn't make any headway towards Tom. He knew he could only get to Tom if he discarded the lifejacket. He also knew, in the back of his mind, that that was about the stupidest thing he could do. He thrust the thought away savagely.

He had not realised how difficult it was to unbuckle a lifejacket while in the water, and his hands were already beginning to lose dexterity as they got the warmth sucked out of them. The harder he fought to unbuckle it, the more firmly it locked and the more desperate he became. With a superhuman effort and more luck than he knew, he managed to slip the buckle and fought to push the inflated sausage off his shoulders. He rolled over and his lifejacket floated away. Instantly he was sucked under the boiling waves without having taken the necessary breath. He forced his way up to the surface and vomited salt water, steadied himself, and struck out for Tom.

Although it was only about five yards, a hidden force was pulling him back, away from Tom. He kicked and struck out harder, his muscles and ribs screaming in pain and his lungs violently complaining at trying to suck in oxygen only to find salt water.

His progress was slow, agonisingly slow, but the gap narrowed. Tom continued to tumble in the waterfall crashing above him and from which he couldn't escape. With a final desperate lunge, he grasped at Tom and grabbed a trailing loop from his lifejacket harness. By now Jack was being sucked under the waterfall of crashing waves and felt himself going down and down. With lungs crying out for oxygen he couldn't stop himself reflexively taking a breath underwater and sucked in half a litre of salt water. He retched and his lungs burned as though sandpapered.

He reached the top of the spin cycle and shot above the waves again. A hard object delivered him a mighty crack across the back of the neck and shoulders, and his free arm went numb. The hard object was part of one of the wooden bench seats from the smashed boat. Attached to it was the foam rubber cushion, which was making a better job of staying afloat than either Jack or Tom. Kicking frantically with his legs, he flung himself bodily towards it and manoeuvred round to the opposite side of it from Tom, with his arm still grasping the loop of Tom's harness across the cushion. Both of them recovered their breath briefly.

The respite was short. They were perilously close to the wreckage of the boat which was slowly and inexorably being broken up against the rocks of Eilean a' Bhealaich. Jack looked up and saw one of the giant twin 300-horsepower engines hovering above him, held up only by a very frail-looking fibreglass transom from which the structural strength had been sucked when the vessel smashed into the rocks.

As the engine began to separate from the transom holding it, Jack kicked his legs with all his might in an attempt to move his raft out of the way. No good, the boiling water was too strong. This time he heard Tom shout out in an agonised voice, 'Dad, look out!' just before the huge block of steel crashed down on Jack's shoulder. He was crushed down into the water as a searing pain shot through the whole of his left side. The flesh of his shoulder opened up. He momentarily glimpsed a jagged edge of bone sticking up at a crazy angle.

In a sea of pain worse than the swirling maelstrom trying to drown him, Jack had a moment of clarity: *Shit, and we so nearly made it!* In panic, he felt his life-force draining out of him.

Alerted by reports from the Scarba lookout, the SBS boats had covered the mile from their standby position to the eastern side of the Grey Dogs in just under ninety seconds. Corporal Gogerty had ordered Marine Dusty Miller from Tango Alpha Two to land with a hand-held radio on the rocky shore of Scarba, just twenty yards from the tumultuous Grey Dogs.

'Tango Alpha One this is Dusty. Target boat's smashed itself to pieces, there are people in the water and the whole thing looks a right shitty mess. Over.'

Gogerty brought both RIBs as close as possible to the boiling sea. With the tidal stream rushing at nine knots to crash down into the maelstrom, they made their approach by turning into the tidal stream at just less than the velocity of the water, slowly approaching the cauldron by the stern.

Gogerty pointed at Marine Geordie Martin. 'That lifebelt with the polypropylene line: get it into the water over the quarter and float it down to the casualties in the water. Lofty,' he turned to the cox, 'watch out for that line and make sure it doesn't end up round the props. I'll fucking have you if we have to be rescued ourselves.' Gogerty gesticulated over to the other boat to tell them that they should do the same, but they were already on the case and their yellow lifebelt was just going over the side.

* * *

Just as Jack was giving up the fight, and Tom was trying vainly to swim with their makeshift raft out of the black hole sucking them all in, Tom saw one of the bright yellow lifebelts thrown down on the cascading water. He made a grab for it and missed, but his arm closed over the polypropylene line to which it was attached, floating on the surface.

'Tango Alpha One, this is Dusty. One of the casualties has grabbed a line – can't see which one, over.'

'Roger that,' said Gogerty. 'Geordie, heave in on your line. Any weight?'

Geordie Martin heaved in without noticeable resistance. 'Not yet, Goggs.'

Gogerty acknowledged, and shouted above the combined noise of the boats' engines and the roar of the waves to the other RIB that they should heave in.

'Goggs,' shouted the driver of the other boat, 'there's weight on our line: we'll heave in.' The line was secured round a rubber cleat and the RIB carefully increased speed with the intention of hauling whoever was holding onto the other end out of the maelstrom into calm waters.

Tom felt the line moving under his arm, and quickly the lifebelt came up to him. He hung on for all he was worth. But as he was hauled towards the crashing wall of water he realised that his father was no longer hanging onto his lifejacket. He twisted round to see where he was. He could see that Jack's energy was all but spent and he was about to give up the game. He had let go of the foam rubber cushion and was disappearing below the waters.

Tom's indecision was brief and agonised. He let go of the lifeline and kicked back towards where he had last seen Jack.

'Dad, Dad' he screamed, the tears streaming down his cheeks saltier and more poignant than any seawater. 'Dad . . .'

Jack continued to be dragged down by the undertow beneath the cascading wave. The water boiled crimson only briefly before the blood pouring from his shoulder was diluted and then swept away. Tom kicked savagely through the last two yards separating them, and lunged down into the water for him, hoping with all his might at least to make contact. His hand grasped nothing but water.

'Dad,' he screamed again, not knowing what else to do and ready to give himself over to helpless grief. His legs encountered a solid object and instinctively he opened them and embraced whatever it was. It was Jack's torso. Tom reached down with all his force working against the buoyancy of his lifejacket and grabbed his father's shirt collar. But Jack was both heavy and waterlogged, and it was all Tom could do to hang onto him. The momentary elation of two seconds ago had vanished, and Tom began to feel the leaden weight of real despair replacing mere terror.

Twenty yards away, on the other side of the cataract of water, Tango Alpha Two had realised something unscheduled had happened.

'Goggs, we've lost the weight on the line,' shouted the corporal.

Christ, muttered Gogerty, now we've lost them. 'Sparks,' he yelled to the radio operator, 'ask Scarba lookout if he can see them.'

The radio operator conversed briefly with the lookout on the top of Scarba and Dusty Miller on the rocks by the Grey Dogs.

'No, Goggs, they can't see no one – they've both gone down.'

43

A police van pulled up behind Grant's car and a sergeant clad in black overalls got out and ran forward.

'Sorry about the delay, sir. I was on another operation and came as quickly as I could.'

It was a measure of the pressure that Grant snapped, 'About time too, Sergeant. Let's get cracking with the briefing.'

As he did so, four constables also dressed in black combat overalls got out of the van and started donning black Kevlar bulletproof vests and black helmets. Three had short Heckler & Koch MP5K-PDW submachine guns, the remaining constable a weighted battering ram.

The briefing complete, Cox spoke to Shona MacLeod, Stuart Sutherland and the uniformed PCs. 'Right,' she said, 'we've not been sat about on our arses waiting for the cavalry to arrive just because we're short of paperwork to do or targets to meet. They will go in first and disarm any and all occupants. Your knife-proof vest is as useless here but it's all you've got. Anyone goes in too close behind or gets in the way is likely to get shot, and if anyone does that I will fucking have them on the naughty step and then your problems will truly start. Crystal?'

There was the usual mumbled 'yes sarge'.

Headed by Sergeant Wallace and followed by the detectives

at a distance induced largely by fear of getting on the wrong side of DS Cox, the firearms team quickly made their way under the shadow of the building to the entrance. They went up the stairs to the second floor and congregated at the stairwell. Once they left the cover of the stairwell it would be fast, furious and noisy. Anything less would be fuck-up territory.

Tom was approaching the end of both his physical and his mental strength. Jack was still below the water and Tom was sure, dimly, that by now his father was dead. But he would not let go – nor could he hold on much longer. Again he saw a yellow lifebelt, just outside the reach of his free hand. He tried to kick towards it, but there was no strength in his kick. He knew that his only chance of survival was to let go of Jack and throw himself towards the yellow lifebelt.

At that moment, the wreck of the boat gave an almighty shudder and rolled off the rocks towards Tom. The resulting small tidal wave swamped him. When his head resurfaced he realised with horror that the lifeline had looped round his neck.

'Tango Alpha One, this is Dusty, over.'
'Alpha One.'
'One of them's got the line – heave in.'
'Roger that. Heaving in.'

At the stairwell Sergeant Wallace checked his team one more time.

'Ready?' They nodded. He looked at Grant. 'Ready?' Grant nodded. 'Right, let's go.'

The officer with the battering ram led the way along the landing, followed by Wallace and the three other armed officers. Grant followed after a slight gap, with his detectives behind him. The group paused while the battering ram shattered the lock with a single, crashing blow. Wallace ran in roaring, 'Armed police!'

He ran to the end of the corridor off the entrance hall, passing four doors. His three officers followed close behind, each taking one of the doors leading off the corridor. The air reverberated with shouts of 'Armed police' and the sounds of wood splintering. Adrenalin and testosterone fought for supremacy.

Sergeant Wallace kicked a door, which smashed open revealing a kitchen and three occupants. He put his gun to his shoulder and roared, 'Armed-police-stand-still-put-your-hands-on-your-head-and-do-it-now!' Two officers followed him into the room and covered the occupants, who were glued to the spot with terror on their faces. Their hands shot up in the air. One lost control of his bowels. Wallace turned to one of his officers and barked 'Yours', before nodding at the other with a peremptory 'Come'. The two of them headed off to find other rooms. In the kitchen the officer started making the occupants lie on the floor, searching and disarming them before handing them over to Grant.

Grant poked his head into the kitchen, DS Cox and DC Sutherland close behind him. Three individuals were lying on the floor with their hands on the backs of their heads. No sign of Jenny.

Meanwhile, the third officer had gone to the remaining door and kicked it in. In the adrenalin-charged excitement Shona Macleod got too close behind him. As he raised his weapon to his shoulder his cry of 'Armed police' died on his lips, as he was knocked backwards by a spray of bullets erupting from an automatic within the room. The majority of the bullets punched his Kevlar vest but one severed his carotid artery. As he spun backwards the blood spurted in a bright crimson fountain, spraying Shona Macleod behind him.

She dodged behind the partition wall for cover, but there was no let-up from the automatic weapon. Bullets thudded through the flimsy plasterboard out into the hallway, criss-crossing Shona's upper body, her black knife-proof vest no match for the bullets while she convulsed and jerked like a demented marionette.

At the sound of the gunfire Sergeant Wallace and one of his officers broke off from their search and ducked out round into the hall to see where the firing was coming from. The scene was mayhem, blood spattered on the walls and the walls themselves erupting in shards of plasterboard. He couldn't see a thing. He hugged the floor to get below the barrage of bullets and raised his weapon to his shoulder, ready to shoot through the walls to where he thought the firing was coming from.

Grant yelled, 'Don't shoot! We don't know where the girl is!'

In a desperate bid to take the weight off the rope round his neck, Tom reached higher up the line, grasped it and took a turn round his hand, hoping he'd reached up and not further down. As the weight came on his hand the line tightened, giving him the double sensation of his hand being cut in half and friction burn as the rope slipped slowly through his grasp. Almost immediately the line tightened round Tom's neck and he was faced again with the horror of garrotting. He pulled the line in with his hand until he felt his muscles bursting, but the instinct to survive drove him on.

Unconsciously his other hand had remained clamped round Jack's shirt collar. The line pulled them both steadily through the wall of water, which continued to crash down from a height of ten feet. Tom was kept afloat only by his lifejacket, although his forward movement, towed by the line, pulled Jack to the surface behind him.

Before they were free of the power of the tidal stream Tom's hand, with the lifeline wound round it, could resist the strain no more. The line cut cruelly through the skin and flesh, through to the bone below the index finger and the little finger. In agony Tom's released his grip but nothing happened: the line was embedded in his flesh. His arm straightened, abandoning all the weight of his body to the loop around his neck.

Jesus! Sergeant Wallace thought, *no one told me this was going to be like the Iranian Embassy siege. Why the hell didn't I bring flash-bangs!*

The firing from within the room ceased momentarily. Wallace

heard the click of an empty chamber and the sound of a magazine being unclipped. He sprang up and charged round the corner and into the room, his weapon at the shoulder. He saw a giant of a man with a Polish PM-84 Glauberyt submachine gun in the process of changing the magazine. He had an instantaneous decision to make: *Shoot the bastard as he surely deserves or warn him and give him the chance to give himself up?*

The decision was made for him. In the instant Wallace appeared, the big man rammed home the fresh magazine and began to raise the weapon again.

Your luck just ran out, Sunny Jim. Wallace squeezed the trigger of his Heckler & Koch twice. As the nine-millimetre parabellum bullets tore into the centre of the man's massive torso he was thrown backwards by the impact and crashed down heavily across a low camp bed behind him. There was a weak groan from underneath him as the occupant of the bed had his breath thumped out of him, and Wallace smelt the sickly-sweet odour of bowels emptying, cutting through the astringent smoke of burnt cordite.

Still aiming his weapon at the big man, he approached to feel the neck artery for a pulse. There was too much flesh there so Wallace had to make do with the wrist. He noted with reluctant satisfaction that there was none – not that he expected there to be any.

Wasting no sympathy on him, Wallace heaved the inert giant off the bed with difficulty to see what was underneath. What he saw shocked him to the core.

44

As the line tightened around Tom's neck and he screamed noiselessly, Tango Alpha Two came alongside. Hands hauled the two of them over the low, inflated bulwarks and dumped them onto the rigid floor of the boat. Marine Sharky Ward, qualified battlefield medic and veteran of Iraq and Afghanistan, assessed the situation quickly.

'How are they, Sharky?' Gogerty asked from the other boat.

'Right old mess, mate. Looks like the old one's had it, but the young one's still alive. Seems like he was trying to strangle himself. Hand's in a pretty bad way.'

'Anything you can do with them or do you need help?'

'Dunno. Snapper,' he said, turning to the other Marine in Tango Alpha Two, 'sort out the lad, will you. Elastoplast, aspirin and tell him to pull himself together. I'll have a go with the old one. Here, someone, give me a hand getting him up onto my shoulder.'

Jack was heaved onto his front and onto Sharky Ward's right shoulder. As Jack's diaphragm became depressed, he belched up copious quantities of water, all over the bottom of the boat. Ward bounced him up and down a couple more times and, satisfied that there was now room for air, dumped him down on the bottom of the boat. Ward didn't get the manoeuvre from any of his training manuals. But then, the manuals didn't tell you half what you needed to know in Helmand.

'Right, let's get some air into him and get that ticker going.' After a few moments' mouth to mouth resuscitation and heart massage he became excited. 'Goggs,' he called over, 'this bleeder might live but we'll need a medevac soonest.'

'Sparks, get on to Clyde Coastguard and request them to relay a request for medevac to *Gannet*. Location, Craobh Haven Marina, one casualty, partial drowning, major loss of blood, severe shock, time-critical.' He turned to the driver of Tango Alpha Two, 'Now, get on over to Craobh Haven Marina for the transfer while I go and sort out that horlicks of a wreckage.'

Within minutes a Sea King helicopter was scrambled from HMS *Gannet* at Prestwick with an ETA of 30 minutes.

Sergeant Wallace saw a young girl with long blonde hair that was filthy, matted and stuck to her face with days-old vomit. She was pale and thin as a ghost. Her lips were peeled back in a rictus exposing her teeth, like a skeleton from which the flesh had all but decayed.

'Sir!' he called urgently.

Grant came running, followed closely by Sutherland. His eyes flicked over the scene. A huge mound of male flesh lay on the floor, inert. One enormous hand still grasped the Glauberyt.

'Is he any threat?'

'Not any more, sir. But it's the girl I'm worried about.'

'OK, thanks sergeant. I'll take it from here. You can go back to securing the rest of the apartment. Did any of your people get hit?'

'Yes, sir. I'll go and take care of them.' Wallace gratefully left the scene. As the father of a teenage girl himself, he was shaken by what he had seen. When he got home tonight he would give his daughter an extra special hug.

'Brenda!' Grant called through. 'We need those medics – now!'

'They're on their way up, Boss. Called them as soon as the shooting started.'

Grant went on to look at the filthy bed and its occupant. His nose wrinkled at the stench. With a gasp of horror he realised this was the girl in the photo Ross had shown him: Jenny. Her skin looked pale and cold, like that of a cadaver. He could see no breathing, no sign of life. *Oh Christ, were we too late after all?* Holding his breath against the stench, he leaned down, listening to hear if she was breathing. He wasn't sure if he could hear or feel anything. He put his fingers against her neck. Again, he couldn't feel anything. Inwardly he groaned.

He'd have that fucking Grimwade.

But right now there was a mess to be cleaned up. He recalled the brief glimpse of bodies in the hallway. One of them was clearly one of the firearms team. But who was the other? He went back to the hallway. The pale walls, what was left of them, were spattered with blood that was already drying to a dull red. Brenda Cox was crouching over Shona MacLeod. Cox looked up as Grant came close.

'How is she?' asked Grant quietly.

DS Cox shook her head, unable to speak.

He allowed himself a few silent moments of utter venom against all violent criminals. He had never before been involved in, much less presided over, such a dismal failure of an operation. Pulling himself together was harder than he would have imagined. He went through into the kitchen and saw Sergeant Wallace crouching next to a body in black combat overalls and boots. He went over to him, put a hand on his shoulder, and asked, 'Any luck?'

'No, sir.' Wallace shook his head sadly. 'Willy McBride, that was his name.'

'Whose name? That evil bastard through there, his name was Davy McBride.'

'Maybe, sir. But my officer was PC Willy McBride. Sod of a world, isn't it?'

After a moment Grant removed his hand and looked round,

needing to get back on track. The three men who had been apprehended in the kitchen were lying face down with their hands cuffed behind their backs. A pile of assorted handguns and knives lay in a pile in the corner. At that moment a fourth man with his hands cuffed behind his back was marched in and made to lie face down.

'Where did you find him?' Grant asked.

'Hiding in the toilet, sir,' replied the officer. Grant felt in no mood for a wisecrack.

Sergeant Wallace got up and went out, taking one of his officers with him. He came back a few minutes later with another three handguns which he added to the pile.

'The premises are secure and all other occupants disarmed. They're all yours now, sir.'

'Thank you, Sergeant. You go back to Springburn now. I'll talk to you in the morning.'

'Thank you sir, but if you don't mind I'll stay here until the ambulance arrives and takes my officer away.'

There was a commotion at what was left of the front door. 'That'll be the medics,' Cox said. She went to the door and brought them in. The first medic looked at the carnage in the hallway. 'Jesus Christ! Who's worst and can be saved?'

'Don't rightly know,' said Grant despondently. 'I think we've got four fatalities.' He pointed at the bodies of Shona Macleod and PC Willy McBride.

'What about that one?' asked the medic, pointing at the mountain that had been Wee Davy McBride.

'Leave him till last. Look at the girl on the bed first. I can't detect any signs of life but I can't be sure.'

The medics got to work and Grant left them to it. It was a bitter and unhappy team that rounded up the four kidnappers and took them back for charging and locking up.

'And no, sergeant, they fucking can't have police bail.'

Shona Macleod wouldn't be getting married two weeks on Saturday.

45

Jack awoke, refreshed and more alert than he had been since they hauled him out of the water. At least his mind was clearer, even if his shoulder ached like blazes. He lay awake for a while, savouring the feeling that he was alive and well. He needed to talk to Sarah, see how Jenny was.

'Nurse!' he bellowed. It came out as little more than a pathetic wheeze, but a passing nursed wheeled in.

'Morning, Mr Ross,' she said, middle-aged and businesslike. 'Sit up,' she ordered, and hauled him upright. He winced and muttered something about Jesus. As she checked his drip he told her his shoulder was sore. Her look was unsympathetic. 'I'll get you some more painkillers.' Angel of bloody mercy, but thankful for small ones.

He asked if she would dig his mobile phone out of his clothes. But then he realised it'd had a major wetting and therefore was probably useless. The nurse tutted, saying that mobile phones were banned in the hospital. Instead she brought him a payphone on wheels.

'Umm, do you know where my trousers are?' he asked.

'You've been unconscious for two days, so you won't be needing them a wee whiley: just you stay in bed a wee bit longer.' He thought she'd been about to add 'young man'.

'No, I need some change for the phone, you see, and I don't have enough in the pockets of these hospital pyjamas. I was hoping I had some in the trousers I was wearing when I came in. So if you could point me in the direction of my clothes I could make use of this trolley thing you so kindly brought along. Don't you think?' He smiled at her innocently.

Her brusque manner suffered a hairline crack and she almost smiled. 'Weren't you dripping wet when you were admitted?'

'I expect so – I wasn't paying a great deal of attention at the time.'

The nurse tutted again, and went off to look for his clothes in the drying room. She was away for quite some time. Normally he would have got impatient after a short while, but he just couldn't be bothered. As the door to his room opened he began to think of all the impatient-type remarks he might have made but just couldn't summon up the energy. But it was not the nurse returning. It was Sarah.

He looked stupidly at her, then at the payphone, then back at her. *Got any change for the phone, love? You see, they won't let me use my mobile and I need to ring . . . Hang on, something not quite right there. Oh bloody hell; I'm in deep trouble here, aren't I?*

His brain wasn't clear enough to sort out all his uncertainties in the right order, but one thing was crystal clear. They still hadn't resolved the Lydia email, hadn't had the necessary row, the grovel, the penance – hadn't cleared the air.

Another uncertainty, riding hard on the heels of Lydia, was Jenny. Sarah had said if he didn't get Jenny back safe and sound she would never speak to him again. And he hadn't got Jenny back at all, safe, sound or otherwise.

He licked his lips. They were dry, cracked. His shoulder was still agony, bloody nuisance.

'Hello,' he said carefully. 'How are you?'

'I'm all right, thank you.'

Oh dear. She hasn't worked these things out in her mind either. He could have done with her showing a bit more feeling either way.

Obviously preferred it if there was a hug, a kiss and a pithy comment about what a pillock he'd been and best he pulled his socks up. Or he would have settled for a rant that would blow itself out and pave the way for a bit of a grovel on his part. But this uncertainty didn't feel all that encouraging. He'd done too much walking on eggshells just recently, and it was doing his bloody feet in.

'How's Jenny? They *have* found her, haven't they?'

'Yes, they've found her. She's in hospital in Glasgow.'

'Is she all right? I mean, silly question, obviously she's not all right if she's in hospital. Is she badly hurt?'

'No. She's just got some . . .' Sarah looked out of the window, as though the word she was struggling for was out there, 'some *recovering* to do. And they wanted to keep her in for observation.'

Jack relaxed against the pillows and muttered his thanks to heaven. After a moment or two he realised Sarah was still standing, uncomfortably, by the bed.

'Er, would you like to sit down?' He indicated an orange plastic stackable chair loafing in the corner. She pulled it over and sat down – just an inch or two further away than he would have liked.

'Look,' he began, 'I realise I've been a right idiot and all that, and I'm terribly sorry.' *God, that's pathetic. But I can't dredge up anything better. Come on, I need some help here.* 'I genuinely thought it would be better for us as a family if we started again on this venture up here . . . '

'After you'd misbehaved with that woman,' Sarah interjected.

'Ah, that,' said Jack. 'Yes, I'm sorry about that. Damn stupid of me, it meant absolutely nothing . . . '

'Oh I know that,' said Sarah. 'It's not that I'm objecting to. Or not that especially. It's that you didn't tell me when . . . when . . .' Her voice and eyes faltered. 'What really hurts,' she continued, her voice so quiet it was almost a whisper, 'is that you took advantage of me, didn't you? Of the situation I was in.' Sarah had her hands on her lap, absently twisting her wedding ring round and round.

Jack chewed his lip. He honestly didn't know whether that was true or not. Looking back to that day in March when Sarah had gushed out everything about Jules when his suspicions were still unformed, his reaction had been based on that single punch to the kidneys. Another man trespassing where only he should tread. That much had been honest. And then, as he realised the situation could only have arisen because he hadn't been much of a husband, he'd started to come off the boil. That also had been honest.

But the question Jack shied away from answering was whether he'd failed to mention his own, very recent trespassing at that point in case it prejudiced his own proposals. He screwed up his eyes in a mixture of shame and denial. Right now would be precisely the wrong time to lose Sarah and the children. After they'd come so far together, and what each of them had been through.

He went as far as he could. He had neither the energy nor the will to dissemble. With his eyes still screwed up and his voice an even hoarser whisper than hers, he said, 'I don't know, love, I really don't know.'

If he was hoping for mercy and forgiveness at that point, he was out of luck.

'And then you get your son and daughter caught up in this dreadful drugs business, with gangsters and what have you. Have you *any* idea what Jenny went through at the hands of those awful men? And Tom almost got drowned.'

Jack could do no more than hang his head. This was a lot worse than he'd expected.

After a terrible silence, she got up and said, 'I'd better be going.'

Her parting kiss felt perfunctory.

46

There was a knock at the door and Charles' head appeared.

'Not interrupting anything, am I?' His head was followed by his long thin body. He carried a plastic supermarket bag with some flowers poking out of it. 'Flowers,' he announced vaguely.

'Flowers,' said Jack flatly. 'Very kind and thoughtful, sailor.'

'Not for you, petal,' said Charles testily, 'they're for Sarah.' He pulled the flowers out of the carrier bag. Spotting an unused glass bed-pan, he took it over to the basin, filled it with water and stuffed the flowers in. 'There you are,' he said, admiring his artistry, 'I'm sure Matron won't miss the vase.' He glanced round the room as though someone might be hiding in the totally inadequate bedside locker. 'Where is she, by the way?'

'Who? Matron?'

'No, you moron, Sarah. Has she been in to see you yet?'

'Afraid so.'

'What's that supposed to mean?'

'Well, she was here about half an hour ago, but not to heal my soul and body. She had a large bucket of salt and took great satisfaction in applying handfuls to my wounds as she told me exactly what she thought of me. It didn't make pretty listening even though she was about right in everything she said. Basically, I agree with her that I don't deserve the family I've got.'

'That's bollocks,' Charles boomed. A passing nurse glanced through the doorway in alarm and hurried on her way. 'She'll come round, don't you worry. I suggest you reorganise your sense of humour with some of this.' With a flourish he produced a bottle of Lagavullin malt whisky from his plastic bag. Spotting a tooth mug by the basin he swilled it out, sniffed it, wrinkled his nose and muttered something about not needing to worry. He splashed a couple of inches of the peaty brown liquid into the mug and handed it to Jack. 'That'll do you more good than all these namby-pamby splints, tubes and bandages.'

Perching on top of an elderly and very functional chest of drawers, he studied Jack as if for the first time, propped up in the bed with tubes coming out of him and bandages swathing his shoulder and arm.

'Well, you did that good and proper, didn't you? You should have your ticket taken away, driving like that. We had lookouts watching what you were doing on the return journey from Iona, and couldn't understand what you were playing at, switching from your perfectly decent course through the Corryvreckan to the Grey Dogs. Just what was going on in your boat?'

Jack was grateful for the whisky. The first mouthful made him cough, but it tasted good.

'I was looking after your operation, matey, that's what I was doing.'

'Oh yes?'

'Oh yes. d'Astignac's planning was much better than ours. He obviously anticipated a welcoming committee, so when he was satisfied you lot were all at Crinan, he told me to go to Oban and then the bugger shot out my radio.'

'He shot out your radio?'

'He did. I've never been so cross in my life.'

'I'll bet. One of your primary safety aids. Not to mention contravention of regulations.'

'Regulations be buggered. No – what I was cross about was that he – or rather his goon – had brought a gun on board without getting my permission first. What skipper would allow that, eh?'

Charles almost fell off the chest of drawers with mirth. When he had calmed down, he asked Jack to carry on.

'Well, I could have altered course to go to the west of Scarba and then up to Fladda, but when he – or rather, Coluzzi – put the gun in Tom's back I sort of blew a fuse. Very quietly.' Jack paused while he eased the position of his shoulder. 'Actually, there was logic in it. Once he'd screwed my radio, there was no way I could tell you to go to Oban instead, and so he was going to get away scot-free with the contraband. No guarantee about getting Jenny back or that I would be free of these scum. Secondly, I didn't like the idea of a gun in Tom's back – and who knows whether d'Astignac would hang onto Tom to guarantee my future good behaviour?'

'Fair point. So what did you do?'

'So I decided to crash the boat, and the Grey Dogs was the ideal place – well, I *thought* it was the ideal place – so that Tom and I would be safe while the others would be far too busy trying to save their own skins to bother about us. I'd say it worked, wouldn't you?'

'You're mad, you know that, don't you? Mad, brave, stupid, ingenious, courageous, inspired – and right. It did work, it saved the operation and we swept up pretty much everyone and everything.'

'So it was worth it?'

'I'll say. We recovered the bodies of three of your passengers. Two were found in the wreckage of your hull, and Coluzzi we picked up along the coast. He was wearing his lifejacket but for some unfathomable reason he'd neglected to inflate it. Can't think why.'

'Can't think why,' Jack agreed.

Charles continued. 'No sign of d'Astignac yet, but no doubt some of him will turn up in the net of a fishing vessel or some-such.'

'So it was a success?'

'Oh, there was more to it than that. Jim Francis in *Vanguard* arrested the freighter that had landed the contraband in the first place, *and* we recovered a number of holdalls from your boat, which provides the evidence we need to secure a successful prosecution. Our friends at the US DEA and the FBI are also able to use that to round up all the big fish in the American company. So politically it was a very satisfying operation. Do you know how much cocaine was on board?'

'Tell me.'

'Well, we recovered a shade over four hundred kilos, and there were probably one or two bags that got away. The wholesale price of four-hundred-plus kilos of pure cocaine delivered into the wholesale market is in the region of ten to fifteen million US. So you made a bit of a hole in their business plan. And then there's street price: well, obviously depending on how much it's cut, it could sell for twenty-five, maybe thirty-five million sterling on the streets of this country.'

Charles paused to let that sink in. Then he continued more quietly.

'That's an awful lot of money in the hands of evil men. And an awful lot of pain and misery on our streets. You saved that, Jack. You personally. If you hadn't done what you did, that pain and misery would be on our streets very soon. So yes, the operation was a modest success, don't you think?'

Yes, Jack was forced to agree, that was a good result. Shitty, painful and expensive, but a good result. Why didn't he feel elated, then?

'What had happened to Jenny? Who kidnapped her and did the police get them?'

'Well, you must remember that I was a bit further removed from the action there, so I can only tell you what Duncan Grant has told me.' He told Jack as much as he knew about the difficulties Grant had in identifying where Jenny was being held, and her rescue.

'Sarah told me she's in the Southern General. Is she badly hurt?'

'I don't think she's been hurt or injured, more not properly looked after. I gather from Duncan Grant that he thought she was a goner, but the hospital thinks it's more a case of just cleaning her up and getting her back to robust health. As far as I recall, she's going home today or tomorrow, so I guess she's fine.'

Jack was going to ask about her baby, but some flicker of warning reminded him that knowledge of Jenny's pregnancy was still closely held. Instead he asked whether the police had made any high-profile arrests.

'Well, they certainly . . .' he paused infinitesimally to get the right word, 'neutralised those who were immediately involved in the kidnap. Whether or not they'll be able to nail the buyers and associated hierarchy here is another matter: you'd have to speak to Grant about that.'

'I don't think he wants to hear from me again, does Mr Grant.'

'Why ever not?'

'When I offered my services to him on Monday, he and his sergeant patted me on the head and told me to go home. They were absolutely right, of course, but I felt such a pillock. And then, when I'd picked up a piece of information and phoned it through to them, the sergeant smacked my wrist and gave me such a talking-to that I felt about five years old again.'

Charles' expression was one of surprise. 'That's not what Duncan said to me.'

'No?'

'Definitely not. He said that he was embarrassed to admit that all the leads they were coming up with trailed off or were blocked, and the information you gave them enabled them to carry out the rescue. So he reckoned you were instrumental in Jenny's rescue – couldn't have done it without you, was what he said to me. Tom was impressed when I told him.'

Jack glowed with a mixture of relief, surprise and pride. 'Well, I'll be damned,' he muttered.

47

Jenny would usually have been thrilled to be home but her energy levels allowed only a warm glow of pleasure. Her normally slim frame contrived to speak of emaciation rather than glowing health. She was taking her chicken soup and scrambled eggs slowly.

Tom had rejected the offer of the same: *his* appetite wasn't in issue. The rib-eye steak lay glistening on his plate, winking at him, as he looked forlornly at his still-bandaged right hand. Sarah had offered to cut it up for him but Jenny got there first. He surprised them both by putting his arm round her and giving her a kiss. 'Thanks, Jen.'

Supper should have been a happy affair but there was an air of grim determination to make it so. An undercurrent of uncertainty was running, like a draught round the ankles. Rain from heavy showers beat an uneven rhythm on the kitchen window.

'Thanks, Mum, that was lovely,' Jenny said as she put her knife and fork down. 'I never thought I'd appreciate sitting at table so much: eating all your meals in bed *so* sucks.'

Sarah laughed. 'I never thought I'd hear you say anything like that: so no more TV meals on the sofa, then?'

'I didn't quite say that, did I?'

The frivolous moment died.

'What happens now, then?' Jenny asked.

Before Sarah could answer, Tom dived in with determination. 'Dad comes home in a couple of days and he gets better, right?'

'That's not what I meant. Mum? You know what I meant?'

Sarah was busying herself clearing the plates away, as if trying to avoid the issue.

'I think your father and I have to have a long talk about the future.' She put down the plates she was carrying, rinsed her hands in the sink and turned to look directly at Jenny as she dried them. 'How do you feel about Dad? After all . . .'

The question hung.

Jenny studied the table surface in front of her and played with grains of salt that had escaped. Her freshly washed hair glinted in an errant shaft of watery sunlight with something approaching its old lustre. 'What he said really hurt, you know?' She glanced up at Sarah. Tom wasn't involved in this. 'I know he can sometimes say stupid things, but I really thought over the last few months up here we were getting somewhere, you know?'

Her gaze fell back to the surface of the table.

'The police came and interviewed me in hospital. Did you know that?' Again she looked up. Sarah didn't answer. 'They told me I'd been used as a pawn in a drug smuggling thing, and Dad's boat was caught up in it.' She paused, as though struggling to make sense of it. 'Honestly, Mum, I don't know how I feel about Dad. I guess my hormones are all over the place what with losing the baby as well, but to be honest I'm a bit frightened of how I'll feel when I see him again. It's this dreadful thing about how awful he was when I told him I was pregnant, and then him being involved in drugs, and leaving me to the mercy of those dreadful men.'

She shivered, shut her eyes and wrapped her arms around herself. Instantly Sarah went over, knelt down by Jenny's chair and hugged her fast.

When Jenny had calmed down Sarah sat down at the table with them.

'Look,' she said, 'one of the options is that we – just the three of us – go back down to Bracknell and pick up our lives down there. The house still hasn't been sold so we can just walk in the front door. We don't have to decide this now, but I want you both to think about it.'

'No.'

Sarah and Jenny both looked at Tom.

'No?' Sarah said. 'I just want you to think about it.'

'No.'

'Why not?'

'No. You've got it all wrong. You've both got it wrong. About Dad, I mean.'

'What've we got wrong, Tom?'

'You think Dad just does silly things, says stupid things. But he doesn't. Dad's . . .' Tom struggled to find the word he wanted. 'He's *colourful*. He's brought some excitement into our lives – well, into mine, anyway. Coming up here was the best thing ever. The boat was the best thing ever. And I'm really pissed off she's gone.'

The women looked at him, astonished. This was, for him, a long speech. And he wasn't finished yet.

'I don't know how we got mixed up with smugglers, but I don't see how we could have worked out they were smugglers before we got sucked in. And then once we were sucked in I don't see how we could have escaped. Dad told me how he'd tried to get out of it but by then they'd grabbed Jenny. He was torn between doing just as they ordered so they'd give Jenny back to us unharmed, or going to the police and playing poker with Jenny's life.

'I don't quite know how it was decided that we had to do the last run, but Dad was frantic with worry. He told me. He told me before he went to Glasgow on Sunday evening with just a photograph of Jenny. Do you know what he was going to do? Do you know what he did? No? Well, I do.'

Tom was all but shouting now. The women were frozen.

'He went to Glasgow with a photo of Jenny to walk the streets at night and talk to junkies, drunks, barmen, pros . . .' he faltered over the word, 'prostitutes, to try to find a lead, someone who could tell him where Jenny might be, or someone who could tell him who might know. And you don't get that kind of information from people like us. You get it from low-life, criminals, drug dealers. And they aren't nice people to know. As Dad found out.'

Sarah's hands flew to her mouth, her eyes wide. 'How?'

'He spent most of the first night walking the streets, talking to all the rough people and getting nothing. And then about three in the morning someone told him where to start looking. I don't know its name, but it was in the east end – you know, where all the gangs and that are. He got about four hours' sleep and then went to see the police and offered his help. They took a statement from him but they didn't let him help them. Can you imagine how badly Dad felt about that? It was probably a stupid thing to do, but it was brave. He spent the rest of the day looking round the area where he was told, so he knew where to start at night when all the bad people are out. He even had to buy some clothes so that he didn't stick out like a dog's – like a sore thumb.

'And then when night-time came awful things started happening. He was going round the pubs with Jenny's photo and asking if anyone knew where she was, and he was warned off. People started telling him not to ask, it wasn't safe for him. But did that put Dad off? No. It made him scared, but he just went on going. And then he got to one place, was warned off again, he went to the Gents and these two men followed him in and peed all over his trousers and told him not to go on asking around. That really scared him. But he didn't give up. He went to the next place, was warned off again, and then as he was coming out, he was grabbed, tied up and put in the boot of a car. They took him to some waste ground, hauled him out of the boot, and . . . and . . .'

Tom faltered, close to tears. He remembered Jack telling him all this on the boat on the way to Iona, remembered his father trembling and eventually crumbling as he relived it.

'And what, Tom?' Sarah asked gently.

Tom looked at them both, almost too choked to speak. He took a deep breath.

'And they beat him up. They punched him, they knocked him down, they kicked him. On the ground.' Tom's tears were now flowing. But he was determined to complete the story.

'Those injuries he's got in the hospital now, half of them came from that beating up. His face was a mess where they punched and kicked him, and he's got half a dozen broken ribs. *But he didn't give up.*' Tom was almost yelling. Sarah and Jenny were holding hands, mesmerised.

Tom wiped his eyes, sniffed, and dropped the volume. 'He was rescued by some street girls. Otherwise he would probably have been killed.' He paused to make sure the others understood that. 'They took him home, bandaged him up and gave him painkillers. He was going to go out on the streets again but they said they would have a much better chance of finding anything out than he would.'

'And did they?'

'Yes. They found out a name and the place where Jenny was being held. Charles told me yesterday in the car that that was the information the police needed to rescue Jenny, and they hadn't been able to get it. Dad gave it to them.'

Sarah and Jenny exchanged glances. 'So what happened next?'

'Well, when he'd had a couple of hours' sleep, he drove back here early Tuesday morning to pick up the boat and do the trip to Iona. He looked a real mess. There was blood caked round his nose, he had a fat lip and the beginning of an enormous black eye. He wasn't walking upright and his breathing was difficult. The cracked ribs, I think. And he stank, I mean really stank. But he was cheerful because he'd been of some use, he'd given the police a lead. And he was all energetic about having a shower and change, and then taking the boat out.'

'But he wasn't fit to do that, surely?'

'Course he wasn't! He didn't even want to take me, he said it was too dangerous to take me along. But there was no way he could do much on the boat: he was a walking wreck. *And* I wanted to come along as well. I wouldn't have missed the excitement for all the chocolate in China – or wherever it comes from.' Tom allowed himself a taut smile.

'It was on the passage out to Iona, when d'Astignac and the others were all in the forward cabin, that Dad told me what had happened. He'd been trying to make like he was OK but he'd had to give up and ask me to do something for him. So I told him I wasn't stupid and asked him all about it. He was pretty cut up about what he'd been through.'

Tom spent a few moments thinking about that time. It had brought him even closer to the father that he'd been discovering these last few months.

'One of the gang drew a gun on me, did you know that?' Hands flew to mouths again, breath sucked in. 'Yeah, d'Astignac changed the destination we had to go back to. Dad tried to radio to the Customs people but they shot out the radio so he couldn't warn anyone. And then one of them whipped out a gun and pointed it at me, and said if Dad didn't do as he was told he'd shoot me.'

'Oh my God!'

'So we changed course for the Grey Dogs. I think it was Dad's intention to crash the boat so that d'Astignac and his gang wouldn't get away after all. And they'd probably drop the gun while they were trying to save their own lives. You see, Dad and me had lifejackets that inflate automatically when you fall into the sea, but they didn't. So it was very smart thinking.'

'But wasn't it dangerous to crash the boat?'

'Well of course it was. But when you've got a mad drug smuggler on your boat pointing a gun at you it's not very safe anyway, is it? I think Dad did good.'

'But how did you both get injured?'

Tom thought for a long moment. Not because he didn't know the answer. But because he didn't have the words to describe the boiling waters, the huge engines crashing down on them, both of them being sucked below the waters by the undertow, releasing their lifejackets so that they could save each other, the agony of the rope around his neck.

'That's a very long story. I've forgotten the number of times Dad risked his life to save me. Just as he did to find Jenny.'

For a while the only sound was the rain lashing against the kitchen window.

'For me, I'm staying up here. With Dad. Aren't we, Mum?'